Paul B. Boyd

Palace
of Strangers

NOVELS BY HILARY MASTERS

Palace of Strangers
An American Marriage
The Common Pasture

Palace
of Strangers

By **HILARY MASTERS**

THE WORLD PUBLISHING COMPANY
New York

Grateful acknowledgment is made to Norma Millay Ellis for permission to quote lines from Sonnet XLI by Edna St. Vincent Millay, *Collected Poems*, Harper & Row. Copyright 1923, 1951 by Edna St. Vincent Millay and Norma Millay Ellis.

Published by The World Publishing Company
Published simultaneously in Canada
by Nelson, Foster & Scott Ltd.
First printing—1971
Copyright © 1971 by Hilary Masters
Library of Congress catalog card number: 70–149424
Printed in the United States of America

WORLD PUBLISHING
TIMES MIRROR

FOR CECIL SCOTT AND RICHARD MAREK

FOR THOU HAST MADE OF A CITY AN HEAP; OF A DE-
FENCED CITY A RUIN: A PALACE OF STRANGERS TO BE NO
CITY; IT SHALL NEVER BE BUILT.

Isaiah 25:2

Palace
of Strangers

Record

Tuesday

Too many people were too young in 1960 to understand what was happening, and too many people were too old in 1968 to *care* what was happening. That leaves a lot of us hung up in the eight years in between.

Pug Connors says it reminds him of the Iliad. Few know he's a "student" of Homer. That's the sort of footnote *Time* takes delight in. "Cool-eyed, six-foot-two John "Pug" Connors, who if he had not won an unprecedented victory for the post would have been called sheriff anyway on the basis of his looks, has been known to quote from the blind Greek poet. 'The Irish and the Greeks have a lot in common,' says the boss of Yost County's outnumbered and struggling Democrats." But he doesn't talk like that.

The old man asked me to stay late today to help prepare an answer to the governor's supplementary tax message. Alma has my dinner warming in the oven. She goes over the events of her day, the comings and goings in the neighborhood, while I shovel in the Swiss steak and peas. She stands by the sink, arms folded under her breast. That funny look on her face as she talks, mystified, almost curious, maybe like the first time she saw me use a knife and fork.

Does she suffer questions about me at the Garden Club, the Saturday Rummy Club? "And how is your son, Mrs. Bryan? Still living with you, is he? He must be how old now?" Women lose face, are marked down, if their sons do not marry.

"The Granbys are back from Florida," she says, reaching down a coffee cup for me.

"How are they?"

"Just fine, though I think Fred has had another stroke. He looks like it."

"Here today and gone tomorrow."

"Oh, I saw Ellen Mapes—what's her married name?" She pours me some coffee.

"Rhodes. She married one of the Rhodes from Arthursburg."

> E. M.—About eighteen when I first had her. Nice breasts though rather wide in the hips. Had a curious cast in her eyes, full lips, slightly prominent teeth. Would become wet quickly. First used sun porch of her house. We screwed one whole summer and then she saw I wasn't serious. I went back to school and she went to some secretarial school. A sweet girl but a very placid lay.

"I understand she's gotten fat," I tell my mother.

"Not that I can tell; her little boy's as cute as a bug's ear."

Watch my mother's back as she cuts pie. It's my turn now. "What did you do today? Did you go downtown?"

"No, I worked around the tulip beds. You better get busy with the garden if you want to have any peas this year."

I promise to plow it this weekend.

"Oh, yes, I knew there was something. Sheriff Connors wants you to call him at home."

Talking to Connors on the phone, talking to any politico on the phone, it is useful to have something to do, something to read or look at. It sometimes takes awhile to get down to business. I look over the argument I'm supposed to rewrite for the Assembly minority. It costs the taxpayers of New York State twelve thousand and five hundred dollars a year for me to put these partisan polemics into something recognizable as English, and then they rarely get to the floor.

The conversation went something like this.

"Oh, hiya," Connors' voice soft and with the usual faint note of surprise that anyone should return his calls at all. "I tried to call you at the office but you were out. How's your mother?"

"Fine."

"Good. I wanted to know if I could put you down for a couple of tickets to our county dinner?"

"Sure." I make a few corrections on the text. The minority leader has a problem with participial clauses.

"Yeah, I think I can get Sorensen up for a speaker," Connors' voice drifts on.

"That's swell."

"Yeah. Well, how have you been? I thought I'd see you at the city committee's function the other night."

"No, I had an appointment."

> R. F.—About 25. Lives in a trailer court with her husband and three-year-old daughter. Husband on night shift at brass mill. Very slender, sharp pointed breasts. We have to use the lounge chair in the "living room" end of the trailer because of the kid sleeping at other end. A real bitch but fucks like a mink.

"That's too bad," Connors continues. "They had a nice turnout. Say what's this bill that gets us federal monies for retarded children?"

"I don't know. Want me to check on it?"

"See if you can get an opinion on how it would apply to just one or two cases. You know? Say, lissen . . ."

I put away the report, just at the crucial point, a raise in the sales tax; Democrats are against a sales tax in theory but vote for them in practice. Has to be carefully worded.

". . . say, lissen, do you know this guy Howard Ferguson?"

"Ferguson? No."

"He runs that ski area up in Alton. I thought you might know him."

"Oh, yes. I've heard of him." No need to ask why.

"He's got a crazy notion about running for Congress."

"For Congress? I thought it was Cade County's turn. I thought Cranston was running?"

"Well it is. I spoke with Captain Billy the other day and Cranston is going to run."

"For Christ's sake . . . you mean we're going to have a primary?"

"Well, I haven't talked to this kid yet. He's got lots of moola, you know. He's young, maybe thirty. Anyway, I thought you might take a run up to see him. Because if he does go, it would be good to have someone like you with him, to help him. You know? To stay with him."

"What did you tell him?"

"Me?? I told you I haven't talked to the kid yet." I could see Connors' gray eyes bugging out indignantly. "I'll call him if you want to see him, that's all. No, I mean it, Tommy, if we go into a primary—it'd be good to have someone like you with him. He's pretty new."

"What about my job with the Legislature?"

"They'll give you a leave. The session is almost over anyway." The arrangements have already been made, the tone in his voice says so. Connors never makes assumptions like that unless he has them wired up.

"It wouldn't be easy," I say.

"I know it, I know it. That's why I thought it would be a good idea to have you there, you know, so too many people don't get hurt." He pauses. "I'd appreciate it," he adds with that soft voice, just a hint of an old-country lilt.

"Okay, I'll see him this weekend."

"Give my regards to your mother."

That initial angry reaction when Connors assured me that my job was already taken care of . . . that it would be waiting for me next session after I do this chore. Just another interchangeable part that can be switched around from one operation to another, whenever needed. Needed.

But beyond the anger, overcoming it; the way my heart skipped a beat. My mind began to add up figures, part of that continuous numbers game that is the basis of politics. An unknown. Ferguson. Young. Money. Putting numbers together that might come up a winner.

Judge Samuel J. Bryan holds court on the cream-colored mantel above the fireplace. Black-robed. The photograph caught the mad light in his eye that served him for a laugh. Judge. Your Honor. Pop. Father. Your Grace?

"But I don't want to be a lawyer, Pop."

"What do you want to do, boy?" Lighting one cigarette from another, the third one of the interview.

"Well, I thought I'd like to try to be a writer."

"Writer. A writer?" Looking across the desk. This court only accepts one plea, and see me later in my chambers. "Listen to me, boy. I'm sending you up there to study law. Get your law degree. You can always be a writer, you can be anything you want to then . . . it's a good basis for anything you want to do. But get that law degree. Understand?"

"Yes, Pop."

Charlie Merrick, under the influence of Ziggy Ellman and Harry James, wanted to play the trumpet. His mother, he told me, insisted he learn to play the piano first. Result: Charlie Merrick never played the trumpet and flunked his first piano recital on a number called "Dancing Daffodils."

"What's the sheriff doing, getting a posse together?" My mother sitting in the reclining lounge chair bought for my father the year before he died. Supposed to help his heart, but nothing could do that. She's reading *House and Garden*. On the table near her is the tall glass with a weak rye and ginger. Judge Bryan looks upon his widow, resting in his chair with her feet up to equalize the blood pressure. "I told you so," says the judicial glint in the eyes.

"Don't turn that up," she snaps. I had turned up the volume on the silent, flickering TV positioned before the fireplace. "I'm waiting for the ten o'clock news."

"Why not turn it off until then?"

"Because I like the light flickering like that. It's homey. Feels like there's a fire in the fireplace. Nobody builds me any fires anymore."

"It's too warm for a fire. I made a fire for you last month," I tell her. I meet His Honor's querulous look again and then look at the other picture, a much older picture, a brownish hue to it. Daisy Bryan. 1930–1939. Polio. Remember her hanging head-down from the old crab apple tree in the backyard. The muscles in the little thighs tensed, face getting pink. Upside-down Daisy. That's all I can remember. The apple tree was cut down a few years ago. She'd be married by now. Give this old lady some grandchildren.

"He'd better stay sober," my mother is saying.

"Pug Connors hasn't had a drink in two years," I tell her. "He wants me to help him out with a candidate." Alma makes a gluffing sound in the back of her throat, her version of I-told-you-so. Settles back with her magazine. Almost every night she thumbs through elaborate, perennial gardens before the flickering light of the silent TV, waiting for the ten o'clock news.

It takes imagination to be a Democrat in upstate New York. It takes imagination to win. It takes imagination to lose also, or it eases the hurt of losing, which is more often. Maybe that's Connors' reason for referring some things to Homer, just as folks in the old days used to go back to the Old Testament—to reach out for some sort of parallel that would seem to make sense of what was happening to them. Pain, hurt, by oneself is bad stuff. To know one does not suffer alone helps. "See my wife over there. She's a greedy, solid block of bitterness. But think of poor old man Lot."

"I tell you, pally," Connors said to me. "Zeus had a lock on destiny. He always knew how things were coming out. But there were all these little gods, mischief-makers, who chose up sides and so destiny was put off for a while. And in the meantime, all the flashy young heroes were knocked off one by one, and it all ended up just the way Zeus knew it would. And so in our present situation after those eight years . . . it's all back to the status quo, to where it was intended to be. What happened in between doesn't count for anything, except maybe for the poetry."

There's no question that Connors has already talked to Ferguson. He's been up to see him in Alton, probably. For some reason, he's talked him into running. Virgins rarely bend over unless asked.

Wednesday

I can imagine Pug Connors opening the doors of his garage. It's still dark. He fumbles with the ignition switch dangling on wires from the dash of the old Chevy pickup. The engine scrapes dryly, cylinders rasping inside the block, and then it cracks to life. He backs out carefully past the long black Cadillac he uses for funerals and other ceremonial occasions. Or when he drives Annie down to Florida to stay with her relatives.

"Let's go, Little Ben," he whispers to the truck, shifting gears and starting off through the pre-dawn streets of Yost. The mornings are very chilly in early April so he would be wearing a red plaid lumberjacket. The gray fedora would be set square across his brow, brim turned up like a pony express rider.

And that's not farfetched. He rode me around in Little Ben a few times during Wriston's Assembly race and it was like being on the last stage to Cheyenne. Wind whistles through the holes in the floorboard, springs grate against cracked members, and all the while Pug crooning to the truck, urging its quivery passage over the hills, around the curves of Route 19; a heavy foot on the lopsided gas pedal. "Let's go, Little Ben."

Once outside the Yost city limits, he'd run into the lights from dairy barns, farmers the only people up at that hour—and those poor pricks down at the brass mill on the night shift. The farmers would be moving among their steaming cattle, coupling and uncoupling throbbing suction hoses from the warm, rubbery teats as a cracked radio hums somewhere in the barn, beats time.

No wonder he started reading Homer. Look at some of the names in his small empire, the outposts he's always checking. Carthage, Delphi, Athens. Then there are others, just for balance. Green River, Sullivan's Corners, Leix. By the time he reached Delphi, the gray line of dawn would be edging the mountains' humps and scoops like some earlier dawn breaking over the sudden, silent graves of dinosaurs.

And all the while he'd be thinking about the fractions, the integers. Roaring through Carthage, only a few lights on in the mail room of the post office, he'd pass an aluminum and glass facade. Empty and out of business, the big window still plastered over with Wriston posters, the store's bankruptcy à la mode is strange beside the sagging, prospering storefronts on either side, a ne'er-do-well with empty pockets held up by plain, prosperous cousins. Connors had bailed the Edwards' boy out, made him election commissioner, and the family won't forget. He hopes they won't forget. They better not forget.

Along the main street of Green River, a couple of hounds dash from the side alley by the Co-Op to wrangle with his wheels. There'd be the ABC appointment to think about. He'd promised it to Lyle Stafford and the Staffords carried some weight. They were also related to a lot of Republicans in Yost.

At the one traffic light in Leix, at the intersection of Routes 19 and 71, the hood of Little Ben shuddering over the trembling ninety-five horses inside, Pug Connors might decide to make a detour. It would be full daylight by now but still early.

Over the spring heaves of a county road and then onto the sloppy ruts of a long muddy lane between two great meadows, he'd push the pickup in second gear. There would be lights on in the farmhouse, in the kitchen. Cows would be stepping through the barn doors into the muddy field, matrons leaving a party, udders slapping between their hind legs. Empty purses. Alerted by the whanging tailgate, a figure might appear in the doorway of the milking parlor just as the Chevy pulls around the drive and stops in the courtyard.

The farmer wears an old baseball cap, a heavy jacket, coveralls, and great rubber boots with open tops flapping. He resembles an old-time aviator ready for the dawn patrol. Pug Connors knocks open the truck's door and steps out. He's also wearing mudders. They meet at the gasoline pump. "Well, what brings you out so early?" the farmer asks. His face would be friendly, unshaven, and the eyes red-rimmed from lack of sleep. "You been on a binge?" Connors gives him the wall-eyed look.

"Not me! Listen, I've been off the stuff for two years," he says taking a deep breath. The morning air is heavy with the smells of rich mud; sweet, warm milk and sloppy, hot cowshit. Connors thinks maybe he would swear off milk, too. "Naw, I had some business up on the mountain and I thought I'd drop by. How's the missus?"

"Monkey business is more like it," the farmer says good-naturedly and turns back to the barn. Pug follows him. Both of them deciding it was a bad day to fly anyway. Inside the farmer bends down and takes a big can of raw milk and dumps it into the bulk cooler. There's probably a hired man around and he carries in more cans from the barn. These are emptied into the cooler.

"How's it going, Ed?" Pug asks, scraping his boots on the hosed-down cement floor.

Ed Van Buskirk—Committeeman, second district of Leix. A good dairy farmer. About three hundred acres and rents more. Milks about 120. Anti-Farm Bureau. Married. One child, a boy. Good Democrat but not too interested in party business.

"Like always."

"How's your boy . . . Carl, isn't it?"

"Oh, he's coming along all right." The genial face becomes somber, reflective. A couple of cows groan trying to push through the yard doorway simultaneously. Ed Van Buskirk waits, listens. The animals work out their impasse, and he turns back to Pug. "The doctors say he tests out to about the fifth grade. I guess it's not as bad as we feared."

"Well, what the hell," Pug says. "You're not any smarter than that." The farmer smiles slightly and watches the hired man scour the aluminum milk cans with disinfectant. "Lissen," Pug continues, pulling up the collar of his lumberjack, for it's very damp in the milk house. "Lissen, the Legislature passed a new law last week that can get us federal money for one of them enrichment programs. Just the thing for Carl. I'll find out about it if you want."

"I'd appreciate that, Pug," Ed says.

"Coming to the committee meeting on the twelfth?" Pug asks in the same conversational tone. As if it didn't matter. "You got the notice, didn't you?" Ed nods, closing the top of the bulk tank.

"I don't think so," he answers slowly.

"Well, will you give me a proxy?" Pug says, taking the fedora off and resetting it on the same line across the brow. "I hear Jim Hurley may want to come up against me for chairman?"

The farmer reacts as if one of his cows had flicked a tail across his face. Jim Hurley, one of the old guard but still with lots of connections. Also he'd grab your shoulder and call you Dan or Bill instead of Ed. Also, all that money made on interest, mortgages. Generously loaned out to farmers in Yost County when local banks cut them off; even more generously collected back.

Pug Connors is silent. He doesn't need to say anything more. He just lets the spell of the name work. (Of course, in some quarters it would have just the opposite effect, but not with Ed Van Buskirk.) Pug gives the man time, granting him the grace, the pretense of making a choice. Both of them know what the answer will be, but a short pause is required by the rules.

"Sure," Ed finally nods, and Pug pulls the printed form from the sheaf of proxies he always carries. "What shall I put down?" the farmer asks.

"Just sign your name," Pug tells him. "I'll fill in the rest of it."

Maybe Pug would make one more stop. At the diner outside of Alton. A couple of early breakfasters sit on the stools, maybe a fisherman or two having eggs before they go after trout. One or two of the town layabouts having their sixth cigarette and third coffee, quietly working on their cancers because that's all they have to do at that hour; they stopped farming long ago. Gracie's behind the counter. She's back running the place now that her husband is dead, and doing very well, I hear. Her boy is in his second year at Cornell.

```
G. S.--My first piece of ass. After the night game
when we beat Hinton for the championship. A couple of
years older than me, already out of school, but still
around. I was crazy with seventeen-year-old heat.
She was very patient. I smelled of Lifebuoy and
wintergreen and she of pancake makeup and cunt. Out
by the reservoir in the back seat of that 1940 Dodge I
had. "Take it easy. Do you have a rubber?" After it
was over, she sat up to fix her hair. Moonlight
caught a stubby nipple peaking through her open
blouse, glistening wet. "Are you really Judge Bryan's
son?" she asked.
```

"Well, hiya, Pug. Long time no see."

"Hi, Gracie."

"How's it going, Pug?"

"Good."

"Say Connors," one of the coffee drinkers turns on his stool. "Who are you guys putting up for Congress? Understand Captain Billy is going to ram Cranston down your throats." There'd be some snuffing, laughter. Wise-ass Republicans.

"Cranston's a good man," Pug would answer, giving them the wide-eye. "DA of Hinton City, well respected. I got news for you . . . we're going to beat you."

"Oh yeah. Breaking all those nigger heads open. That's a good way to get votes."

"Hey, what kind of a place are you running?" he asks Gracie. It's seven o'clock in the morning but her face is made up for a midnight fiesta. "A citizen comes in for refreshment and he gets a political diatribe."

"No, honestly," the town wise-ass continues, a little worried now that he might have gone too far. After all, even he might need a favor sometime from the Democratic county chairman. "Listen, I wish you luck, Pug. I really mean it. You know I voted for you both times for sheriff. You were the best sheriff we ever had."

"You better believe it," Pug says, fixing an eye on the Lions Club clock behind the counter. It would be time to go. Once more in Little Ben, some fiddling with the loose ignition wires, the motor clunks, gasps, and comes to life. He crawls through Alton behind a school bus on its morning pickups. Just beyond town he cuts off and heads toward the base of Ellis Mountain where the ski area is located. It rises over the village like a great green tidal wave.

Tailgate clanging, three fenders twittering, Little Ben sloughs and side-slips down the dirt road and into the pseudo-Austrian mountain village built around the base. Everything would be closed up, shuttered; the development appearing more artificial in its seasonal desertion. Bouncing on the hard seat, Pug Connors is humming, the gray eyes squint mischievously. "Almost there, Little Ben." And then he might start to laugh, a low cackle in the back of his throat, thinking back to the dum-dum at the diner. "That son of a bitch never voted for a Democrat in his life!"

```
(Howard Ferguson--31--Played basketball for Alton.
All-State center. One year at Syracuse. Old family.
Father a farmer. Went into contracting business on
his own. Added onto family farm at base of Ellis
Mountain and started ski area six years ago. Voted
Outstanding Young Man by N.Y. Jaycee's. Treasurer
Alton Lions Club. All kinds of business, civic
organizations. Married. No children. Supposedly
loaded. Nothing on him.)
```

All right, let's look at the numbers again. Our congressional district is made up of Yost, Cade, and Sinnemok counties, about 150,000 registered voters. In Yost county, we got, in round numbers:

15,000	Republicans
8,000	Democrats
6,000	"Independents"
500	Liberals

Sinnemok much smaller and the bulk in Captain Billyland. And a note about those independents. Some "afraid" to enroll because of their jobs. Some don't care. Somebody said, people get the government they deserve.

Okay. So we come up with a candidate that will attract the independents, hold what we have, and maybe pick up a few of the Republicans. That's our county. That's after a primary. But a primary against Cranston, Captain Billy's boy? Connors must be nuts. Maybe he *is* off the wagon.

Or else . . . maybe this is a hand job.

```
(Everett "Jack" Cranston--47--Married.  Four kids.
LLD from Fordham.  Grand Knight, Columbus.  School on
scholarships, family ran a small hardware store in the
bottoms of Hinton.  Started with Capt. Billy just out
of law school.  City council president.  DA of Cade
County three terms.  Kept the National Guard out of
Hinton during the riot, handled it on his own.  Lots
of press on that.  Arrested the "ringleaders" on some
charge.  Hard man on law and order . . . pulls a raid
on the State U. when things get dull.  Nothing on
him.)
```

Just back from Tiny's. Something screwy's going on. Wriston may jump in. The Home Spot smelled of chitterlings and greens, Wednesday special. Tiny gets bigger, therefore blacker every day. He's going to have to push the bar out more so he can move behind it. He's like one of those puzzles carved of a single piece of wood with a ball rolling around inside a box. Except out of ebony.

Question: if Tiny had made All-State tackle that year would he have gone on to college or would he be here anyway, running numbers and keeping things generally clean in the fourth ward?

One Saturday afternoon after I had been smeared for a loss and we were walking toward the sidelines, losing the ball on downs:

"What's the matter with you on that play?" I asked him. "You missed your man."

"No, I didn't miss him," he smiled.

"How'd he get by you?"

"I let him," he giggled.

"You let him? How come?"

"I just didn't like the way you looked at me in the huddle," he replied in that wispy voice.

Behind the bar, up with the dusty bottles of crème de menthe and the Cherry Heering, are three pictures. A triptych of flashy young heroes: the two Kennedys and Martin Luther King. On the TV, the late news has an interview with Matthew P. Wriston. I'm watching, amazed. You never are completely prepared in this business. He's talking judiciously into the microphone, crumpled face awry. ". . . somewhat necessary that we of the Democratic Party develop candidates who draw their moral sustenance from the will of the people and the issues, rather than from the rule of a few lordly overseers of the public trust."

"Mr. Wriston," reporter off camera, "as one of the more successful Democratic candidates in the district, do you see yourself in this congressional race?"

"Well," Wriston edges a smile, a twinkle in the dark eyes, "there is some relevancy to the congressional seat. As to my part in it, I really have made no decision as yet, except to precipitate some quiet hectoring from the sidelines . . ."

"Have you. . . ?" The guy was green, wasn't aware of Wriston's weighty pauses.

". . . for the moment, it's probably best to adopt a wait-and-see attitude, and see what candidates are being considered before we take the next step."

"You said 'we.' Have you discussed your candidacy with any party leaders?"

"I wouldn't care to use the term candidacy," the poker face breaks. "That's a rather formal, somewhat intimidating category, especially for a Democrat around here." A knowing wink for reporter and camera. "But I have made my views known to those in responsible positions in the Democratic Party and I think there's no misunderstanding among them as to my position. The issues this year are too important. They must be taken directly to the people."

"That was an exclusive Channel Twelve newsbreak," studio announcer, "in which prominent Yost County Democrat, Matthew L. Wriston, all but announced his intentions . . ."

"Well how about that," Tiny says, bringing me another beer. "You look surprised."

"A little."

"I thought you might have written his statement."

"Wriston writes his own speeches," I tell him.

"Aren't you and him together anymore?" he asks.

"That was just for the Assembly race."

Just before I left, I ask Tiny, "What do you think of Wriston as a candidate? Better than Cranston, isn't he? Remember that riot in Hinton?" Tiny shrugs, a gentle swell of the huge shoulders.

"What difference does it make?" he answers. "I think I'm going to give up voting for Lent." His words reach the other end of the bar, turning a patron away from the spring training reports.

"You can say that again, brother."

Up above, Jack Kennedy looks quizzical, Bobby looks eager. In the middle, Martin Luther looks doubtful about the whole business.

One last note. Connors must have known about Wriston. "Made my views known to those in responsible positions." It *is* a hand job. Know more after tomorrow.

R. F. doesn't answer. Maybe the old man came home and killed both her and the kid. Couldn't blame him, but it would be a loss of good stuff. Well, as old Sam Pepys used to say . . . and so to bed.

Thursday

By eleven thirty, every morning the Legislature is in session, there are four large pitchers of Bloody Marys ready on the bar of the Knickerbocker across from the Capitol. Most eat in the backroom. There's a good deal of table-hopping, back-thumping, shouldergripping, and studied whisperings. More might get accomplished here than in the chambers of either the Senate or the Assembly. It's always a shock to an outsider who might wander in for lunch to see this big happy family of legislators and lobbyists relaxing after their strenuous morning efforts on the public stool.

I took Alma here to lunch when she was shopping in Albany one day. She surveyed the room with prim disapproval. She was so flustered by some of the pairing of tablemates that she had trouble with her chicken salad.

"Isn't that So-and-so?" she asked, indicating an upstate Senator whose contributions in last year's session was a bill that would have suspended the right of habeas corpus. I nodded. "Well, what's he doing eating with him?" His luncheon companion was a young liberal Assemblyman from New York, one of those bright boys who supposedly had had the ear of Bob Kennedy.

Yeah, how about that AFL-CIO lobbyist who's made a mint investing in the "other side," well-earned tips, who when he's not boasting about his personal fortune says, "Oh, I wish he was still alive, all right. You know why? So the son of a bitch could be shot again!"

Connors was right. The Old Man called me in, thanked me for my efforts, wished me luck, and said he'd look forward to working with me next session. So I'm cleaning out my desk, a little pissed off by the way things move sometimes without a gesture from me, like Peter Pan's shadow dancing around him, come loose and not sewn on, and also thinking of what Tiny said last night about giving up and more particularly of what I said to him about what "they" *owed* us, the two black boys Connors had made deputies, etc. Everyone in the business knows what Tiny was saying is true. But you forget it, you have to in order to keep going. It lies there in the back of your mind like a dull brown ache that you intend to take a pill for sometime, but in the meantime there's more immediate, pressing problems such as how to raise a few thousand bucks for some television spots. How to put an unknown, inexperienced yokel into the halls of Congress.

So when I'm cleaning out my desk and Connors calls to say he's buying lunch, I say, "You're goddamn right you are."

I'm already in the backroom of the Knickerbocker at a table when he comes in, the gray hat on a cocky slant across his brow.

He puts a big arm around a diminutive, aging waitress and propels her along with him to the table.

"Be a sweetheart," he whispers in her ear as if he were pleading for her most sacred treasure, "and get this boy a drink. Bourbon and water. And I'll have a bottle of your best ginger ale."

She leaves, ruffled but not ungrateful—it's remarkable the number of people who fall for that Irish bullshit, myself included—and Connors sits down, carefully removes his hat, puts it on a chair, and smoothes down the thinning black hair across the big skull.

"Well," he says, "how's your mother?"

"All right, cut the crap," I answer. "What's all this about Wriston?" I get that wild-horse eye.

"I only know what I read in the papers this morning."

"Did he talk to you about it?"

"Well, I met with him a couple of weeks ago and we talked about a lot of things. Minkus was there too. You know how Matt Wriston is, it's hard to know what he's saying sometimes. He did say that . . ."

We are interrupted by one of the Speaker's deputies, one of those smooth Republicans that look and smell like they spend several hours a day in a high-class Italian barber shop. He mentions to Pug a job opening in the Assembly record room if he had anybody for it.

"Gee, thanks, pally," Connors says, then to me, "Do you know anybody that could use a job?"

"Let's get back to Wriston," I tell him. "Did he actually say he wanted to go for Congress?"

"You know how he is. He was playing Achilles in the tent. But it's not up to just me, you know. There are two other chairmen in the district." And he gives me a look that's supposed to be significant.

"But what about this guy Ferguson?" I wait until the waitress serves the drinks. "Are we going to have a three-way primary?"

"Search me," Connors says, throwing open his coat as if it were part of the offer. "He's a nice kid. Lots of money. He wants to try it. He's got potential."

"So you have talked to him?" I say. He just looks at me and grins. "Potential. Potential for what? In a three-way primary Billy Brown's outfit would grind us up."

"Well, I got to think of the future. But don't get me wrong, because I got to stay neutral if we got both Wriston and Ferguson going—but with the right exposure, this kid could go places later on. That's why I thought you'd be interested. Build him up. Get him around."

"So, I'm to cover for you, is that it?" He sips his ginger ale and looks over the room. "What about Captain Billy? How's he going to like opposition?"

"What can he say?" Pug answers, hands spread wide, eyes popping. "I'm neutral and you're just doing a job, that's all. He'll understand. Believe me."

A trim blonde in her late thirties stops at the table. "Hello, Pu-ug," she sounds as if she's slowly rolling off of him. "Where have you been? We don't see you anymore."

"Oh, I'm over in Public Works this year," he tells her. "Hey, d'you know Tommy Bryan?" She nods briefly to me.

"Sure, hi," I say though I've never seen her before. Hair in a stiff beehive, a size twelve firmly corsetted and the face and hands flawlessly enameled. She is one of several score of secretaries who click-clack around the marble halls of the Capitol, like courtesans trying to find the bathroom in an old palace.

"Don't be a stranger now," she drawls as she leaves.

"She's one of Senator Rickett's secretaries," Pug tells me. "I hear she's pretty good," and he rolls his eyes. "Are you interested?"

"No," I tell him, though curious about the extent of his influence had I said yes. "Let's get back. I still don't understand. If we put up Ferguson . . ."

"Look, pally," Connors says with that melancholy look which means he's leveling. "I just thought you'd do this favor for me with no questions asked. If you don't want to, feel free. I think you'd be doing a favor for yourself. The kid's a comer, I can tell. But more important, it's a favor for me, you know?"

So there was the magic word. The oath one swore on the battered shield at the Round Table. The ultimate call-in. He looked at me for a moment and then leaned over and talked into the ashtray between us.

"I heard this morning that Cranston will announce on Monday. That means Wriston will come out about a week later. It'll take him that long to put together the right words. This is Thursday. You got the weekend to sell Ferguson. It's got to stick. Our county committee meeting is on the twelfth. We got to hold Ferguson until then."

"And then?"

"Who knows?" The fur pieces over his eyes jump. "Wriston might drop out. Or he might go for petitions to get on the ballot. But the important thing is if there is going to be a split, at least we got one of them, control one half. And who knows," he gives me a poster smile, "We might even beat old Captain Billy, if it comes to that."

About favors. Loyalty. It can tear you apart sometimes. But it makes everything go.

When I dropped out of law school for Korea, hoping that would solve — ultimately solve — my problems, Pug Connors was about to make his first run for sheriff. Out of Korea and still alive . . . think of saying that.

"Well, what are you going to do now, write the great American novel, I suppose?" Eyes pierced the cloud of cigarette smoke hanging over his desk. A constant cloud.

"I don't know, Pop. There's an opening with the AP in Albany. I might try that."

"A newspaperman, eh? Well I guess that's all right. It's not like practicing law, but there have been newspapermen who've gone on successfully into politics."

"I don't know that I'm so interested in politics, Pop."

"Eh? What's that? Of course you're interested. I tell you what to do. You take that job in Albany and in a couple of years, Sheriff Connors is up for re-election. You help him with that. You'll learn a lot from him, and he won't forget. Pug Connors never forgets a favor. He's a little ordinary but he's a solid Democrat."

"But . . ."

"But!" The feet come up and the silk-hosed ankles cross on the desk. "What the hell do you want out of life, boy? Don't you want to amount to anything? You'll meet the best people in the world in politics, also the worst. But the best are the best of the best. That's what you're going to do."

So I did Pug Connors a favor a few years ago. And he's done me a lot of favors since. We're just a big daisy-chain of favors, everybody doing everybody else.

Saturday

Overheard in Albany the other day:

FIRST MAN: He's one smart Jew-boy.
SECOND MAN: All Jews are smart.
FIRST MAN: What kind of a statement is that?
What are you, prejudiced???

"I thought you were going to plow the garden today," Alma says.

"I have to go up to Alton, I'll plow the garden tomorrow," says he, handing her his favorite fly rod. She stands in the kitchen like an old vaudevillian, sloppy slippers, faded wrapper — a small neat figure with fire in her eye and a fishing pole in her hand. He finds his boots. If he gets away early enough he can do some fishing. There are a couple of streams up near Ellis Mountain that only he knows about.

Driving up to Alton I go over what Pug told me the other day about the meeting with Wriston. It was several weeks ago, in March, during that freak blizzard. I remember the day because Alma called me in Albany. "Don't try to come home for supper." Imagine that.

"Pugilist-faced Thomas H. Bryan received a phone call from his mother on an afternoon in March, saying the weather was too bad for him to drive back to the pleasant, clapboard *petite maison* his father's astute judication of the law had built. Simultaneously, a meeting was being held in the law offices of Mathew P. Wriston above the Vista Theater in downtown Yost. HAD HE BUT KNOWN. . . ."

The stores along Wentworth Street had big Easter bunnies and enormous paper flowers in their windows though the annual commercial rebirth seemed threatened by an unexpected turn of winter.

Pug was the first to arrive. He flirts with Mrs. Arnett in the outside office. Probably asks about her daughter, a nurse over in Vietnam. Then Ernie Minkus arrives, pushing out his hand, palm down in that way he has so you never know whether you're supposed to shake it or get on your knees and kiss it.

```
Ernest Minkus—-About 45.  County chairman of Sinnemok
County Democratic Party.  Lives off his chairmanship
by milking postmasters, office holders, etc. though
supposedly runs a real estate office. Has been known
to take from Republicans as well and is a yes-man for
Capt. Billy.  When Wriston ran for Assembly, we gave
him $2,000 for "expenses" and got tickets to six
church suppers in return.  Also got tremendous
shellacking.  Nothing on him—-that can be proved.
```

"What's going on?" he asks Connors.

"Ya got me," Pug answers. Then some key committeemen from Yost wander in, men with large blocks of votes behind them. They see Pug and immediately sense they shouldn't be there. Wriston is foolish enough to invite them, as if to show strength to Connors and Minkus.

Popular candidates, such as Wriston, think that they build up credits of loyalty with committeemen, but they forget that there are years of favors to be paid off by most of these people — sons in trouble with police, jobs for brothers-in-law, etc. — that are never paid off. And the slips are held by Pug Connors.

"Come in, gentlemen."Matt Wriston's figure in the door of his office. When I worked for Wriston I used to enjoy going to his office. It was a peaceful haven in the noise of a campaign. He goes with his office. Though one might guess his clients paid a fearful price, more often than would be expected, for the cozy clutter of the room; and that the counselor's famed gift of language was but a hyperbolic intervention while he searched through the piles of legal documents spilling on the uneven floor, the briefs and manuals strewn about the furniture, the books open on the velour-covered sofa, for the one simple, declarative point that would decisively win the day. Lincoln, FDR, Jack Kennedy, and even Lyndon Johnson, personally inscribed, are on the wall. Two diplomas, Cornell and Columbia.

Wriston completes the picture. He's great in the courtroom, wonderful to listen to. An old-time polish that's rare these days: the way he negligently leans on the jury rail to talk in a dry, witty manner. When Matt Wriston rises to say, "Your Honor" it makes the third-degree burglary he might be defending sound like a turning-point in constitutional law. There are kind souls among us who attribute the small number of acquittals he wins to the implacable will of the system.

"Gentlemen." They were all settled now, the committeemen standing by the door, still undecided whether they should stay. "I'm sorry to bring you out on a day like this, Ernie," he says pointedly to Minkus. "I'm truly grateful for you coming here today. Truly grateful."

And that's a mistake. To tell someone like Ernie Minkus you're *truly grateful* is no pleasantry. In his mind the phrase means a few bucks at some later date.

"I note," the counselor continues, "that Cade County is not represented, but it would seem not impertinent to conjecture that the points of this discussion will be made known to them."

Nobody says anything. Minkus has a bland look on his porcine face, the look of a church warden who's been told the collection plate is being tapped. Pug probably plays with the gray fedora in his lap and looks benign. The committeemen are certain now that they shouldn't be there and look around, hoping to hear someone cry "Fire." Wriston continues. I see him turning to the window, hands clasped behind his back, up under his suit jacket. He spent more time talking to me this way during the Assembly campaign than to my face.

"In any event, those of you who have been concerned enough to answer my invitation are the prime movers of our party (Not Captain Billy???!!) and make it what it is" — a suggestive, soft addition — "what it is today. I don't need to tell you gentlemen,

I'm sure," turning back to them so the black eyes move from one face to the next, "that there is a confluence of issues and events joining today which make it imperative . . ."

"What's on your mind, Matt?" Pug Connors interrupts.

One time in 1962, during the Assembly campaign, Wriston, Connors, and I were having a beer together and he was all wound up with his courtroom language when Pug said, "Look, Matt, there's just you, Tommy, and me here. Just tell us straight out what you mean."

"Yes, quite right, John," Wriston said, one of the few to call Connors by his Christian name. The lawyer's smile goes with the weather outside and I can see him pull at his upper lip, reflecting. Then Pug said he came right out with it. "I don't think we, as Democrats, can afford to have Jack Cranston be our candidate for Congress." Boom.

The committeemen shift their feet in silent agony. Pug and Minkus don't move a muscle. Models of polite attention and their equivocal silence unsettles Wriston. He probably anticipated some arguments, probably had a briefcase full of points prepared.

"Let me put it this way," he continues. "We can no longer afford business as usual. With Abe Kleinsinger resigning, we have a splendid chance to elect a Democrat. But we've got to present candidates who are responsive to people's needs and not those who are at the beck and call of the courthouse gang. Jack Cranston does not answer these qualifications."

"Let me get something straight," Minkus leans forward on the sofa, little fat belly pressing on his knees. "If I remember correct, you nominated Cranston at the judiciary convention."

"That's quite right, Ernie," Wriston says, grateful to explain this subtlety. "But the office of supreme court judge removes a man, in great degree, from outside control. Cranston would have made a good judge, and I would nominate him again — with honor — but not for Congress." It's too delicate a point for Minkus. "Gentlemen, need I remind you that there's a new sense of politics alerted in the country today. If we are to have a successful candidate he must be a man who is tuned in to this new sense — he must be independent, no ties with the old gang. He must be able to excite the imagination of the young people, he must be able to identify with the outcasts, the put-downs of our society."

Pug told me that at this point Wriston even gestured to the pile of briefs on his desk, the legal errata of his clients, most of whom were doomed to serve time, with or without his help.

Lawyers are like doctors: they make the inevitable less painful.

"Gentlemen," Wriston leans on the desk, a heavy lock of salt-and-pepper hair falling over the dark eyes. "Jack Cranston cannot be that man even if he wanted to be. You know it and I know it."

"Well, Matt," Pug asks then, "do you have anybody else in mind?" Connors told me he had to give Wriston credit: the question almost broke him up, but he clenched his jaw. His stern expression didn't crack.

"John, you and I have had our differences in the past, but I like to think they have always been for the good of the party. Now you boys (suddenly it's from gentlemen to boys) know that I have no great means and that my support in the party organization would probably be minimal, but I'll tell you one thing. I'll be . . ." and he pauses dramatically, decides it's okay, since it's not a courtroom, to use the words, ". . . I'll be goddamned if I'm going to sit on my ass and let bosses manipulate and debauch the people's will. The issues must be taken to the people."

"Now let's get this straight," Minkus says nervously, clearing his throat. "If Cranston is put up, you'll go to a primary?"

"Ernie, if there is no other viable alternative, I shall give it serious . . . serious consideration. Would you support me?" Wriston asks, thereby giving them all a taste of the new politics. Candidates never ask party leaders direct questions. That's what aides are for.

"Well, gee, Matt," Ernie says laughing, wriggling on the sofa as if he might be wearing a girdle and it's ridden up. "You put me in a hell of a spot. I'd have to stay neutral in something like that. You know what I mean? Of course you have a lot of friends in Sinnemok because of the Assembly race you ran. Lot of people still remember you. But I couldn't come out and endorse you in so many words. Don't get me wrong," he adds quickly. "I think what you're saying makes a lot of sense. A little competition is good for us all. Yes . . . hmmm." And he looks to Pug to say something.

Pug has that cool light in his eye, the broad face relaxed and not unfriendly as he slouches against the arm of the old sofa. The fedora is on his knee. "I don't know," he says softly. "You got lots of friends around here of course, and what you say about the organization might be true. I'm in the same position as Ernie, though of course, you *are* from Yost County."

"That's right," Wriston says, a finger spearing the point.

"Do you think you'd get the Liberal nomination? Have you talked with them yet?" Pug would ask.

"Of course not," Wriston answers with affronted honor. "My first responsibility is to you gentlemen. But I think it goes without saying that I would almost certainly receive their endorsement."

Damn right he talks to Connors and Co. first. Total Liberal enrollment in the whole district is just about fifteen hundred. Run only with them is like putting a 2:10 horse against a 2:05.

"I'm sure you will," Pug says. "Well, when are you gonna announce?"

"I won't say anything until you think I should," Wriston says.

"Oh, don't wait for me," Pug tells him, wide-eyed. "In a situation like this, you're going to be on your own for a while."

"But ultimately, John," Wriston says, asking for an acquittal, "I can count on your support."

"Like you say," Pug Connors says, hefting his bulk up, "if there's no other visible candidate."

"I said viable," Wriston corrects him, amused by the county chairman's unfamiliarity with the language. No Homer friend he.

Everyone was eager to leave then, taking his cue from Connors: The city committeemen hesitated at the door and then darted out like fish spooked by a shadow on their pool. Downstairs, Minkus and Pug stood under the theater marquee, the committeemen waiting for them with the strained expressions of men at the scene of a disaster. They're told to stay loose. Pug and Minkus pledge to attend each other's county dinners. Everyone was bound to silence, but someone put a call in to Cade County. Minkus? Pug Connors?

```
Matthew P. Wriston--About 50.  Lawyer.  Made a strong
run for Assembly in 1962.  Out of nearly 50 thousand
votes he only lost by about two thousand, in a 3 to 1
Republican area.  Following among young and
idealistic.  Married, two children.  No bad habits.
Nothing on him.  Wife formerly a Bennett, which means
a little money.  Strong willed, temper, which means a
drawback in some areas while some say she should run
for office and not him.  He can be unpredictable,
quixotic.  In some ways a good candidate though a lot
of unknown qualities.
```

Our county is as beautiful as any in the state. Especially this time of year. Driving up to Alton today to meet Ferguson I come face to face with it and wonder why I'm in this business. The mountains form a bluish green backdrop for the spring turning in the farm fields, a tiny fuzz hanging over the promise of timothy and oats and trefoil. Sometimes above the new fields of corn there's a simmering haze, as if the seeds below were giving off fumes prior to the soft explosion of green shoots.

On the dairy farms, cows are out in pasture, though most are still being fed silage at long troughs, for it is early yet and the fields not ready for grazing. Some troughs are placed outside the fences along the road and the cattle stand with heads thrust through the rails, eyes glazed and flanks quivering in the spring sun, to chew a heady mixture of corn and grain. I have to stop for some to amble off the highway because a fence has been knocked down by a winter storm or city hunters and is yet to be mended.

On up through Carthage, Delphi, and Green River, I cross several streams where I used to fish but no more. The headwaters I know very well, in the mountains where they fall like silvery ribbons from a bride's bouquet, but down here they are old and soiled, one already dried up nearly, though they are not the sluggish sewers they become down near the city of Yost.

From the Yost chamber of commerce brochure: "The Metco Copper Mill and the Universal Paper Co. account for Yost County having an annual paycheck twelve percent higher than the state average."

"You know what the difference is between a black man who picks apples down in Cade County and one who works in the copper tube plant up here?" Tiny once asked me. "One's a nigger with $125.60 minimum per week in his pocket and the other's just a nigger."

The higher you go, the soil becomes poorer because of shale and slate. This area, around Athens, was one of small farms settled by the Finns and Poles, who had been pushed up toward the top of the county by the prosperous Dutch and Irish who had got to the fertile lowlands first.

And because they were small farms, none of them more than about a hundred acres at most, and because the soil was poor and for many other reasons (perhaps in one catastrophic year, the spring rains on the mountain lasted a week longer than down below, so that corn planting was held up, making for a poor harvest, which in turn meant silage would have to be bought for the winter at a cost the farmer could never make back) most of these places are now owned by summer people, people up from New York, and the Finns and Poles all went down the mountainside to work in the mills around Yost, a total erosion.

It's easy not to see the bankruptcy that occurred here. *Clematis jackmani* grows wild over the roofs of the old farmhouses that sparkle with fresh paint; the Latvian gingerbread and corner posts are painted lavender and yellow and pink, vying with the borders and beds of daffodils, a few early tulips. The barns have new sills under them, new siding, a few skylights in one or two and several bear hex signs which are not indigenous to our area, so their spells are probably ineffectual.

But the fields tell the story. Apple orchards prune themselves with arthritic attrition. The slopes, not much to begin with, are blurred by scrub cedars; thistles and tansy spread over the fields like greenish purpling bruises, as red-tail hawks mount the wind like flakes from an old fire.

Up near Alton, one comes to much timber and this is pretty wild, lots of good hunting still left. There is partridge and supposedly more deer than when the Iroquois was around, but the deer are small because the wolves have long gone. No fox live here anymore, but now and then you hear reports of a big cat being heard at night. Near the pass that runs down to Sullivan's Corners there's a swath cut through the woods; a wide, man-made avenue being reclaimed with soft persistence by creeper vines and saplings.

The old railway bed going back to the forest and this sign of unprogress makes you wonder. The Age of Steam returning, being overtaken, finally outdistanced by the Jurassic. If the locomotive, those big ten-wheelers that used to snort and loom in these passes with cargoes of milk cans, mail, and visiting cousins, if they can disappear forever into the woods, what arborescence awaits us all?

There are great tracks cut through the timber up the sides of Ellis Mountain, too, but of a grade no Pacific could master. Steel structures resembling power-line towers support heavy cables for the two chair lifts that rise from the base to the summit. What a day this has been. First Alma on my back about the goddamned garden, and then driving up here to meet Ferguson to put the blocks to him, get him hot for Congress.

And that's a funny thing. The use of expressions in politics normally associated with sex. What's the connection? For example, it's disconcerting for someone not in the family to hear a grown, very square type say, "So-and-so has a hard-on for me." It means the other guy hates him for some reason and is out to try to "fuck" him in some way. The verb "to fuck" supposedly has to do with the "act of love," but we somehow have given it a violent connotation.

So I'm at the Ferstock ski area. A fake Alpine village that in the off-season looks like an old Hollywood set built for a movie with Walter Slezak. There's nobody around when I park, but I can hear the sounds of construction. There are a few A-frames and a large condominium beneath a ledge that faces the mountainside. Up on this rock promontory there are two houses, one completed, the other almost finished, and when I get out of the car, I see a coveralled workman rise and then kneel, disappear beyond the roof line of one. There's the systematic rap-rap of a hammer driving home roofing nails.

"Hey," I shout. The rap-rap continues. "Hello up there!" The hammering stops and the workman comes to the edge of the roof, looks down at me. Surprise, surprise. Pug Connors forgot to tell me anything about Howard Ferguson's wife. She looks like a blond chorus girl, a refugee from some old, wacky production number honoring the WPA.

"Hi," she says, brushing at a lock, still holding a hammer in the other hand. Her hair is tied with a blue ribbon. "I didn't hear you."

"I'm looking for Mr. Ferguson," I say. "Is he around?"

"He's up on the mountain," she gestures to the peak. "You must be Mr. Bryan. I'll get him for you." She drops the hammer, disappears for a moment, and then returns holding a walkie-talkie. "Hello, Howie . . . Howie . . ." She looks at me, grins a little toothily, shrugs. "Howie . . ."

"Yeah, sweetie . . ." a voice crackles over the set.

"That Mr. Bryan is here."

"Okay, I'll be right down." Then the voice breaks clearly through the static, "Geronimo!" and I quickly turn back to the mountain. No one jumps.

From below, the young woman seems very tall and later, seeing them together, this turns out to be true. And there's no doubt about her other dimensions, even in the loose, one-piece coverall. On a shorter woman, her build might be called voluptuous. Not on her.

"What do you think about your husband getting into politics?" I ask her. She has already picked up her hammer to go back to the job.

"Well, whatever Howie wants to do, he usually does," she says. I guess her to be about twenty-five, knowing Ferguson's age. The heart-shaped face is that of a sophisticated teen-ager. Eyes brown and precisely outlined in dark mascara. That's all for makeup, but nailing down a roof wearing mascara?

"Well, how do you feel about it?" I say, anxious to keep this caryatid talking. She brushes off on the coveralls, showing the indent of waist, curve of hip. I'll have to ask Connors if there was ever a minor Greek goddess who was patroness for roof layers.

"Well," she twirls the hammer and catches it in mid-air, "if he wants to do it, I suppose he will. Say, will you excuse me? I've got to finish this section of roof before lunch or else." She disappears over the roof line, the tap-tap resumes, leaving me to wonder what her fate would be if the task were not finished.

She reminds me a lot of M., except for the face which with M. was prettier in an old-fashioned way. Not as *cute*. But in height, build, and a very feminine but altogether hearty exuberance. Came close to marrying M. She was a great girl with wonderful thighs. She said her hands would go numb when she came. Probably has varicose veins by now.

One of the lifts had begun to operate, empty chairs moving up the mountainside, passing others descending. So my first look this morning at Howie Ferguson, this hand job of a candidate, is from a distance, as he rides down from the mountaintop. He sits in the center of a chair, workboots dangling in space. His arms rest on the back of the seat. Halfway down, the arms raise over his head, fists in the air, and a second or two later the sound floats across the valley. Tarzan's yell. Good Christ! But the hammering above me doesn't miss a beat. I half-expected an answering cry.

I pick my way among the puddles and mud flats to my car, arriving just as a dilapidated jeep roars around a phony Swiss hut, Ferguson at the wheel, plowing up the mud, splashing pools of water on the hood, and brakes up short beside me.

"We got to get this fucking road paved," he says right off. "Hi," he says, so it had to be a family usage, and his large, calloused hand is surprisingly gentle. "Wait a minute," he says and stands up on the seat. "Hey, hon, how are you doing?" he shouts.

She comes to the edge of the roof, one leg canted in at the knee, hammer in hand, and takes some roofing nails from her mouth. "Okay," she shouts back. "I'm almost finished."

"Well, keep at it," he shouts back, and then to me, as he drops back behind the wheel, "Got to keep them busy, don't you know." He winks and grins and I see an inkling of what Connors means. IF HE IS SERIOUS ABOUT FERGUSON?

So I get in and we splash down the road, Ferguson driving with his knees nearly up to his chin. The rattle of the jeep is augmented by the clash of junk in the back seat. Pieces of steel cable, heavy drills, mammoth wrenches and other construction tools. Maybe Connors' attraction for this kid is based on their mutual taste in vehicles?

Ferguson makes a LeMans downshift and we tear up what seems to be a thirty-degree incline; jounce to a stop beneath the overhang of a very modern house. "Better than a 9-G pull-out," he laughs.

He must be about six feet four. Hazel eyes. Dimples and blushes when he grins! Self-effacing, toe-kicker. Built like a minor god (Is he meant to be Connors' Hector?). Seeing him in the flesh I remember now watching him play basketball about ten years ago. Maybe more.

He shows me through the first floor of the house for about a half hour. It's muddy so we take off our shoes, but I get the feeling that shoes are never worn inside. Wall-to-wall carpet so thick it seems alive. It fights back. As a matter of fact there's no furniture at all but only piles of cushions in various colors, hassocks and pillows. You could categorize the interior design and furnishings as somewhere between Late Spartan and Early Sybarite.

The house is ingenious. It all seems to be suspended on different levels from four huge beams that rise like pilings up through a laminated roof. The living room has a large circular depression in the center lined with pillows and in the middle of this area is an altarlike hearth, an open platform over which hangs a metal shield suspended by a copper chimney. The mountain can be seen through one glass wall and the other walls, windowless, are of raw cedar and hung with the stuffed heads of animals, glass eyes looking out on the wilderness they had carelessly enjoyed.

"You see this bathroom?" He opens a door in the hallway. "It comes in a unit, just like a big cube, and you just set the whole thing into the framework, put a couple of twists onto the bolts," he makes a quick wrench in the air, "and there you have it. Same goes for the kitchen, stove, sink, fridge : . . everything in a box and you just hook it up.

"Of course, when I build this model for other people, I use steel girders instead of these," he thumps one of the support timbers and leads the way down into the cushioned bowl of the living room. "Steel is cheaper, easier to work with, and this house was only my experimental model. My aim," he says stretching out on the circular rim, "my aim is to build a completely disposable house."

"Disposable house?" And there is a temporary quality to the place with all of its luxurious padding, temporary in terms of location, as if it might take off while we're sitting there. I look up at the suspended platform of the second floor. A corkscrew of a stairway spirals up to what seems to be bedrooms, and one gets the impression of a coiled spring about to smash through the laminated roof.

"Sure," he continues. "Everything is disposable these days, so why not a house. Especially the way people move around. All you got to do is unscrew the crapper and the kitchen—they're the most important rooms in a house anyway—throw them on a truck and just plug 'em in at the next place. Nothing to it," he tells me, and I believe him.

"Well now," he turns on the dimples. "Pug Connors says you're supposed to talk me into running for Congress." It's a good-natured challenge which I'm suddenly in no mood to meet. How about a disposable candidate?

"Well, Pug sometimes gets these ideas," I answer.

"You could have knocked me over when he came up here with that one. Is he on the sauce again?"

"No. But he tries to find new faces. He must think you have the potential or he wouldn't have mentioned it."

"Shit," Howie says, grinning. "Me running for Congress."

"You don't think you can do it?" I ask, for his eyes were not convincing.

"Well, I've got no experience."

"You have to start somewhere."

"Yeah, but Congress. I was only thinking of trying for town councilman up here. But Congress. Shit, that's really serious."

"It's all serious," I tell him. He sits up, arms on knees, face in his hands and looks out at the mountain.

"You know me and the old lady have got this thing going pretty good now. We got it down to a system so we can build a house or two a year and sit back and collect the rents on the condominiums and so even with a bad year on the slopes we got it made. What the hell do I want to run for office for—especially Congress? This councilman deal was just so I could keep my eye on the fucking zoning board." He makes a breathy, gagging noise that seems to serve him for a laugh. "Why, shit, my accountants tell me that in a couple of years I'm going to be in the millionaire bracket, at least on paper. Just think of that." I think about it, though I'm not as amazed by the idea as he seems to be.

"So, I don't know about this Congress business. What about this guy Cranston? He's supposed to run, I thought."

"Probably," I tell him. "It means you'd have to go through a primary for the nomination."

"Well, shit, he's backed by that old boss down in Cade, isn't he?"

"Captain Billy. Yes."

"Well, what would I be doing challenging him? I thought Connors and everybody else around here took their orders from him?"

"Not always. Sometimes there are disagreements. Maybe Pug wants to change things." I try to think of other reasons, possibilities, for it's a question I can't answer. "Strange things happen in politics and to people in politics," I finally say, hoping the oracular will get by.

"But how could I win a primary against the machine?" he asks, squeezing a pillow.

"First off, remember a machine is just an organization that functions reasonably well, elects a fair amount of candidates, and delivers a certain amount of services to the people. It has weaknesses, defects like any other organization.

"The fact that you're unknown," I tell him "is a good asset, provided you get to be known. I mean," for there's a dumb look on his face, "people like a newcomer in politics, no strings and all that, but you'll have to get around the district, get acquainted. You have youth, good looks, a good image," he actually blushes . . . think of that. "You're also a self-made man and that goes over big. Also from the looks of her, your wife will be a great asset."

"She's a bitch, ain't she?" he gags again.

"By the way, where did you meet? How long have you been married?" I ask. You never know about these things.

They tell the story about old Pete Haviland when he was county chairman—this must be about thirty years ago—who had this perfect candidate for county clerk; big family, well respected, church warden, good business. The Republicans did some digging and discovered that there was some irregularity, a mistake on his marriage license, and of course whispered around that the couple were not married and their four or five children were all bastards. It wrecked him, ruined his business, the whole family had to move away. We lost the election too.

"She was a blind date at school," Ferguson says eagerly. "Neither of us could find anybody tall enough and so we just went ka-boom. That was six years ago. We've been married five. Dropped her right in her tracks, you might say. Couldn't afford to let that one get away."

"Where was this?"

"Where was what?"

"Where were you married?"

"In Syracuse," he answers.

"Children?"

"Naw," he gets up, pulls his shirt off over his head and sits back down. "We got no time for children. Shit, you saw her today. She's the best damn worker I got. And the cheapest," he laughs. "Well, you're the politician; what do you think my chances would be?"

"Pretty slim," I tell him truthfully.

Truthful, yes, but you know how someone like Ferguson might react. The ski area, the disposable house, the big cats on the wall.

There were footsteps outside. The front door opens, closes, and then comes the sound of pans and cutlery in the kitchen, some switches clicked. "Hey, hon," her voice from the kitchen. "Is Mr. Bryan staying for lunch?"

"I don't know. Can you stay for lunch?" he relays the question as if I were at a distance. Before I can answer there's the soft pad of feet, her head pokes around the doorway.

"It's just an old casserole I made last night, but it's sometimes better heated up," she tells me. It's as if I've been invited to a hot, shoeless game of Monopoly. I say yes.

"You get that roof finished?" he barks, winking at me. She's back in the kitchen.

"Um'hm." She returns.

"Christ almighty, look at yourself, woman. You look like a common laborer and here I am sitting with an important politician. Go get yourself cleaned up. How am I going to be a Congressman with you looking like that?"

She looks damned good; nevertheless, she ascends the spiral staircase and goes into the bedroom.

"Well, okay," he continues. "Say everybody's crazy enough to pick me in the primary. Then there's the real election. What's the opposition like? Who are the Republicans going to put up now that Kleinsinger has resigned?"

"The talk seems to point to Assemblyman Green."

"What's he like?"

"Not much. But don't worry about him yet. Let's get through the primary first." There's a buzzing sound, like an insect against the ceiling. My eyes follow the noise to the half-opened door at the top of the landing. She's unzipped the coverall and her smooth body squirms from the old blue skin, brown bare shoulders first, then golden breasts in quivering proportions that would have disheartened Praxiteles. It's only a quick glimpse, for I look away just as the door is nudged shut by her toe.

"How about a drink?" Howie asks.

"Not a bad idea," I answer.

"Well, could I beat this Green?" he asks, returning from the kitchen with a couple of Scotches. "He's been in the Legislature. He's got the experience. He's got an edge in the enrollment figures hasn't he?"

"Well, Yost and Sinnemok are part of the assembly district so he's known around here. But not Cade, so you'd both start more or less even down there. And that's where the big vote is *and* our organizational strength. You'd have an edge there."

"If I get through the primary."

"Yes. Also Green has a lousy record in the Legislature. Just a glorified messenger boy. I've campaigned against him before. Matt Wriston ran against him, so I know his weaknesses."

"How did Wriston do?" He's grinning. The kid has some cute spots in him after all.

"Well, he lost but . . . look, let's not worry about Green until the time comes," I tell him. The door on the landing opens and she emerges, hands putting pins into the high mound of corn silk. I figure she's only had time to pull on the beige stretch pants and slip the dark blue turtleneck over what I had just seen. The descent of the stairs is a moving marvel, hands still busy at the top of her head, the face a demure valentine, and the nature of the spiral slowly turning her completely around twice with everything rolling at random.

"Let's eat," Howie says, jumping up from the pit, grabs her with a playful swat on the butt. She returns an elbow into his stomach which he counters with a forearm smash on her shoulder. For a moment, I expect a preprandial free-for-all, wondering if I were expected to share in the fun as I am the leftover casserole. It would be no contest, me between the two of them. In her stocking feet, she's just under the six-foot mark. Her femininity is as developed as her size and she soons begs for quarter, letting him push her into the kitchen.

The kitchen also looks out over the mountain and we sit on plastic chairs around an oval formica-topped table, the first pieces of real furniture I've seen. As we eat, he talks about the new ski run he's building, points out the toy-sized bulldozer way at the top of the mountain, a wake of busted timber behind it. There's an easygoing manliness about him, a security, that strengthens the intense, somewhat boyish enthusiasm in his voice. He's got appeal, no question about it, if it can be put across. If we really *want* to put it across.

A lot of candidates are terrific in small groups and lousy in the more important large crowds. Harriman was an example of that.

They review business details as we eat; health department permits for a new sewer line, zoning appeals, mortgages, bank notes. She seems to do all the bookkeeping for the corporation. It's tasty chicken and mushroom casserole, too. The girl can cook. "Want some catsup?" he offers and then dumps an appalling amount of it on his own plate. She doesn't seem to notice or mind.

"Let me show you the rest of the house," he says, picking at his teeth. "Designed this staircase myself," he says going ahead. "I checked a book out of the library on ironmongering . . . nothing to it."

There's only one room upstairs, two if the oversized pink-tiled bathroom is counted. But the bedroom, where my gaze had been attracted a short while ago, turns out to be like the rest of the house. Deep carpet, built-in cabinets, sliding panel closets, and only two pieces of furniture. An enormous, translucent plastic armchair lolls in one corner like a beach toy and in the center of the room is a round bed that must be about eight feet in diameter. The empty husk of coveralls drapes over the edge.

"We can get into it from a different side every night," Ferguson tells me with unaffected delight, even pointing.

But the curious quality of this stark room is the amount of light, for there are no windows, not the usual kind, but only small gun-ports which the self-taught architect has inserted in the walls at ceiling level. It doesn't seem enough, and then a glimmering catches my eye and explains the even illumination. Fixed to the ceiling above the round bed is a plate-glass mirror about six feet square.

"I know what you mean," Ferguson says soberly, for I have unconsciously started, grunted with surprise. "It doesn't look right, does it? But I looked all over and couldn't find a *round* mirror that was big enough for the bed."

"Bryan, any truth to the rumor your candidate and his wife have an enormous mirror over their bed?"

"That's an outright, dirty lie." How about: "Mr. and Mrs.

Ferguson have never shown me their bedroom?" Or how about: "Doesn't everybody???" Oh, Christ!!

Ferguson drives me down to my car. His wife stays behind, the roofing job finished, and there are probably chores to keep her busy inside the house for the rest of the day. Maybe the mirror needs polishing. He shuts off the jeep engine and we sit in the silence of the Austrian village he's founded. A foot braces against the frame of the car.

"Well," he says after a while. "What do you think? Should I run?"

"No," I tell him. "Why should you want to get into this business. Why? You've got everything a man would want in this world. You can take off anytime you want. You owe nothing to nobody. Also, you'd probably get your block knocked off, if not in the primary then later." I came pretty close to saying more, but I had the sudden urge to go fishing, to get up there behind the mountain where the clear streams were, and try out a new Phoebe.

As I watched his face, he looked pretty stupid, the expression on it. The jaw dropped slightly, the eyes sort of glazed and the tongue curled back in the mouth to push against a molar. It was, the more I watched, quite the reverse. He was calculating, thinking something out. Then the look was gone.

"You know," he looks up at the mountain. "He skiied here once." I didn't have to ask who he meant. A chill went through me. "He was a real heller, wasn't he? Did you know Bobby?"

"Oh, I met him once or twice. I can't say I knew him."

"What he lacked in style he made up in balls. He took that mountain like nobody I ever saw." He stops talking, still looking at the mountain as if the marks of the Kennedy *schuss* were indelibly traced on it. I get out and walk to my car. There are harps and happy sounds inside of me. The sun is beautiful, everything is beautiful. I see rainbows flashing on the end of the line. I've done my duty, I've done my favor. I'm free! And then the son of a bitch calls out, "Hey. What should I call you?"

"What do you mean?"

"Well, manager, agent – advisor or what?"

"You mean you're going to go for it?" I ask. The line goes slack and a catbird mocks me.

"Shit, why not?" he giggles, and I'm surprised he doesn't jump up in the seat and give the Tarzan yell again.

"Well, officially," I return to the jeep. And, by God, he puts his hand out—Scouts forever. "Officially, I'll be your campaign manager. But you can call me Tommy. Or Bryan. By the way, what's your wife's name?" And he blushes at the oversight.

"Helen," he says. That was a foolish question, I should have known.

Those damned Kennedys. With their self-righteous sacrifice and service. Their personal *cum populo* holy crusades. The McCarthys, the Stevensons—none of them have the same effect, they appeal to the loonies, the bleeding hearts—the well-meaners—those liberal types who come out of the petunia beds every so often to support some guy they know is going to lose simply because they like to lose, it *shows* them the "system" is no good. They want to be shown every now and then.

But the Kennedys. They're different. How many kids like Ferguson have been brought into the family because of them? Cluttered up the stage with kids like this, get me mixed up with such amateurs. Knocking their brains out for what—nothing. NOTHING. And here I am. What the hell favor do I owe Connors to get me into this? When was the last time he went down for me? I've got to get out!

Sunday

Well, it wasn't easy with the head I had this morning but the goddamn garden is in. . . . ALL In. I planted everything, much to Alma's disapproval. But it looks like I'll be busy later on.

"You're not going to put the corn in now, are you? And beans too?" She asks, seeing all the packets of seeds I plunk down. My head rattles similarly, dry seeds rasping.

"Let's live dangerously this year, Alma," I say. It was so balmy today, deceptively warm perhaps, for there's still a good chance of frost before April is over.

She had just planted lettuce and straddled the row, her feet in an old pair of my waders, tops cut down. She gave me a scowly look from beneath the floppy brim of the flowered sun hat. I turned away from her and leaned into the small cultivator, turning the moist earth.

"Seems like a waste of good seed to me," she calls after me, but whether she refers to the corn or to me is anybody's guess.

Last night at Tiny's we kept things pretty much on the "old days" level. The old games. How once Hayes Singer scored on a busted play and must have run about 170 yards, back and forth across the field. Safe things like that. Several mean-looking boys in the corner booth giving me the eye. "I'm going to give your place a bad name if I hang out here anymore," I tell him. Tiny just smiles and goes back to watching Perry Mason.

It's funny that we never had a vegetable garden until after my father died. My mother had only been interested in flowers up till then, had won prizes at the county fair for her asters. This year we've put in a smaller garden, not quite all the way to the back fence but still filling the space between the lilac bushes and the garage.

Two kinds of lettuce, peas, green beans—beets this year instead of carrots—and then the corn. Two rows of Golden Bantam, so by late August we'll have to buy more from the stands, but that's all right. There's something about planting corn, and watching it grow. The stalks are stately and appealing, the greenness a refreshment, and the silvery tassels seem to reach out, tease something inside me. To place a few dry kernels in the earth's warm lap, shape a mound over them, pat it down—it's probably one of the last personal mystical experiences left around.

Wouldn't any farmer laugh to read the above. Their experiences are far from mystical. Dawn to dusk, backbreaking labor planting a couple of hundred acres of the stuff and then worry for three or four months about rains or drought. Or to get through all that and to look out some afternoon and see a sudden hailstorm slashing down the tall green stalks like an invisible scythe. There goes the herd, the mortgage, the loan for the new silo—it all depends on those green shoots coming to full harvest. On the other hand, they must feel something of the mystical way I do or else they wouldn't be farmers.

I'm on my second boiler-maker when these boys amble over and start to talk. It's funny these days. You look into a black face, into dark expressionless eyes and you immediately think— look out, bad stuff! Then that face smiles, begins to talk in a light, feathery tone, and you wonder how far apart we are, how bad it really is.

One of these kids had recognized me from Wriston's campaign. He had been a poster runner, and must have been in grade school then. They are in a group calling themselves the Peaceables, some kind of an activist bunch in the fourth ward. Very inquisitive about Wriston running for Congress. I was noncommittal. I bought them some beer and they all sidled up, just a bunch of young, friendly college boys—they go to the State University down in Cade—rubbing shoulders with the old pro. Just a bunch of young, friendly black boys trading quips with the white man. Crap. To think I'm responsible for getting them interested at all and now they're going to turn around and work against us probably. "Here, sonny, here's fifty cents; put these posters on everything that doesn't move in the fourth ward."

While one of them was talking to me knowledgeably about the urban renewal mess down in Hinton and how Wriston could make some votes out of it—a smooth-faced kid with some sort of a medallion hanging from a heavy chain around his neck (Why do they have to wear all that junk anyway? Just to remind us of *their* origins?), all I was thinking of was cunt. I was wondering if any of them knew of a girl, some buttery brown-skin darling just laying around humming to herself. They're so serious—about everything, even cunt. Well, they have reason to be, but do they have to be so goddamned prim, almost prissy. If I had said, "Boys do you know where I can get a piece of ass to-night?" they would have blushed purple.

Of course I knew where I could go, or thought I did.

So we are taking a chance this spring with the garden. I push the cultivator, purging the fumes of last night at the same time. I told Alma a little bit about Ferguson. She wasn't too impressed, muttering to herself as she stooped over to put in the peas. Once or twice angrily flipping back the hat brim from her face.

"It's better if you talk to me, Alma," I finally say. "What's the matter?"

"Oh, I just mourn the day, mourn the day you ever got mixed up in this business. Your father used to think it was so wonderful taking you around with him as a boy and I told him . . . I told him," she repeats the admonition while tamping down the earth, "I said, 'Samuel, it's enough that you're in this dirty business but don't get the boy in it too. Let him go.' I told him. 'You'll be sorry,' I said."

"Well, was he?" She doesn't answer but takes a few steps and picks up a hoe and begins to dig another trench, hacking the earth.

"What does your son do, Mrs. Bryan?" she asks herself. "My son is a public servant," she answers. "That is, when he isn't trying to get votes for numbskulls and crooks."

"Calm down," I tell her. "You're planting those peas too close together."

"My mind is not on it." She straightens up, dusts off her hands, and it seems she's through for the day—through with everything—but then picks up a packet of flowering sweet peas she likes to sow among the others. "Connors is up to something with this deal," she continues. "You know it. I don't see why you've forsaken Matt Wriston, if he wants to run. You worked for him once before; thought the world of him. God knows he deserves this chance." Her voice startles me. Momentarily it had lost its grumpy crackle and was the clear, sweet voice of a young woman.

"People don't always get what they deserve," I say. "Anyway, Wriston just isn't congressional material, just as___"

"Balderdash! I suppose this house builder is?" she snaps.

The Peaceables were around me, hanging on every word I dropped—nice boys but green. Green black boys. Their cachet tickets were being punched. I could hear them talk in the next couple of days, "Ran into Tommy Bryan—you know him—and he said . . ."

So I played it to the hilt. Inevitably . . . INEVITABLY . . . one of them asked, "Did you know him?" gesturing up to the Saints of the crème de menthe. Or he may have made it easier, I can't remember, and said, "You knew him, didn't you?"

"Who? Bobby?" I say. "Sure."

"What was he like?" A coming together around me, a press of yearning, crying, bombed-out blacks.

"Shy. Very shy," I answer slowly, reflectively. A few heads bob, nod recognition. Yes, they had read that somewhere too; now it was being confirmed. Where had I read it? "But the coolest pair of eyes you ever looked into." No crap there. "Tough-minded, very tough-minded," so says Schlesinger, but he likes that word. Everything is tough this or that. "Fantastic ability to grasp and put himself into situations, roles that were far away from his own experience." Oh, they knew that, they knew that. Yes. Yes.

And do you know what I was thinking about all this time, Bob Kennedy, while I delivered this eulogy to you in Tiny's Home Spot at around midnight? I was thinking of the reflections in that mirror on the ceiling, of those two gorgeous creatures rolling around on that round bed and I was thinking of them both— BOTH. I must be going queer, but I couldn't separate the vision of those long, tapering thighs, those high bouncy breasts from the hard-pounding butt and muscled back belonging to "our next Congressman." I couldn't think of one without the other, together —all four of them, two on the bed and two in the mirror.

So I break out of my Nubian court and I go to the pay phone and call R. She's about to go to sleep and anyway, she says, it's the wrong time of the month. But she hears something in my voice and says, "Well, come on over, I'll think of something."

"No, I don't want that," I say, meaning I need the whole bang-up course and not just a little nibbling on the antipasto, but she gets the wrong idea.

"Well, screw you, you bastard!" she says, insulted, and hangs up.

"You know there's something I never told you," my mother says this morning. We were sitting on the bench at the end of the yard, resting, the garden all planted. She was looking at the back of the house with a strange expression as if she were seeing it, not for the first time, but with a fresh eye.

"What's that?" I ask, cuddling her a little bit. She had been glum, silently angry with me, and now she's suddenly laughing, kittenish. "What haven't you told me?"

"Well," she says, pushing me away and getting up. "Your father voted for Eisenhower—both times." And she picks up the hoe, a rake, and starts for the house.

"There may be a bad Democrat now and then, but they are never as bad as Republicans." That was the saying in our house, my father's dictum. Sometimes the same thought took variations or was amplified such as, "You know what Republicans are, don't you, boy? They're Whigs, that's what they are." The word was given a hard "g." Whi-G. He would come down on it with all the weight of his years on the bench. Whi-G.

"But what about Lincoln, Pop? He was a pretty good President."

"Lincoln," he'd exclaim, putting his feet up on the desk. Delicate ankles sheathed in dark blue silk. "Lincoln! Why he wasn't a Republican, he was an ambitious Kentucky Democrat. He's the only good one they've ever had—the first and the last good one. Wasn't he? Eh, wasn't he?" And he'd fix me with that eye that was known to melt down the guilty, inept attorneys, and all other idiots unlucky enough to come before him. They would become anonymous pools. My father never laughed, not out loud, that is. He would sometimes smile and if you looked close there'd be a 20,000-candle-power gleam in his eyes, as if all the ha-has in the world were rotating around inside his skull.

"Listen," he'd continue. "They may say a lot about Democrats sometimes." First year in law school, and I was putting the Billy Brown machine on my newly found and fashioned moral rack. "But the Republicans are the only ones who have stolen a Presidential election. Stolen from Governor Tilden to keep themselves out of prison. Didn't they? Eh? You know the history." Then he lit another cigarette, muttering, "Sons of bitches," almost as if the Tilden-Hayes campaign had been the month before.

"When we get a party organization going good, *they* call it a machine," he continued. "But nobody ever hears about a Republican machine. Oh no! They call them something else, something more dignified. Now let me tell you about Billy Brown," he said, recrossing his ankles and brushing cigarette ash from his vest.

"You can't win elections without getting people to vote for you. And how do you do that? You offer them something; hope, a dream of something . . . and *then* you do your damnedest to deliver. That's what Billy Brown has done. He's delivered. Maybe not a lot for this or that group, but something for everybody. He's spread it around. Take the judicial now. I would never have been on the court were it not for what some people call a 'deal' he made with the Republicans. And why not? There are a number of good men, of both parties, that would never get on the bench if it were put to a majority vote—they belong to the wrong minority party in their area. But Captain Billy calls everybody together and says, 'Okay, you got a man here—we'll endorse him, if you back our man Bryan up in Yost.' That was smart politics, but it took the court out of politics too and brought balance to the bench."

"Yeah, but he's still the one to make the decisions. He picked you, for example."

"Now look here," he said, snubbing out the cigarette to play with the half-empty package. "Just remember one thing. The Democrats started out as the party of aristocrats and they became the party of the people. Those two elements are the mainstay of the party; they're still there, the aristocrats—whether they are of the mind or class it doesn't matter—and the people. What's in between is what the Republican Party is made up of— Whi-G trash!

"But I tell you one thing," he said, deciding on another cigarette. "There's something that's even worse."

"What's that, Pop?"

"Beware, my boy, of the green-eyed liberal." And his eyes burned merrily through the smoke.

Tiny had turned out the lights and locked the door and a few of us still sat around, stonily watching Gary Cooper trying to smuggle a scientist out of Nazi Germany. The Peaceables had left long ago, probably back to their poli-sci textbooks. No cunt-crazy kids they. There was nothing on the news about anything.

So I drive by R.'s trailer around three—two hours before her husband is scheduled to come home from the night shift. She says he smells of copper. Two hours for something that will take but a few minutes, the way I feel. No lights, of course. And I just sit in the car, thinking of her offer, and how pitiful, how very pitiful. Because she's not really fond of going down and does it mechanically, with no passion. Maybe she learned to do it in high school, in order to compete with other, prettier girls, and now everybody goes down, almost—and there's the irony. But so she offered tonight, exposed that soft part of herself usually kept inside the flinty shell, and I slammed her. I'll send her some flowers tomorrow, something gaudy like a potted begonia. She likes things like that. I'm sorry, R. We've come to the end of our rutty relationship, I fear.

Driving home last night, I came up on the small rise above Yost. It startled me, for I thought it was a big fire. It was just a low haze catching the moon, the yellow sodium lights, reflecting it. But at first glance it looked as if the whole city was on fire. At least, the garden is all in, frost or not.

Thursday

First the note I got from Matt Wriston on Monday. No, that wasn't first. First was talking to Pug Connors on Monday. "Did you see him?" he asks on the phone. "What do you think?"

"He's lovely," I say.

"No, whatta you think?"

"He's a nice boy. He'll photograph well. He's eager. He's going to go for it."

"Gee, that's swell, pally," Connors says. "Did you meet his wife?" And there's a soft chuckle.

"Yes."

"She's something, isn't she? Now look," the voice becomes very plain, "I got lots to do. Our convention is in ten days. Minkus hasn't decided yet about his but the Cade County committee is going to meet the following Monday. You get him down to meet some of those guys down there. I'll send you a list. You know the ones in Sinnemok. But get him around. There's some church suppers coming up. Get him started, you know."

I know.

Then Wriston's letter.

Dear Tommy,

    Strictly confidential, but I wonder if we couldn't get together to talk about some of the problems I feel concern us both. It would be best if you come to my house where we could talk frankly and with no fear of interruption. Needless to say, it would be just the two of us with the addition of the fair Emily. How does Wednesday night suit you?

Sincerely,
Matt
Matthew P. Wriston

Bridesmaid Bryan. How many more little *accouchements* will you assist with? Their passion can be understood, but explain the passion of the matchmaker, the pimp. His eye is on the keyhole.

It's mostly routine right now. This is the best part, laying it all out on paper before personalities get into it. This is the science before everything goes haywire.

I get out the lists of committeemen in Sinnemok County. Check off the ones I remember talking against Minkus. We can get some of those to at least give Ferguson some show there. Pug will take care of Yost. Cade is something else with the old man. Pug apparently will help with that too.

IMPORTANT: Try to set up a tour of the University in Cade before the committee meeting. Contact the *Register-Herald* and see if we can't get a story and some pictures. If we can get some of the kids interested in Ferguson that would look good.

Primary is June 14! A little more than two months. Maybe I can get him in as a judge at the Apple Blossom Festival in Sinnemok, get some TV.

But the budget comes first. We'll have to hit the media hard to get his name around and to show the fence-sitters a big cock. I figure around twenty thousand. That's for openers. He doesn't flick an eye when I show him the budget, but that's today—go back to last night.

Go back to Tuesday morning. Alma in the kitchen fixing me scrambled eggs. It unsettles her to have me around the house during the day, even though I spend most of the time on the sun porch where I have all my files, papers. My own phone.

"They had a frost up in Albany last night," she says, looking out the window over the sink, looking out at our garden.

"That was Albany," I tell her.

"Yes, it was a warning, though," she says. Just then the phone in the sun porch rings. It's one of the boys on the newspaper.

"Hey, Bryan, what's this about the Yost Democrats putting up this guy Ferguson from Alton for Congress?"

"Search me. Where'd you hear that?" No need to ask that. Pug Connors and his Magic Balloon.

"Oh, come on. What's it all about? We're going to do a story on it anyway. Does this mean a break with Captain Billy?"

"I really don't know," I tell him truthfully.

I really like Emily Wriston and wished she liked me. Black hair slightly graying around the soft peach of a face. The assured way she moves around; a sly awareness that she's above all this crap. She opens the door for me last night and gives me an amused look, as if I were some sort of a drunk that's always showing up for a glass of water. But I was invited, Emily. Your husband invited me, because he wants to put his head on the block again.

The counselor is in his study, a beautiful room thanks to her money and his pretentions. Lots of books. The stereo hi-fi tuned to baroque chamber music. Wriston greets me with that wry smile, the same look he gives on election eves — screwed again — and hands me the evening paper. "I suppose you've seen this," he says. Too polite or too cagey to say what he really means.

With Purcell in the background I read it again, just for show.

FERGUSON SEEN AS COUNTY DEMS CHOICE

There are indications that Yost County Democrats may go their own way when they meet April 12th by endorsing Howard Ferguson, Alton contractor, as a candidate for Congress.

If so, it may indicate a break with "Captain" Billy Brown, Cade County Democratic leader and acknowledged boss of the three-county congressional district, that includes Sinnemok as well as Yost.

John Connors, Yost County Democratic Chariman, could not be reached for comment on the move. Mr. Ferguson is a 31-year-old contractor and builder who has developed Ellis Mountain into one of the state's leading ski areas. Two years ago he was chosen one of New York State's Outstanding Young Men by the Junior Chamber of Commerce, and has long been involved in civic affairs in the mountain area.

In the past the relationship between "Captain" Brown and the local Democrats has been a close one, but there have been indications that all was not . . .

"What about it?" Wriston asks, handing me a bourbon. Emily has come and gone twice, leaving a tray of small sandwiches and a bowl of ice.

"I only know what I read in the papers," I say.

"Oh, come now, Tommy." He stands over me for a time and then goes to the fireplace, leans on the mantel. Lawyers always seem to have to lean on something when they talk, maybe their hands are so calloused from the jury rail they can only talk that way. "I suppose it is useless for me to try to reach you now," he begins and then gives me much the same spiel he gave to Connors and the rest in his office. Except he throws in our old relationship. Well, I did work for him, worked for him hard. And not just for the money. He was a good candidate and I liked him. But times have changed.

"You sound very serious," I finally say.

"I am very serious, very serious indeed. Can you imagine this area being represented by a man like Cranston?"

"Well, you nominated him for the Supreme Court once," I say, and he gives me a sharp look; he's had the same question twice in one week. Not counting the times he's asked himself.

"Yes, well, I had to do that," he answers. "You understand. But not Congress. No. Goddamnit. No." He puts his drink on the mantel and looks down in the fireplace. There's no fire, which is a slip-up, but then it's warm tonight too. "Also, there was no chance of him winning the Supreme Court."

"You seem certain he would win for Congress?" He nods several times.

"He would win," he answers. "We couldn't beat Abe, but he's out of the picture now, and if they put Green up — why I nearly beat him, in his own district. With Cade thrown in against him, any Democrat would have a chance. Even Cranston."

"The conditional is not my favorite tense," I say and he smiles. His dark eyes soften up a bit. "So what are you going to do? Are you going to go through with it?"

And he seems to make up his mind right then. He nods his head. "Yes. I've got some following. I can get the petitions needed. I'll split things up if I have to. Rather a nonentity like Green in Washington than that slick tool Cranston."

"That sounds like treason," I say, but I'm not angry. You have to be able to judge to be angry and who does that anymore. Anyway, you can't get mad at a guy who warns you beforehand he's going to double-cross. But he goes on.

"Treason to whom?" he says. "I've done my share. When was the last time a Democrat carried Yost before me? This is an act of conscience," he says.

Oh, yeah . . . we've heard that before.

Later, I think it's funny. Why do all these guys fight for the privilege of having their heads knocked off. There's just an outside chance we might take Congress but it's outside and here they all are clamoring over each other for it. Excepting Cranston, of course, he's been told and promised something later. He may get a judgeship if he loses, because he'd have to give up as DA to run. But the Fergusons and Wristons — I'll never understand them.

If I were Matt Wriston I'd stay home with my plump, rich wife and listen to the Brandeburg Concerto on the hi-fi.

"It's the greatest poker game in the world, boy. And you'll meet the worst people in the world but also the best. And I'll tell you something else, boy," after a few kaf-kafs over the weed. "When you walk into a room and there's suddenly several hundred people on their feet, screaming and applauding simply because you walked in — well, it gets to any man."

Yes, Your Honor, but did it ever occur to you that they're on their feet not so much for you but for themselves too. It makes them feel goose-pimply good.

This morning I was telling Pug Connors about Matt Wriston, especially about the hi-fi because Connors was in his shop making some adjustments on a shortwave receiver. It must be for a friend, or more likely for some votes, because the craft he learned in the Navy is more of a hobby than a business these days.

But I was telling him about the evening and especially how at one point there was this sudden wish-wash of hash on the hi-fi, Corelli struggling against the waves of interference and ultimately swamped in a tumult of hound-dog guitar and cornball lyrics. Wriston had ignored the first sounds, tried to talk over them, then finally jumped to his feet and stalked to the tuner, his face almost yellow and fingers trembling with anger. He failed to bring back the chamber music clean.

"That's one reason I want to go to Congress," he muttered. "The first thing I'd do is to investigate the FCC and find out why the public air is crammed with junk. All decent music is overwhelmed."

Connors smiles and looks around his workshop for something, finds the cover to the set and fits it over the glowing exposed tubes. "And you wonder why I don't back him. Can you wonder, telling me something like that? All that needs to be done and all he really worries about is his own special music."

"Come on, Pug. There's more to him than that."

"I don't think so," Connors says, making a few fine adjustments with a long, slender screwdriver. "So he wanted you to

work for him" He makes the last adjustment. "Do you want to?"
And he gives me a wide-eyed, beagle look.

"No." And I'm about to go over the budget I've worked up —
that I'm taking up to Ferguson — when the intercom plips on and
Annie tells him from the house, "Johnnie — You have a phone
call."

"Who is it?" he asks the box on the wall.

"I think it's Captain Billy," her voice comes back. Pug goes to
the extension phone on the bench, switches it on, but doesn't
pick it up. Just rests his hand on it and looks at me and smiles.
And waits.

"Okay," I finally say. "I'll check in with you if Ferguson
doesn't buy the package."

"You do that, pally," he says. When I pull out of the driveway
past Little Ben, I can see him through the window of his shop.
Talking on the phone and smiling.

The florist didn't have any begonias. But they had a pot of lilies left over from Easter. So I sent those to R. Sort of appropri-
ate at that.

I'd give anything to know what was said in that phone conversation. If only I were one of those big-shot political writers: how
they use all sorts of cross references, actual quotes from both
sides gleaned in early-morning booze sessions — then maybe only
second- or third-hand.

I can imagine the old man propped up in the hospital bed as
he must have been strapped into a Spad in World War I, his life
ticking over very slowly, tubes dripping life essences into him at
one end while more tubes drained off the wastes at the other.
He'd hold the phone in his right hand, and a cigar stub about
three inches long would be in his left. His voice would be high,
reedy, and very precise.

Someone once told me that Jack Kennedy said talking to Captain Billy on the phone was like talking to a pookah through a
door crack. Are pookahs good luck or is that a banshee?

"Hello there, Pug. I understand you've got a boy up there that wants to be a Congressman?"

"Seems like that, Captain."

"What's he like?"

"Young. Big bankroll. Very presentable. No experience."

"That makes it a little difficult, don't you know?"

"I know . . . I know. I've tried to talk him out of it, but he's got the bug."

"There'll be a place on the Bridge Authority in a few years. He's a contractor. It would be good for him."

"I don't think that would work, Captain. He's really hot for Congress."

"Well, I got commitments down here. I hate to see this, Pug. We got a good shot this year with Abe Kleinsinger out."

"I know it, but what can I do. He's already been around talking to some of my boys. He seems determined to get petitions even. There's no hard feelings in this, Captain."

"Sure, Pug, no hard feelings. Well, keep in touch." And the connection goes dead, suddenly as if the wire had been cut.

It was more likely like this:

"Good morning, Pug, how's it going?"

"Just fine, Captain. He's going for it."

"That's splendid. Any response from the other?"

"I just heard that he's definitely in."

"Well, things are coming along. So that's fine. You must bring this new boy of yours down. I'd like to meet him. It will be good seasoning for him anyway for something in the future."

"I think so too," Pug might say, then smiles as the old man continues.

"I hope your county convention won't be too lopsided."

"I'm going to knock Cranston's block off," Pug says. There's probably a whiskery rattle at the other end. Pug waits until the old man catches his breath. "I can't wait to see Jim Hurley's face."

"Try to be kind to Jim, Pug. He's done us some favors down here. He's still important to us."

"Yeah, sure."

"Well, it sounds good. Keep in touch."

But most likely, it went like this:

"Look here, Pug," the thin voice says. "Have you heard from the state chairman yet?"

"About the state committeemen? Yes."

"Well what do you think?" Captain Billy asks. "I know we don't share an assembly district but I think it's important that each county have two on the state committee rather than just this business of two from each AD."

"I agree," says Pug.

Connors had a hell of a time holding his state committee post last time and finally had to make some kind of an arrangement with Minkus. Wonder what that cost him?

Estimated Expenditures – Primary, Howard Ferguson

Item: Outdoor Advertising Displays

25 locations, mostly in Cade County, at $110 per spot for month of May and first two weeks of June.
Artwork and printing of sheets, about $1000 extra.

$3750

"Shit," Howie Ferguson says, "here I am contributing to these bastards spoiling the countryside. That's one of the first things I'm going to do when I get to Congress is put a ban on billboards."

"Well, wait until you get to Congress," I say, thinking between him and Wriston, the sights and sounds of America are going to be radically changed. "Anyway, you have to have them."

"Is that what I'm paying you?" he says, looking up from the ledger sheet I had given him.

"Too much?"

"No, it doesn't seem like enough," he says.

"Don't worry; if you win, I want a good job. I'll be your legislative assistant." He gets a nutty grin on his face. The term delights him – makes it sound as if he's already elected, then he looks back at the sheet.

"Hey, hon," he shouts to his wife in the kitchen. "We're going to buy five hundred dollars worth of balloons! How about that! The kid loves balloons," he says to me, winking.

He reads on down the list. Buttons, bumper strips, newspaper ads, brochures, radio and TV spots, telephone canvassers, headquarters (rent and expenses). A dark red, troubled look floods the Jack Armstrong face and he throws the budget on the cushions.

"What's that item, Primary Day Expenses—four thousand dollars? What are we going to do, buy votes?"

"No, no," I assure him. "You have to have workers to get out the vote for you. Rent cars, pay poll watchers in every district. Many of them take off from their own jobs and you have to make it up to them."

"Where do all these people come from?"

"I have a list," I tell him.

"Okay," he sighs. Then, "Jesus Christ, this democracy business is goddamned expensive. I guess you want a check. Hey, Helen," he shouts again, but she must have been listening because she's already in the room, a large multiple checkbook in her arms.

Note for Ferguson: About wife's clothes.

Does she have to wear them so short? The electorate likes a little sex but it should be hinted, not thrown at them all spread-eagled and up to the hairs. This morning, her dress (?) ended just where the long thighs began, the legs sheathed in bluish gray hose. Hair in a ponytail. A child bride. A child bride with size 38 hangers.

They sit on the soft rim of the living-room pit—Ken and Barbie dolls, only life-size. And there is a pathetic eagerness on Helen's face. Wifely pride maybe. Maybe a Young Married's *Good Housekeeping* interest in civic affairs blooming in her round cheeks. Or maybe Helen Ferguson already pictures herself leading the other congressional wives in a frug contest on the Capitol steps. Anyway, that's the way she looks when she hands him the checkbook, even opens it for him. I can see her neat handwriting, everything carefully accounted. When he takes up a ball-point pen, studiously licks the tip, I have to get up and turn away, look up the slope of the mountain. There's a pool up there I haven't got to yet and I should be there now, play-ing the shallows.

"Do I make this out to the county committee?" he asks.

"No," I tell him gently. "This being a primary, the committee can't be involved, not officially. Just make it out to cash." So just like that he makes out a check for the preliminary expen-ses — fifteen thousand BUCKS!

It's no better when I look around at them. They are looking at me as if I were a scoutmaster briefing them on the spring cook-out. "We'll fix someone up for you as a finance chairman," I say, taking the check from him. They both fall back on the cush-ions together. One big arm around her.

"Well, I guess we're in business," he says. "You better get used to it, hon." A normal-sized girl would have been crushed by the squeeze he puts on her.

"What?" she says, adroitly breaking the hold and sitting on the edge of the conversation pit. The dress is up all the way, exposing a pearly blue buttock.

"Just call me Mr. Congressman from now on."

"Oh, Mr. Congressman," she says in an affected, teeny-bopper voice. I'm reminded of Zasu Pitts! How about that? They pause in their wrestling match to say good-bye, wave me to the door. When I pull away in the car, I almost swear a slight tremor shakes the ground.

Conversation pit, hell! Their store of talk must be exhausted in a few minutes; drainage ditches, the merits of steel pilings over wood supports, interest payments, etc. Then what? Down into the pit. By the fire. Do they use the different levels or just work their way around the cushioned lip in an endless, concen-tric fuck?

This is nuts.

Note for Ferguson: Clean up his language. He probably isn't aware of what he's saying half the time. Uses it the way he does catsup.

"Mr. Ferguson, our library committee is very interested in this bill that would give us more federal aid. What's your opinion on that?"

"Well, shit, lady, books are fucking important!"

Of course if we *do* get through the primary — let's say Connors is serious — we got a lot going for us. Cade would line up behind us, no funny business there IF WE WIN! Pug could count on the deputies he put on civil service. There's also the county highway boys we could use. He's never called in, that I know of, the slip he holds on that statutory rape he quashed for Lucas' son. Having the county highway Super working for us quietly, even though the board of supervisors appointed him, should be worth a couple of thousand votes.

Yes, even though Roy Lucas was killed near Wonsan, just a few miles from where I was and at about the same time, his old man would still acknowledge the debt. Family honor and all that. I wonder, when Roy stepped on that mine did he think that fourteen-year-old nookie had been worth it? I hear she's married to a teacher over in Rensselaer. Some kids.

There's only that little prick Minkus to worry about.

Tonight, Alma: "Well, how's the campaign going? She settles down in the lounge chair. Zip! Up go her feet. It's remarkable that the small, fragile head can counterbalance the rest of her. There's a letter for me on the mantel. Blue stationery and a neat, feminine hand.

Dear Mr. Bryan,

   You don't know me but I was the secretary of the Yost County Democratic Young Democratic Club when you spoke to us after President Kennedy was killed. I just want to express my surprise on hearing that you are now cooperating with Mr. Connors in working against Matthew Wriston's candidacy for Congress. He's a man ideally suited for the job, a man who in every respect is in the tradition of the person you eulogized for us in 1963 and who . . .

Well, crap. Some of Matt's hacks at work already.

"Who's the letter from?" my mother asks over *House Beautiful*.

"I don't know," I answer. "You want the return address so you can write her?"

"Why on earth would I want to do that?" she snaps, the chair seesaws a bit.

Laura Kuslowski, formerly Patrovich. Never heard of her; formerly or otherwise.

Next week is Alma's birthday. She'll be sixty-seven.

Friday

I was going into the courthouse today — to pick up a set of new enrollment lists — and saw this huge beetle on the steps. Very large. Brown. It had two large antennae with small leaflike appendages and two sharp miniature tusks. One of its wings was damaged so it couldn't fly. It would run in a circle, then try its one good wing only to ground loop; then crawl a bit more, then buzz around again. Crawl, buzz; crawl, buzz. It resembled a windup toy, programmed to run in circles, a single wing vibrating at predetermined intervals. Never seen a bug quite like this one.

Sunday

We just might have something with Ferguson. I had him out all this weekend, starting Friday night at the firemen's convention down in Green River. He was a bit shy at first, a little hesitant about putting his hand out and pronouncing his name, but he'll get over that. The important thing is the way he's able to talk to people — all kinds — once he gets started. He made a good impression with the firemen, I think, and that was quite a coup since they were from towns from all over the CD.

I like the way he plays everything. With some, Ferguson has a self-depreciatory manner that makes them feel at ease — he's no better than they are. With the pros, he's eager, earnest, with lots to learn. Or seems to. With women, he gawks, gaggles and blushes, but manly for all of it. Yet none of it seems calculated, very natural.

And he can *talk!* A remarkable number of topics, knowledgeably. Hunting. Building business. That was expected. But banking, financing, the stock market — he really scored with a banker we met at a clambake in Arthursburg yesterday:

"What do you think of this Amalgamated Research Inc. (whatever its name was)?" he asks this old coot. Eyebrows shoot up.

"Strange you should ask that. Our trust department has been looking into that," the banker answers.

"I'm a little leery of it myself," Ferguson says, tongue flipping back over the molars. "It zoomed up so quick I saw a piece in *Barron's* last week about this Coast outfit that's been taking over these think-tanks and though no names were mentioned it sounded suspicious . . ."

"Yes, yes. We came to a similar conclusion," the banker said, and I watched his eyes come back to Ferguson, take a second, more careful look.

And there was the scene at the barbecue put on by the Polish Sportsmen Club. "There I was," Howie told them, "coming around this old wall, pitch-black — way before dawn — and I come nose to nose with this buck that had been sleeping on the other side. Ya-whoop! We both jump about ten feet and take off in opposite directions. Well, shit, I just turn around and go home to bed!" Four or five of them double over. Eyes gleaming with the fun of it and a glint of something else too. With all the tall tales told, a man that can tell a story like this on himself must be some hunter. Bull's-eye!

He even swapped recipes with a couple of women today at the St. Mary's turkey dinner. Something about how Helen made dressing, some spice she uses that caught the ladies by surprise.

"Well, I just must try that," one of them said. "Your wife is

not with you today, Mr. Ferguson?" she asks, looking around
the basement hall.

"No, ma'am," Howie answers. I have to turn away as I hear
him say, "She's at home fixing some draperies."

Was that for real?

I took Red Tompkins up with me Friday morning to make
some pictures. By the time we got to Alton it was about eleven
o'clock and the sun was very hot. Tompkins said he had been up
to the ski bowl before on some photo assignment for a travel
agency but he had never met the owners. Funny guy, Tompkins.
Pale face, pointed ears, and little pink nostrils. He looked
around the place with a mixture of envy and disdain: Peter Rabbit on the outside of an insurmountable fence.

I feel sorry for Tompkins and he's a damned good photographer besides. He never laid a hand on any of those high school
girls, just took nudies of them. The guys at the newspaper said
his wife always accompanied him to the motel he used for a
"studio." So what was the harm. *Chacun a son ragoût!*

We climb up the stairs to the sun deck around the house. First
into view comes the pointed crown of a straw hat, then on the
top tread, the rest of Helen Ferguson. Tompkins makes a
gurgling noise, turns it into a belch, and looks away. Below
the broad-brimmed coolie hat, she's wearing an enormous
pair of sunglasses and a tiny yellow bikini. She's been reading
a book.

"Oh, hi," she slips off the lounge chair and stands up with a
slithery sound.

"We might be early," I apologize.

"Oh, that's all right. I just heard Howie, he's on his way
down." She turns, bends over, and picks up the walkie-talkie on
the deck. Tompkins is humming to himself, busily checking,
rechecking the settings on his Leica. But I look.

"Come on in," Helen continues. "I've made some iced tea."

She leads us in the house, walkie-talkie in one hand, the book held over the smooth expanse of golden belly, almost a gesture of modesty.

And the book shielding the glorious Ferguson navel! Daniel Bell's *The End of Ideology*. Considering its position, it occurred to me that it was serving an ancillary but no less apt usage, unplanned by its author.

And there were more books inside. After we had taken off our shoes and stepped in, it looks as if Howie has ransacked several libraries, whole sections of biography, history, and government rifled and the booty spilled all over the carpet. The kitchen table has a stack of memoirs and political biography. George Kennan sprawls open in the hallway, and when I use the bathroom later, a volume of Dean Acheson leans against Harold Laski's *American Presidency*, two tipsy pragmatists on the dirty clothes hamper. The ubiquitous Galbraith hangs over a lower tread of the stairs and William F. Buckley saucers a large coffee mug.

More books are scattered around the fire pit and these of a more sober type, as if theory and anecdotes were being supplemented by facts and statistics. Tables and booklets issued by state and federal bureaus of commerce, agriculture, etc. Population, labor surveys. Joint legislature committee reports on transportation, conservation . . . everything.

We watch Helen go up the stairs. ("I'll just change," she said, lowered lashes making soft shadows on the round cheeks.) I know what Tompkins is thinking, but I also remember Howie proudly showing me this wrought-iron staircase, saying how he learned to make it from a library book on ironmongering.

Do you suppose after a serpentine screw by firelight, and while catching their breath for another go-around, they pick up a few manuals, leaf through the histories and theories? I can hear Ferguson, perhaps sampling a passage with a playful slap on the gorgeous ass, "Hey, hon, listen to what this guy Moynihan says here!"

The conversation pit has come full round; the ultimate evolution of that impulse bred on *Projects for Boys and Girls* and weaned on *Popular Mechanics*.

Anyway, we got a great shot of Howie on top that big No. 12 Cat that he wheels around like an MG. It will look great on a billboard. And some nice shots of him and Helen together on the porch, the mountain behind them. She came back looking like a cool million. Real class there. (Kept wondering how Tompkins' gelded imagination would react if I had told him about the mirror.)

The only minus of the weekend popped up where it was least expected – at Cade State U. For some reason, his age maybe, I thought Howie might come on strong with these college kids, but the minute we stepped on the campus he showed a nervousness, an insecurity – for the first time. Almost had to push him into the Student Union building, and he approached them with a stiff-legged awkwardness. It's strange, but with all his accomplishments and natural abilities, he must feel very sensitive about his one year of college.

Of course, the groovies in Anaemia didn't help any. What a bunch of smart, nasty little snot-noses. Howie dutifully and not without courage goes from table to table, introducing himself, telling what he was doing there. What was he doing there? Some would laugh in his face but most just gave him the cool deadpan, though behind the eyes was an oh-so-merry light. But the worst were establishment types, neat haircuts, ties, etc., who kept pressing Ferguson for comments on such things as the industrial-military complex, the missile gap, etc. The light behind their eyes was not at all merry, but goddamn scary. He took it pretty well, though I could see he was a little hurt. But he didn't get mad, which I was glad to see.

RFK used to say, "Don't get mad, get even."

Of course, these small-time Einsteins are going to come streaming to Wriston's unsullied banner. They'll turn over for a guy like that while giving someone like Howie the finger.

•

Really enjoyed the little session with Minkus. Howie, naturally, wasn't aware of what was going on and just sat in the corner of the cheesy real estate office with that stupid look on his face. We paid a duty call, a formality to inform Minkus that we were going to court some of his committeemen.

"Sure," he says. "I'll even give you a list of them if you want." He smiles like a Woolworth Buddha, something you might burn incense in but be afraid to leave the house with it going.

"I have a list," I tell him.

"Oh great," he says, then looking Howie over again, assaying his worth, possibilities. "There's a few suppers you might want to attend, also some barbecues. I'll give you a list of them." He's talking deep in his throat the way he does when he's being important, "As I would for any candidate, you know." The eyes pop with the effort to be fair.

"That's fine," I answer. "How much are the tickets? I remember the tickets for church suppers down here come fairly high."

"Oh, please, Tommy, c'mon," integrity speared to the core. "Everybody has expenses. That's how it is you know," he tells Howie, making him part of the family. Ferguson smiles like an angel. A dumb angel.

I don't say anything. The three of us sit there listening to the clack-click-clack-click of Minkus' secretary, a woman he's been using for a pincushion for several years now. She has prick marks all over her. I look over the inscriptions of the different lodge awards, Lions Club service plaques, the trophies won by bowling teams sponsored by the Tru-Value Real Estate, Inc. Small gold figures about to deliver small gold bombs. Minkus finally gets nervous, his voice goes up, becomes fluttery.

"You've never run for office before?" he asks Howie, but before he can answer I interrupt.

"How are we going to do down here with your committee?"

"Well, Tommy, I can't tell," Minkus shrugs, hands apart. "I'm sure you'll get the vote of some of the committeemen who have a gripe with me at this particular moment. You can't please everybody in this business," he smiles at Ferguson. "Yes, you'll get those. Maybe one or two extra, depending on the impression Howie makes in the next, what is it?"—he carefully refers to a calendar, though he knows the date—"oh the next ten days or so. Not much time. Why don't you have a little get-together for the Sinnemok committee, a get-acquainted party. I could get a keg of beer, put on some food, have a little music. You know, make it a sociable evening."

"Are you in the catering business now, also?" I say.

"No, no. Don't get me wrong," he whines. "I have to stay out of this. Then there's Wriston to worry about. He's been around I hear."

"Oh, yeah. Has he been down here?" Howie asks.

"Just relax," I tell him, and get up. There are handshakes all around. Minkus shows us out the door.

Later in the car: "You know that might not be a bad idea?"

"What's that?" I ask.

"Have Minkus throw a party so I can meet all the committeemen at once."

"You've got better ways to spend a thousand bucks." We ride in silence for a few minutes.

"No kidding," he finally says, the light coming on. "Is that what that was all about? Well, shit. I sure am green, aren't I."

I didn't say anything, just drove.

Tuesday

Spent most of yesterday in Albany. Took the brochure for Howie into the printer, along with Tompkins' picture showing Ferguson close up. Stopped by and saw the Old Man and helped his nephew who's filling in my place on the advisory committee with a position paper on consumer protection.

It's funny. I've been away from the Capitol only about two weeks but it's as if I were an old grad back for a reunion. Walking the halls again. The old faces. And the talk.

"Hello there, Senator."

"Why, hello, Tommy. How's it going?"

"Good. How's it going with you?"

"Good . . . good."

"Long time no see, Tommy? How's it going?"

"Good. How's it going with you?"
"Good."

"Hear it's going good with you, Bryan?"
"I think he'll be a good candidate."
"That's good."
"How are you going to do?"
"Pretty good."

Around noon I go to Pug's office but he's not there. Assistant to the Deputy, Reclamation and Supply, Department of Public Works: $17,500 per annum. How does he get these jobs? Mabel says he called in sick and gives me a wide-eye. She's been his secretary for so long, following him from one department to another, that she's beginning to look like him, use the same expression. Over in the corner is this young girl with stacks of material in front of her, making notes. Mabel introduces me. She's some kid on spring recess from Skidmore who's doing a paper on mass transportation. Nice legs. Cute upturned nose. Very blond and wearing a dark blue dress with a prim, white collar around the neck.

Howie got a kick out of the brochure material I had prepared. It was probably akin to seeing his picture in the yearbook for the first time. It makes everything official for him.

> Howard Ferguson is a native of Yost County, a graduate of Alton Central High School where he was an All-State selection in basketball. He attended Syracuse University to study engineering. . .

"Shit, it was mechanical drawing. I had a basketball scholarship and blew it."
"That's all right," I assure him. "Technically it comes under engineering, and you didn't blow it. You withdrew to start your own business."

> In 1964, Mr. Ferguson broke ground on Ellis Mountain and, with the enterprise and ingenuity that are part of his

success story, has turned the area into one of the major ski
areas of the Northeast. The Ferstock Corporation, of
which he is president . . .

"You see," he says eagerly, "I took part of my name and part
of the old lady's maiden name and that's how . . ."

. . . employs fifty men year around in the different construction and maintenance jobs that he has created. During
the winter more than twice that number are employed, making the corporation one of the largest industrial employers of
the county.

"Also one of the largest taxpayers. Some days I feel like selling off the whole fucking thing and taking the old lady to Florida."
"Now is there anything else we can say about you? The Jay-
cee award is there, your club memberships."
"Shit, I don't know."
"And that's something else. When we go around, try to tone
down your language. It's automatic with you, so be careful. You
know?" He blushes and looks away. "Now, c'mon, isn't there
something else we can say? Some personal philosophy about
government that you've thought about." I look around at all the
books in the living room.
"You think it up," he says petulantly. "You're the expert."

"Just as I've built what I have with my own two hands,"
the young contractor said recently, "I believe the people of
this district should be given the opportunity to build their
future with their own hands. I run for Congress because I
want to put my hand on the future."

GIVE HOWIE A HAND

FERGUSON FOR CONGRESS

Well, I've seen worse slogans and it's a starter.

I spent some time in the Legislature library before I see the
state chairman. The *Britannica*, the *Book of Knowledge* . . .
None of them had pictures of anything that resembled the beetle

I saw the other day. One came close, the stag beetle, but the spiky horns were longer than the one I saw on the courthouse steps. One article in the—I think the set was called *Our Living World*—began, "Beetles are the Smiths of the insect world." Now what the hell does that mean?

The state chairman generally spends Monday afternoons in Albany, checking up, having meetings with the Democrat legislators. Pug had suggested I stop by and see him, let him know what is going on. I just catch him, he's on his way to meet with some legislators over at the Capitol. So we ride down the elevator of the DeWitt Clinton together, he listening silently, pained. Another goddamn primary, he's thinking. Why can't the Republicans be so lucky!

In the lobby we talk for a while longer and over his shoulder I see Miss Skidmore at the news counter. She looks over, sees me, and her Dresden blue eyes take in who I'm talking to. I feel her little poli-sci instincts turn on.

"Watch out for that prick, Minkus, Tommy," The state chairman is saying. "I sure would like to get rid of him."

"Why don't you?" I say. She's turned away now, leafing through a *Newsweek*. High hips and straight back.

"I've got to stay neutral," he tells me.

At sixty-six, going on sixty-seven, Alma's legs are still slim and straight, none of that funny bowlegged look some thin women get when they age. Her back seems to have a steel rod down it. She must have been around twenty-five when I was born. There's a picture of her upstairs in the attic standing by the Judge in front of the family Buick, the high running board almost at the backs of her knees. She's got one foot crossed in front of the other, leaning forward into the camera with a girlish grin. His Honor stands a little behind her, the straw Panama pulled low over his eyes, and the loop of watch chain across his vest the only semblance of a smile on him.

I remember that car and that straw hat vividly.

"Where are we going, Pop?"

"We're going to take a run up to Sullivan's Corner to see some people. Maybe buy some of that good cheese up there, eh? Here, boy, put my hat in the back seat there." Route 19 is just a two-lane road then, big slabs of concrete with tar in the joints, winding, and gently rising into the hills. The Judge's pink hands on the big wooden wheel, a cigarette between his lips, the immense head glistening beneath the velour canopy of the square roof. The spokes of the wheels sometimes would lull me to sleep with the whir and whash they made. The car smelled like an old, musty sofa you might find in a deserted summer house.

Sometimes we'd come to the crossing at Purchase just as the noon train would come through, steaming toward its connection in Albany with the Twentieth Century. He'd sit at the crossing, motor idling, an arm across the back of the seat and sigh, as if the iron wheels click-clacking by meant something special.

Well, suppose you were a poor boy, working at Fielding's hardware store during the day and then taking the afternoon train to Albany to study law at night; then getting what sleep you could on the milk and mail train coming back at two in the morning. And then suppose later on, when you've become reasonably well off, respected, and with some influence, you sit by a railroad siding and watch one of those boiling, slick-pistoned monsters pile by, sit and watch its power and perfection with the intelligence and foresight that tells you it's only got a few years left to run. Wouldn't you sigh?

Miss Skidmore sits prettily on the stool of the hotel bar, just off of the lobby. She's damn smart and I find that rosebud face is deceiving, for there's a cool reckoning inside. She's majoring in political science — what did I tell ya??? — and is fascinated with politics AND politicians.

I do her a real favor by introducing her to the smoothie who lobbies for the Teamsters and she fires some sharp questions about mass transportation. I'm roaring inside. He stands by her, his bleary eyes glued to the bumps underneath the blue frock, as she's half turned on the stool to talk to him. Her dress slides way up her thighs which are very slender, but still okay. He makes a point on one of them with his cigarette-holding hand. It's time to go. Not just because of him, but I see that funny look in her eyes, sort of glazed, frightened; like a rabbit looking at a snake.

So I take her down to Jack's for a steak and tell her about Ferguson and the campaign. She's *just* fascinated. It helps that a few people stop by the table.

"Oh, Assemblyman, this is Miss . . ." Or—

"Want you to meet Miss S., Jerry. She's doing a piece on mass transportation. Maybe you can help her out."

"Be my pleasure. I have to fly up to Buffalo with the governor tomorrow, but come see me the day after. You bring her in, Tommy, make sure she gets in, you know?" Miss Skidmore purrs over her T-bone.

"Young lady," the courtly clerk of the Senate admonishes her, "I'm sorry to see you in such bad company. The most corrupt politician in the state. How's it going, Tommy?" a squeeze on my shoulder.

"Good."

"I don't see how you do it, Bryan," he says, another squeeze.

She orders cheese for dessert and as she picks up crumbles of Roquefort with her fingers, (elegant, perfect nails of light pink) I see I'm getting the look. She blinks once or twice, trying to clear the big blues, but to no avail. I ask her how long her term recess is and wouldn't it be more interesting for her to see how a congressional primary is shaped up. I mean, you can read about mass transportation in any old office but to see grass-roots American politics at work—how about that? She said she'd think about it. Leaning on the table, little white collar around her throat, she looks like one of those awful, sweet calendar pictures of a kid at First Communion. Except she's stoned on the wine.

The general store at Sullivan's Corners sold marvelous cheese in those days. The Judge would steer the Buick into the small lot by the store and nose up to the siding, cut the engine. Suddenly it would be very hot in the car. Hot and more of a smell of old carpet and cushion.

"Here, boy," handing me a dollar, "go inside and get your mother a pound of cheese and buy yourself some jawbreakers." Usually, as I got out of the car, someone would be approaching and I'd hear him say. "Hello, there, Oscar. Get in and we'll talk a bit."

"Thank you, Judge."

There are a lot of phony stores now like the one that used to be at Sullivan's Corners, but they are nowhere the same. It's the people inside the store, clerks and customers, that make the difference. Old man Schuster staggering around, already a little high on home brew and reaching into the candy jar with fingers stained with the guts and blood of the pig he'd just slaughtered. That was half of it. Sucking on that rootbeer barrel, thinking of it speckled with gore. Almost sacrificial.

"There you are, Tommy. Never put more than one in your mouth at a time," he'd always warn and one of the farmers sitting or leaning against the nail bins would cackle. It would be midday and they would sit around talking crops and bulls or make arrangements to borrow a piece of equipment or maybe speculate what the new city people had paid for so-and-so's place. One would be holding a five-pound bag of flour, another a sack of six-pennies, or perhaps another had the new *Saturday Evening Post* tucked into the top of his bib-overalls — all of these being "tickets" purchased for a bit of sociability, a small recess in the eighteen-hour day.

Sometimes Aunt Mae would come in. Whose aunt she was I never knew, but she'd come in wearing a longish crepe dress of a flowery print that I associated then with those huge flowers in South American jungles that were known to eat grown men alive. There'd be a smallish, black straw hat set tight to her thinning hair, the pin surely embedded deep in her skull. Purse clutched tight to her scrawny bosom, she would tiptoe the heavy black shoes over the creaking boards of the floor. All dressed up like this, every time, although she had just trotted over from her two rooms back of the barber shop, come over to peek in her mailbox and if there were no mail, which was usual, no circulars promoting hearing aids or cure-alls, she'd say:

"I'll just have an eighth of a pound of your gunpowder tea, Mr. Schuster. Now, just an eighth, mind you," she'd emphasize, as if Schuster ever gave anything away for nothing.

Schuster died just after the war, leaving an enormous estate which was administered by the Judge. Much of it, Pop told me, was made by the loans he advanced to the farmers sitting around his store — their lands and herds being the collateral, which he would inevitably get.

"Well, how are you today, Aunt Mae?" one of the farmers would ask, winking at a companion. And they'd sit back, straight-faced, as she'd recite a litany of ills, aches, pains, and mishaps that had occurred to her since last she had been asked—which might have been yesterday. Then she'd always add, "But my bowels are good."

Holding the cheese in my hands, testing how many times I could let it slip and still catch it before it would thud softly on the floor, the slick butcher paper eventually besting me, I'd lean against the sloping glass of the candy case and listen to the talk, hear old man Schuster hack and slash on some carcass inside the big cooler at the rear, panting, "There! There, you son of a bitch. . . there!" or I'd stare up into the dim heights of the place where old-fashioned plows and corn planters were suspended on ropes, like the rusted armor of Crusaders.

Ultimately someone would come in, or peer through the screen to say, "Young Tommy Bryan in there? Tell him his dad's ready to go." Another person would be getting out of the back door of the Buick as I went out, not Oscar who had got in when I left the Judge, but another man. Perhaps, there had been several occupants in that back seat since I left, and my father sitting behind the wheel, facing front, wiping his forehead with a handkerchief, and nodding to the departing man through the tiny rear-view mirror.

That's a funny thing about those old cars—the small, tiny rear-view mirrors they all had. Does it *really* have to do with safety? It's almost as if none of them in those days thought or cared about what was behind, what might be catching up to them.

At home, we'd wheel into the cement driveway, my mother's rhododendrons only about at the level of the car windows then, and the Judge would pull into the garage, know precisely where to stop on the turntable he had installed in the floor, and I would get to push it around so the big, flat chest of the Buick's radiator was turned toward the street. One more task, one more treat for me.

"Boy, get me my hat." And I'd open the square door to the rear seat, the heavy metal panel swinging easily on the vaultlike hinges. I'd bring him the straw Panama that had been on the back seat. When I first did this, I remember saying, "Pop, where did this money come from?"

Once, there was a pint bottle of homemade applejack misshaping the crown as if the hat were full of water. "People ask my opinion about things," he told me that first time. "When you get older and are a lawyer they'll ask your opinion too, you understand? And they sometimes feel grateful and want to show their respect and thanks. That's the way some people show their thanks for you doing them a favor. And, son," he looked down at me with those merry, merry eyes, "this embarrasses your mother, so we won't mention it, eh?"

I was only about nine that first time, and I guess I was lucky. Some boys don't find out about their fathers, if at all, until much later and that can be pretty bad. When you're older.

Last night at the Thruway Motel, after Miss Skidmore and I had sketched out a curriculum for her seminar in grass-roots politics, she was peeling off her pantyhose—a certifiable blond at both ends,—she laughed as if she had just thought of something, some appointment she was missing.

"What?" I asked her, fixing the door to the bathroom so we'd have a little light.

"You may not believe this," she says, "but I've never done this before—not quite like this." And I laughed a little, and unsnapped my shorts. But I was thinking how many times I've heard that phrase and how it must be the feminine version of, "What's a nice girl like you doing in a place like this?"

M. S.—About 19 or 20, very slender but with a nice
build. Nipples are blunted, inverted. Upper middle-
class, good school and "good" family. A springy,
enthusiastic fuck. But also cool in manner, not
withdrawn, but as if she were selecting her pleasures
from a jewelry tray in Cartier's. "I've never quite
done everything," she tells me with a calm
defensiveness. The next morning I want to say "You
mean, like not in the ears?"

Scored a real coup today. Got Ferguson invited to talk to the Hinton City Rotary next week, of course, not on his candidacy, but as the developer of Ferstock ski area. Tompkins is taking some more color shots of the place and with the winter scenes he took for the travel agency we can put together a show to give Howie a little exposure down there before the Cade County establishment.

Pug called tonight to say he'd heard some good reports of our excursions over the weekend, especially from Cade. I mentioned the bad time we had at the University and he promises to put an arm on someone so that when we go back again, we'll have some official entry.

The secret of Howie Ferguson may be to get him to meet as many people as possible, person to person. He's no good on a platform and would be horrible in a debate. But he comes across like a ton in person. But is there time?

"Where have you been? I've been trying to get you all day?" I ask him on the phone.

"Oh, Helen and me have been doing a little politicking," he answers, laughing. Icy prickles along my arms.

"What do you mean? What have you been doing?"

"Well, we drove down to Sinnemok County today," he says, with all the moxie of Tom Swift, "and she drove the car and I just went door to door and introduced myself. We did all of Cairo, Pumpkin Hollow, and half of Flatrock. Have to go back to finish Flatrock."

"You mean you just went to every house?"

"Yeah. How about that? Boy, the people down there are awful nice. Almost all of them wished me luck."

"Howie, that was a waste of time. Three out of every four people you talked to today were Republicans. Not one of them can vote for you in June."

"Yeah, but they can in November, can't they?"

Of course they wished him luck. Behind those gentle, amiable faces were the thoughts, "Knock yourself to pieces, you no-good Democrat bastard."

Never forget that old bore that Wriston met somewhere when he was running. You could see that she had been a charter member of the Clochehat Gang that marched on Washington in the Army of Temperance.

"My grandfather served in the Union Army," she fiercely said, "and I still believe what he told me. Democrats are the dregs of our society, a threat to the Union."

One of the few times I've ever seen Matt Wriston speechless.

College girls these days really shock me. It must be the pill that's done it. When I was up at Ithaca there was always a little talk about Bennington girls and when a guy showed up at a dance with a girl from there, you always felt certain that he was getting some. But today, every one of them is like a Bennington girl. It's as if morality went out the window with Trojans. And they're all from the so-called better families!

Harvey Washington. He's one of those Peaceables I met at Tiny's the other night. He was back there tonight and looking a little sheepish, shying away from me at first. He had heard of our visit to Cade State and knows now which way I'm going.

"I don't quite understand you," I tell him after he finally comes down to the end of the bar. "Ferguson is your kind of person, a guy who knows what it's like to make it on his own. Wriston has a lot of fine ideas, I grant you, but he's up there on the mountaintop looking down."

"You may be right, Mr. Bryan," he says scratching his head, "but Matt Wriston has done a lot for us down here. We know him. We don't know Ferguson."

"Do me a favor, will you? Keep an open mind until I bring Howie down here. I want you to meet him, Harvey. Will you do that? Maybe you can arrange a meeting down at the Abyssinian. Okay?"

"All right," he says but not enthusiastically and he quickly finishes the beer I bought him, anxious to leave all of a sudden.

So the news comes on and I move down at the other end of the bar to watch it. There comes old Matt Wriston, dented armor all shined up, patched.

"I hereby announce my resolute and determined candidacy for the Democratic nomination for the congressional seat representing the people of the . . ."

"Want me to turn it up?" Tiny says to me, a glow in his dark eyes.

"I can hear it fine," I tell him.

". . . . reason I offer myself," Wriston continues. People like him are always offering themselves. ". . . is because there are too many people who, it might be said, are losing faith in our democratic system of government, and I want to prove to them — at least I trust I will be able to prove to them — that it is still a viable means for them through which they may seek the answers and remedies for their problems."

"Now ain't that just ducky," I say to Tiny.

"What's that?"

"What a hell of a thing to say. He knows he doesn't have a chance, so he's going to take the whole goddamn business down with him. Talk about cynical politicians."

"Well, he speaks the truth," my big black friendly bartender answers. The boy-soprano's voice coming out of that big bear always fascinates me. "There's lots of people who are beginning to think we're on a bum lure. You know you were talking the other night," he leans over the bar, looks past me out through the neon beer sign to the street, "you mentioned about Pug Connors appointing a couple of our brothers as deputies."

"That's right," I say, "and they're still there because he put the whole department on civil service. That's important."

"Sure," he smiles dreamily, "but you and I know those two black boys were only put on the force for the votes it would get."

"Votes! You're goddamn right it was for the votes. What the hell do you think it's all about? For Christ's sake was he supposed to do it for . . . for love?"

And Tiny looks at me for a moment, still smiling like a baby picture but his eyes lumps of coal, lusterless chunks. Then he shrugs and walks to the other end.

Okay, let's figure it out. Wriston hasn't got them yet, but say he has the black vote. What does that mean? Down in Cade, only about a third, and that's being generous, a third of the migrants are enrolled, are registered. There aren't that many in Sinnemok and here there's a pretty good enrollment—only because Pug Connors drove, bought, and pushed them to the polls. But in the overall there's maybe two thousand—and that's being generous. Not much in the total, but in a close race it could make a difference, depending on how Wriston draws elsewhere. Of course, most of them stay home in a primary—you can figure that Captain Billy's people would keep 'em home down there unless they were sure of the vote. So *that* number would be subtracted from Wriston. So, screw them! . . . But I'd hate to see it happen.

What really made me mad was not Tiny, though, but what I saw on the television. Wriston had taped his announcement this afternoon, in his office, surrounded by a couple of committee-men he could drag out—a couple of them have always had a hard-on for Pug—and some of those young kids that are always running after him AND right behind him who's standing there with a big grin on his face, yuk-yuking it up, but open-minded Harvey Washington. No wonder he was in such a hurry to get away before the news went on. What kind of a dishonest, two-faced way is that to act???

Just spoke to Miss Skidmore. She'd be "delighted" to go around with me as I try to sweat some committeemen in Cade County. She'll be delighted, all right.

Alma's birthday on Thursday. Maybe she would like a begonia.

Friday

Wednesday morning Pug catches me at the radio station. I'm laying out a spot-saturation program for Howie. "Where's your boy?" he asks me. Suddenly, Ferguson is *my* boy. "Get hold of him right away. The paper just called. Wriston has given them a statement saying that Howie's a shill for Captain Billy to split the vote up. You've got to get an answer in, but it's got to come from him. Direct."

Well, where is our wandering boy? Helen points me in the direction of Arthursburg but I spend about an hour on the phone, calling around. It's like trying to track down the pony express.

"Ferguson? He was through here about an hour ago."

"I heard he was up around the Corners at two o'clock."

In between time, I'm calling the paper. No, they can't hold up the press until I find him. "What's the matter, Bryan, did you lose your candidate?" the deskman snickers. Big-shot journalism grad. "Maybe he can't answer what Wriston says."

Finally . . . finally, I locate him doing his Fuller Brush act in the first ward of Hinton City. Tell him not to move, just stay where he is — a used-car lot. Then call the paper back. Okay, wise-ass, you want to talk to my candidate, I'll take you to him where he's campaigning.

"No kidding, campaigning?" Genuine surprise in his voice, but now he's on the defensive and has to even up. They assign one of their pocket-size scribes, but that's okay. I drive him down to Hinton and we get there an hour later.

Howie has that turned-on, bright-eyed exhaustion. "Hell, I could have met a hundred or more people in the time you took to get here," he says right off. And it's magic time. Zowie! So we miss being in the same issue with Wriston's charge. But yesterday's edition: it's our turn. What a score!

> If Howard Ferguson is a "bogus" candidate as charged by Matthew Wriston yesterday, an attempt by the Brown machine to deny him the congressional nomination, it seems that no one has told the young Alton builder and ski-resort owner.

Now that's what I call a kitchen-sink lead; every "w" but where represented.

> This reporter followed Mr. Ferguson from four o'clock in the afternoon until long after dark, while he made an exhaustive, door-to-door confrontation with the voters of Hinton City, the capital of Captain Billy Brown's political empire. Ferguson was a Daniel in the lion's den, and obviously enjoying every minute of it.
> With seemingly inexhaustible energy and enthusiasm, the Democratic hopeful bounded up steps, rang doorbells, introduced himself, and chatted a few minutes with whoever answered.

With *whomsoever*. "How d'ya do. My name's Howie Ferguson and I want to run for Congress. Just wanted to come by and say hello." Eyes boggle—some of them had never seen a candidate in the flesh before—for anything, let alone Congress. "Yes, ma'am, I think you're right." He was fearless with dogs, would walk right past yapping and snarling mutts and they'd turn and look after him, silent and puzzled. "No, sir, I've never held any office before, but I think it's important for all of us to get into this business of governing ourselves in one way or another."

"Is he doing this every day?" the reporter panted. "Every day," I say evenly.

> . . . .most places the youthful candidate was offered coffee and at supper time there were several invitations that he sit down and share a meal. The response was generally

warm and friendly and if the voters who met Howard Ferguson today thought he was anything but an eager young
man with an apparent overwhelming determination to serve
them in Congress, many of them have probably changed
their minds by now.

That proves what a lousy paper we have here. Editorializing
like that in a news story. But it's GREAT. The printer had already locked up our brochure but I get him to insert a small
quote from the piece: "Howard Ferguson . . . an eager young
man with an apparent overwhelming determination to serve . . .
in Congress — Yost *Daily Sentinel*" . . . Bull's-eye!

"That's a great piece, pally," Connors says, putting aside the
paper. We meet early at the Sunray Diner in Athens, Connors
taking up all one side of a back booth. "You set it up good."

"I didn't have to set anything up," I tell him. "I just had to
find him." Eyebrows raise slowly toward the upturned hat brim.

"You mean he's really doing this?" I nod and a laugh starts
way down.

"Is that going to upset any of your plans?" I ask; he looks out
the window, seriously contemplates the Shell station on the
opposite corner.

"What plans? There are no plans," he says carefully. How did
you locate the accused, Sheriff? Just routine police work, just
routine. "Well, it looks like we've got a candidate, doesn't it?"
he says after a moment and brings the mug of coffee up to sip it.
"Here's the list I told you about for Sinnemok. A couple of
guys here will give you a vote just to screw Minkus. Of
course " — the lids droop over the gray eyes — " with a little moo-
lah, Minkus would give you a very nice showing.

"Oh, yeah," he continues. "I talked with a friend over in
Education and he's going to get a contact with the Cade State
President — a man named Harmon. Give him until next week
and then call this Harmon. He'll give Howie a nice tour of the
place. You can do the rest of it, yourself. Which reminds me
also that Captain Billy wants to meet Ferguson — your appointment" — he pauses to pull out an old envelope scribbled over
with names, numbers, and notes — "your appointment is three
o'clock on the ninth."

"What's this all about?"

"He just wants to meet him, that's all." And I get the wild-horse look. "How's your mother?" he asks.

"Just fine," I say. "Today is her birthday as a matter of fact. She's sixty-seven."

"Isn't that grand," he says, tossing a dollar on the table and getting up.

When Pug wheels out of the parking lot in Little Ben, I go into the phone booth to find out where the *wunderkind* was chopping them up. Surprisingly, he answers the phone.

"Where are you?" I tell him. "Come on up, we got something to show you," he says, gagging. *We* got something to show you! Maybe a new way to use that brass hood over the fireplace.

There are five of them and they come trotting out of the kitchen hand and hand and around the carpeted level above the pit. They're all about fourteen or fifteen, short short blue skirts and a fairly uniform—well matched, you might say—breast confor-mation pushing out white sweaters—each with a large blue let-ter: H-O-W-I-E.

So they enter, trippingly on their toes, to stand in line, a knee turned in coyly here and there. "All right, girls," Helen says like an older sister who majored in Phys. Ed. But she's a little ner-vous too.

> "Give a hand
> H – H – H
> Give a hand
> O – O – O
> Give a hand,
> Dubba-U – Dubba-U
> Give a hand
> I – I – I
> Give a hand,
> EEEEEEEeeeee!
> Give a hand
> TO HOWIE!"

Well, Christ, you can just imagine. And Ferguson? You could market his grin on a Wheaties box.

"Ain't that something?" he says. "The old lady thought it up and got the girls together. She sewed on the letters and everything." So it wasn't draperies after all. "What do you think?" he then says, face sobering a bit.

"It's great," I finally say. "We can use them for rallies and such."

"That's what Helen said," he says eagerly. While we've been talking, she's been going over some of the finer points of the technique, dropping to a knee, arms jerking quickly in and out and, of course, shoving those big works out at us. It was a demonstration the kids would be able to emulate in kind only.

"So how's the campaign going, chief?" Howie asks. "Hey," he rushes on, "we really scored with that newspaper piece, huh?"

"That turned out pretty good. Tell me, what do you say to these people when you go to the door?"

"Oh, we just talk," he says, becoming earnest, a sixth-grade look on his face.

"About what? You don't promise things, do you?"

"Naw, sh——shoot, what could I promise anybody?"

The cheerleaders have gone upstairs to change clothes. We go over his talk for the Rotary, compare schedules and appointments. I tell him about the date with Captain Billy.

"No kidding?" he says. "What's he want to see me for?"

"He just wants to meet you. After all, your name is getting around pretty good." That pleases him.

It's just occurred to me. Those five high-schoolers changed their clothes in that bedroom with the mirror over the round bed!! Probably smoothed down their hair in it. Yet, when they came downstairs, there was no hint that anything was unusual. It was just, "Good-bye, Mrs. Ferguson, Mr. Ferguson, Mr. What-you-may-call-it . . ." and out. Not a sign. Not a token blush. Nothing. Are they all getting like this now? I mean, are mirrors over beds commonplace even to the readers of *Teen-Age Romance*?

"But I did want to ask you something," Howie is continuing. Helen plumps and stacks some cushions and then settles on the floor, listening. I see on her face that they've been discussing something and now he's going to ask my opinion. "What about issues?"

"Issues?"

"Yeah, you know, issues. Shouldn't I have some issues."

"Well, for the moment, your main problem is one of anonymity — of getting acquainted with the people. This door-to-door business you're doing is a good way to overcome that. Don't worry about any issues."

"Yeah, but are people just going to vote for me because they like me, how I look or talk about the weather? I've been thinking about issues quite a lot lately."

"Like what, for example?"

"Well, there's the war, of course. Then there's the urban renewal problem in Hinton. It's going too slow and the money is not getting to the right place. And we're not getting the federal money we should for our highways around here." He pauses for a moment, going over some list in his mind.

"There's the problem of medical services in rural areas," Helen suggests.

"Yeah, that's right — there just aren't enough doctors around here, can't attract them. And another thing," he continues, her remark pulling the plug in his memory. "We got all those old railroad beds, and the remaining trains are going to quit running in a few years . . . in terms of the future, we're going to be part of the Eastern Megalopolis and a network of mass transportation will be necessary. We ought to prepare for that by buying up all these old tracks and saving them for the future. Cheaper to buy them up now than to let them be torn up and then put new ones down later."

"What was it you called it last night, Howie?" Helen asks, shifting on the pile, an odalisque.

"Oh, well, it was just an idea, you know," he answers, blushing, "but we could call it a Rail Bank — you know, like Soil Bank?" There are several long seconds of silence.

"It sounds good," I finally say. "Why don't you put some of these ideas down on paper and we'll go over them. But for the moment, personal appearances are your big play. Don't worry about issues. In fact the fewer issues the better. People get confused with too many issues."

Put it down on paper. A classic dodge used on hot-shot kids that come up to the Legislature as aides who take their "no-show" jobs seriously and have a new idea for everything. In the halls, in the cafeteria, around conference tables, they are constantly coming up with these ideas, as if the Continental Congress were held only the day before. "Look, why don't you draw up a position paper on that and submit it to the committee." Yeah, yeah. Off they go, crazy with Realpolitik lust and are rarely heard from again. Perhaps there's a secret room beneath the "million-dollar staircase" of the Capitol, where all these guys are scribbling, reviewing old pieces of legislature, feverishly exchanging ideas. Some of them young but others old and gray now — and all of them very happy.

Matter of fact, an awful lot of it does get printed up as proposed legislation. Tons of it every year, ten-foot stacks of "great ideas" on the desk of every legislator.

"What are they trying to do to us?" remember Joe Garvin said once. "I got to get back to my shoe store by Easter or I'll be out of business!"

And that's funny. Originally the two- or three-month session was so farmers (most of the Assemblymen and Senators then were farmers) could get back for spring plowing. Now it's to sell shoes.

I meet the noon bus in Hinton and Miss Skidmore hops off, sandaled feet tredding the grit and debris of the station floor. She's fresh and crisply pretty in a yellow spring suit, a tulip in a cinderbed. A Pacific-Orient airline bag holds all her essentials and she greets me as if I were the trusted family overseer, sent down in the ranch wagon to pick her up.

Most of the afternoon is spent going around Cade County, seeing committeemen, according to the list Pug Connors has given me. Most are noncommittal. Some promise their vote — too easily. Others are afraid to say anything. Miss S. stays in the car, one elegant leg over the other — taking notes!

"It's fascinating the way you talk to some of these people," she says. We've just left a guy who runs a filling station down near Prussian's Run. "You don't seem to respect them an awful lot. Do you?"

"Sure I respect them, but I want them too."

"And the two things are not compatable?"

"I tell you, boy, committeemen are the unsung heroes of this business. They do all the grubby work and for what? Nothing. Oh, sure, there are some who will take a few bucks now and then, but they are in the minority. Most of them work day and night, day and night—and only to serve the party."

"Yeah, but, Pop, there's the matter of ego-fulfillment."

"Ego-fulfillment?" eyes shoot across. Zap! "What the hell are you talking about?"

Nolo contendere, Your Honor.

We go by the State U. at Cade to follow up the contact Connors made. Who did he talk to, I wonder? I feel sorry for the president—really—a man who's worked hard in his profession; lots of credits in his folder, and almost bowing from the waist when I come in his office. Yes, they'd be delighted to give Mr. Ferguson a tour of the new dorm. Perhaps he'd like to talk to the Lincoln Club, the undergraduate political-science club? Grand. Fine. Marvelous. At your service. Anything to oblige. Give me one of those unschooled, ignorant, slightly dishonest committeemen any day.

Miss S. walking around the campus outside, very much at home with her notebook as if she were on her way to English 690:

English 690: THE GREATEST!

The ten greatest books in world literature as selected by the editors of the *New York Review* and programmed by Univac for the ultimate in speed reading.

But also, looking down her retroussé nose, a short look but enough of a put-down, at the facilities and enrollment of this public, tax-supported, everybody-in normal school.

"Strange mixture of architecture," she says when I come out of the Administration Building. "You say this college is only three years old. But some of these buildings are positively antediluvian."

"This used to be a fancy girls' school, a junior college," I tell her.

"What happened to it?"

"The owners didn't pay their taxes, so the state took it over."

"My goodness," she says, looking around with a new respect. She wasn't wrong after all. Her tuned-up nostrils *had* smelled the lingering odor of class.

"That's what happens," I say, putting her in the car. "We eventually take over everything," and her eyes give me the blue-plate special.

The rest of the day, she pumps me for the facts on the Cade County organization, the enrollment statistics, the breakdown on the vote we expect from the committee — all the while taking notes.

Captain Billy's adventures with the Lafayette Escadrille bore her. So does the romance of his brother's saloon in the Bottoms of Hinton City. She's up on this genre! She's read the similar stories of Pendergast or O'Connell or Curley. She's checked out all that stuff and wants the facts.

"Now Cranston will be endorsed by both Cade and Sinnemok committees. Your man will be endorsed by Yost. So then you circulate petitions to get his name on the ballot and go to a primary. Just looking at the figures," she looks down at her lap, "with your man and this Wriston running, it looks like Cranston is a cinch to win."

"That's the way it looks in figures," I agree. She's silent and I turn, see her nibbling the full lip. "It's not always that simple. One day you get a winner and the next day he might well not exist. Anything can happen. Maybe Cranston hasn't paid his income tax or maybe he'll keel over with a stroke. Who knows?"

"You make it sound as if it's all so dependent on chance . . ."

"Miss Skidmore, where have you been the last few years?"

That's the trouble with a lot of us. We've got so used to thinking in terms of the individual lately, we forget about the system

—even though there has been proof after proof that individuals can come and go but the system still provides. It's like Connors and the Iliad—Zeus and the status quo. But maybe the poetry in between is essential, just to keep us going.

But all this participatory democracy crap—it's dangerous. It puts too much on the—THERE'S NO OTHER WORD FOR IT—charismatic. Say the guy loses or is knocked off: then no one wants to participate anymore. Say the guy wins and is a jerk; that could be the end of democracy.

And yet . . . and yet . . .

Along about ten o'clock after we've played bouncy-bouncy a couple of times in the Glenview Arms, I remember it's Alma's birthday.

"Hi, just wanted to call you to wish you a happy birthday."

"Um-huh. Thank you," she says, something more in her voice than the length of the Bell System between us. She's probably worrying that I won't get off the phone before the ten o'clock news comes on. "Where are you?" I tell her. "Did you have anything to eat?" Yes, I say, eyeing the delighted Miss S. who just then comes back from the bathroom. She's wearing a belted scarlet housecoat that comes halfway down the firm, trim thighs. She claims to be a first line forward on the field hockey team.

"I didn't forget you," I tell Alma. "But I got tied up down here and couldn't get away until now."

"Nonsense," she answers. "Birthdays are a hardship at my age." Pause, one—two—kick, "Got a nice bouquet of flowers from Sheriff Connors, though. Will you be home for supper tomorrow night?"

"No. Well, many happy returns of the day," I say.

"Thank you. Thank you for calling, Tommy," she says to me as if I were the newspaper boy down the street, who phoned to apologize for missing the front porch. Miss S. is a red blur on the end of the bed and I have to blink several times before she's in focus. She sits, one leg folded under, the mini-robe looped open at the top, showing one upper-class tit jig-a-liging in cadence with the emery board. We're like an old married couple, settling down to a night before the tube. The news comes on and there's *my boy* taking shape, walking up some front steps. Cut to a close-up: Ferguson at door, talking to a giggly, moony-eyed housefrau.

I raised hell with Channel 12 about all the coverage they had been giving Wriston, so they apparently caught up with Howie.

Note for Ferguson: Hereafter, always contact me immediately if newspaper or TV people want an interview.

". . . . conducting a unique, shoe-leather campaign for the Democratic congressional nomination in . . ."

Fortunately, no audio with Ferguson, just pictures of him ringing doorbells and the announcer speaking. Towhead has stopped her cuticle care and is watching intently. Ferguson looks about eighteen years old on the screen. And there's a great shot of him talking with some guys at a filling station. Not bad. Not all smiles, I mean, but serious listening.

"Son of a bitch," he tells me this morning. "I only went in there to take a piss and I thought those guys would never get through taking pictures. I had to do it three times for them, walk up to the pumps and shake hands all around. THREE goddamn times, and all the while, my bladder's about to bust."

"What do you think of him?" I ask Miss S. Her eyes linger over the TV image.

"Sincere," she says finally, still not looking away. "And square."

"Do I detect a note of pity in your voice?" She shrugs and petulantly returns to her nails. She resembles the low earner of the house, the girl who's next on the boat for Buenos Aires.

"You asked me and I told you," she says.

ABOUT ISSUES

1. Southeast Asia involvement. Stay away from all foreign involvement topics. Say they're wasteful of life and

money. Say we have to withdraw as soon as *possible*. That's the key word. But this is a dead issue now. Look at those guys who got to Congress on an anti-Vietnam platform, they're not saying much about it now. These little wars are like colds we've learned to endure — with sympathy.

2. Urban renewal is foundering in Hinton City because there is not enough money, and *not* because the money is being funneled somewhere else. Say you'll get more money for it.

3. These other ideas of yours, the rural medical plan and the Rail Bank, are good ideas but don't talk about them too much. Use them as incidental material, something you might mention to an interested group.

4. The main issue for you to exploit, portray, is your youth and eagerness to serve. Your vitality. The know-how that has made Ferstock, put to use for the people of the district.

5. Remember: issues tend to confuse if not bore people. Just be yourself. Keep up this door-to-door campaigning. This impresses a lot of people, makes them think you *deserve* to be their Congressman.

Out of the goodness of his heart, Minkus had Howie invited to talk to his Women's Democratic Club last night. The invitation was phoned about three hours before the ladies met and it's the kind of a trick Minkus always pulls. Offer an invite but make it nearly impossible to get there. He could say later, "Sure, I cooperated; I invited him to talk to my Women's Club, didn't I?" But we made it!

What a bunch of bags! Howie was okay. It was a waste of time, of course. None of the femmes are committeemen and they all do Minkus' bidding anyway, but it was good practice for him. He played it easy and friendly. Gave them a few jokes they could laugh at. It was a pizza and beer meeting in the backroom of a place called Bull Tongue Inn and he starts right off with an old one.

"Want to apologize to you ladies for being late, but me and Tommy got lost up the road and we saw this car parked on the shoulder and he goes over to it to ask directions of the couple inside and he says, 'Say, how far is the Bull Tongue Inn?' and . . .''

Well, they laughed till the tears poured. Big thick splitting whoops and faces breaking up in armpits. There's something disgusting about fifty- and sixty-year-old women laughing at jokes like that. I wonder if Alma would have broken up if she had been there. (Without me, of course.)

Anyway, it was good practice for him.

Of the 150,000 enrolled voters in the district, over half are women. About 82,000. If we could just get Howie around enough to meet them it would be great. The Vulva Vote would counteract Wriston's Black Vote. But how about the Black Vulva Vote?

𝔉riday

Laura Patrovich Kuslowski. I met her Tuesday. Not bad. Unfortunately, she might be one of those marching types, working for Wriston. Not really my type — too petite.

We had a frost last night. Alma this morning, making her I-told-you-so click-clacks, looking out the window as I eat my scrambled eggs. But only the peas are up and they can take it. Nothing else should be bothered. The corn should be okay.

"Saw your Mr. Ferguson on TV last night," she says.

"And?"

"He's a nice-looking boy," she says. "His wife is a little sharp-looking though."

Being vice-president of the Yost County Industrial Development Committee, Howie was able to cut the ribbon for the opening of the copper mill's new addition. I thought Helen looked great, though her dress was still a little short.

"That's just the style these days, Alma. All young women dress like that now."

"I'm not talking about her dress," she says.

On Sunday I put Miss S. on the bus for Saratoga and she looks as fresh as when I met her on Thursday. Which figures because that yellow outfit was on a hanger more than it was on her.

She hops up the step of the bus, turns around and says, "Thanks for a marvelous time. I really learned a lot."

Which was a pleasant formality and nothing more.

I read a piece awhile back, written by a woman too, about the relationship between women and power, especially in the political sense. She made one reference to the occurrences of well-adjusted, generally straight girls going haywire in the rarefied atmosphere of politics. So right!

```
XY--About 20.  Never knew her name.  At the '66
Buffalo convention.  She was working for Samuels, I
think.  A little on the plump side with breasts that
would not be so great after a few kids but were very
fine then.  Yearbook smile.  A crazy, pneumatic
screw.  Between fucks, I had to make some phone calls
and this seemed to get her worked up.  So I pretended
to call Harriman's suite once, and she blew me as I
talked . . .
"CONSULT YOUR DIRECTORY OR DIAL YOUR OPERATOR FOR
LOCAL ASSISTANCE."  A nice kid but nuts.
```

I suppose Howie expected Captain Billy to live in some sort of a mansion or small castle with guards around it because he seemed surprised when we parked in front of the modest frame house on Maple Avenue. There are several cars pulled up at the curb, one with a fireman chauffeur behind the wheel. A couple of guys sit on the railing of the sprawling porch, taking the sun, and if it weren't for the sun, it looks as if a wake is shaping up.

Inside, the old floral design looks like the pattern had been printed on brown wrapping paper. The rock maple sofa and chair suite and the three harp-backed Sheraton chairs are all taken by the usual audience of job holders and/or seekers, party officials, and candidates who pay their visits to Captain Billy every afternoon but Sunday between the hours of two and six.

Howie whispers something to me and again I am reminded of a wake, for as one steps across the threshold from the hall, between the large sliding doors of oak, it's as if a switch is thrown. The hush is marred by a few grunts of recognition or maybe by a brief exchange on the Yankee's chances or how some pitcher is shaping up.

I'm also reminded of a doctor's office, the waiting room filled by a lot of old patients — the average age in the room, including Ferguson, must be over sixty — waiting for the results of a final test.

Then there's Phil or Jimmy or Billy, the two or three aides I can never tell apart, supervising the room, keeping the schedule of appointments to the minute with all the unobtrusive but no less efficient dispatch of funeral directors at a well-organized burial, and all looking like twins or identical triplets — or is it quadruplets? — I'm not sure how many there really are. They're in their late forties or early fifties, big men with boyish faces under short-cropped silvery hair and button eyes, always smiling big deep-dimpled flushes of good fellowship and casually calling everyone by first name.

Heavy signet rings flash, encrusted cuff links glint when they put their hand to a doorknob; a foot in Italian leather presses the bottom of the door and the left shoulder is uptight — a slight pause and then everything opens in one smooth motion. Up against the wall!

Looking at Howie in this room yesterday, well, it was something. He looked more like a young repairman who had come in to fix the telephone. He ambles around, flips through the magazines on the table, inspects the curios on the mantel — china bulldogs in various sizes and positions — and checks out the enormous steam radiator in the corner with a professional bemused interest.

My first visit here — Pug Connors brought me — it was wintertime and that big steamer was hissing and spitting. It must have been 105 in the room, which smelled of stale tobacco and old men's underwear.

"Hey, look at this!" Howie's voice shatters the silence. Papers rustle, one old guy jerks out his watch but doesn't look at it, just puts it back. Ferguson is grinning, pointing to the framed photographs of Billy Brown and his flying comrades beside their World War I crates. "Isn't that Rickenbacker?" he asks, once more disturbing the clubroom. Yes, I nod, it's Rickenbacker. Howie bends close for another look and whistles.

Our turn comes. Frank or Ralph or Steve conducts us through the curtained French doors by the fireplace, some of the same old men still sitting where they were when we came in. Perhaps their turn never comes. Perhaps they come every afternoon only to sit around like crickets near a hearth.

Then down the hall with that perpetual odor of cabbage and pine oil disinfectant and to a polished oak door at the end. The well-tailored shoulder rests against the door, the hand goes to the knob, the foot to the jamb — Ferguson not knowing the ritual nearly falls over the guy's back — and then we're in Captain Billy's room.

He looked damn good, I told Pug last night, and I wasn't kidding. Though I suppose to be objective, one would have to say there were differences from the face that appears in the pages of the *Register Herald*, an official photograph taken about twenty years ago.

Red Tompkins told me there was a standing offer of $500, made by the Hinton paper to any photographer who could get a contemporary picture of Captain Billy. "Are you going to try?" I ask him, and he just looks at me.

But I wonder what Howie thinks, having just looked at the picture of the handsome, daredevil pilot outside and to now come face to face with the present version. The large aquiline nose is thinner along the bridge and it has a red sponge tip. The cold blue eyes are watery and the mouth is smaller, tighter. The remnant of the thick, dark hair passes as a shadow over the dark blue veins of a head that seems too large, an unnatural tumescence set upon the skeletal body that barely makes a shape beneath the bedcovers.

There was no need to describe the room to Connors and I certainly wasn't going to tell him my feeling as I look at all the flasks of fluids suspended over the old man's head, rubber syringes at the ready. I've seen it all several times before, the jars at the foot of the bed, on the floor, with the red rubber hoses snaking up to disappear beneath the counterpane, the odor of disinfectant and something else that always reminds me of caramel. But yesterday, I am looking at all the plasmas and solutions, all the paraphernalia and tubes, I wonder if the whole works are not so much to keep the body alive — because the corpus has become really just another fluid pipe — but are to keep this enormous head blinking and nodding and thinking and laughing and making noises with the frayed reed, embedded halfway down the neck pipe.

Certainly didn't say that to Pug.

"Hello there, Tommy. How are you?" the whiskery sound greets us.

"Just fine, Captain. You look good."

"Oh, crap," he says, waving away the compliment with the cigar stub. He takes a puff and puts it to smolder in the big marble ashtray by his bed. All the while, the blue eyes sweep up and down Howie, zero in on the face.

It was quite a look, and I can imagine him looking at, say, young FDR (no, that would be too early for *the* look — but maybe Lehman or perhaps Bob Wagner's father or maybe Jack Kennedy). I could read his eyes. "Well, here's another one."

"So, this is the boy that wants to run for Congress, eh? C'mere, son."

"Like you to meet Howard Ferguson, Captain," I say, a hand in Howie's back pushing him toward the bed. Howie takes the scrap of hand that's offered, takes it gently and looks down at the old man.

I'm getting carried away. It's not a scrap of hand at all. The Captain's hands, in addition to his head, are very operative, well developed and strong.

"You're a big kid, aren't you?" Captain Billy says, looking up. There's a tinkle of liquid against the glass. Amber fluid is trickling into the jug beneath the bed. "So you want to get into politics?"

"Yes, sir."

"Well, I tell you, boy, you'll meet some of the worst people in the world but you'll also meet the best." The head turns toward me. "Who's going to nominate him down here?"

"Well, we've asked this man Stacey from . . ."

"From Arthursburg," he says, chomping on the cigar. "Yes, he's all right. Go on."

"I spoke to several committeemen down in the Bottoms districts and I was wondering about Emmett Wade for a seconding speech." There was no comment, so I add, "How's that sound?"

Still no answer. Howie hangs over the bed, jaw slack and swallowing his tongue. Captain Billy's eyes dull, the mouth purses and a few more drops splash in the jug. Then he relaxes and takes a deep breath.

"Well, Stacey's okay, but I suppose with Wade you were thinking about getting a colored boy in the lineup." I nod. "Well, I don't know. Being Negro it might cause him some trouble seconding . . . what's your first name again?"

"Howard, but people call me . . ."

". . . seconding Howard's nomination. Also, it might cause *you* some undue problems around here with the Italians, you know, whereas it wouldn't bother us. Anyway, I got something for Emmet Wade to do already." He pauses, considers telling us about it and then adds, "Someone's got to move the nominations closed, and I think Wade would be the proper man to do it. You follow me?"

"That's perfect," I say, and his twinkle joins my laugh. Howie looks dumb, back and forth between us. "Well, who can you give us for a seconding speech?" I ask.

"I'll get someone for you," he says as the phone rings. "Yes . . . yes . . . no . . . yes . . . no . . . all right." That was all of it. It took him longer, with several slapdash attempts, to replace the phone.

"This is just in the family, you understand," Captain Billy says, the other hand working the cigar, "but I always thought Jack Kennedy made a mistake smooching up to the darkies. Of course times change. Well, how many votes are you going to get down here?" he asks Howie who still stands by the bed.

I remember the Judge saying to me every Christmas, "Well, what's Santa going to bring you tomorrow?" Was it before or after the first hat trick I realized His Honor knew all along what Santa was going to bring? Can't remember. But it was the same tone of voice with Captain Billy.

"We're pretty sure of at least nineteen," I tell him. "How's that sound?"

"That's about right," he answers, one – two puffs, "Give or take a couple."

The door opens behind us. Our time is up and one of those baby-faced goons is standing, waiting to show us out the side door. I nudge Howie but the phone rings again and Captain Billy says, "Wait a minute" as he picks it up. "Yes . . . yes . . . I haven't decided yet . . . no . . . all right.

"Well, boy," he says to Howie, who helps him hang up the instrument this time. "I have a feeling you're going to like politics, eh? I have a feeling you're going to be in the family for a while."

"Well, I hope to . . ."

"You're going to do all right too, I can tell," the old man continues. "C'mere. Want to show you something," he pulls Howie close to the bed. With the cigar hand, he throws off the coverlet to reveal the scrawny hips and legs naked beneath the bed jacket. It barely resembles a penis, and only recognizable because of its place in the groin. A grayish mass of genitals, given shape and substance by the tape around it and by the red hose inserted in the urethra.

Howie Ferguson's head snaps back slightly but he stands his ground, looks down with a scarlet face. And as we watch, the shriveled organ seems to work on the tube, a rippling spasm along the length as if it were trying to swallow more of the small hose and a few seconds later, more urine trickles into the jar.

"Hell of a rig, eh?" Captain Billy says proudly.

"Remember all those funerals we used to go to?" I said to Alma this morning. And it was true, we did go to a lot of funerals. There seemed to be a wake a week when I was a boy. All over an area of three or four counties. I grew up with two sets of friends and acquaintances; the ones I knew in school, Livingston High School, and the ones I got to know and played with at all the funerals we attended. We all belonged to families connected in some way with Democratic politics.

We youngsters knew the nooks and crannies of every funeral home in the Sinnemok Valley; where the best places were for hide-and-seek, which funeral director would let us play among the caskets stored in the basement — and there was that unspoken rule, never use the water fountain in such places. But our thirsts were always quenched with lemonade or sometimes there might be ginger ale left over from the adults' highballs.

I remember these occasions always in the dusk of long summer evenings, though mortality must have set the stage in other seasons. Perhaps we kids were only taken in good weather, when we could run around and not get in the way of the bereaved or those conducting serious business.

A group of men on the darkening front porches, the glow of cigars and the murmuring of voices, my father's dry tones among them; a general laying on of hands and clasping of shoulders, an occasional slow shake of head. And in the background, drifting through the screen door from inside would be, most always, the incessant drone of the Rosary. Sometimes, an enormous Buick would pull up, a thick-necked driver would get out to open the door for the occupant in the rear, while the men on the porch would automatically arrange themselves into a reception committee. "Hello there, Captain. How's it going, Captain?"

"Good. Good."

"What was the name of the guy who sat up?" I asked Alma.

Pouring me more coffee, she paused, thought for a moment, and then smiled with remembrance.

"Oh, yes. Jimmy Houlihan."

Jimmy Houlihan. He kept a fancy woman in the Broadmoor Apartments in Hinton City. How fancy she really was is subject to question; but she had a *chaise longue* in her bedroom and in those days no one in our area had ever seen a *chaise longue* except maybe in a movie with Norma Shearer. Anyway, Houlihan died while relaxing on that *chaise longue*, his inamorata absent, probably out buying unguents and negligees. It must have been a rather long shopping spree, for it was several days before they discovered Houlihan, stiff on the Louis Quinze.

The undertaker did a marvelous job. We kids studied the corpse at length on the night of the wake, since we knew the circumstances. Houlihan looked as if he were one of those lamb chops you could get at an Albany restaurant, wrapped in garlands of paper flowers that hid the straps holding him down.

Since we always got out at the first rattle of the beads, we were playing out in the yard when it happened. But my mother was there. Apparently, halfway through a Hail Mary, someone looked and saw Houlihan partially sitting up. Not all the way up but just a little, the big Norman nose poked above the edge of the open coffin as if he were about to turn and peer down at all them on their knees to say, "What the hell is going on here?"

There was a sudden exodus. Windows, doors—every opening in the house utilized. Out on the lawn, we watched with open-mouth amazement and fright: those candles we lit for a game of "ghost" among the caskets stored in the basement: maybe they had set the place on fire. The place was cleared in a minute, each kid yanked up by the hand and the motors of the LaSalles, Packards, and Buicks roaring to life, gears clashing, dust flying.

The poor Houlihan widow, deceived by the man in life, was then deserted by his friends in death, for she buried him alone the next day, watching the remains lowered into the earth without a friend to lean upon, and perhaps wondering herself about the irrepressible spirit once more tied down, and being put underground. My father had a case in court that day.

"We don't go to many funerals anymore," I said to Alma this morning.

"Everybody's dead," she answered and started to do the dishes.

But not *everybody*. "He doesn't show that to just anyone," Tom or Wally or Charlie whispers to Ferguson and me as we went out the side door. And I suppose it was a mark of some distinction to have seen the Brown Testaments.

I was thinking tonight of that room, Ferguson standing by the bed, looking down at that old crotch and of the gleam in Captain Billy's eyes. And I believe it; not everybody is treated to the sight. It was some sort of ceremony, reserved for only a few deemed worthy of a screwy act of fealty.

I'm thinking also of that sick room with all the pictures on the walls, the great and the near-great, a private portrait gallery representative of the last forty years of the Democratic Party. From the "Happy Warrior" to LBJ, they were all there with men like Champ Clark and Jim Farley in between, and even my father up there just beneath Harry Truman, and I wonder how many of them had been treated to the view. Howie Ferguson is in distinguished company indeed.

"I don't understand," Howie says. We are driving back from Hinton and he's been silent up until now, watching the scenery.

"What?" I say, thinking I couldn't explain the old man's actions either.

"Well, what's all this business about asking him for someone to nominate me and second me? I thought we were in competition with each other. I'm running against his man Cranston, aren't I?"

"Yes."

"Well, why is he being so accommodating? Giving us people like that?"

"It's not a matter of accommodation, he's just being practical. Don't worry, once these county conventions are over with, you can expect him to try to destroy you. But the papers are going to be there, it's a public meeting. He wants, and we want, everything to go smoothly. No arguments or yelling on the floor. It would look bad. Therefore, we line everything up beforehand." Howie doesn't say anything again until we cross the Yost County line, but for twenty miles he's had that stupid look in his face. He's thinking. Then at Carthage:

"What was this business about having that colored guy close the nominations?" he asks.

I take my time. "We expect that Matt Wriston might draw

well in the black vote. In Cade County, where there is a heavy black vote, the idea is to have a Negro make the motion to close the nominations."

A few more miles of silence. "Hey," he says suddenly, "you mean that Matt Wriston won't even have a chance to be nominated down there? The nominations will be closed . . . and by a black man?"

"Something like that," I tell him.

"Well, that's not very fair, is it? Is it?" Again I don't answer, and I'm about to say something when he starts to laugh, that quick gasping chortle. "Well, I'll be a son of a bitch," he says. "That's really something. But," he hesitates, "won't his people raise a stink about that the night of the meeting?"

"Probably."

"That will make waves, won't it? The newspapers there and all."

"Probably." It only takes him about half a mile this time.

"Ah, I see," he says, slipping down in the seat. "Never argue with the referees, it looks bad for the school. Is that it?"

"Something like that," I say.

"What's that place?" he says, straightening up in his seat.

"That's the Rose-a-Sharon Nursing Home," I tell him. "Lots of old people, you know."

"Let's go back."

"Go back?"

"Yes, let's go back. I haven't been there yet," he says.

"There's no sense going in there, Howie. It's a waste of time."

"You're on salary, Bryan. Turn the car around and let's go back," he says with a voice that's new to me.

"You better watch out for him," Alma tells me at breakfast. I had been explaining to her why I was late for supper last night. Ferguson was determined to go from bed to bed in the nursing home, saying hello and grinning. I gave up after the first hallway, the smells were too much. And all of those old people—none of them knew who the hell he was!

But he went on. "Look," I say "nobody can vote by absentee in a primary, this is a waste of time." He just shrugs and walks in and introduces himself to Mrs. Hennings who looks startled, especially a little apprehensive to see me there. What's up, she's wondering. Of course, she okays the visit.

"Look," I try again as we're waiting in the hallway — she has to get some of them off the evening bedpan before we go through — "even when it comes down to November, you don't have to worry about these people. Mrs. Hennings gets their absentees filled out for Pug Connors all the time. Don't you understand me?" And he gives me a look I'll never forget. The hazel eyes become sad, there's a distance in them — not cool or unfriendly though they might look like that at first — but a distance as if he were looking at something far, far away and not just down at me. Where have I seen that look before?

"What do you mean watch out for him?" I ask. I finish my coffee and bring the cup to her at the sink.

"He may not be what you think he is," Alma says, and her back gets even straighter.

I wonder if Miss S. has typed up all of her notes yet. It should make quite a term paper if she includes everything.

Speaking of everything and Miss S., maybe I ought to go see Doc Brook for a checkup. His speech to Rotary last year about the rate of clap among college girls, especially those from so-called upper-middle income families, being so high and increasing!

Maybe this Laura Patrovich Kuslowski would test positive with all of her goodie-goodie participations in democracy. What is she, a widow? Not divorced. Come to think of it, no. With a name like that and from around here, she's not upper-middle class.

"You don't remember me," she says with a bat of heavy black lashes — not demurely but with a slow burn, a slight flush of anger in the high-boned cheeks — but at what is she angry?? "You don't remember me, Mr. Bryan, but we met several years ago at the Yost County Democratic Club. I just wrote you a letter recently," and she smiles, looks away as if she had scored some points.

Aside from this encounter, we had a good day at Cade State. Tompkins trailed along, snapping pictures of Howie talking to students, to teachers, to the men working on the new dorms. This last was very good, because Ferguson was at home among the brick layers and President Harmon went with us. We got a shot of Howie, Harmon, and the construction boss that I'm certain the Hinton paper will take.

> President Clarence Harmon reviews the plans of the new dormitory complex to be built at Cade State University with Democratic congressional hopeful Howard Ferguson. Chief construction engineer James Finney looks on. Mr. Ferguson, who is challenging District Attorney Everett Cranston for the Democratic nomination for the post, paid a visit to the campus last Thursday.

When I had those pictures made of Matt Wriston for his Assembly race three years ago, we played on his Lincolnesque appearance and there was the same picture, a few of the same old posters—with "For Assembly" scratched out and "For Congress" lettered in—there was the Raymond Massey of Yost County looking down on us wisely and benignly from around the walls of the Student Union lounge where the Lincoln Club met after lunch. It was a sandbag.

The thing that really pisses me off about these new participatory Democrats is their high moral tone on the one hand, and at the same time, the sneaky little tricks they're always pulling. They're not really very decent about anything. Absolutely no manners.

"Of course," LPK says in her introduction, "when you have some posters ready, Mr. Ferguson, we'll be happy to hang them up also—we are a nonpartisan club." Sure they are, but they couldn't wait to hang Matt up there until after Ferguson spoke to them. What a nice, friendly, nonpartisan greeting! Not to mention the little card table she had set up in the corner for the nonpartisan convenience of the nonpartisan club members to sign up as nonpartisan volunteers for Wriston.

"It's a little early to get petitions, isn't it?" I say to her before the meeting begins.

"This is all legal," this slant-eyed piece answers. "We're just collecting names for volunteers. If they're over twenty-one they can sign petitions *and* circulate them." And she has a look on her as if there's some secret joke that's vastly, oh so vastly amusing. But she won't meet my eyes, glances away.

The whole operation was rigged—even the questions. I can imagine her and some of the bright-eyed boys there—my old buddy Harvey Washington among them—having a caucus beforehand to dream up the cute ones.

"What is your meaning of the word 'possible' when you say we must get out of entanglements such as Indo-China as soon as possible?"

"What's your reaction to student demands for broader participation in administrative decisions?"

"Do you feel there should be a more immediate request-response ratio in our political system?"

Poor Howie. He stumbles, gurgles, and gags. None of his answers satisfies them, he doesn't even understand some of the questions. Then he gets onto something, there's almost an audible click in his head.

"I have to agree with Moynihan," he says and a few heads turn to each other, "that there are hazards in using sociological techniques, originally designed for institutional evaluations, as programs for action."

What a mouthful! Did he understand what he was saying? It didn't matter, because none of them did either. Thanks to the Yost County library, a bit of political maneuvering was being fashioned before us. He had broken their drive. He had stood under the basket, picked up the rebound, and zapped the ball the length of the court for a snowbird.

Then he kept going, didn't let them recover, and starts talking about his rural medical plan. "These large issues you've raised are important, but also important for a Congressman are the local problems for which solutions have to be made on the spot; hand-work you might say. Now the folks up in the little town of Leix in my county went together and built a small medical clinic. But . . ."

And it's story time with milk and cookies. They are fascinated. How hard it is to get doctors to practice medicine in rural communities. Why not offer scholarships with the understanding that a certain amount of practice be conducted in small towns . . .

". . . after all, if a country like Mexico can do this, I don't see why we can't." Mexico? Where'd he read about that? Then the tongue goes to the back molars and I stiffen up. I can hear a plus for socialized medicine coming out. ". . . for about one hundred seventy-five years training officers for the Army at West Point and a little less time, officers for the Navy at Annapolis. All to have a capable and well-trained group of professionals for the Army and Navy for out national defense. It seems only reasonable to me that we need a large corps of medical professionals for our national health defense. If we can okay a bunch of professionals who are trained to kill for us, we ought to be able to okay another group of professionals who are going to heal us."

That ball just rolled around and around and around the rim and then in the silence dropped through the net. But there were no cheers, just silent astonishment as if two points had been made by a blind basket-case. Miss or is it Mrs. Kuslowski looks up at him, green eyes squinting.

Her cheekbones are set high, giving her a faintly Oriental or maybe Slavic look, as if she were perpetually flinching from an expected blow. I wonder if she's hooked up with the Kuslowskis down in Slab City. That's a big family and used to regularly deliver a big vote. Nice legs for a small girl, though she has that peasant build that could get dumpy later on. She moves slowly in contrast to her eyes that shift restlessly.

"And another thing," Ferguson continues. "Projections indicate the population of this area will double by the year 2000, but there's no preparation for mass transportation . . ." A buzzer rings somewhere, and a few get up and tiptoe out. More interestingly, several others make a move to go but sit back. Howie gives them his pitch on the Rail Bank. "Some of you probably drive more than an hour to get here and it seems likely, from the growth plans I saw today, this will become an important educational center—there should be some provision for rapid, public mass transportation." He paused; I could sense statistics rising into his mouth, but he waits too long.

"I'm sorry, Mr. Ferguson," she's on her feet, little feet which make her legs look better than they are. "But our time period has expired and many of us have classes. On behalf . . ."

"I thought you did pretty good," I answered his question. We were driving over to meet Captain Billy.

"Do you really think so?" he said, slumped down. "I don't know. They were awful smart. Some of those questions, why, shit, I didn't even know what they were talking about."

"Neither did they," I told him. "It was all out of books. You're way ahead on personal experience. That's your strength, personalize these questions."

"She was kind of cute, the little Polack," he said, looking at me. "She must be working for Wriston."

"Don't worry about her. And don't say 'Polack.' "

"Well, shit, that's what she is, isn't she?"

"I don't know what she is," I tell him. And I fill him in on Billy Brown.

Just one week from tonight: our county committee meeting. Then comes Minkus', and then Cade County. Howie will take ours easily. He'll get about nineteen votes in Cade, "give or take two," and in Sinnemok, maybe about eleven—who cares about that.

Then we go to the petitions. Hate petitions. Also Wriston's people are the sort that will check out every damn signature.

Got the proofs for the billboards today. They're going to look pretty good. Close-up of Howie sitting on the bulldozer, grinning. We should put FERGUSON in blue and the FOR CONGRESS in red.

Rented the old candy store for a headquarters. It's not large, but a good location next door to the telephone company office. Mrs. Avery agrees to manage it.

"How's Betty Jane?" I ask her, not curious but just to make conversation.

"She's just fine, Tommy. I heard from her yesterday. She has a nice little bookstore in Elmira."

Hello there, Betty Jane. Who's making you cry in Elmira?? Elmira?!!!

```
B. J. A.--About 23. Virgin. A plain, wholesome
type, in the neighborhood. I was on the AP in Albany
and she at SUNY. Was always writing funny little
poems and sending them to me after each bang. One of
those women that makes bad fiction real: she
"blossomed" after being fucked regularly. Then I
started hearing wedding bells. Remember the night on
bench below Capitol when I told her we were through.
She cried and then almost begged. There were the
lights of the DeWitt Clinton across from us. So I led
her into the lobby and up to the room for one last
bang. Nearly chewed my lips off and I tasted her
tears. Or was it my blood? I didn't treat her very
well, I guess. A nice, friendly girl.
```

Was that late summer? Yes, because it was just after Betty Jane that one of the guys came into our cubicle and threw a tear-off from the wire on my desk.

ALERT UPSTATE (34−25) SAMUEL J. BRYAN, FORMER YOST COUNTY JUDGE AND PROMINENT IN UPSTATE DEMOCRATIC PARTY CIRCLES TAKEN TO YOST COUNTY MEMORIAL HOSPITAL APPROX. 3:30 PM FOLLOWING POSSIBLE STROKE IN OFFICE. OBIT FOLLOWS

BF 16982

It was just like Alma to let me find out that way, or I guess she was pretty busy, too busy to call me. If you can say sitting outside the emergency-care room waiting is to be busy.

When I came out of the elevator, she was still there, looking like one of those pictures of immigrant women waiting on Ellis Island for their ticket to the land of the free. And she was dressed to the teeth. Hat, gloves, her best dark blue dress with

the white piping on the collar and smelling of "Evening in Paris."
I remember her wearing the same outfit when the Judge was
campaigning.

As I came up to her she didn't move, and I wasn't sure she
saw me until she reached up, took one of my hands, patted it,
and said, "He's all right, Tommy. He's going to live."

Then Doc Brook came out to say they were moving him into
a room now and we could see him but he was very tired, and
might not be too aware of things. So a few minutes later, they
showed us into a room and there he was, magically in a bed with
all the tubes and jugs already in place, breath steady but a little
ragged. Eyes closed, the face somehow smaller on the pillow,
and everything tucked in neatly.

Nevertheless, my mother moved around the bed, testing,
redoing the precise, expert folds of the hospital corners, making
sure the sheet and coverlet were smooth, then paused at bedside; one lavender gloved hand by the shape of his hips. I'll never
forget the look on her face.

Very sweet. A half smile on her lips and her eyes smoky; an
anticipatory glint in them. She stood like this, minute after minute, silently just looking at him this way, looking at that unconscious visage, with the cramp behind the broad brow slowly
loosening up, the brain regaining its flexibility. She looked as if
she expected the eyes to flutter, to open, and the mouth move,
to say — say what? "Alma. Alma. Why don't we get married?"
"All right, Sam, if you think it's a good idea." "I do. I think it's
a good idea."

But of course that didn't happen. Doc Brook said the next
twelve hours were critical, so we stayed on, and along about
four in the morning, Alma not having moved at all, except for an
occasional subtle shift from one foot to the other — there was a
deep sigh and the eyes were suddenly open with all the old fierce
intensity. Now she was nervous, the soft look gone along with
the memory or perhaps with her imagination of a memory, and
she picked over the counterpane, opened and snapped her purse,
reached in under her dress to adjust a shoulder strap of some
undergarment.

His mouth smacked a few times and hung down funnily at the
left corner. His eyes took in the room, the gleaming steel carafe

at bedside, the vanilla walls and the mocha draperies hanging straight down over the window.

"Well, schift," he said finally, and I remember thinking it was one of the few times I'd ever heard him swear or try to swear.

"Now, Sam," my mother said, patting his arm. "Just rest yourself. Doctor Brook says it was just a small one and you're going to be on your feet in no time."

He looks at her with those mad eyes and then slowly, judiciously inspects the rig of bottles suspended over his head. He tries to straighten his mouth out and Alma takes her handkerchief and wipes off some drool from the slack corner. Then the diamond brilliance dulls, there's a general relaxation of neck muscles, and his body seems to disappear a bit into the mattress. "That's right," Alma tells him, giving him permission almost. "Just rest."

And then during another silent, systematic inspection of the new environment, his eyes come across me as I stand just behind Alma — they move past and then return.

"Whosth that?"

"It's Tommy," my mother tells him.

Saturday

Dear Mr. Bryan,

On behalf of the members of the Lincoln Club, I want to express our appreciation for the opportunity of meeting Mr. Howard Ferguson and to listen to his views.

You will agree with our belief, I know, that it's important for college students to become involved with the political process and even though some of us feel we can't support Mr. Ferguson's candidacy it was productive, I feel, to have an exchange of opinions.

Thank you again.

Sincerely,
Laura (Patrovich) Kuslowski

Had a few with Spook Waldorf at Jack's the other P.M.
He had just flown the governor back from that conference in

Puerto Rico and we got to talking about what would happen if Spook should screw up a landing some rainy night and we'd end up with that sanctimonious prig moving onto the second floor.

Waldorf talked about the in-flight recorder the government has built into all commercial air liners, saying that when they play the tape back after a fatal crash, the last recorded words of the pilot are almost always, "Aw, shit."

Makes me wonder. Perhaps there's an enormous tape recorder continuously running somewhere, an endless belt taking down in thirty-minute sequences everything that is happening during this mindless carom through the dark, which is not to imply that we're the one scratch shot in this game of billiards — but the tape keeps going, copying all the laughter, the screams, the grunts, the sneezes and farts, AND the words, the words, the words. . . .

Alma and I spent the morning in the garden, removing the paper "hats" she had put over the beans last night and hoeing. There was no frost last night.

I was feeling good. Ferguson was supposed to be campaigning down in Sinnemok and then over to Cade County for a state police barbecue this afternoon. He did well with his picture show for the Hinton Rotary on Thursday. And there had been no frost around here last night.

Everything going like clockwork and it was one of those moments I enjoy most in a campaign; where you've done everything you can according to schedule and you rest in a quiet, peaceful lull — in the horny hands of fate. Like noon on Election Day, a momentary lull before the anxiety begins to build up again, what the results will be when the machines are opened nine hours later.

She serves me a farm dinner at noon, pot roast, carrots, browned potatoes, coleslaw, and apple pie, but doesn't sit down. "Aren't you going to eat?" I say.

"I'm never hungry this time of day," she answers, fussing around me.

"Well, at least sit down. You make me nervous waiting on me like this. It's like with . . ." and I stop and just a flick in her eyes betrays the fact she knew what I was about to say.

"Do you want your coffee now?" she asks and just then the phone rings.

It's while I'm talking to Pug Connors that I remember where I saw that same far-horizon look Howie gave me the other night.

It was just after the Indiana primary and he had come back to New York and invited us down to lunch at that high-rise he lived in across from the UN. He had aged about ten years. He expressed his appreciation to us for coming out for him, especially those of us from the upstate where he was really hated. Said he knew what it meant and the risks we were taking to do it. But he promised that after California, he'd come back and make it up to us and that we were going to win . . . so, he said. Just ignore the cute remarks and when he came back to New York we'd put the fire under their tails. Well, he came back.

"What are you doing today?" Pug asks.

"I was thinking of doing some fishing," I tell him. Everything was going so well; I have this Bucktail that nothing has ever struck and I just had a feeling that if I could get to Emerson Creek — this would be the day an underslung-jawed monster would snap onto it, as we say, BUT . . .

"Could you pick up some proxies for me?" my county chairman asks.

So I go after other fish.

It's at Miller's Store I run into her again. Not really, but she's just left and left with Ed Miller's proxy for Wriston.

"How was I supposed to know?" Ed Miller tells me, trying to keep the razor-blade display card between us, keeping busy filling orders. I just stand there, patiently, a salesman obstinately in the way, some of the customers eyeing me curiously. "She just comes in and says she's working for Wriston, and I just figured that Wriston was okay. You know? I thought it was okay with Pug, to do it?"

I just stand there. Miller fills an order, rings up a sale. Waits on another customer, turns to the shelf behind him and takes down some soup. Drops a can, picks it up. Turns back. Then he goes into the walk-in cooler to grind some hamburger and I remain by the paper goods. Maybe he'll stay in there all day. He'd like to, I'm sure. But he comes back with the ground round, and the last customer is gone, leaving us alone; Miller nervously wiping his hands on the white apron.

Scenes like this sadden me and I will never understand them. I mean what devilish contract was it that a man like Ed Miller signed in blood to throw him in such a state? He's got a nice little superette there. He's a Boy Scout leader, his wife plays the organ in church. His two boys are good kids. Yet, he just goes to pieces in a situation like this.

> I, *Edmund Miller*, a duly elected committeeman of the *1st* (District/Ward) of the (Town/City) of *Athens* do here by appoint *"Just leave it blank, Ed"* to act for me in all business that will come before the meeting of the County Committee of the Democratic Party of the County of Yost to be held on the _____ day of _____, 19_____.
> All proxies given by me heretofore are hereby revoked.
>
>

"Just sign it, Ed."
(SIGNATURE)

>
> *"We'll fill in the date"*
> (DATE)

"Who is this Laura Kuslowski?" I ask Connors. "Her maiden name was Patrovich."

"I remember a Patrovich girl who used to be active in the Young Democrats. Relative of George Stamski."

"That's her," I say. "Who's she married to?"

He gets up and walks over to the water cooler in the corner of the election commissioner's office. He draws off a cup. It's noon time and the girls are out to lunch and we have the place to ourselves. "I don't know," he says after a few sips. "Let's look her up."

The sixth ward of Yost is where most of the Polish settled when their farms failed up on the mountain. He pulls out the index file cards but there's no (Kuslowski, Laura) registered in the sixth. There's lots of other Kuslowskis and several Patrovichs but no Lauras of either strain.

"She must have moved out," Pug says. "Let's see." He holds up a card. "I think I remember now. Here's old Stan Kuslowski. One of his boys married a Patrovich girl. Yeah, that's right." He slips the card back in place and closes the file. "I believe the kid was killed in Vietnam."

"Oh, yeah?"

"If she's the same one," he looks over at me, a glint in the cool eyes. "You interested?"

"No, hell no. It's just that she's working for Wriston. Everywhere I've been in the last week or so, she's either there or just left. She had Ed Miller in a real bind."

"What's she look like?" he asks, smiling.

And I try to describe her, in general terms.

Tonight we scored one of those coups that you dream about. There was a Little League playoff in Delphi, our county champions playing a team from Sinnemok. I fixed it for Howie to present the trophy to the kids, using his own athletic background as a wedge.

"Ladies and gentlemen, to present the trophy, one of Yost County's all-time basketball greats . . . Howie Ferguson!" Splatter of applause. "Come up here, Howie—understand you're trying to be a politician these days . . ." and that's all, but it was enough. Howie looks good and does well with the presentation. It's over quickly.

But what I didn't count on were the five cheerleaders being on hand. That was Helen's idea, I guess, and seeing them in the parking lot behind the grandstand, fluffing their hair and pulling down the white sweaters—well, people don't like politics intruding too much. Especially into Little League!

"Well, sh——, shoot," my candidate says to me. "The home team has got to have some cheerleaders, don't they?" And he looks at me and grins. And I see Helen talking to the legionnaire running the show, pointing to the girls, and he's nodding his head, eyes swiveting from her to the five teeny-boppers prancing around, doing their warmup exercises.

So it's real smooth. Not a word about Howie running for any-thing, excepting that half-a-joke in the introduction. (And that cost a fifty-dollar donation to the Legion Camp Fund. Candi-dates sometimes get the idea that people say these things be-cause they're such nice fellows. Yet, when asked where all the money goes, it's hard to explain and sometimes you only hurt their feelings when you do. Unnecessarily.)

So all through the game, they were along the third-base line, with about 1,500 people looking at them. H-O-W-I-E. In their enthusiasm and careless fervor it would sometimes come out W-O-H-I-E or E-O-W-H-I.

"Look, girls," I tell them during the third inning. "You're going to have to remember your place and stay in line. It makes no sense at all if you jump around and get all mixed up."

"Yes, Mr. Bryan."

"Yes, Mr. Bryan." Warm little eyes over pert breasts. Oh me, oh my!

And, by God, we even got a picture out of it. The paper had sent over a photographer just for the game but the kid knew an extra dividend when he saw one. How many of these Little League games had he been sent to, but with nothing like this? So there it was: Howie bending way down to hand the trophy to the nine-year-old Mickey Mantle and the girls arm-in-arm behind, floradora fashion and the five budding billboards where they should be. H-O-W-I-E.

The widow Kuslowski was nowhere to be seen. I kept looking up in the stands, expecting to see her in the crowd handing out Wriston brochures. She missed up on this one, which just goes to show how amateurs overlook an opportunity.

I am very tired. But it is almost three A.M. Over in the corner of the sun porch, by the French windows, are two boxes of gray notebooks like this one. The Bryan Memoirs. I've become a squirrel in a nest of clippings, enrollment sheets, position papers, canceled checks, receipts, index cards, voting records, and phone numbers for people who don't answer anymore, like 202-225-4451 — which someday I'll have to draw a line through.

A squirrel with hot nuts. "Don't you need anybody? I need

somebody to love." The big difference is when Columbus touched shore in the Caribbean, there were some human faces peering through the plantain and the sailors went back to the Old World with the clap which was some sort of measure of human exchange.

But on the Moon or Mars or Venus or any of those alluring islets, there's just nobody. We might as well face it; we're all alone. They lie around us, deceiving us with their glitter.

The Judge, Alma, and I all taking a trip in the new Buick right after he "retired" from the bench. Out in Oklahoma or maybe it was Kansas; we'd see great tall buildings on the horizon, way in the flat distance; a great metropolis shining in the western sun. The heat seemed to be a cutting edge, planing the prairie even more, finishing the job roughly done by the ice long ago. And we'd keep driving and driving, wondering what city it was, for there was nothing on the road map—a new city that had appeared overnight or at least after the AAA maps had been printed.

Finally coming into the outskirts by the railroad siding, one or two dusty hopper cars on the spur, their trapdoors hanging open, and the whole downtown section of this splendid city composed of three or four concrete grain silos, cylindrical storage bins rising to the height of a twenty-story building with maybe a dilapidated watchman's shack on the other side of town—a distance of about ten feet from the silos—and nobody around. Absolutely nobody.

Through the rear window of the Buick, I'd watch the mute, humanless skyscrapers recede, unbelieving of what I had seen until the distance my father's heavy foot put between us somehow "peopled" the place once again. And then to turn around and see another skyline rising in the distance, sparkling indentations in the blue mouth of the sky; the same anticipations repeated to meet the same disappointment. We must have driven all day without seeing a soul, through a dozen of those empty, deserted places. That's what it's like out there.

Saturday

A week has elapsed and though there have been the usual chores, not much has happened except for last night. Miss Skidmore did show up. After saying on the phone she wasn't sure she wanted to watch the county committee meeting, she walks in just as I'm filling out the proxies. I hear her finishing school voice outside the sheriff's office, inquiring for me.

(Earlier: Pug Connors unlocks the office of the sheriff and leads me into his old domain, looking around to see what changes had been made. The calendar is different, that's about all, but maybe that's enough. "Here," he says, handing me the papers, "put your name as the proxy on those you didn't witness and Joe Cummings on those you did. Put today's date on all of them. Also, the time," he adds, one heavy lid dipping momentarily.

"How about seven fifty-nine," I ask, "or is that cutting it too close?" But he doesn't think that's so funny. "Seven thirty will do," he says softly and goes across the main hall to the Election Bureau to set up the agenda with Wriston and Jim Hurley and others.)

She's been in the sun, her bare legs are tanned and they look very good, crossed, the line of muscle along one thigh tensing, one calf pleasingly flared. She sits across from me and lights a cigarette.

"What are you doing?" she asks, and I tell her. "Aren't proxies supposed to be dated the day they are given?"

"The proxy with the most recent date is the valid one," I tell her, and the blue eyes widen, narrow, then return to normal size.

"That's not what I asked," she says.

"I know, but that's the answer."

"Oh," she says and I look up. She's got a little girl smile on her—a wicked little girl smile like that night in the motel after we had watched the late news and she had finished her nails and was brushing her hair (it's remarkable; the similarity between these upper-class broads and whores—how they reach for a hairbrush or a nail file or bottle of cologne between tricks), and she looks down at me, at my flagged cock, and says, "Do you want some head?" And when I ask what's that, she gives that little smile as if I'm some sort of green kid who's just been told the truth about storks. So, still holding onto the hairbrush, she bends down and starts on it. But "head?" My God, what's the world coming to?

I ignore her look and continue filling in the proxies, my name or Cummings' name at the top, the date and time at the bottom. The foyer outside is noisy with committeemen. Soles and heels clatter on the marble floor; greetings and small talk echo hollowly. An assembly of the horse guards. I've just about finished when Connors' slap shoe approaches and he opens the door.

"Done?" he asks.

"Just about," I answer and make introductions. Off comes the gray hat and he almost bows over her hand. The charm is strong enough to make Miss S. pink prettily; sit up straighter. The smile on her lips, halfway to amused contempt, froze and had to rearrange itself into something else. She didn't see the way he rolled his eyes behind her. "Okay, let's go," he told me.

YOST DEMS CHOOSE FERGUSON

PARTY SPLIT IS INDICATED

Alton contractor Howard Ferguson was given an overwhelming endorsement last night by the Yost County Democratic Committee in his bid for Congress. Meeting at the county courthouse, Democratic committeemen gave their votes to Mr. Ferguson in a better than 2-to-1 margin over his nearest rival, Matthew L. Wriston, Yost attorney, and a crushing 10-to-1 margin over Everett Cranston, Cade County District Attorney who has the support of the Brown organization.

The great difference in the vote might indicate that Mr. Ferguson's bid represents more than a favorite son's candidacy and that Yost County Democrats have decided to challenge the wishes of "Captain" Billy Brown who has ruled the Democratic Party of the entire Sinnemok Valley for several decades.

Two more county conventions yet remain, in Sinnemok and in Cade, and it is thought unlikely that he will carry either of these. However, the size of last night's vote would indicate that a primary, at least between Mr. Ferguson and Mr. Cranston, is a certainty, and that Mr. Wriston might possibly make it a three-way split.

Some observers felt that Mr. Ferguson was given some assistance in his victory by a crushing show of muscle from the county organization under the leadership of John "Pug" Connors.

Though Mr. Connors ostensibly claimed neutrality it became increasingly obvious as one after another of forty proxies were presented in support of the ski-resort owner's bid, that the Democratic chairman had more than a passing interest in the Alton man's candidacy.

Matthew L. Wriston spoke eloquently and at length, using what he termed, "certain evidences of a prearranged, prepackaged rout of democratic principles" as the substance of his remarks.

"In no small way," the attorney told the 32 committeemen who attended the meeting, "we here tonight are witnessing the end of the Democratic Party—if, and I say this most earnestly, if we permit this travesty."

When asked after the vote if he would enter a primary, Mr. Wriston answered, "The die has been cast. It is somewhat academic since I had sworn myself to challenge the bossism that is destroying our party. Whether it is a boss in Cade County or one here in Yost is immaterial.

"What is germane is that the issues must be taken to the people. I am not a man of means, but I shall carry this fight on with all the resources at my disposal."

The final tally, each committeeman casting a weighted vote based on the number of ballots received by the last Democratic gubernatorial candidate in his district, was: Ferguson, 1,302; Wriston, 612; Cranston 103.

No wonder the average citizen thinks politics is mysterious if not dishonest . . . with reporting like that. If this had been the Republican county committee meeting, the newspaper would have given more space—"in depth," as they like to say. Fortunately Jim Hurley's speech nominating Cranston was omitted. He sputtered and spat, pulling that turkey gobbler neck up to warn about "lawless elements" trying to wreck Our Party. He praised Cranston for his handling of the riot in Hinton City last year.

"They don't run things yet," he nearly shouted at one point and I looked at Harvey Washington sitting along the back row. To be objective, Harvey's cool cocoa expression was preferable to the Hurley apoplectic flush.

Naturally, the paper used some of Wriston's rhetoric—always a favorite with the copy desks in the area. But they completely ignored Howie's little speech. I suppose they regard him as just "another" picked out by Pug Connors for some obscure reason, maybe for a big contribution. Well, maybe so.

He stood in front, just before the high judge's bench—which was empty—the first time most of them had seen "their" candidate in the flesh, looking like the team captain promising victory next Saturday to the school assembly. He delivered the words I had suggested: JFK . . . inspiration, hard campaign . . . work in every area, etc. When he'd recited the concluding sentence I went back to the proxies, arranging them in roll-call order, but there was no applause. Ferguson was still standing there, that strange, hangdog look on his face, the empty sky in his eyes.

"Now I know what a lot of folks are saying," he continues. Pug Connors looks up at him with the smile of a big Irish china doll, ready to go to smithereens.

"I know," our impromptu candidate says, "that people are saying that there's something phony about me being in this race, that maybe I shouldn't be in it at all. Well," he pauses, throws a look toward me which I try to hold, try to transmit, a command—SIT DOWN!

"Well, that reminds me of a cave we have up on the mountain."

A couple of committeemen put down the newspapers they were reading. A cave on the mountain? What's this all about— some sort of story hour? Laura Kuslowski has been chattering in the rear, sotto voce, but she's stopped too—green eyes in slits, bemused anticipation; waiting for the All-State chump to say something that can be used against him later. The long, slim pendulum of Miss S.'s crossed leg stops its monotonous clocking of democracy.

"I used to play in this cave when I was a kid," Howie continues soberly. "Or rather I tried to play in it. Because there were bushes around the entrance and there were always birds and squirrels in these bushes. They were mostly jackdaws and blue jays. Anyway, everytime I'd try to go inside this cave, they'd set up a big racket, jabbering and calling and I didn't know—any better but to let them scare me off. Then one day, I guess I was about twelve years old, it came to me that I had as much right to go in that cave as they did—in fact"—and he makes a slight fist and throws it through the air, a dice-throwing motion or maybe the follow-through of a slider—"in fact, they never went inside this cave themselves, but just hung around outside and scared everybody else off. So, this one day I just went up to it and walked right in."

You could hear the automatic flusher gurgling in the men's room on the second floor. Connors still looks up at Ferguson, a strange light in his eyes. Wriston: a sad, reflective look on his face — you could weigh the pity he was turning out. Howie takes a couple of deep breaths and continues.

"I'm not afraid of that cave anymore and I'm here to tell you tonight, to say that it belongs to all of us. We don't have to worry about the birds who make all the noise at the entrance. They've never been inside, they don't know what it's all about. I'm here to ask you all tonight" — artful use of the Kennedy repetitive declaration — "to ask all of you to come with me inside that cave. So," and he blushes, his eyes seem to refocus, roll around the room, "so, that's all I got to say." And he sits down abruptly, the back of his size 17 neck scarlet.

Then they clapped, not terribly long or loud but there was a ring of genuine appreciation. Whether they understood him or not, he had told them something new and they liked it. It had been different. The tingles along my spine were flinty trapezoids.

But does that sort of thing make our sterling local press?

One of the girls on the desk who puts together social notes when she's not clipping and blue-lining the canned food-fashion-foolidoo-doo crap could have done a few paragraphs for the *Sentinel* on the little scene that transpired in the lobby. In order of their height: Helen Ferguson, Miss Skidmore, and Laura Kuslowski.

> The candidate's wife, the ever-popular Helen Ferguson who still practices several hours a day before the mirror twirling the old baton, was wearing a light summer suit of blue linen with white blouse, orange accessories of simply fab jaw-breaker beads and pumps that accentuated the noted Ferguson legs for general delight.
>
> Miss S., one of the more brilliant head-mistresses of our time, underplayed her classical blond beauty with a simple line shirt-waist jersey in dark mustard, the modified Bryonesque collar in hunter green that was carried over in low-heeled suede shoes that sported oversize brass buckles. Her only jewelry was a strand of pearls — rumored to have been plucked one by one by her devoted dah-dah from the sea-slippery fingers of bare-breasted divers off of Kunnihoihoi.
>
> The third member of this engaging trio, widow of the slain war hero from the sixth ward, confided to us that she made the smart

Peter Pan blouse in lavender paisley herself. Laura Kuslowski, who is just throwing herself completely into all sorts of civic and social activities this season, complimented her handiwork with a black miniskirt that proved the Patrovich underpinnings were both sound and sight. On-the-go, in-the-know Laura's accessories included a very sensible but no less wild clipboard in brown Masonite that had just oodles of fascinating doodles and figures.

"What did Laura Kuslowski have to say to you?" I asked Helen later. We were at the party Howie threw at the Lafayette Hotel.

"Oh, she just said how much she had enjoyed Howie's talk," she answered. "I think she meant it. She seems very nice. And funny."

"Funny? What do you mean, funny?" She crushed an ice cube, thinking or perhaps wondering if she should repeat it. Laura: talking, laughing with people across the room. Campaigning on Howie's time!!

"She asked your friend," Helen finally says, "if she was rooting for anyone tonight. But it was the way she said it. It was funny. I wish she was working with us. I like her."

The party at the Lafayette had been Pug's idea. Naturally Wriston didn't show, but she does, sitting down to chat with committeemen. But it was as if Wriston had won! She has a little courage. Or else she just doesn't care at all.

Contrast her behavior with Jim Hurley's blow up on the courthouse steps.

"What the hell's going on here, Connors?"

"What's that, Jim?" Some of the departing committeemen pause on the steps and the walk.

"You call a meeting," Hurley is almost shouting, "but you don't give enough notification, enough time. We had no time to talk to anybody, to get out proxies! What are you trying to pull?" Hurley's voice goes up as his neck stretches, the strain on his windpipe seeming to pare the sound.

"Now don't get a hard-on, Jim," Connors answers, gently

adjusting the gray fedora, once, twice, and then at last satisfied with the position. "I'm neutral in this business," he adds, eyes glittering.

"Neutral," the old man gasps, "you're about as neutral as a nigger at a cockfight! This won't end here. You'll regret this, Connors," Hurley says, and stomps off toward the black Lincoln waiting at the curb. He turns around and comes back a few steps, finger waving, makes a few thick consonant sounds, a guttural slipping of dentures, finally repeats, "You'll regret this." Now he makes it to the car, says, "Let's go!" to his driver.

"I enjoyed that," Pug says, as we watch the limousine pull away.

"You're not drinking," I said to Miss S.

"No, I have to drive back to Saratoga tonight."

"Tonight? You're not staying over?" The blond fall swings with the negative. "I thought you were . . ."

"I have an eight o'clock class tomorrow morning," she said simply.

"There's a lot of ground we haven't covered yet in our seminar?" And she smiled, stroked the pearls.

"I think," she said, "we've touched all the major points." And then she got up, a little too quick and I think one word or two may make her stay over, but it wouldn't be the same.

"Don't bother," she said, "I can find my way out," and side-stepped through a crowd, pelvis pulled in as if the merest contact with a strange body would send her into an uncontrollable yet unwanted frenzy. She walked out under the old, stained mural depicting General Lafayette among fluttering handkerchiefs, circa 1784, during his first farewell tour of America.

I think, Laura K., I have you to thank for my chaste night. Whatever you said in the lobby of the courthouse — and why?

It's human nature to want to win, or to be with a winner. To be a Democrat upstate means this urge often goes unsatisfied. Maybe that's why we have so many primaries, so that at least some of us can win, be with a winner sometime, even at the expense of another Democrat. Every now and then you just have to beat somebody.

Reduce this to a smaller fraction: Howie Ferguson's trivial victory last night — not even a primary but just a county convention, set up at that, still had that magical effect. Committeemen surrounded him rubbing their hands, chuckling, jostling for place as if he were a stove in a wintry place. And he did glow, laughing and bowing and swaying under the impact of all the meaningless, congratulatory remarks.

Pug was gone, having made a brief appearance to "legitimize" the party, so committeemen would know it was okay to be there. Helen sat with some wives, one or two leaning toward her eagerly, perhaps to catch the thin mint of a secret falling from the candy-box face. Others, the realists of the group, slumped sullenly in their chairs, casting suspicious side-looks at the beautiful young woman beside them. And what a look? If there is a magic here, could it go in reverse: what may Helen Ferguson look like by Primary Day as a result of the radiation I saw flashed at her last night . . . not to mention November?

November? Yes, why not. I'm beginning to feel something, smell something about this kid. It's too early but still . . . Or maybe I'm caught up in the cheap euphoria generated by last night's party.

Conversation at the makeshift bar in the rear, beneath Stuart's portrait of George W.

BRYAN: Don't you ever quit? C'mon rest a moment. Have a drink.

LAURA K.:   The smug assurance of the victor. Is that it? You and Pug Connors taught me a lot tonight, Mr. Bryan.

BRYAN: Why so formal?

LAURA: (She shrugs — a pause) How did you break your nose?

BRYAN: What kind of question is that? Now it's my turn: what are you studying in school?

LAURA: I'm going to law school. I was about to go to college when Frank and I were married. Then the baby came . . .

BRYAN: The baby?

LAURA: Sure, my little boy. Anyway, I graduate this spring. Then law school. Maybe.

According to the Yost County Historical Society, the General was supposed to have paced a final *rondeau* in the room where Howie Ferguson presided over the cold cuts. Since the oldest part of the hotel dates back only to about 1820, there are those who claim the Marquis made his adieus in the tack room of an old livery stable. When it burned down, the present hotel was built on the site. It's all irrelevant, for when urban renewal comes to Yost, the whole business is going to be torn down for some low-rent high risers. Maybe the DAR will put up a small plaque.

The rooms upstairs have not been used, for many years. The old halls creak underfoot, floor boards slant and the doors to some of the rooms hang open, brass numbers and locks gone and sold long ago. It's like moving through an old ship, a wreck that's been picked clean and has a slight list to the decks, suggesting the final, crazy skew to the bottom.

What was I doing up there, wandering about those condemned sagging rooms, finishing my beer? Was it to get away from downstairs, to get away from a scene that had suddenly become tedious, boring—too tempting? Yes, partly. Also the wild fantasy that Miss S. may have changed her mind and that behind one of these doors her golden fuzz was glowing in the dark. I check each room; see only the messages scribbled by other voyagers momentarily becalmed: symbols, computations, lists of needs; all of them exposed in the unnatural light of the Vista's marquee across the street. In the backrooms, matches are needed.

Each room becomes a page, in a forlorn but rather commonplace diary; here by the wall phone some numbers, indecipherable code. What was the message: a plea for help perhaps. At the top of a closet: a homosexual's impassioned request for dimensions that, if ever realized, would effect his self-destruction.

There were numerous valentines; initialed, properly arrowed and meticulously dated, confessing to more ordinary loves, easier achieved if no less ardent.

Some rooms were empty pages where ostensibly nothing of note had occurred; though their blank guilessness was somehow ominous as if the events of their day or night were too terrible, too tragic or perverse to even commit to the secret sharing walls. There was one I liked best, two insertions in different handwriting. Beside the light square shadow where a mirror may have hung, someone had written, "The 93rd Airborne Division Was Here!"

Cocky, the one man representing the whole — a lonely soldier setting his cap smartly, checking his uniform in the mirror then suddenly reaching for a pencil to leave his proud mark, his kilroy. Or perhaps, in the back of his mind he made an association with Pershing, the old melodramatic utterance working down through the ranks and the years to a single GI standing in a room in this small city, but the vibrations still strong enough and he leans forward; Hotel Lafayette, We Are Here. But moved by devotion to the larger group, to name names before turning out the light, he wrote instead, "The 93rd Airborne Division Was Here!"

"And this is the only GODDAMNED PLACE YOU'VE EVER BEEN!" a sloping, different hand had written beneath.

It was the first time I had ever spied upon these mementos, though not the first walk I had taken through the deserted halls. And this was the reason, of course, the browsing and musing merely being a subterfuge to get me up to room 312. The shape of the letters on the oak door visible, the room bathed in the amber glow of the new sodium lights installed on Sixth Street. It is a large room and in the center a four-by-eight piece of plywood rests on a pair of sawhorses, left over from the last salesman who set out his samples.

This room has some claim to uniqueness, for in addition to its happenchance piece of furniture, it also boasts a little art in the form of a large calendar from the New York Central Railroad Co.; a big diesel pulling a long freight train and every car is reproduced in the mirror waters of the Hudson River. The page was turned to November — 1961.

Maybe Pug Connors is serious about Howie—the fact that Connors picked the Lafayette for this little victory celebration. There are much better places in town. For old time's sake? No, not Pug Connors. For luck? Perhaps, but something more; a ritual? There had been a magic, magic had been wrought in this place before—spells had been concocted in this room over hands of five-card stud.

Room 312. Those in the game during its heyday were (1) Pug Connors when he was city chairman, before he ran for sheriff. (2) Jesse Daniels, former mayor of the city of Yost; (3) Earl Stone, assistant DA; (4) George Van Arsdale, vice-president of the Merchants & Farmers; (5) and (6) I'm not sure about, but (7) would be the Judge.

The seven-sided table would be set up where the plywood-sawhorse affair is now. Every Thursday. They would gather at five o'clock and play knock rummy for fifty cents a point until Jackson brought up their supper. When the kitchen at the Lafayette closed down, the old bellhop would bring over corned beef and cabbage from the New York Café. After supper, five-card stud would be played, with an occasional hand of draw.

The mystery of this game was so strong that it drew the Judge from his bed, put him back on his feet in a brevity of time that Doc Brook termed miraculous. Alma was dismayed, unhappy to lose her patient. She had nursed him, fed and washed him on the sun porch where a bed had been set up. She supported his first shuffling, baby steps; each excursion longer than the last until he finally could go all the way to the downstairs bathroom and back without her. The obnoxious bedpan was put away. He had become an old man.

I got home early one day from Albany, it was a Thursday, to hear Alma pleading, arguing. He half sat, half leaned on the edge of the bed, wearing just trousers. There was a slight hump in his back, just below the neck, and the shoulders, almost womanly in their whiteness and texture, were held with an exaggerated military squareness—slack flesh draped on a hanger.

"Come here, Tommy," he said, without turning his head. "I want you to do these shoes for me."

"Oh, very well," said Alma, kneeling on the floor to loop and tie the laces. "If you are determined to go." So I drove him down to the Lafayette. One year, another went by. Connors, no longer in the game because of his office, up for re-election then — I ran his campaign. Arnold, the hardware dealer, takes his place at the table.

The calendar is unmarked as are the walls on 312, as if to underscore the seriousness of the business conducted here, business where nothing was ever written down. It was in 1962 anyway but the NYC thoughtfully provides a smaller calendar of the succeeding year, printed on the card under the sheet for December — 1961. A look into the future, a whole year laid out by the numbers. There were four Thursdays in the month of April, 1962. It was the first Thursday, the fifth. The calendar is unmarked.

Something else I never thought of until now: the way that game just kept on going while the hotel slowly closed down, went out of business around it. First the restaurant closed, but they kept on playing, bringing food in from across the street. Then the lobby was cut up by plywood partitions into several small offices. The bar had several owners before it finally shut down. But the game continued.

The clientele changed also; shoe salesmen, the usual whores, drifters, and bums, then no one. The room clerk was let go. But the cards continued to be shuffled and dealt in room 312, the maneuvering went on. At last, only the old banquet hall was to remain open, made available by Hunt and Clark Realty as a public service for groups that needed such space. The game was over by then.

Sunday

Conversation at breakfast.

ALMA: Well, it's happened, hasn't it?

BRYAN: What?

ALMA: The frost. Look at that garden. That corn won't grow at all now.

BRYAN: We'll plant more corn. It doesn't look so bad to me.

ALMA: It looks bad to me. I told you it was too early.

BRYAN: Yes, I remember you did.

ALMA: Did what?

BRYAN: Said it was too early.

It's a big night at Tiny's Home Spot. The holy trinity looking down on us and I'm feeling whiter than usual. Harvey Washington introduces me to his girl, a cool, defiant-looking chick with an Afro hairdo. So, he does have a girl after all. But so serious.

"That was quite a show you put on last night," he says. Then adds good-naturedly, "You really taught us a lesson."

One thing I can't stand is the pretentious good-sportsmanship displayed by the ignorant and the amateurs in this business. They rarely get mad. They only laugh and say, "Boy, you really whacked me that time."

"What I don't understand," I say at one point, "is why you're going down the line with Wriston. Cranston is the real enemy, not Howie Ferguson. All you're going to do is split the vote. You're giving the primary to the very guy you want to beat."

"But it's a whole new thing now, Tommy," he says, suddenly serious, adjusting the horn rims. His girl stares stonily ahead, not seeing her own beautiful reflection in the blue mirror behind the bar. "Actually, there's not that much difference among the three of them: Cranston, Ferguson, and Wriston. Not as far as *we're* concerned." And he gives me a sorghum look. "But it's the way Wriston is doing it that's important. Cranston and you guys are going about it in the same old way; all these committeemen, nominating speeches, the deals—that's a lot of old shit, Tommy. It don't appeal to the real, baby."

"And Wriston does, baby?"

"Forget about Wriston," he says, and his fingers flick poor old Matt into oblivion. "It's the *way* he's doing it that counts. He went out on a limb, all by himself. He made the break. He's the man," he adds softly, "right now."

"He's going to take all of us with him—down." It suddenly occurs to me that our differences are not just those of color and this makes me feel better, makes me feel better toward H. Washington. Strange.

"You still don't understand," he says patiently. "It's the *way* he's doing it that makes him important. That's all."

Oh, I understand. The exemplary life. Form is all-important, not content; the separation is made. In fact, there's no division to be made since it's all form. All bellowing and shouting. But what I don't understand is the type of examples that are chosen, are idolized. Successful failures!

"It's no great secret what you're doing," I say. Tiny is leaning over the bar, a sleepy-boy expression. "You want to prove the system bad in terms of how badly you're mangled by it. A big grand, gratuitous gesture. But who are you proving it to? *You* already know. Who else? The very guys who are going to chop you up. It's like geese walking to the water in a world of foxes. You guys—of all people—ought to know about things like that." His girl gives me a stony stare, cigarette smoke jetting from wide, flared nostrils. A beautiful brown dragon. Cold fire.

J. L.--About 25. Part-time hooker and showgirl I met
in San Francisco on way home from Korea. Very tall,
boyishly slim. Only Negro girl I've made it with.
Had five wild days with her. She'd get off around
four a.m. from the club she was working and then we'd
go to her place and fuck until noon. Did fantastic
things with her tongue. Cunt rather dry but hot and
she could ball herself up, feet crossed over my neck.
Seemed to get more of a charge out of me sucking her
tits--caramel apples with black, rubbery tips-- than
stuffing her. Her pimp boyfriend busted us up, as
well as my nose, when he found out she had only
charged me the first time around. She was okay but,
all in all, there are better ones.

Martin Luther seemed embarrassed; a fast middleweight who had been beefed up quickly to make lightheavy by weigh-in time. But his managers, that flashy brother team from Boston, looked very optimistic.

"That is funny, isn't it?" Harvey Washington says. "I think the gesture, to use your terms, the gesture is important—that there must be someone still out there who's going to pay attention right now. While you, of all people, Tommy, don't believe there is. You ain't keeping the faith no more, baby?"

"Don't give me that shit," I say. His girl has gone back to looking at herself in the mirror. "I was keeping the faith, as you call it, when you were pitching pennies on Walnut Street. Who the hell do you think has been keeping the faith all these years?" And they all laugh. Even Tiny has a little smile. What was so funny about that?

"Something I always wanted to tell you," Washington says, containing his yuks. "When you used to hire me and other kids to distribute pamphlets, put up posters—fifty cents a run, remember?—we used to take all that stuff, and hand out a few and throw the rest of it over Bronstein's fence. I bet if you go down to his junkyard today, you could still find some old posters for Connors or—who was that guy who ran for coroner then?"

"Brewster. So what. I knew that. What are you trying to say: that you've matured? You've become a big boy now and take politics seriously? But you haven't. You're still going to the dump. Except this time you're taking more than posters. You're putting yourself on the pile now."

"Let's burn the dump." It's Tiny that says that. Tiny! I can't believe my ears.

"What's gotten into you!" I say. "What are you going to do, change your name? Tiny X?" I am only joking but no one laughs now. It seems like everyone in the place heard me. There's only the sound of a tap running in the sink behind the bar. Then Tiny reaches out and taps his fist against my forehead, lightly but a precise one-two, and the place eases up.

It's a gesture from the old days. When I'd miss a hole or call a bad play, he'd come back to the huddle and give me a tattoo on my helmet. But I wasn't wearing a helmet last night.

Dear Laura Kuslowski,

It seems I owe you a letter, an answer to your question, why I'm helping Ferguson and not Wriston. If you had hung around Friday night at the Lafayette I could have told you then. I was in the mood to talk the other night, but you had left when I came back from a stroll. Actually I was upstairs, indulging myself with the luxury of nostalgia in derelict surroundings. That's bad stuff. So I had hoped to talk to you.

```
Kuslowski, Laura P.  126 North 3rd St., Apt.  2B Birth
7/12/46.  Marital Status: Widow.  Children: Jacob
2/9/67.  Enrollment: Democrat.
```

So reads your card in the Election Bureau index. You moved up from the sixth ward into the second, Laura? I know the building you live in, the Ace Cleaners is on the ground floor. Right? And I know inside. Your apartment is in the rear. Old Man Kruger used to live on the third floor, just above you. You don't remember him; he used to be a committeeman in the second.

And I know your old neighborhood too, Laura. Palinski's Market there on the corner of Frye and First. The 3rd Co. Pumper Station House near the old school—I guess you must have gone to that school, it was still up, wasn't it? You probably went to St. Mary's Church with Father Reagan. (Father Reagan was an old friend of my father's, kept trying to convert him. He used to say, "With a name like Bryan and not in the Church? Why, man, what befell your family?") All along Clark, from Second to the city limits, were the furniture factories, enormous buildings of dark brick like the wall of a medieval town, to protect the uptight citizens of the fourth ward, on the other side, from the spicy breaths and loose habits in the sixth. Slab City. They became copper mills just before the war.

I carried more baskets of food up on the front porches of the sixth ward than any ten-year-old in history and I remember the Patrovich house, or at least one of them. It had a small porch with very steep steps up to it, no grass on the top of the small terrace, and a scrawny collie-favored mongrel slept under the porch, who growled without ever opening his eyes. Right?

"Happy Thanksgiving from Judge Bryan and all your friends at the Yost Democratic Club," was what I was supposed to say. In the baskets would be a small turkey, a peck of potatoes, canned peas, a small bag of flour, a tin of lard, and a can of cooked pumpkin. Most of the time I'd just plunk down the basket outside the door, ring the bell and run, as if it were Halloween and a prank had been pulled. I'd catch hell from whoever was driving the car.

I remember one time the goods had been delivered this way and when I got back to the car, a kid had run out on the porch, broken open the bag of flour, and was dusting himself and the cats that were always around. "It's snowing, it's snowing," he kept singsonging. I wanted to go back with a replacement but the driver wouldn't let me, we had a schedule to keep. "But how can they make pumpkin pie without flour?" I asked.

"Listen, kid," he said. He was a thin, consumptive Irishman named Creeley. "Listen, kid, most of these people sell this stuff to buy cornmeal. They don't even know what a pumpkin pie looks like."

Well now, Laura, where was I? I was trying to answer your letter, answer your question: why I'm working for Ferguson and not Wriston.

But first let me compliment you on the way you handled yourself at Friday night's meeting. When we had got to Leix on the roll call and it became obvious how it was going, I looked over at you. There was a slight smile on your face, and your eyes had pulled up. All those proxies—we let you have a couple, do you know that?—coming in and you merely nodded to yourself a few times and grinned. No one could feel sorry for you the way you looked and that's what was good about it. About you. Let me tell you something about Pug Connors. I don't agree with this way of doing it, but he reacts with a shotgun blast when a peashooter would have done the job. That's only in politics, because, if you remember, he reacted just the opposite as sheriff.

Then later, over at the Lafayette, you came to the party as if Wriston had been the winner. Between you and me, you may have picked up a few workers Friday night: taken them from us. You behaved very well, lot better than some of the so-called pros that night, and I wanted to talk to you more.

But what kind of a question was that: how did I break my

nose? Once in school, I got creamed going around end – this was in the days when only bleeders wore face masks – and a second time the job was done by the boyfriend of a girl I was dating. Both of them were Negroes, or what's the new term, Afro-Americans? Maybe that's significant. In fact, there's very little about me that hasn't been broken up.

"I can show you scars," he said, "but I would rather talk about grasshoppers." That may not be the exact quote, but do you remember that scene during the retreat on the Italian front? I have a feeling you'd be laughing at this, at me.

All right then, let's talk about beetles. I've been reading up on beetles lately. Did you know, Laura, that beetles, who are the Smiths of the insect world – that beetles bite while other insects suck? Beetles bite. The world sucks.

Maybe I should call you up, L. P. Kuslowski – 623-1167. Why list it that way – to avoid heavy breathing on the line? Or is this the new liberated woman way of doing it? Maybe, L. P., I should call you up and tell you why I'm going with Ferguson.

Are you as "liberated" as you seem? No sign of any man around you these days. And I've done some checking. Frank was wiped out when, a couple of years ago, wasn't it? That's a long time to wear the weeds and you don't look the placid type, if you know what I mean. But why do you get involved in this business? Yes, go on and become a lawyer, if that's what you want to do? Raise your kid, find some guy to marry – maybe another lawyer; you could have a family firm – BUT why get mixed up in all this business? Do you know what a yard is? Do you know how to fix an absentee? Do you really want to learn?

Maybe this is part of the answer to your question. You're raising a kid by yourself, you're finishing college and want to go to law school – you're going to go on. You're what – twenty-five??

Again, I don't mean to belittle you and maybe you'll believe me when I say I hope you don't become serious. To answer your question, Laura: I'm working for Ferguson because this is what I do. It's what I do.

But in the meantime, you're going to mess things up, you're going to make a lot of unnecessary trouble, cause a few heads to be knocked together, waste a lot of time and money for what? It's all going to come out the way it's supposed to. Old Zeus-Connors had it all laid out long beforehand, you should know that. You're only fighting a delaying action. . . . and what will happen to you in the meantime?

I just dialed your number, L. P. No answer. Where's the kid, staying with relatives? Where are you at 11:35 P.M., Sunday night? Do you have a date? Are you out lining up Wriston's petitions? Getting your student corps together? It won't work, Laura. It's not going to work. All for nothing.

Well, since you won't answer me tonight, I won't send this note. We're going to beat hell out of you. Howie Ferguson is going to win this primary, but if he doesn't Cranston will. So either way, you lose.

Yours sincerely,
T. J. Bryan

RAW DATA:

Unevaluated

"Yes, of course I remember your uncle." That's Matt Wriston's voice. "It's probably because of men like George Stamski, of how they were used by the system that I intend to confront the Billy Browns and the Pug Connors." We can imagine Matt Wriston standing by his office window, observing the sluggish flow of traffic moving between the levees of dirty snow piled on either side of Wentworth Avenue. Hands clasped behind his back, he would rock back and forth on his heels as he tells her how grateful he is for keeping the appointment on a day like this. For it would be February once again.

The girl would sit impatiently on the edge of a chair. Her head bends at an angle and a shimmering curtain of black hair momentarily masks the large amber eyes that accent the broad, Slavic face.

(Haven't her eyes been green up until now? Moreover, this sort of third-person narrative is no longer convincing. What are your credentials for describing this scene? How do you know what is happening?)

Actually, the eyes are of a grayish green, somewhat the color of large seedless grapes that appear in midsummer. But in certain light conditions, such as the obscure lighting we associate with the attorney's office, her eyes might very well appear amber.

Her face would be blank, expressionless, excepting the movement of these eyes, and her mouth — which some would call *quattrocento* and others merely sullen — sustains a fixed pout. She is as affected by the lawyer's rhetoric as she is by the melting snow running down the slicky length of the green patent leather boots that fit her legs to mid-thigh.

"With Kleinsinger retiring, we've got a damn good chance of putting a Democrat in Congress now." Wriston has turned around, hands hanging by their fingers from the vest's pockets. "And we can be assured, Laura, that the officially endorsed Democratic candidate for that office will be Everett "Jack" Cranston, that noted district attorney who has made full use of wire-tapping in the name of public order."

The attorney might pause and turn his face to the shelves of law books, spines cracked; then turn away to sort, rearrange the piles of briefs and memoranda on the desk, his eyes glancing always at the girl to assess any response to his words. The green toe of one boot noiselessly taps the worn carpet. Even though it is February, her miniskirt comes just below her hips and the long military-like outer coat is almost regally thrown open so Wriston can hardly avoid seeing that her thighs are . . .

(Just a minute. This material is repetitive; the way Wriston stands and talks, the shabby, dusty atmosphere of his office — again description.)

But the structured cliché of Wriston and his surroundings is just another of those episodes in a conventional drama that the girl, Laura, would have been trying to escape since Frank Kuslowski was killed, When she buried him, she thought she had also buried the last remains of the urge to be part of a predictable pattern, had performed the last rite or devotion to the expected. Her behavior at Kuslowski's grave is still remembered, talked about.

The legionnaires presented her with the folded flag that had been on his coffin and she threw up. Vomited on the flag. Her reaction was attributed to grief, shock; after all, they had been married little more than a year and her young figure was only just then being gently misshaped by the baby.

But she had been quite calm and cool inside even though the stars wheeled dizzily on the blue field. It was something else. As each sour string of mucus played out, she thought of it as a poison her system was voiding, a poison that neither Frank Kuslowski nor her Uncle Georgie Stamski had been lucky enough to expel.

His eyes glance sideways at the girl to assess any response to his words, and he might pull a soiled handkerchief from the side pocket of the jacket to wipe an unperspiring face. When he returns the handkerchief some of it would hang out of the pocket; as much an emblem of Matt Wriston as anything.

"Let me drive you home," Matt Wriston again. "Maybe I can talk you into joining me, to give time to this little revolt." So she would precede him down the creaking stairs to the street and wait under the canopy of the Vista Theater's marquee while he brings his car around.

(If she's going to the State University in Cade County, below Yost, and if she also works in this cocktail lounge near Albany, wouldn't she need a car of her own?)

"Since your car is getting snow tires put on, I can drive you home," Matt Wriston could say. "Maybe I can talk you into joining this little revolt. Just show me the way and we'll pick up little Jake in no time."

Her son by Kuslowski is one of those faceless, nearly anonymous three-year-olds. Black hair, her feline, angled eyes but with the long high-bridged nose that was his father's. When she's in school, and when she works weekends at the Gilded Cage, Laura puts little Jake in the care of her unmarried older sister, Marie. She's late to pick him up, and as Wriston drives she prepares herself for her sister's grumbling, a surface disturbance that marks the sunken vessel of the older woman's resentment.

"The lady lawyer," her father sometimes referred to her, but in old Jake Patrovich's confusion and scorn, there was often a grudging respect.

"You should make more time for yourself, Laura," her mother used to say while chopping cabbage. Laura would have done her homework on the cold enameled top of that kitchen table. Make more time to do what – find another husband, settle down, take over the cabbage division?

On the other hand, she exploited her family's ambivalence; borrowed money from them for the down payment on the car and daily handed Little Jake over to her sister. There was an unspoken agreement, a deal; for if she ever got her degree, ever got by her bar exams, she knew that she would be expected to handle all the legal work for the entire sixth ward. Free.

But people were always talking to her about time, she who seemed to have so little of it, as if she had lost some sense or faculty and these well-meaning but thoughtless possessors of time constantly described the ever-changing position of the clock's hands, the color of the hours. Make time for herself!

Time was a dividend – the only one, perhaps, awarded to people who did what was expected of them. Moreover, it seemed to Laura that the people she knew who seemed to have the most time were those who lived carefully proscribed lives; took the same walks, stared from the same windows at the same hour of day – moved through life in shifts and as much ruled by these shifts as was her father regulated by those at the copper mill that determined his sleeping and waking hours. Like inmates of a prison, they all seemed to have lots of time.

Indeed, could one make time at all? Time. Love. Could any of these be made or do they just exist apart, perhaps in contiguous fields that one might move through but never really possess or . . .

(Why the abstract discussion? We were in Matt Wriston's car going to pick up Laura's little boy. Can we go back to that?)

"When you go to Albany for your law," Wriston again, "I think I can give you some help. There's a couple of judges up there who could use a smart girl like you for a clerk. Pay wouldn't be much but it would be better than waiting on tables at that cocktail lounge. What's the name of it, the Bird Cage?"

"The Gilded Cage," Laura.

"Heard about any problems on campus this spring?" Wriston. "Gosh, that's all we need is another riot down at Cade State. You know, if we could get those youngsters involved with a political campaign, it might channel those impulses into constructive areas. It would be good for them, not to mention the great assistance it would be to me. That's why I need you to help me, Laura. If you have the time.

"We're in a precarious moment of our history. I'm sure I have no need to tell you that," says the lawyer perhaps as she lifts Little Jake into the front seat. She would smile and Wriston assumes it is to acknowledge the rightness of his comment. But she might have been thinking something else. He had apparently not stopped talking, his voice continuing to fill the damp, heated interior of the car while upstairs in Marie's apartment she stuffed rubbery legs and arms into a snowsuit, ignoring her sister's peevish complaints. So when she returned with the boy, the flow of words made Wriston seem plugged into, driven by the same system that pushes the wipers back and forth, back and forth across the windshield, piling up freezing slush on either side of a small fan-shaped aperture through which only the lawyer could see.

"There are laws on the books right now," he would be turning up toward Third and Wentworth, "which could put this country into a dictatorship overnight. It's frightening. This wire-tap bill that Cranston used so effectively to stop the black demonstrators last year, it might be good for you to study the wording of that statute, Laura. You may have to defend someone against it someday. And what, after all, is a conspiracy? About what we're doing right now, Laura? Someone could interpret the law to put us in jail for just what we're doing now. A man like Cranston could tap your phone – for forty-eight hours – without a court order, if he declares it an emergency."

The car has stopped at the curb beside her apartment building, a four-storied structure that is one of the tallest components of the Yost skyline, excepting the usual church steeples. The windows of the Ace Cleaners on the street level are opaqued with condensation, Mrs. Stone moves among the hanging garments inside, an amorphous shape on a running patchwork of pastels. "So, think about it, Laura," Matt Wriston leans over to open the door. "We've got some time yet."

There's that mention of time once more, she thinks as she takes Little Jake by the hand to . . . "Wriston showed up in the doorway of the Student Union, looking like some professor that had just been stiffed, you know? Like his course in Polysaturates 101 was still in the catalog but nobody had signed up, you know. And we were sitting around inside, Laura is with us, see, and as soon as she sees him standing in the doorway with that old raincoat on and that gray hat all bent up . . ."

(Who's this talking? Not the same narrator?)

". . . her eyes turn up at the corners and she sort of tippy-taps a little message under the table with her boots."

"Hey, man. You know anybody that's balled the widow-chick?"

"Not me. You know Laura don't have time for that scene. Anyway, she finally gets up and greets this noted counselor and they split, she and this overt-practicing attorney like it was an appointment, you know. But it wasn't. He just popped in like that as she was dropping her café.

"I happened to have some business in Hinton, he told her when they stepped outside, and thought I'd drop by, baby, maybe give you a lift home so we could have a little rap."

(What's this!!? How can this new voice presumably that of a student, know what was said between Laura and Matt Wriston?)

"Man, how do you know what this cat talked to her about?"

"Laura told me the next day. She said they walked across campus, all the way to the parking lot where he had left his car. Where her car was too, see. And all the while he kept trying to talk her into working for him if he should run for Congress, see.

"This place has certainly grown, he said brilliantly, looking

around at old Guv. Hiyafeller's answer to Bologna. And lookee
dat, he says. Strange how only a few miles closer to the equator
can make such a difference. Those daffodils are about ready to
bust out and the ones in our garden have only just poked up.
There's energy down here we lack in the north, in Yost County.
Wild."

*(Daffodils about to bloom? We were just in the month of Feb-
ruary? And would Wriston use a term like bust out? And lookee
dat and wild?)*

"So they go along together, Laura not saying much, you
know, like always. Yes, sir, Mr. Counselor repeats, there's a
source of energy down here that we don't have in Yost County,
and I don't mean Captain Billy Brown. I mean all these young
people."

"Hot dog, man. All out for vespers at the YM of the CA! You
know, baby, I got creamed for Gene."

"Anyway, they had stopped at the intersection of the paths in
the green, see, so that Wriston could spread out his arms—
spread and raise them in one of those all-embracing gestures,
you know. What a source of energy they could be, Laura, he
says, meaning us, see. They were once before, they revitalized
the whole system. And they look up to you, they'll follow you,
Laura. That's what he told her. Even though thirty years separate us, I know it, baby, we share the same objectives, the same
causes. This immoral intervention in foreign hang-ups, for example.

"And right there, she told me, he stops and gives her meaning-
ful look No. 42A. You are a widow-chick whose old man got
scratched over in Slantville—I know how you still must hurt, so
help me get to Congress, baby, it'll make you feel better. You
know?

"It's tearing us apart, Mr. Wriston continues when they get to
the parking lot. Have you ever seen the set of wheels he makes
do with? Old dusty-rusty and he's supposed to be loaded, too, or
his wife. Anyway, he's been saying how we're being busted up.
Just because we've managed to keep things going for two
hundred years don't mean this country is going to go on forever,
you know. The Constitution . . ."

"The what?"

"The Constitution, baby, guarantees almost everything but
the continued existence of the Constitution, he tells her."

"Professor, sir. Would you kindly run through that one again?"

"What he was saying is that the authority of the Constitution is subject to the razor-edge whim of the people. So, power to the people. Right?

"I sometimes think, Laura, this baby goes on and on, that the great mass of Americans don't understand, maybe couldn't care less about our system of government. Democracy, you know. But then there's this other group, see, who dig it but don't like it, see—and would just as soon scrap it for something else. That leaves a very small groovy group, like you young people . . ."

"Oh, man. He's too much."

"Wait a minute, you got to get all of it . . . you young people who are firmly committed, dedicated to democratic principles. We've been lucky so far, he nods, in these two centuries because somehow we've kept the first two groups apart—the ones that don't understand and the ones who do but don't like the system—we've kept them apart, off-balance. But it can't happen forever, I'm afraid."

"So, is that it? What next?"

"Nothing more. The Great Defender hops in his wagon and cuts. The widow-chick soaks up the sun for a little bit and then pulls out."

. . . around the desk to lean against it, arms folded over the narrow chest, and looks down upon her, thinking that the damp spot on the rug might probably leave a greenish stain, though the leather of her boots looked of good quality.

"That was a remarkable group of men who fashioned this government. And though the term 'elitist' is not . . . Laura worked here just on weekends, but we got to know each other pretty well—that is, I thought so until this incident I am telling you about . . . cute in her red feathers. Really a knockout with her coloring and she doesn't have to use any padding like some of them I know. Anyway, we all felt sorry for her, losing her husband in Vietnam like that, and raising her little boy all by herself—it was easy to see there was something different about her.

"She gave the customers just enough but no more. Many times saw her turn a few of them down flat. Sure, there's the house rule about that, but a few I can mention are not so particular about following it, if you know what I mean.

"Well, I'm not the one to point any fingers. After all, if a girl needs a little extra cash for the rent or well, for whatever reason, who I am to say nay. We're born with a natural little money-maker. And most of the guys are a little past their prime any-way, from up on the Hill, you see, so by the time a girl gets to the room they're so worked up from looking at everything you just put a hand on them and they go off. Or so I'm told. And some of the girls also pretend they're out of action so nothing really intimate takes place. Don't you know.

"This one evening—I was serving these two gentlemen at number eight, one of them was a Senator because the other one kept saying, Senator this and that to him. But they were very funny types, lots of jokes and all eyes, you know what I mean. The Senator says something about having a small party later and when I come back with another round—both were drinking Chi-vas Twelve, very plush—there's the room key placed by the ashtray. I think it was number forty-three, yes, forty-three—that's the unit that has a broken soap dish in the john.

"Anyhow, they inquired about the dark-haired, little redbird. Laura. So when I had retired to the Perch, Laura is leaning against her swing and I tell her about them, pointing them out. Well, she turns to me, those eyes narrowing, and I feel more of a canary than I'm dressed like—well, she turns and says, Okay, but I don't fuck. . . . this gentleman comes in, rather depressed-looking in the dim light. Of course, the reddish gloom in the Cage makes everyone look a little peculiar but him especially. And he slumps into the banquette, without removing his raincoat and puts a battered hat beside him. I bend over to serve him, don't you know, and he doesn't even regard me but looks around and asks for Mrs. Kuslowski.

"And that's another rule that's sometimes broken, trading off tables, but the manager is a good guy as long as we don't make a habit of it. So I send Laura over to him and they talk for a little bit and she brings him a drink from the bar. She tells me he's a lawyer from her home town and I think it probably has some-thing to do with her late husband's estate.

"Well, I forget about it, it's a busy night. But just as I'm leav-ing after closing—well, you could have floored me with a feather. There's the two of them out in the parking lot in the moon-light. There's still a lot of traffic on the Thruway and this so-called lawyer is standing by a car, his hat on crooked and look-ing up at the stars. I can see he's talking and Laura is standing there by him, holding her coat closed at the neck, for she's still wearing her feathers – another rule some of us don't observe, the costume is not to be worn outside the premises – but there are the two of them. I can't hear what he's saying or promising her, you know what I mean, but just as I locate the car license I'm looking for, I hear her say, "Yes. All right. I'll do it." Just like that, mind you, and after she said what she did to me. Just as calm and cool as can be. "All right. I'll do it." And without any feeling or anything and this man, this so-called lawyer, nothing. I tell you, it's always a wonder."

(Is there another report on her?)

"Have you ever wondered what becomes of the girl saxophone players in high school bands? I mean those who were assigned the alto or tenor instrument and who marched every Saturday at half time, between the clarinets and the brass, dutifully puffing out something reminiscent of 'On, Wisconsin.' Or if you did not go to football games, perhaps you saw some of them sitting in the second row on the right beneath the conductor's benevolent baton, toes tapping as they crisply fingered the peppy measures of R.B. Hall's 'New Colonial' . . . stood for a moment in the center of the room as she slipped on the nearly floor-length coat. There was a last glimpse of the girl's thighs above the flared tops of the boots, strangely vulnerable and unsettling when viewed from behind.

"Since your car is getting new snow tires . . ."

". . . do you suppose? After the last commencement concert, and the school instruments are returned, do they continue their music? The saxophone is not an instrument that can slip gracefully into the average housewife's day. Far easier to pause on the piano bench for a few clattery preludes, or a guitar can be plucked while waiting for the coffee to reheat. But a saxophone must be taken out of its case. It must be assembled. The reed must be adjusted. And then, probably just then, the children come in from school to stare at their mother standing in the living room, breathing heavily on this funny-looking instrument.

"And though it was necessary to assign many of them to it, I've always thought the saxophone to be a very unfeminine instrument. Piccolos, flutes, and clarinets – yes, quite definitely. Naturally, violins and all string instruments. There's even something appealing, if not amusing, about a young girl pressing her lips against the brass mouthpiece of a trumpet. But a saxophone! A mutant in the first place. I've always thought it a pretentious instrument, one that betrays its basic awkwardness of sound and shape when held and blown by a pubescent female. It's so touching, so ungainly. I don't know."

(I don't know either. What the hell is going on here? This is some sort of a music teacher?)

" . . . history teacher also. I still think of her by her maiden name, Patrovich, Laura had been a very good student. Alert, responsive, capable of grasping concepts as well as particulars. And it was only a few years after she had graduated, already a widow and a mother, that she appears at my office to say that she was going back to finish college, go to law school. She asked me if I knew of a used alto saxophone that she could buy for little, and would I also advise her on what practice manuals to use.

"Why such an attractive young woman would resume the solitary fingering of the saxophone is beyond me. Surely Laura can have her pick of any of those firm, resilient young men who are her classmates but she prefers to be alone, to practice chords and scales with breathy blasts, lips pursed around the vibrating mouthpiece. Of course, I arranged for her to buy a Conn from the school, at a fraction of its cost.

"Last spring, Laura returned a practice book I had loaned her. This was a year ago—and she had an enormous bruise on one thigh—and she seemed proud of this blemish. This was a week after the student riots at Cade State and she said two policemen had dragged her down the steps of the library she and the others had occupied. It was difficult to imagine her in such a rebellious atmosphere; she seemed so petite, so feminine.

"Actually, she told me, her eyes sliding from side to side, actually, most revolutionaries have a very feminine character. Surely she was joking, I thought, but the sullen seriousness of her mouth, the shift of eyes said otherwise.

"Actually the profile of the status quo is of a pronounced masculine nature, probably dating back to when *Homo Erectus* first appeared, she paused, looked directly at me for just a fraction. Just a flicker of an eyelash, and then resumed the restless inspection of the ceiling, the corners of the room. I have a theory, she continued, that it was when men—not man—but when men stood up on two legs permanently that they realized how unprotected they were in that position, that they could be damaged, had something to lose. Therefore, and she crossed her legs and made a cursory examination of the purplish splotch, pulling back the short skirt to its ultimate, the defiant defense of the existing order is really a masculine trait. Most revolutionaries believe they have nothing to lose when they stand up. So to rebel is feminine. And for just a moment I thought that small, downward curving mouth was about to lift on the wings of a rare smile—for she had once more looked directly into my eyes— surely she was joking. But she was very serious, her eyes glanced off once more in their melancholy search around the office. We have nothing to lose when we stand up, she repeated, though whether she meant revolutionaries, in general, or females in particular I shall never know."

. . . to talk a little bit about this uncle Matt Wriston mentioned earlier.

(Yes, it might be a good idea to have a little bit down about this George Stamski, since Wriston has already mentioned him and he seems to have some relevance to Laura's character.)

There's hardly anything down on him. He died young. Some in the sixth ward still say he died, at the age of forty-one, with everything to live for. Not an untypical life.

"It's another Stamski festival," he'd announce after leading an assault on the neighborhood ice cream store. He'd have to shout over the clamor and screams of Laura's playmates making their demands, for his voice was rather light.

"What are we celebrating today, Uncle Georgie?"

"Whaddaya mean, what are we celebrating? Don't you kids know your history? Today is the anniversary of Freddie Chopin writing the *Polonaise.* I might have forgot it myself had not my good friend, Joe Iturbi, called me from Hollywood." He'd wink at the guy putting the sundaes together.

And it might have been true. After all, Uncle Georgie's own life closely resembled movies they had seen at the Princess on Saturday afternoons; war heroes played by Van Johnson becoming friends with movie stars and celebrities. There is still a photograph on the Patrovich parlor mantel showing George Stamski being awarded the Silver Star by a general. Stiff in his jump boots, chest swelled out to meet the presentation. To Laura, as a child, he resembled one of those inflated toys that continually rebound, right themselves when knocked over.

The Schenectady *Star* had used the same picture and not long after the society section headlined the announced nuptials of George Stamski and the former Mary Greco. This was also part of the movie.

The Yost *Sentinel* had just carried old man Greco's obituary when George Stamski was discharged. Everyone in the sixth ward said it was a perfect match, it was fate. After all, a man was needed to manage all the property Joe Greco left his daughter. The old man had died as foundations for the new shopping center were being dug on the old truck farm, the corner gas station. It seemed right, perhaps ordained, that the same war that had made Greco's daughter a widow had now returned a hero husband to her, and who, incidentally, could manage the booming new business. "Conspicuous gallantry."

SOCIAL NOTES

Mr. and Mrs. George Stamski, 126 Askew Terrace, have returned to the city from a winter honeymoon in Miami, Fla. Mary Stamski says she's eager to assume her duties with the Altar Society at St. Mary's. She's formerly Mary Greco. The couple have purchased a condominium in Florida and expect to winter there every year.

Uncle George and Aunt Mary's house on Askew Terrace was the only one with a well-kept lawn and the first to enclose the front porch with glass jalousies. A contractor was brought in from Albany to build the swimming pool in the backyard. One year there was a full-page ad in the *Sentinel*, run by Reece's Hardware showing Uncle Georgie taking ownership of one of the first color TVs in the city of Yost.

STAMSKI NAMED CHAIRMAN

ST. MARY'S FUND DRIVE

Mr. George Stamski, 126 Askew Terrace, prominent businessman and civic leader, has been named chairman of the annual fund drive for the St. Mary's School Building Program.
The goal for this year is $125,000. "We're going to make it and then some," the popular war hero announced yesterday. Plans for the new . . .

But the drive was a flop. Each year Uncle Georgie had always been the largest contributor, so people figured they didn't have to give anything the year he was the chairman. Later on, the Charles Novak American Legion Post, No. 824, elected him commander and that was the year Memorial Day was just barely observed and only then due to the strenuous, last-minute efforts of some of the older members.

Some said that Good-time George Stamski was living too high to pay attention to such matters. Others observed the post was named after Mary Greco's first husband, the one she had lost on the beach at Anzio. Maybe this fact had sapped the second husband's enthusiasm. . . .

"Marie, you're the oldest, mama used to say, so if anything happens to me, you'll have to take care of the others, especially Laura. Especially Laura. She was always special, but I do what Mama asked me to do which is why I still help Laura all I can. But she got her big ideas from Uncle Georgie – the big-shot living off of Aunt Mary's money. Mama's little brother, so he was another one who could do no wrong and Laura was his pet, so it was everything carried to the *nth* degree. Honestly, it was something.

"But he's always so gay, so much fun, Mama would say, her eyes bright, somehow younger-looking, but then she'd turn right around and start talking – with the others – about Aunt Mary's cooking: how she generally forgot the sage in the dumplings or maybe overcooked the sauerkraut for the *bigos*. And somehow I always got the feeling that these women in our kitchen – even Mama – silently blamed Uncle Georgie for his wife's bad cooking. Wouldn't you know.

"One year just before Christmas – it was early in the morning and we were all lined up in the hallway waiting for the bathroom – Laura so tiny in her slip, shivering – and we heard Papa come home. He was on the night shift at the mill then, so he had not been home the evening before when the big express truck rolled up before our house with all those boxes from Miami. We heard Mama take him into the parlor where all the packages had been stacked up. A wall of them with spilling ribbons that completely hid the small Christmas tree set up on the sewing machine table. Honestly, it was something. Mama was conducting Papa on a tour, pointing out this or that package and who it was for – I could hear all this since, being the oldest, I was standing at the end of the line by the top of the stairs—and finally I heard him say, Well, he can afford it, and something else that I didn't quite catch because Mama hushed him up.

"And then he came up the stairs, heavy step on step, and we quickly dropped back and he went on by without saying a word, looking straight ahead. He was so tired and upset. He passed us standing along the hall, a dark, rumpled figure—giving off the damp smell of the mill, that bitter, metallic odor. And after he walked into their room, I heard a crunch of springs, for he must have just thrown himself on the bed without undressing and it was like the smell of him and the sounds of the springs had become one solid, heavy thing.

"That was the year Papa gave Laura her first pair of roller skates—and, wouldn't you know, they were taken apart and lost long before the snow had melted and she could use them on the sidewalk. I bet she doesn't at all remember what was in those boxes that came from Miami—box after box, mostly for her, honestly. She doesn't remember, probably. . . ."

"Sure, George Stamski. Good-time Georgie. It's funny I hadn't thought about him for some time until the other night at that meeting at Matt Wriston's house when he introduced me to this girl—I was beginning to wonder who she was, dressed like that, you know—and Wriston introduces her as George Stamski's niece.

"And Laura, this is one of the best damn town chairman in the whole county, Worthy Kershaw, he says to her about me, you know.

"Well, Matt Wriston is very generous, very kind, though I will admit that when I get behind a candidate I give it all I got. You can ask anybody about Worthy Kershaw. And I'd do anything for Wriston, so when he asked me to get some people together— ones he could trust—just to have a little talk, I had a hunch it had something to do with going for Congress. And I was right.

"So I got Mary Tate. Remember, Pug Connors dumped her as state committeewoman a few years back. And Jack Simmons from the city of Yost, the Whalen brothers from over in Purchase, and a few others like that, and everyone in that room had a reason to support Matt, especially if it meant taking a crack at Connors. Jack Simmons, for example, he could have been mayor of Yost if Connors had not laid down that year. Never mind about me, I've got my reasons too.

"And it was very nice at Matt's that night. He's a real gentleman but he can be like the rest of us when he wants to be. I think if it weren't for his wife – now don't get me wrong; I like Emily, she's a real lady – but I think Matt unbends a little when she's not around. You know?

"Anyway, he had a fire going in the fireplace in that room they have with all those books, even though it was kinda warm the other night. But that room looks real nice with a fire in it. I sometimes wonder if Matt has read all those books he had in that room. And you think of the money that went just into those books, not to mention the velvet draperies and all that fine furniture. I took down one of the books, looked at it and the flap inside had the price printed on it. Five dollars! And it was poetry at that. Multiply that by all the books in that room.

"So Emily Wriston serves us coffee and little cakes. Matt offers some whiskey around and we settle back as comfortably as you can in that antique furniture they have. We were all listening for him to say it, and I was looking over this niece of old George Stamski who was standing to one side in a corner – and good thing she was standing because I wouldn't know where any of us men would have looked if she had sat down . . . let me take your coat, Laura." The dazzling revelation, almost as if she had been stark naked, except for the green boots, underneath the long, drab maxicoat . . .

". . . just wonderful, Matt, Mary Tate is saying, patting her knees. She tugs her skirt down a little bit, maybe to make up for this girl in the corner. Course to be fair, and don't get me wrong 'cause I like her, but old Mary hasn't got an awful lot anyone has wanted to look at in a long time.

"Can't wait to see the look on Connors' face when you do announce, Jack Simpson says. I sure would like to beat that son of a bitch. Matt doesn't answer but just smiles in that grave, sly way of his and gives the log another nudge. He'd make a helluva judge.

"We'll have a little money, Matt says modestly, but more important are the spontaneous, voluntary efforts of people such as each of you . . . and he pauses and looks around the room at each of us. I can't say about the others but I felt a real thrill

from the look he gave me. Your backing is more valuable to me
than the support of those that can be bought. Because your
backing cannot be bought.

"That's right, Matt, Mary clapped her hands and nodded,
looked around the room. Well, I wasn't so sure that there might
not be one or two in that room that couldn't be bought, including
our former state committeewoman."

"Pug Connors first ran for sheriff—1950 or 1951, wasn't it?
Yeah, he was city chairman of Yost, then, remember? And naturally he was trying to find someone to run against Henry Sherman for city treasurer. He was up that same year, too. Well,
Jesus, Henry Sherman! The best vote-getter the Republicans
ever had. He was a helluva guy; I voted for him a couple of
times myself."

"I would have done the same thing Pug did then, he had to fill
the ticket. If Sherman ran unopposed he would be free to help
old Sheriff Roejan campaign against Pug, and a lot of people listened to Henry Sherman."

"Say, do you remember that story they used to tell about old
Hicks Roejan?"

"What one was that?"

"Well, that time they raided a roadhouse below Green River
and they were booking those people for gambling, and there was
some women among them . . ."

*(Now what the hell is going on here? Who are these people?
And what does this story have to do with Laura Kuslowski, her
uncle George Stamski, or Matt Wriston's campaign?)*

". . . and old Sheriff Roejan so loaded that he doesn't hear
the deputy so he said, swiveling around in that big leather chair,
he said, What's that?!

"I said, the deputy repeated, that one of them women we arrested says she's got to have some Kotex in the morning.

"And so old Roejan thinks for a moment, falling back in his
chair even more, and he says—he says, you go tell her that
she's going to eat corn flakes like everybody else!"

"No, I'd forgot that story. But he was a colorful old coot,
drunk that he was, and teamed up with a vote-getter like Henry
Sherman; well, you can appreciate Pug Connors' position. But
who was going to run against Sherman?"

"And that's where George Stamski comes into the picture?"

"Right. A dream candidate. He was a war hero, won some kind of a medal; what was the medal he won?"

"Purple Heart."

"Naw, not the Purple Heart, everybody's got one of them. For Christ's sake, what was that medal? Anyway, it was an important one. Also, he had married old Pete Greco's daughter and had plenty of the moola, you know. And he was a popular man—you know, they were always asking him to raise money for various things. So, he *was* a Polack from Slab City—it was a whole new ball game after the war. People were thinking different. More democratical."

"Man-oh-man, what a campaign that was. That sixth ward really came alive. Even the kids got into the act. I bet anything this girl at Wriston's the other night was one of those kids that swarmed out of Slab City all over Yost, handing out handbills for Good-time George Stamski."

"I remember that material. It showed a picture of him getting this medal pinned on him by some general, and down underneath it there were the words, "Conspicuous and Capable.""

"No, no. *Conspicuously Capable*, not Conspicuous *and* Capable. Where was I?"

(A good question. Are we still at the meeting at Wriston's house? It sounds more like a barroom conversation.)

". . . right. Sherman never had to work so hard in his life and, by God, it wasn't just the sixth ward that was voting for Stamski, I think he carried the second and the third too. He didn't win, but it was a helluva fight. Of course, Pug knocked off old Roejan and became sheriff."

"The strategy worked?"

"Yes, and something else happened too, and don't you forget it. Since that day, the sixth ward has been one of the strongest Democratic wards in the city. Them people down there were so grateful that Connors had given one of their own a chance . . . why, hell, my brother worked down at the mill, in the office, you know, and he told me those Polacks would punch that time clock after Stamski's run like they were daring it to punch back."

"Good-time Georgie Stamski. I remember him coming into the legion post and standing down at the end of the bar. Setting up drinks for everybody, like he was always campaigning."

"And he always had an occasion if you asked him, remember? What are we drinking to tonight, Georgie, someone would ask. We're celebrating the victory of Casmir the Fourth over the Turks, I can remember him saying. . . ."

(How would this sort of character know this obscure historical detail?)

" . . . the victory of some Polack king or other over somebody. I can hear him saying."

"Wintered in Florida, died in Florida."

"Had everything to live for and just died one day at forty-one."

"Heart?"

"I don't think they ever knew. He just walked into an elevator one day in this big Miami apartment hotel they lived in during the winter, and when it got up to his floor and the doors opened, he was on the floor, stone dead."

"I heard the elevator was going down, and he fell out into the lobby."

"What kind of nonsense is that? The elevator was going up."

"And I tell you what else I've heard. That Stamski paid Pug Connors three thousand dollars just for the privilege of having his name on the ballot and having his head kicked in by Henry Sherman."

"I wouldn't know anything about that . . ."

". . . only thing I can think of is that Laura may have heard Mama and some of the other women gossiping in the kitchen about Aunt Mary. She often did her homework on the kitchen table before supper. Laura was always very serious about her studies. But whatever she heard about Aunt Mary must have got all twisted up wrong because at Uncle Georgie's funeral, Laura turned to me—it's peculiar to think she was just about a year or two away from burying her own husband—and she looks at me with those eyes she got from Mama, and she says, I know why he died, Marie. He starved to death. Honestly . . ."

". . . How do you think you'd do in a primary down in Cade County? Jack Simpson is asking Wriston. He's always been on the realistic side, you know. But the funny thing I don't remember exactly what Matt answered and you know I bet no one else does either. It's not important right now and maybe all we'd like to do is just kick old Pug Connors in the ass a little bit. Just sting him.

"I suppose Tommy Bryan will work with you again? Mary Tate said, patting up some of her hair. And when Matt shook his head, I saw the Whalen boys look at each other and I knew they had just slipped into the doubtful column. Meanwhile, this sexy-looking niece of Good-time George Stamski is still standing in the corner of the room, just looking around . . ."

. . . breathing heavily on the instrument; sulky curvature of mouth pursed around the vibrating reed and she bends at the waist to finger an exercise in Cragun's Method . . .

(What's happened to the political campaign?)

. . . the deepening twilight of the April evening, the most modern, most handsome county office building in the state and the pride of the Cade County Democrats — a square block of dark gray glass, ten stories tall, one of the tallest buildings in Hinton City, and in the deepening twilight of the April evening, the Polaroid glass walls grow denser, the structure assumes the nature of a huge, glistening block of obsidian, impenetrable and somehow ominous. On an overcast day, the county office building lends a funereal accent to the Hinton City skyline, a gigantic gravestone . . .

. . . would-be committeemen, politicians, hangers-on standing crowding the flagstoned entranceway, sitting around the edge of the huge planter in the center, puffing on cigarettes and cigars and tossing them into the shrubbery or the blooming tulips of the huge planter in the center . . . hacking, wheezing, laughing, punching shoulders, hitching up pants over beer bellies . . . clusters of men standing beneath the flush mounted lights of the portico, small pin-beam instruments . . . in the black glass of the foyer. A double image of this girl, nervously picking at a seam of the shirtwaist, smoothing the dark hair; reflecting, doubling the confusion of her brow above remarkable eyes and then turns around to view this arcade full of hacking, spitting, puffing committeemen, politicians, hangers-on. She would be alone and knows few there. She would know Tommy Bryan and Howie Ferguson who stand with a group of men beneath one of the pin-lights of the portico.

"Who's the girl? A reporter?" someone asks.

Bryan would have just introduced Howie Ferguson to Stan Rosenfeld, the former circuit court judge who will probably be "Jack" Cranston's campaign manager, when this dark-haired girl in a lavender shirtwaist mini walks among them in the courtyard, strolls leisurely over to the entranceway and checks herself over in the mirrorlike wall and then just as leisurely pivots around to observe them coolly, somewhat like a well-fed insolent cat.

"Who's the girl? A reporter?" Stan Rosenfeld asks Bryan.

No, he would tell them who she is and some eyebrows go up, not so much honoring Matt Wriston's political acumen for selecting such an associate but rather what a tidy piece like this sees in Matt Wriston.

One of several problems connected with the construction of the new county office building had to do with the two elevators. They work fine but they cost more than had been originally budgeted—some one hundred thousand more . . . that was the problem. In fact, the whole building cost nearly a million dollars more than had been originally estimated, but the Democratic majority in the county legislature stood firm. Well, there had been some labor problems and material tie-ups and one thing or another. The money just goes.

But the elevator works fine; a smooth, silent, effortless ascent from the lobby to the legislative chamber on the tenth floor during which Laura would feel immersed in an emphysemic longing—a lingering wheezing—all talk suspended within the elevator rising smoothly on its greased cables, a special tribute to her presence. And just before they reach the tenth floor—say when the illuminated numerals above the door go from 7 to 8—someone leans down and asks, "Did you drive down by yourself?" That might be Ferguson, and without looking she knows their ears turn upon her, scan the dead-stillness within the rising cube for the first warning *vibrato* of her answer. She would merely nod.

Now pictures are being taken outside the chamber, large doors of smooth paneled walnut, twelve feet high, extruded aluminum fittings, handles. Rosenfeld and Bryan introduce Ferguson and Cranston to each other, set them up for the photographer from the Hinton *Register Herald.* Handshake and face front with smiles. Pop! The district attorney knows how to look directly into the camera lens, to concentrate, wide-eyed. Howie looks over, beyond the photographer's right shoulder—caught off-guard so his eyes blink with the flash.

It would be a bad picture. Though Cranston is shorter and

much older than Ferguson, it will look like the DA is leading a young blind man by the hand. The older man's smile is confident, benevolent — Howie's as if he had just stepped in something squishy.

But what caught Ferguson's attention, made him flick his eyes up and over the photographer's shoulder was a group of students that had greeted Laura K. when she stepped out of the elevator.

Let's say there are about a dozen of them; no beards but most with long hair and some of the girls wearing rather baggy, outsized dungaree shirts and pants, others normally dressed. Castro caneworkers. Four or five hold long, shivery pieces of wooden lathe to which old posters of Wriston from his Assembly campaign have been stapled. FOR CONGRESS has been printed on strips of cardboard and stapled over FOR ASSEMBLY — an effortless advancement. They gather around Laura for instructions, mouths slack and eyes dull behind the granny glasses. HEY — HEY — WRISTON'S RIGHT! HEY — HEY — WRISTON'S RIGHT! It was this impromptu cheer that attracted Howie Ferguson's attention just as the shutter clicked.

(It's only logical to assume that it also attracted the attention of the deputy on duty that night. Perhaps he has been keeping an eye on this group of possible troublemakers — perhaps he had been along on that raid District Attorney Cranston had ordered on Cade State last year. He might still flush with the memory of the things they found out there; the way some of these kids live, girls as well as boys, all sense of decency gone. And the language, the filth that some of the girls used when they had only been doing their duty — so this deputy has been watching them closely, standing in one corner of the green marble hallway and when they started to chant, he quickly moved over to them.)

"Who's the spokesman for this group?" he would ask, hands on his hips, the wide pearl handle of the .38 angled at his waist. Naturally, he asks the question of the one black student among them.

"I suppose I am," Laura says hesitantly. The lawman is ruffled, he had hoped that it would be — if not Harvey Washington — one of the boys with flowing locks, but here's this good-looking girl.

"Well, I'm sorry, miss, but we can't have demonstrations up here. There's serious business going on tonight and there's got to be decorum around here. You can demonstrate all you want outside the building but not . . ."

"What's the matter, Deputy?" Bryan's voice. The officer would wheel around.

"It's these kids here, causing a disturbance," the man says. He would look Tommy Bryan over.

"They have a right to be here," Bryan tells him. "Mrs. Kuslowski is representing a potential nominee, Matthew Wriston. There's been no disturbance."

(This is Cade County and not Yost. Would Bryan be so well known down here that a minor official like a sheriff's deputy would not wonder who the hell he is, butting in?)

Just at that moment, a stocky, red-faced man holding several folders of papers might edge through the crowd to squeeze Bryan's arm and says, "Hozitgoin', Tommy?" The deputy's eyes would blink, his lips come together and the back of his neck gets redder. He's apparently made a mistake since the man with the papers knows Tommy Bryan. This would be the secretary of the Cade County Democratic Committee. His name is Seymour Miller. "Hozitgoin', Tommy?"

"Just fine, Cy. I was just telling the deputy that Mrs. Kuslowski and her people had a right to be here."

"By all means," Miller replies, wheezily croons. "But if you want to check with your superiors . . . ah," he searches the policeman's shirtfront for a name, ". . . ah, Deputy Coons, why not do so."

"No, it's all right, I guess."

"Go ahead," Miller smiles ominously. Heavy-lidded eyes peer through thick-lensed spectacles. "Perhaps you should consult your superiors."

"Well, what the hell do I care what they do," the policeman says, walking away.

"My apologies," Miller continues smoothly, "but this is a fortuitous meeting, Mrs. Kuslowski. We've just had an executive meeting with the various representatives of the different nominees. The committeeman who is to place Mr. Wriston's name in nomination was present."

"Jim Irving?" Laura asks.

"Yes, Jim Irving," Miller intones with the benevolence of a brass idol. "I don't believe you've met him have you? Here, permit me." He reaches an arm behind him and pulls a man from the crowd, a gesture that would remind one of a magician passing his hand behind his back to produce a bouquet of paper flowers. The committeeman is tall and frail with a long face that waggles as he talks. Somber eyes placed high in his face, he reminds Tommy . . .

(Reminds Tommy?)

. . . reminiscent of a dog who wants to be friendly but whose past treatment has made him very wary.

"Jim Irving . . . Laura Kuslowski. And you probably know Tommy Bryan." Through the introductions, this committeeman furiously nods his head and makes slight bows from his long waist, as if the joints of his body were secured with string. "Jim," Cy Miller continues importantly, "I was about to tell Laura, here, that we have just had an executive meeting at which you were a participant and that lots were drawn, secret lots all fair and square, and that you drew the number three position to put Mr. Wriston's name up. Is that right, Jim? That's how it happened, is that right?"

"Right . . . right," the committeeman replied, his body jerking up and down affirmatively.

"And your man is going up second, Tommy," Cy Miller says. "Listen, do you have a minute?" and the two of them push through the crowd outside the door of the chamber.

"Sure would be a good thing if Mr. Wriston were here," Jim Irving says to Laura. The man is trying to smile as he talks. It is a painful effort.

"It's not necessary that he be here," Laura says.

"Oh, I know . . . I know," Irving does that peculiar string-doll jerk again. "But it would make it look better, you know. Are you sure . . ."

"I'm not a coward, Laura," Wriston's voice, "but I can see no viable reason, no positive gain for us if I were to show up only to personally suffer some sort of humiliation at the hands of Captain Billy's gang. You saw what Pug Connors did to me here in my own county. Ernie Minkus has done the same."

(Have the Sinnemok County Democrats held their meeting yet?)

". . . Ernie Minkus has already called me saying that there would be some 'expenses' if I wanted to show well in Sinnemok.

Politics is something like a courtship in that there might be any number of embarrassing moments but the suitor who appears to be the least ridiculous, rather than the most acceptable, often takes the prize. In any event, Jim Irving will be there. He'll put my name in nomination and he's arranged for a second. It doesn't matter. We are going the petition route anyway – we just need this for the record. And who knows – we might pick up a lot of sympathy. . . ."

". . . look better, you know, if Mr. Wriston were here. Are you sure you want to go through with this?" Irving would ask. Just then there is a harsh rapping for order inside the chamber.

The smells of the lavish legislative chamber are those of newly installed materials; wood, paint, fiber, and cement. The smoke and sweat of parliamentary procedure have not yet permeated the sand-colored carpet or stained the swivel chairs of orange vinyl. These chairs are arranged in six rows, nine to a row, each with its companion walnut desk before it. They more than accommodate the thirty-five representatives elected to the Cade County Legislature, surplus seats anticipating future growth and redistricting. But there are not enough chairs for all of the 155 members of the Democratic Committee, and many of them must stand around the room, or lean against the white marble veneer of the rear wall.

It might be a little pretentious on the part of Pug Connors or even a Captain Billy, to refer to such a small assembly as a convention but the committeemen who lounge in the orange vinyl swivel chairs lose no importance from being in a small organization. Certainly their sense of importance is undiminished. They display a curious authority inspecting the modern desks – even the contents of the drawers are gone through with a bemused thoroughness. Some pivot in the chairs to make a solemn scrutiny of the glass and heavy drapery while others loosen belts and prop feet upon the walnut desk tops to stare at the carpeted dais and its elegant podium. The official seal of Cade County has been chiseled into the walnut wall above, but the artisan has made the emblematical beaver resemble a chipmunk.

This collection of men and women, meeting infrequently, are an ulterior parliament; one with responsibility to few outside the room and disconnected from any regulatory suffrage, though it might seem otherwise from the many bylaws and rules laid down by the secretary of state. However, they are, as their attitude implies, the rightful owners and occupants of this chamber. It is they who permit the elected representatives to use it for their legislative sessions. Even Jim Irving, arms crossed tightly around himself, gives off this sense of ownership as he talks to several other committeemen. He's managed to evade Laura Kuslowski, momentarily, as she's caught in the jam of people at the doorway; committeemen and spectators, her retinue of students pressing behind, the standards of Matthew Wriston held above, several copies of the forlorn, Lincolnesque face weaving and bobbing on the thin strips of wood.

(Let's get the meeting started.)

Cy Miller stands before the podium at a long table somewhat like a clerk's desk before a judge's bench. The folders of papers have been neatly laid down on the table. There are several books there, one of them probably *Roberts' Rules of Order.* A heavy ashtray of cut-glass already contains several cigarette butts, three cigar remains, a couple of chewing gum wrappers.

"Ladies and gentlemen . . . ladies and gentlemen." Miller's raspy voice, soft in normal conversation, develops the edge of a steel file when raised. With one finger he readjusts the heavy glasses on his nose and raps the heavy ashtray on the tabletop a few times. "Ladies and gentlemen."

A committeeman might come to the desk, maybe it's Jim Irving, and the two of them consult briefly. Miller shakes his head, the committeeman departs but turns back to hear what the party official says as an afterthought and both men agree, heads bob.

"Ladies and gentlemen." One-two-three taps of the glass ashtray on the tabletop. Miller is not unusually short but he would have to go on tiptoe to place several sheets of paper on the raised podium; probably the agenda and some announcements the meeting's chairman is to make. Someone in the front row might make a joke at Miller's expense but when he turns around, comes back to the table, he acknowledges the wisecrack and says something that apparently is even funnier.

"Ladies and gentlemen." Again, the glass dish cracks against the tabletop. Yet another committeeman approaches him for a consultation; a folder of papers is sifted, the required information is found, verified. The man departs.

"All right, folks," the secretary rasps, "some of us *want* to go home tonight." And the meeting would come to order with laughter. "As you know, Chairman Brown is indisposed and is unable to attend, so . . ."

"Mr. Secretary." The voice of a committeeman. "It's my great privilege and honor to nominate as temporary chairman that distinguished Democrat and lady whom we've all known and respect, our honorable Vice-Chairlady, Peggy Collins."

There would be several seconds while, almost simultaneously, another voice is moving the nominations be closed and that the secretary cast one vote for Peggy Collins.

(Can't this elaborate parliamentary procedure be cut if this woman is the vice-chairlady of the committee? Wouldn't it be one of the duties of her office to assume the chair at these meetings when the actual chairman is absent? In fact, as Captain Billy's infirmities have been noted, it would seem her taking over the gavel at these committee meetings would be a regular occurrence.)

The glint in Cy Miller's eyes indicates he's aware of the gratuitous nature of all these motions; however, they are important to the sense of the meeting, to the sense of participation by the different members who make them. It gives them something to do. So he says, "All those in favor," while arranging the papers on his table, smiling.

Peggy Collins will have been waiting patiently for the superfluous vote that accords her position, and though this takes place at every meeting, she steps to the chair with a near-maidenly expression of unexpected pleasure.

(Near-maidenly indeed. What was the name of that vice-chairwoman of the state committee a few years back . . . Rita Something-or-Other . . . who was talking to a meeting of Democratic committeewomen at Grossinger's and she's supposed to have said, "Ladies, your job is to get out in your neighborhoods and work for our Democratic candidates, and not to get in bed and screw them.")

. . . the short, peppy steps with which she ascends the dais to the applause of a standing ovation. The way she smiles with a near-maidenly expression of unexpected pleasure.

Heavy bracelets clank at her wrists as she confers with Cy Miller, who once again goes on tiptoe before the podium. Perhaps in her fifties, she is on the heavy side though compact:

even compressed would be an apt word, for it would relate her body configuration with the cap of dark hair tightly baked on a small skull. There is a solid, grumous quality to her mass, the result of a lifelong consumption of the fare at political banquets. And when she says, "Let us rise and pledge allegiance to the flag," it's a melodious, fruity voice with an attractive hint of hoarseness. A contralto manqué.

Each item on the agenda is introduced, reported, and amplified, discussed and amended to be discussed once more, and finally resolved during a continuous activity on the floor. Committeemen and bystanders meet, confer, and seem to roll off and around each other like corpuscles to rejoin other groups as the sluggish flow of the meeting moves along. Tommy Bryan talks head to head with Howie Ferguson, one hand on the candidate's arm. Laura has finally pushed her way into the chamber, locates her man Irving and goes to him. He hugs himself tighter, head jerks recognition. District Attorney Cranston holds court in a far corner, occasionally giving up a nervous inspection of cufflinks to take the hand of a supporter.

"Come on . . . let's get on with it!" a voice out in the hall shouts.

(And he's right. What a tedious piece of business!)

But what Laura's young friends are not aware of, perhaps because they are antagonistic to as well as ignorant of the business, is that as the meeting is put together, piece by piece, the structure of the party also is put together. Simultaneously. Each piece of its construction is tiresomely singled out, inspected — the stresses and strengths assayed — and then miraculously reassembled before the eyes of the committeemen.

What those single-minded youngsters in the hallway forget is that the nominating of a congressional candidate is only one item on the agenda of this meeting, and not a terribly important one at that, it is an incidental piece of business. After all, this assembly has seen candidates come and go and the names of all sorts of candidates, including those running for the Presidency, have been placed in nomination here, voted upon, and the next item under New Business taken up.

But if permanence, or at least a sense of permanence, is somehow dependent upon continuity and repetition, then the familiar litany of the agenda at such meetings, all motions and responses

proscribed by the hallowed Robert's Rules, has an almost universal appeal.

*(Who says so? Can we get on with the meeting. Mrs. Collins
was about to receive nominations.)*

". . . for Congress. By prearrangement with the representatives of all the candidates, nominating speeches are not to exceed five minutes with only one seconding speech not to exceed
three. Nominees, if they wish, may address the committee but
with a time limit of five minutes. I now declare the floor open for
nomination."

An elderly, distinguished man in the front row rises and . . .

*(This is all running long. Can we cut some of this out? The
DA, Ferguson, and Wriston are to be nominated. Cranston is to
be overwhelmingly endorsed. Can't these details be eliminated.
It tends to be boring.)*

Democracy is always boring. It is the most tedious of all
forms of government. Perhaps extremists on the left or the right
wish to discard democratic forms not because they disagree with
the methods or aims but because they do not possess a well-
developed attention span. They are like ice-hockey fans being
forced to sit through several days of a cricket match. Media-
massaged minds crave excitement, slam-bang action, an unre-
flective pursuit of big scores rather than the meticulous making
of plays.

Very well. Spike Cranston has been nominated and seconded.
Howard Ferguson has been nominated and seconded. Incidentally, he gives the same speech as he did to the Yost County
Committee, including the bit about the birds outside the cave.
But he is a little more polished, his voice stronger. He has become more sure of himself in a week's time and receives nice
applause. Okay.

Vice-Chairlady Collins peers over the walnut podium, applies
the scrap of linen to her nose once again. The committeemen
talk among themselves, some swivel aimlessly in their chairs,
others exchange newspapers. There's a recess atmosphere. At
this point Laura Kuslowski expects to hear Wriston's name
placed in nomination. Where's her man?

(Unexpectedly detained in the men's room?)

No, but he might look like he'd want to go there. Irving's
against the far wall, still hugging his thin chest, as if without this

embrace his ribs would clatter to the floor. Laura motions to him, he would avoid her look.

"Madame Chairman." This well-modulated voice would belong to a black committeeman sitting down front. "I move that the nominations be closed." There are several, instantaneous seconding motions.

"There's a motion that the nominations be . . ." catcalls and boos echo in the hall outside, startling Mrs. Collins. Her small, round face becomes pink and the skin tightens. "Just a minute, just a minute," she raps for order.

HEY . . . HEY . . . WRISTON'S RIGHT . . . HEY . . . HEY . . . WRISTON'S RIGHT!

"We will have order here," Mrs. Collins shrills from the podium.

Meanwhile, as the kids still shout outside in the doorway, Mrs. Collins raps for order and we can imagine Laura pushing her way across the room to where Jim Irving is standing. He looks around for a way out but cannot move.

"Gosh, I'm sorry, Mrs. . . . ah . . . Mrs. . . . Kuzz-lowsdy. They just got the motion in before I had a chance to . . ."

"Listen," Laura says, eyes narrowing like a cat before a fire. "Make a motion to reopen the nomination."

"I was afraid that this . . ."

"Make it," she says, her long, sharp fingers jab the man's vulnerable ribs. Order is gradually being restored. Wriston's image no longer nods in the doorway. Mrs. Collins continues to rap the gavel, two or three extra wallops smack flatly in the sound-proofed chamber, amplified by the microphone built into the podium.

"Now then," she huffs, apparently winded by her use of the gavel. "We will . . ."

"Ah . . . ah . . . Madame Chairman," Irving is speaking. He steps forward hesitantly, like a man in a straitjacket. Mrs. Collins looks down upon him, her small rosebud of a mouth a venomous pink. "Umm . . . Madame Chairman . . . I would like to move the . . . make a motion that the renominations . . . that the *nomi*nations be reopened." The orange chairs turn to play curious, amused looks over Laura and the quivering committeeman beside her.

There would be a conference at the podium, Mrs. Collins

leaning over to talk to Cy Miller. They might be joined by a third man, perhaps the committee's parliamentarian. There's a good deal of head-shaking and nodding. Finally, Mrs. Collins straightens up, the parliamentarian returns to his seat and Miller comes back to his desk, though to stand, eyes surveying the room.

"We have a motion to reopen the nominations," Mrs. Collins. "The chair is not entirely convinced that this motion is in order or privileged to the previous motion; however, to facilitate matters and as a gesture . . . to be sure that all have a fair hearing" —a pause as she will look down at Laura with a stiff, motherly smile—"the chair will accept the motion to reopen the nominations." A deep breath that threatens to burst her nylon armor. "Do I hear a second?" she asks.

Several committeemen, as if cued, jump up and face the meeting and together with the party secretary make a careful examination of the membership. The air-conditioning whirs, a newspaper rustles, someone clears his throat.

"Very well," Mrs. Collins announces, "hearing no second, the motion dies. Now we shall. . ."

"Motion to reconsider the question!"

(Is this Laura's voice? What exactly is happening here? The whole tedium of this meeting has dulled the interest and it sounds as if something important has happened that hasn't been heard.)

WHACK, WHACK, WHACK—goes the gavel. "Just a minute!" Mrs. Collins shrills. "Only members of this committee are permitted to address the chair. I shall ask the sergeant at arms to remove anyone who interrupts these proceedings."

"Make a motion to reconsider," Laura urges Jim Irving. The committeeman would try to step away from her, and he looks as if he's shaking apart. "Don't you see," she obviously doesn't care who hears her, "they're trying to close us out. Make a motion to reconsider," she repeats. "It takes precedence."

"What the hell is going on here?" This angry voice belongs to a committeeman in the front row. He's probably one of those who had stood up before. "This is serious business. We're not a bunch of children playing games here tonight!" Angry agreements, some applause. The man would turn around to the podium. "Madame Chairman, let's get on with the business before us so we can all get home to our children and families." Much applause.

"The motion has been made and seconded," Mrs. Collins nearly carols, "that the nominations be closed. All those in favor."

"Aye!"

"Opposed?" Whack! "Nominations have been closed. Balloting will proceed."

(My God, she must be furious, eyes like emerald chips. I can imagine her leaving the building, not even waiting for the vote, heels crick-cracking the marble foyer with a militant cadence. Is this how the process begins; that is, from a motivated to a mobilated female — radicalization? In the lobby at the revolving door, there's an impasse. Some man steps aside to let her go first and if she had a gun she would have shot him on the spot. She motions quickly, impatiently for him to precede her. He stands puzzled, immobile, and she finally — with a curse — brushes past him, exasperated with him and herself and with whatever system of chance or history that had brought them together, simultaneously, at the revolving door.

But where are her supporters, those bright-eyed youngsters who had stood outside the chamber, waving Wriston's posters? Have they been arrested, thrown into the shiny new cell blocks located in the basement of the Cade County Office Building? Undergoing systematic beatings by the police?)

No, no, no. At the revolving door, a custodian stands with broom in hand, posing for a photographer. He pretends to sweep up the poster-standards of Matt Wriston that were discarded by Laura's fellow students on their way out of the building. They left before she, and had taken the elevator down to the lobby. The motions and counter-motions proved what some of them had been saying all along. . . .

"Democracy ain't worth shit, man! Let's split before they start stomping us."

"Yes, I know . . . I know," Laura tries to argue with them outside the chamber. "But don't you think we can learn something, the technique, so that later on we can . . ."

"Practice don't make perfect, baby," another youthful voice. "It just multiplies the bad answers. We got to get a whole new rig." And then probably with a toss of his curly mane, the speaker leads them down to the lobby where they disdainfully toss the posters of Matt Wriston into a pile by the revolving door . . . and wonders if this is how the process begins, the transition from motivated to mobilated female; that it is not the Peggy Collins or the Tommy Bryans of the world that are to blame, not even the system that turns on the radicalization of a Laura Kuslowski but it is the Matt Wristons that start the process.

Once through the revolving door, the anger in her throat like sour milk, Laura looks for a telephone to call Wriston to give him the result of the meeting, a result he expected, waiting for her call in the cozy library, a fire in the grate, a book in hand — perhaps a book of poetry in his hand as he waits by the fire in his cozy library for the news of his anticipated humiliation.

There would be a bank of public telephones in the foyer of the office building, along the wall where the custodian is posing with the torn and discarded posters, but she would be too distracted by the man at the revolving door. Moreover, she probably felt as if she were suffocating in the air-conditioned atmosphere of the new building, as if the filtered air had been neutered and the impurities, the filaments and flecks in ordinary air which sustained her, had been screened out. Her lungs seemed ready to burst. And so she steps into the revolving door, presses against the anodized aluminum bar, and makes the circular trip out into the air of the April evening, out into the heavier, more fertile air of the April evening and looks for a phone to call Wriston. There's a public phone booth at the corner. . . .

"You mustn't feel this way," Laura tells them, though knowing that they must. "We can learn something, the technique, so that later on we can use it ourselves."

"Practice don't make perfect, Laura," Harvey Washington would say to her, as . . .

It is hard to identify the voices of young people today and it would be very possible that when Laura pushed through the revolving door, lungs bursting for air, Harvey Washington and several friends would be waiting in a car at the curb. There would be a couple of young men in the back seat and in the front, beside Harvey, would be a girl with an Afro hairdo who seems to be humming to herself, looking straight ahead through the windshield as Harvey is saying, "Practice don't make perfect, baby. It just multiplies the bad answers. How long have we been practicing, Laura? Same old tune and lots of practice and it's got us nowhere. We could see that tonight. It looks to us like Whitey's going to start fighting among himself and we'd only get stomped in the middle. So we're going to split."

"But can't we work together?" Laura would still try to argue, but the girl in the car says something softly, the words indistinguishable though the tone clear. The boys in the back seat laugh. Even Washington smiles, then shakes his head.

"Listen, Laura," there's a vague tenderness in his voice, "this is your scene, right now. It's not ours. I hope you make it, baby. I honestly hope you make it . . . but we don't need no more practice. Okay? . . ."

There's a public phone booth at the corner. Just as Laura pushes through the revolving door, lungs bursting, a car with several white youths pulls away from the curb before the office building, horn blaring and the occupants inside shouting something obscene, though whether their oaths were meant for her, or the outcome of the meeting, or even if they were a part of this scene at all—Laura does not know.

There would be music in the cozy library. Matt Wriston sits by the fire, a book of poetry in hand, waiting for her call giving him the result of his most recent humiliation; so when she says to him, "Maybe they're right," thinking the rest to herself; perhaps as imperfect, even corrupt as the system is; some of the old instinct, the old harsh honesty remains to cut out the weak, the indecisive . . . those who prefer the cadenced logic of the Mozart she hears in the background to the sweat and smoke of grubby power.

"What?" Wriston is saying. "Just a minute, let me lower this music." And Laura turns around within the illuminated aluminum and glass cage of the phone booth. She would be able to see down the block. The meeting will be over and the courtyard of the office building is slowly being occupied with moving shadows.

"Now, Laura," Wriston's voice comes back over the subdued contrapuntal whisper of strings and woodwinds. "What were you saying?"

"I was just wondering if you really want to go through with this now," she will say. The lights on the tenth floor of the office building are being turned off. The number of people in the courtyard will have increased, spilling over the curb into the street.

"Yes, more now than ever." Wriston answers. "Don't you? Aren't you angered by this treatment? They must be brought to account for what they have done. Every one of them. They have used the party for their own selfish interests. Too many great men have given . . ." The enormous glass beaker of a building has been drained of committeemen, spectators, newsmen, officials. Its dark sides reflect downtown lights as people continue to mill about, some stroll away, others congregating by the mirrored entranceway.

Laura would revolve within the illuminated phone booth, holding the silvery flex cable that transmits Wriston's voice. She might slump wearily against the booth, for she is suddenly very tired. There are long columns of mathematical additions penciled on the vertical strips of aluminum molding. On the small steel shelf beneath the instrument is scratched, **June and Rocky—Forever!**

"But maybe I'm not the right person for you in this job," she finally says into the mouthpiece.

"Nonsense. Poppycock. You mustn't be discouraged. It's precisely to get people like Harvey Washington back into the picture that I am putting myself up. We must bring a halt to this terrible division, these suspicions and hatreds that are unraveling the very . . ."

Laura might see District Attorney Cranston wave good-bye to all and step into the black limousine that pulls into the curb; the gestures of an easy victor. A commonplace afterthought; oh, and by the way, thanks, fellows. She would also see Ferguson, standing beneath one of those pin-spots in the ceiling of the portico, smiling and bowing, accepting handshakes. He doesn't look hurt too badly, not a winner but maybe not much of a loser either.

"What was the size of the vote for Ferguson?" Wriston asks her and she tells him she doesn't know, for she had left before the balloting began.

"People are essentially fair-minded," Wriston again. "They will resent this little episode tonight. We can use it to our advantage. There are people in our area, Democrats, who have never been given a choice and we are giving them this opportunity. They will be grateful, Laura . . . you'll be surprised at the result because we are going to win. These county conventions are really meaningless, only useful on a short-term basis. I shall promptly call a friend on the newspaper down there and give him a statement on my reaction to our treatment . . ."

(Perhaps during a slow revolution within the cage of the phone booth, holding the silvery flex cable, she will see Tommy

*Bryan wading from the pool of people at the base of the office
building, coming toward the corner, deliberately moving toward
her. She momentarily considers unscrewing the forty-watt bulb
in the ceiling of the booth, or even breaking it with something,
but it is too late. He will have already seen her.)*

". . . would it be too much to say that a scouring job is required, Laura?" Wriston's voice comes through the silvery teth-
er that holds her in this illuminated booth as Tommy Bryan
stands outside. He idly takes a turn around it, as if inspecting it
for holes through which she might escape. ". . . no better at
Minkus' meeting since I've refused to pay him off." A *pizzicato*
flourish concludes the music in the background. "So don't worry," the voice is saying as her eyes meet Bryan's through the
glass for one–two–three seconds, then he looks down at his
shoes and she turns her gaze down the street. The splayed nose,
softened by the shadows, would not seem so brutal or brutal-
ized. ". . . the petitions lined up. They're what's important. And
it might be well for me not to address your student group–not
right now. Issues are more important than personalities. I'd ad-
vance the suggestion that we're in the trouble we're in now because of an overreliance on personality. It's better to get your
people issue-oriented first," the attorney says, accompanied by
the clear, sweet phrase of a violin.

*(Tommy Bryan might turn his back to wave to a departing
Ferguson and remain that way, still effectively blocking the
door. Laura could study his back, stitch by stitch up the main
seam of the raincoat. She'd see his hair lies thickly over the ears,
though less from any sense of style than from an aversion to
barbering–she might guess. There's a bald spot, about the size
of a nickel where the strands swirl to a vortex on the crown.)*

Wriston has initiated an exchange that will terminate with,
"Good-bye. Keep in touch," as a crazy blanket of static obliter-
ates the background music. But Laura would continue to hold
the instrument to her ear, to hang onto the supple, metal leash
and nod her head or mumble into the dead connection. Bryan
studies the sky above Hinton City, a storm seems to be brewing,
paces carefully around the phone booth and resumes his post
outside the door.

Laura laughs. Wriston has never been so funny, so pungent,
so much in command of both his thoughts and the background

music and she might chuckle again, having observed the first laugh had caused Bryan to glance anxiously through the glass. She would turn away from him indifferently, pulling on the flex cord with one hand, tightening it, and it seems to draw him around the perimeter of the aluminum and glass cage so that he faces her once more through the other side as she mumbles, "Yes . . . yes . . . all right . . . um-huh . . ." into the unhearing receptacle and permits her eyes to meet his once again, no real connection there either. The blue eyes on the other side of the glass are set far apart, or the broken nose makes them seem so, or perhaps whatever smashed the nose had also pushed the eyes farther apart.

Now he's making gestures through the glass, hands and fingers in some foreign pantomine, and she stares dully at him with those large cat's eyes and shifts her feet, takes the one step permitted by the confines of the cubicle and casually turns away. He follows and she laughs as if Wriston has said something unusually funny . . . laughs, wondering which one of them was caught, caged. Ostensibly she was the one enclosed but it depended on one's point of view. Perhaps the lion in the zoo, pacing, pacing, pacing regards the creatures on the other side of the bars as the ones in captivity. After all, he did not come to see them; they had come to see him, are there because of him. His apparent lack of freedom is actually . . . funny. But this charade can no longer be supported, endured, or believed. Interminable as Wriston can be, he would not talk all night to a phone booth on a corner in Hinton City, especially if the call were made collect to his number. "Yes, I'll call him," she says, aware of Bryan's figure behind her left shoulder as she continues the slow, clockwise rotation within the illuminated cubicle. "I'll call him right now," she says into the dead receptacle and hangs up. Coolly she looks through her purse and finds a dime, drops it into the slot—Ding-Ding—and then, carefully counting off the numbers under her breath, fingers a random selection of seven digits on the instrument's dial. . . .

(What a Bitch! Let's make that booth a giant rotisserie and she is turning on the spit, being done slowly to a fine turn by the forty-watt bulb in the ceiling. Broiled well-done in a public square!)

. . . to say, hello-hello, Mr. Wriston asked me to call you, as the canned voice in her ear drones, "for assistance consult your local directory or dial one-one-oh for a service operator . . . Iyam sorry but you have reached a wrong number . . ."

But he might be gone. Nowhere in sight. As if he had never been there. Perhaps it had been all her imagination, that he had been waiting there outside. As she continues to talk to the recorded harpy, she scans the full circumference of her isolation. He is nowhere in sight. The streets are dark, empty. There is thunder and it seems about to rain . . . the air had become muggy, redolent of moist particles of soot and other pollutants that swirl in the deepening twilight of the April evening around the most modern, most handsome county office building in the state and the pride of . . . breath, fingers a random selection of seven digits on the instrument's keys that shape into the opening sweep of "You Blew the Flame Out in My Heart," or perhaps Strayhorn's "Day-Dream," standing in the living room of her apartment over the Ace Cleaners and bending into the alto sax. Then down to serious business; Volume Two of *Rubank's Method, Advanced*, is flipped open, one bare foot begins tapping, nostrils flare wide to inhale as the heavy upper lip closes around . . . being broiled to a fine turn by the forty-watt bulb in the ceiling, well-done in the public square, and finally surrenders the receptacle, gives up the silvery flex cord that had supported her and she takes a lungful of air she hopes will be enough to last and grasps the anodized aluminum handle of the door. Pulls it open. He's waiting for her.

(Has he just come back? Earlier it was indicated he had left.)

The problem is to get her out of that phone booth. If Laura can open the door and step out then Bryan can just as easily be there, perhaps to ask her to have a drink at the bar across the street. Maybe that's where he had disappeared to, to watch her from the front window, and come back when she hung up; reached for the door handle.

And she would accompany him, a bit intrigued, perhaps to show her independence also. Personal revolutions of the spirit, of the personality or mind, can result in bleak disasters, sometimes dangerous, unless given recognition, encouragement, along the way. Laura has had little of either and she sensed in Bryan someone who might not only recognize what she was trying to do, but whose approval was somehow important to her.

". . . weeping all week about Jack Kennedy. . . . showed up and talked to us and what you said put together with Dallas must have challenged me." This is Laura. She might look around the bar, as if fearful someone would find them together.

"You torchbearers have had a rough time these last ten years." Bryan laughs.

"Episodes like this evening don't help any," Laura seriously. "Why was this necessary to do? Why are you sitting here now with me—just to rub it in more."

"Like I told you, I need a ride home," Bryan replies solemnly.

"But more important, why are you here?"

"I really don't know," Laura says. "Perhaps," the idea would pull her up straight on the bar stool. "Perhaps, it's just to show you that I'm different. A few beers and a little inside talk on the great and near-great the famous Tommy Bryan has known are not going to make me fall over like one of those nunnery bums you go around with."

"Nunnery bums?" Bryan's large hands would wrap around the edge of the bar as he laughs. Laura is straight-faced, in fact his amusement seems to perplex her.

She would have been thinking of that delicate blonde with Bryan the other night, whose fine bones seemed to glow beneath her skin, who seemed to print each word into the air, rather than talk.

". . . whether you mean to be or not, but you're funny," Bryan's voice. He pulls at his nose and she half expects it to pop back to its original shape.

". . . humorless. Your whole generation is humorless," Bryan again. "And these songs of yours," he might gesture toward the car radio. "All this crap about Lu-Uve and Free-Dumb. How sentimental can you get? If you're going to go that way, give me back the old symbols—Mother and the Flag. Now they're something you can sink your teeth into. But Lu-Uve," he crooned out the car window. "For Christ's sake, don't any of you laugh at anything anymore? No wonder the McCarthys and the Wristons attract you. No wonder the Agnews and the Nixons can scatter you." . . . answered the door with the sax hanging around her neck from a lanyard.

"My God, that *was* you I heard coming up the steps," Bryan again. "You play that thing?"

"Yes," her voice, in the doorway. Seeing him on the landing, she might think she had expected to see him, though she hadn't really thought about it. "What is it?" she asks. Little Jake peers around her legs at the man on the landing. "What do you want?" "I'm sorry to interrupt," Bryan. "But I thought you might like to come out to the shopping plaza with me this Saturday – bring the boy. We'll even let you hand out Wriston flyers to the crowd."

"Why? What's going on?" She would impatiently tap on the brass keys of the alto.

"We've got a little rally set up for Howie. But it might be fun for you and the boy. A little music," he nods at the blunderbuss muzzle of the saxophone aimed at him, "and just some fun. We call it," he scratched his forehead as if to remember what the term was, "we call it the Apollo Act." He would smile.

"Saturday. I don't know. I have lots . . ."

"Say, you really do play that thing?" he asks again, probably interrupting her before she can say no to the invitation. "I mean how long have you been playing it?"

"Since high school," she would shrug, her face sullen as she looked down at her son. One foot on the instep of the other, she leans against the doorway, not asking him in, not moving out of the way, nothing inviting about her eyes or manner. "What did you call it again?" her eyes now lift coolly to meet his.

"What?"

"This business Saturday."

"We call it . . ."

. . . fascinating by the exact minuteness of their reproduction, the early morning noises of the city rise to Springhill Avenue.

"My bedroom used to be upstairs in front." He might motion out the car window toward the dark house, set among rhododendrons and lilacs. "Sometimes at night, like now, I'd look out those windows at this strip of grass down the middle of the street and – maybe because of its half-round shape right here in front of the house, but I'd sometimes imagine it was a big thermometer and the degrees it measured, the temperature it registered somehow had to do with things in our house. Except it had green fluid instead of the usual red."

"Talk about being sentimental," Laura.

"And here's something else you might think sentimental," he

said. "You ought to get Matt Wriston to come out in support of saving the old Lafayette Hotel."

"Why would anyone want to save that pile of brick?"

"Well, most of the influential Republicans around here are members of the Historical Society, and if Wriston should get by the primary, he might pick up some votes from it."

"Why don't you have your man do this?"

"It wouldn't be his image. He's a contractor, you know—all for building new stuff."

"That old hotel means something to you, doesn't it. It means a lot to you, doesn't it? Why?" The pugilistic profile looks morose in the leaf-shrouded light. . . .

Constitution, Laura, guarantees almost everything except the continuance of the Constitution . . . have some Kotex . . . AND GENTLEMEN, some of us *want* to go home tonight . . . the process begins . . . "What did you call it again?" she asked.

"We call it the Apollo Act," Bryan replied, perhaps only then giving it a name . . . Laura begins to laugh, regretfully, for her amusement takes the buzz off her excitement, pulls it down from the high wire it had been ascending step by step. "No more," she says. "Stop already," but he persists, the flattened nose ironing the smooth skin of her belly as his mouth pursues a white on white striation to the most perfectly fashioned coign where he fits upon his brow the feathery frontlet, a ceremonial headpiece for devotions. "I've lost it," she tells him. . . .

(Is this the Apollo Act?)

"What kind of act?" Laura asking. This would be the Friday night after the Cade County meeting and she has just checked into the Gilded Cage. Bryan has phoned her at work.

"The Apollo Act," his voice comes over the wire. "The boy might get a kick out of it. I'll even let you hand out Wriston's brochures. I hear the printer has finally finished them." One of the canaries might be helping her dress, pulling up the zipper of the red, feathered corselet as she talks on the backstage phone. Other preparations were being made around her; seams in wide mesh opera hose checked, straightened. Powder dusting gelatinous breasts. The feathery frontlets of their birdlike calling would be fitted around their brows: here the yellow plumes of the canaries, over there the ochery papillote of a bite-sized lark. A bluebird smooths the silvery-gray plumage that tops the sparrowlike dun beneath. Naturally, there is the crisp fimbria of the one obligatory but no less appealing blackbird. "The what kind of act?" Laura.

It would be Saturday week and in the Buy-Rite parking lot, just off of Route 83. Traffic would be backed up both east and west. Farmers, people from Yost, others from out in the country, all had come to do their Saturday shopping. Bumper to bumper, the cars edge forward in two lines toward the entrances. A group of deputies in the distinctive uniforms of the Yost County sheriff's office direct them into the jammed area. Fortunately, the weather is fine and cool. Something is going on in the parking lot.

(The men's uniforms, a two-tone maroon, with yellow piping, were designed by Pug Connors when he was sheriff. "We got to get away from the old ways of doing things, the old ways of approaching law enforcement," he explained to the Yost Lions Club one noontime. "And the first step is to dump these baby-blue uniforms.")

The lines of cars extend nearly a mile both east and west. Some become disgusted, others have appointments. There are milking hours to keep or doctors' offices to visit, and they pull out of line, turn around and go somewhere else, maybe even try the dilapidated downtown section of Yost for their needs or perhaps they might drive all the way to Sinnemok to the new complex with an A&P.

"Listen, Tommy, I'd like to help you out, but Saturday is our big day." This is the manager of the shopping center, some weeks before.

"I know that, Elmer, that's why we want to be here."

"But for Christ's sake, what will happen to those people who can't get in? No. I just can't do it. The home office will shit bricks if I do something like that. No, don't make the gesture, Tommy. You couldn't even try to pay me the money I'd lose."

"Listen to me, Elmer. Last winter when we had that blizzard and the state plows threw up those mountains of snow and ice across your entrances out here, who was it that got the county highway boys out here and dug you out? Who was it that called Charlie Lucas and told him to get his boys out here — who said it was a county emergency that this major food supply center was closed off? Who did that for you, Elmer?"

"Okay, so Pug Connors made a few phone calls. But that was last winter, Tommy."

"Just a minute, Elmer. Winter's coming again, you know. I'll tell you what might happen this winter. Both of those exits are going to be blocked up. And nobody's going to call Lucas for you. And don't think you can get to Lucas. Don't think you can use that Republican brother-in-law of yours, because *they* know that Pug Connors has been up your ass to the short hairs, and they don't take sloppy seconds. You understand me now, Elmer? I just want to be perfectly frank with you. I just want it clearly understood what will . . ."

"Oh, what the hell do I care," he would say. "Burn the fucking place down for all I care."

"GIVE . . . AN AITCH! . . . H H H H hh . . .
GIVE . . . AN . . . OH! . . . O O O O ooo . . ."

Laura would begin to laugh. He had skipped down the stairs of her apartment before she could say yes or no, had given her time to think it over. Then he had called her at the club a few days later. He had said it might be fun for Little Jake, at least given her this justification.

The five young girls wearing letter sweaters would be doing the boogaloo on a raised platform in the center of the parking lot, accompanied by a four-piece rock group. In spite of their gyrations, their jerks and twists, the girls managed to stay in line to spell, H-O-W-I-E, correctly.

Bryan has probably driven along the shoulder of the highway, right past the long line of autos to leave the stymied hornblowers in his privileged dust. He waves a greeting to the deputy who motions him through the entrance, and parks in a reserved section near the platform. There is a mass of people in the parking lot who are unaccountably a part of this calamitous demonstration, participating without knowing it, slack-jawed and attempting to defend their ears against the shattering amplification. Laura might feel awkward, but Little Jake starts to jump on the front seat of the car, head bobbing with the amplified beat.

On the other side of the platform would be a silver van dispensing free coffee and donuts. There are large pictures on either side of its panel body. Howie Ferguson with his hand thrust out, "Give a Hand to Howie." A green balloon rises from the crowd, ascends the uncertain air of early May to be swept north by some high current. A strange harbinger.

"Balloon. Balloon." Little Jake had pressed his face against the windshield.

"All right if the kid is seen carrying a Ferguson balloon?" Bryan asks her. Laura shrugs and looks away. "What happened to that old smile" Bryan taunts. "Good Christ, is the quest for the Tru-Blu Award such a joyless journey?"

(Are there any accounts of this scene?)

". . . had asked one of the Whalen brothers to attend this rally just to keep tabs on what Bryan and Connors were up to, but not trusting either of them after the way they acted at Matt's home the other night and also Mrs. Kershaw had some shopping to do, so we wheel in there kind of early just to observe the developments.

"I see Tommy Bryan's Impala ease into one of the reserve places and who should be in the front seat but this niece of George Stamski's, the one that had been at Matt's house the other night. They get out – she's got this little boy with her – and Bryan says something to her and goes off and she just stands by the car, with that look on her face. She always looks – not quite mad, but suspicious of everything. Even when she smiles it's somehow being critical. You know?

"Compare her to Helen Ferguson, they're two different animals though both about the same age. I was standing by this portable canteen having A CUP WITH HOWIE, like the sign invited, and up on the bandstand were these little girls in short skirts waving their fannies at us and all this loud noise they call music these days, and now and then you could see Mrs. Ferguson up on the platform or standing on the ground behind it, talking to Pug Connors or greeting Tommy Bryan when he walks over. You can see by a shiver down that long spine that she's just raring to take off to the music herself and wouldn't that be something. A few bumps and punch from those tits and she'd mow down everybody in this parking lot.

"Talk about the making of a candidate – how about making the candidate's wife? Even while I'm standing there, guess who comes up to me? That old dried-up son of a bitch Morehead; you know, he's the Republican town chairman of Athens. Hey,

there, Worthy, he says to me, are you working for this Ferguson? I sort of nod, noncommittal like. Well, I tell you, he cackles, if you can get him through the primary I might give him a vote myself. Any boy that can top something like that every night can't be all bad — even though he is a Democrat. . . .
"How many do you suppose were in that lot on Saturday? Couple a thousand? Probably. They all look like people waking up to find some army occupying the town square. Bryan came back with this balloon and ties it on the Kuslowski kid's wrist. Did I say she's got on this lemon-colored pair of slacks and a white sweater? They talk for a while, but she still looks mad about something. Bryan kind of hangs over her like he's amused or especially interested in everything she does.
"Then he comes back to the bandstand, all the while these little girls on it jumping around, and some of the boys come up to him, Harvie Merrick and them, and then this announcer from WHYO shows up and I know who's running things for sure because he's a nephew on Pug Connor's wife's side. Hello there, Worthy. There's a tap on my shoulder and it's the Great Man himself. Hello there, Pug, I says. Nice show you got here. He gives me that wide-eyed look; not my show, he says. He takes his hat off and smooths down his hair. He's getting kind of thin up there. Say, he says, looking like someone in the first pew, say, have you seen the Whalen brothers lately?
"Well, that little needle cleared a lot of things up for me. No, why, I says. Well, he says, I got some tickets to the banquet for them, and haven't been able to pass them on. How's Matt doing, he asks? If you need anything just let me know. Matter of fact, I got some materials that Matt could use. Like what, I says? Well, I got a couple of boxes of envelopes left over from his Assembly race. Got his name on them, you know.
"Meanwhile this nephew of his by marriage has been talking over the microphone up on the bandstand, saying how Ferguson would show up any minute, and inviting everyone to have coffee and donuts. Then he introduces Helen Ferguson and she bounces up on the stage, the kid in the band rolls the drums over like she was going to start stripping right there. She doesn't say anything, just waves at the crowd, looking part afraid, part doped up.
"Where's Ferguson, I needle Connors. These people aren't going to wait around all day. I hear he's got a dozen of these

functions set up all over the district, Pug answers. Probably held
up somewhere, he says looking up at the sky. Listen, he says,
that was an awful shame the way Matt was treated down in
Cade County the other night. And he pulls down one side of his
mouth, but his eyes are big and gleaming. Hell of a note, he
adds. You see the difference between them and me. Matt had a
fair shake with our committee, didn't he? Nominated and voted
on. Right? Sure, I think, and clobbered by that pocketful of
proxies you carry around with you all the time. He must sleep
with all those proxies tucked under his pillow like those cow-
boys in the movies with their pistols under their blanket rolls –
in case somebody tries to sneak up on him during the night.

"Of course what upsets me about Matt doing something like
this is I wonder if he's not doing it just to slam me in some way,
he says. I guess he's still got a hard-on from that business in '64,
Pug says, looking around the crowd.

"Now I've heard nothing about 1964. Have you heard anything about 1964? I never heard anything about Wriston and
1964. Connors stands there watching a balloon rise up in the air,
squinting into the sun. So, okay, I finally say, what about 1964?
Oh you know about 1964, Connors says. No, I don't know about
1964, I says. You don't know about 1964? he asks like I'd just
said the world was flat. No, how the hell would I know about
1964, I answer. Oh, I thought Wriston might have told you, he
answers and looks away. I finish my coffee and crumple up the
paper cup, throw it in the trash barrel by the truck. This big
hand of Ferguson's in the picture looks like he's about to give us
the business.

"So, what happened in 1964, I finally ask? And he tells me the
story that Matt had wanted to run for district attorney that year
but that he, Connors, had already promised Bernie Berryman
that he could run for DA. Also, Wriston had just run for Assembly in 1962, and he, Connors, felt he had to spread things
around, 'cause we only got five Democrat lawyers in the whole
county. But he, Wriston, never forgave him for this, because he
figured that he would have won, what with the Johnson land-
slide – after all, Berryman came within eight-hundred votes. So,
according to him, Connors, Matt has always held a grudge
against him and is making this primary just to get even. Do you
believe that?

"This ain't no easy job, Pug is saying. You can't please every-

body all the time and you're bound to make some enemies.
Yeah, I thought, but you can't buy anybody off with just a couple hundred printed envelopes, for Christ's sake. . . ."
". . . lost it," she tells him. "Ouch!"
"A beetle bite," Bryan's voice.

> GIVE . . . AN . . . EYE . . . I-I-I-i-i-i
> GIVE . . . AN . . . EEEEEEEEEeeeeeeee . . .
> GIVE A HAND TO HOW-eeee . . ."

**. . . Ferguson will be here very soon. Just heard that Howie
Ferguson will be here any minute. Don't go away, folks, stay
and greet this fascinating young man, our next Congressman,
Howie Ferguson. Have a cup of coffee, fresh donuts. Let's have
a song, boys.**
"Uncle John is standing over by the coffee wagon talking with
a guy. Things are getting pretty tight. We had a good crowd up
to ten minutes ago, but the edges are getting ragged, people drifting away. The lines of cars on the highway have all but gone.
The cheerleaders are exhausted, sweat's pouring down their
faces and one of the amplifiers for the band has just blown.
Where the hell is this Ferguson?
"Uncle John walks around the perimeter of the crowd, and
behind the platform, and I see him talking with several men, all
of them looking at their watches. Some shrug their shoulders.
The boys finish the piece and I tell them to keep playing and
they hang out their tongues but jump back into it.
"Next time I look, Uncle John is over with a girl in yellow
slacks, talking to her—she comes up to about his waist—just
when there is this ominous lull in the crowd. Ominous because it
means the rally is over. It's over and finished. The time had
peaked and we are on the down side. And no Ferguson. Uncle
John looks up at me and makes a gesture, but the kids on the
platform just can't do anymore for a while. A couple of the girls
are even holding each other up, staggering around.
"So he suddenly grabs this little kid sitting on a car hood. He
cradles the kid in one arm and steps forward. Off comes the hat,
and placed over his heart, over the little boy's legs. The kid's got
a balloon tied to one wrist and this bobs around over Uncle
John's head. In the middle of this awful quiet, he starts to sing
'*God Bless America.*'

"What a move! I'm up at the mike in a flash and pick it up with an 'alltogetherfolks' and in no time we have everybody in the parking lot froze on the spot, whether they are singing or not.

"Second time around, and there's a speck in the sky, moving fast toward us, gradually taking on the shape of a helicopter. It makes a wide circle around the parking lot and then slices in, slanting down toward the platform, finally hovering above us. The chopper sucking up breaths from hundreds of open mouths.

"Here's Howie!" I kept screaming into the mike but didn't need to because interest was hot, saucered on those upturned faces, staring at this big green maple bud just rotating lazily over our heads. Then all of a sudden this figure inside the bubble waves, and automatically nearly everybody in the crowd waves back. The side of the cockpit opens up. A few women scream, most everybody else gasps as this guy just steps out into mid-air – right out of the helicopter and then you see he's got one foot in this stirrup and the cable slowly playing off the winch inside the aircraft. He rides it down just as cool as anything, like one of those construction workers using a steel girder. The band is playing, the cheerleaders jumping and squealing. He's holding onto the cable with one hand and sort of waves the other one over us like a benediction – and he's grinning from ear to ear. I keep shouting into the mike, **Here's** *HOWIE*. **Our next Congressman, ladies and gentlemen** . . . *Howie Ferguson. Here's HOWIE* . . . What kind of act?? . . . WHOPPA-WHOPPA-WHOP-CHINGA-CHINGA-CHING-CHING might make her think of the sewing machine always going in the front parlor, or so it seemed, as her mother constantly reworked dresses, pants, blouses; mending them to be worn by the next in line. She could hear the cheer several blocks down, a band was playing and she could imagine Howie Ferguson descending on his steel thread, though she is thinking of her mother bending over the whirring, ping-ping of that old Singer, sewing the scraps into one crazy pattern quilt.

She would be kneeling on the floor by the front windows of her apartment. The shade, pulled over the mellow light of the May afternoon, gently, tentatively lifts to graze, caress one arm, part of a bare breast, then falls back. She is full of the ingredients of contentment; yet, she would not be content. Hearing the band up the street playing "My Beautiful Balloon," the unofficial

Ferguson theme song, she remembers the scene two weeks ago in the parking lot when Bryan looked across at her from that platform, as Ferguson did his Apollo Act; Bryan looking at her and clapping his hands. He had been applauding her and when she looked puzzled he pressed his fingers elaborately against his cheeks and pressed up, stringing his lips into a smile. Hands to her face, her own fingers felt the lines of a smile. She had been smiling without knowing it. And this perhaps was wrong. To smile unknowingly, to feel contentment without a purpose.

In the corner, the alto saxophone gleamed in the shade-pulled gloom of midafternoon, placed on its stand by the stereo and tape deck where she had slipped out of her sandals and where Bryan, patience and boredom meeting in mutual attrition, had come to her and calmly unbuttoned the long row of buttons down the back of the one-piece culotte so that the garment slipped forward over her arms and she could no longer play. . . .

(What are we to suppose here and from whose point of view? Through whose imagination is this information being transmitted? Are we to suppose that Laura has confided in someone, perhaps a trusted teacher at Cade State University—has described to this person her past and present, and the facts of her life are so very different from those of the teacher that they excite a compulsion to reproduce them as an act of possession?)

. . . last of the Don Byas had murmured, fluttered into silence in the living room, but still turned over and over behind her eyes into ever tightening spirals as his lips pursued a not inharmonious counterpoint, preparing the reed of the mouthpiece before taking a position, moving in to take possession. Up the street the cheers have begun and Laura would vainly fight the distraction, as if a fly were buzzing in the room and were about to light upon her tensed, arched torso.

GIVE . . . AN . . . OH!! . . . O-O-O-o-o-o-

(There should be some development preliminary to such a scene, something to prepare us. For example, it is possible that Bryan would bring her by his house and Laura meets his mother. Maybe this could be on their way to one of those fishing holes he's always talking about. As we understand her, one of the first

*things Laura might notice about Mrs. Bryan's kitchen would be
the paint on the woodwork. It would be an ivory, semigloss enam-
el the texture of smooth caramel and of a depth and luster that
indicate the number of times it had been rubbed and recoated,
rubbed and recoated by a team of painters that must have worked
full-time, around the clock. Ultimately, the actual structure
beneath this smooth, creamy surface has become incidental, if
not forgotten.)*

"Maw, this is Laura. And that's Little Jake."

"Hello, Laura," Mrs. Bryan would say as she leans the hoe
against the garden fence. She would be smaller than Laura had
imagined, a trim, sun-browned woman in her late sixties with
clear bluish gray eyes. She led the way from the garden to the
back porch with a gracious half-turn, a wave of arm and a curiously prompt intimacy about her, like one of those volunteer
ladies who guide tourists through restored homes.

Maybe all the girls Tommy Bryan has brought to sit in his
mother's jonquil-and-ivory-trimmed kitchen have assumed one
amorphous shape in the old lady's eyes; each one coming
through the back door as Laura has done, each one to drink
coffee at the kitchen table beside the refrigerator, each one waiting for her son to make his phone calls in the sun parlor before
the two of them left for someplace. Alma Bryan would be as
kind to Laura as she would be to the next one.

*(But would there have been others who had brought children
with them? Mrs. Bryan's behavior toward Little Jake bespeaks
practice or proves an instinct, for there would be a polished
sportiveness, a grandmotherly casualness by a woman who was
not a grandmother in the way she bent over the child and magically fanned out three oatmeal cookies before his serious face.
She would remove her sunbonnet, check the tight bun of hair,
pour some coffee for herself, and join Laura at the table. The
few words between them would avoid particulars, any unique
reference that might focus, embarrass the temporary association.
For the most part they sip their coffee and listen to Bryan's side
of the phone conversation. Alma Bryan checks her hair once
again. Laura picks up a piece of cookie the boy dropped. There
might be a nervous exchange of looks between the two women
as they hear him hang up, hear him walk through the house toward the kitchen.)*

"Where the hell are those extra pair of waders, Alma?" he might say, suddenly in the room with them. He would disappear into the small closet by the pantry.

"If you want to find anything in there," his mother would speak over her shoulder, "do it calmly and stop rooting around." To have spoken this way before Laura, a stranger, upset her and the older woman tried to cover her chagrin with a good-humored wink. "Going fishing?"

"Yeah. Maybe." His voice would be muffled, deep in the closet.

"That's nice," his mother replied evenly. "It sounded like good news on the telephone," she would say.

"Maybe," he said, coming out of the closet with a small pair of green rubber boots—far too small for him. The blue eyes were bright. "Here." Plop, go the boots at Laura's feet. "Try these on," he would say. "Go ahead." And she would slip off her loafers and pull on the waders up over her jeans as Bryan told his mother about the phone call. "The newspaper down in Hinton City has published an editorial today praising Howie's idea about stacking up trailers for temporary housing in the urban renewal project down there. Funny how he pulled that idea out of his head yesterday during that TV interview. . . ."

(Wouldn't it also be possible that he might have heard the results of some poll? "That was a report on the last poll we had made. As of May fifteenth Howie has a mean recognizable factor of twenty-two per cent, Cranston has thirty-seven and your white knight," he would look at Laura, "has nine. In two weeks time he's come up nearly ten points in the district while Cranston has remained the same. And we have nearly a month to go yet.")

Or he might tell them he had been talking to Pug Connors. There is a report the Brown machine is showing signs of a split, not vis-à-vis the primary but that maybe Howie could exploit this family squabble in some way, pick up some committeemen down there who were disgruntled, angry, or felt slighted by Captain Billy. "Do they fit?" he would ask Laura.

She would nod, thinking some men preferred particular shades of hair, or height or builds but apparently one of Tommy Bryan's specifications in girls was small feet. Fortunately, and the adverb would assume a surprising shape in her thoughts, but fortunately she could slip into the boots, on the large side of a six, with some room to spare. She might stand up and stomp about the kitchen, perhaps to show him they were a little loose, while imagining the unfortunate girl with large feet and the awkward scene that ensued when the rubbery, obstinate footwear refused to fit. Maybe old Alma Bryan had gone down on her knees to wrestle with them, to assist the tug and pull on the unyielding buskins. One more Cinderella wiped out.

("What's so funny?" Bryan might ask, for she had been smiling again without knowing it. She would shake her head. "If we're lucky," he told his mother, "we can take it to so-and-so's place to eat it.")

Julius' Place. A small roadside tavern, located ten miles from Leix, known by a certain few for its part-time chef, Ralph Kuphal, who when sober—and this same qualification also set his hours of employment—has a fantastic way with fresh-caught trout and spiced crab also. This is one of several places around Yost County that could be considered a Tommy Bryan hangout. Behind the pseudo log cabin structure of the tavern, tall oaks and wild hedges discreetly mask several small cottages with dimensions only slightly more than the narrow cots within. Remnants of the days of the "auto court," they are yet serviceable and have their use.

(Okay—it's Julius' Place.)

But it would be necessary for him to tell his mother where they might go. Bryan must always be available to the county chairman, not to mention Howie Ferguson. And if they do not catch a good fish, Bryan will be sure to drop by Julius', have a beer with the owner, and leave the name or phone number of another spot where he can be reached. Even though this is a Saturday.

Candidates attend barbecues, clambakes, church bazaars, and fairs on weekends. But managers can sometimes ease up on Saturdays. If there are headlines to be grabbed, they have already been grabbed on Friday. If the other side grabbed them then there's time on Sunday to think of an answer.

All the hectic scheduling and maneuvering is done for one week, and Sunday—on which no one campaigns—is reserved for making and readjusting the subsequent weeks's strategy. The week ends on Friday; begins on Sunday. But Saturday is usually all Bryan's, barring a party function like a dinner or a meeting.

(OK — OK — OK. So on this Saturday morning or early after-noon, Tommy Bryan will turn to his mother, and tell her that he can be reached later at Julius' Place and if not there, the caller will be given another number.)

"You're welcome back here," Alma Bryan would say to him, though obviously talking to the girl. "It's been nice to meet you Laura. Come back again," she adds in a homely, offhand manner that sounds sincere. Laura takes the rather formal handshake and picks up the multipurpose boots under her arm — she would have changed back to the loafers — shepherds Little Jake out of the room.

When they pull out from Springhill Avenue, she might say to him, "As a matter of fact, the boots are a little too big for me."

"That's okay," he might reply, completely missing her thought.

(There's something that's beyond my understanding and we might as well bring it up here. Indeed, it would seem apt, antici-pating certain subsequent events, to bring it up here. It is this: what is the attraction or even the interest for this girl in this middle-aged man who still lives with his mother? Tommy Bryan, so far described, is a man of rather ordinary talents, a spokes-man but never the speaker, an aide but never a principal. Not that Laura Kuslowski is so extraordinary but Bryan comes off a little on the meager side, nor does she seem the type to be at-tracted to him for the third-rate glamour or excitement that goes with his occupation.)

Perhaps none of Bryan's women are attracted to him because of his job. But we can make some distinctions. For example, he is certainly different in status and background from the men she knew in Slab City. He is also different from the men she serves at the Gilded Cage, soft-looking types who stare at her with a brazen insouciance while exchanging information on important deals in loud, self-conscious voices.

Nor does Bryan resemble any of her classmates at Cade State University; fuzzy, strangely brittle young men who put her off even more, put more of a distance between her and them as there might be between her and Bryan by referring to her as "the widow-chick." Her apparel of self-sufficiency has the same ef-fect upon them as the brief red costume has upon the older ones who could be her classmates' fathers. They all wish to use her or put an identity upon her of their own design.

(Get back to the fishing trip.)

It is not likely that Laura would remember her grandfather's farm, the old man having sold it a few years before she was born and moving from the mountain down to live with an unmarried daughter. She might remember him sitting in the dark, sour-smelling parlor of her Aunt Rosa's, cursing the *heinie Kaplotz* who had cheated him of a good price when his hundred mountain-side acres were finally auctioned.

His farm must have been similar to the ones they pass this Saturday morning on the way to Bryan's favorite trout hole; deserted places on the middle slope with crops of thistles and hawthorns thriving in the untilled shale and with rocks the size of small heifers warming in the May sun. Bryan tells her how to date the construction of a barn by its design, most of those they pass have a hip roof. Around one turn they come upon a field of meadow iris, and he pulls to the shoulder and stops. Little Jake picks some. A small bluish flower grows in the ditch by the road and Bryan brings some to her. It is called Innocence, he says.

"Are those hawks?" Laura asks, for he had talked of hawks earlier. The only animals she could remember from her childhood, not counting the dogs and generations of cats for whom the sixth ward was less a preserve than a province, but the only *real* animals she could remember were a family of squirrels that had made their nest in the front gutter just outside her window. All one early spring, she would lie in bed before her mother woke them for school to watch the squirrels washing and feeding and taking care of each other. But the spring rains came, and their nest blocked the gutter, backed up the run-off water so it ran into the front hall. Her father had cursed them in that calm, bitter tone that was far worse than if he had shouted. He set out rat poison on the roof which also killed one of her cats.

"No, those are crows," Bryan answers, following her point-ing. "Hawks don't flap that much. Here we're coming into Al-ton. Want to stop and see Howie Ferguson?"

"I thought there was to be no politics today," she says.

"Right. Anyway, he wouldn't be around. He's supposed to be down at that farm machinery fair in Sinnemok. Unless Ernie

Minkus has put up a few roadblocks." He might notice her shiver slightly, the classic small mouth askew with scorn. "What's the matter, you don't like Mr. Minkus?"

"He just gives me the creeps," she says. "His hands would be greasy. It's people like him who make politics bad."

"It's people like Ernie Minkus that make politics," Bryan says, stopping for the one traffic light in Alton. "Who the hell would want to be chairman of the dinky little Democratic Party of Sinnemok County? It's one thing to be a Jack English in Nassau or a Crangle from Erie or a Billy Brown of Cade—but Sinnemok? Do you know what the total Democratic enrollment is down there? A little over three thousand as against nearly twelve for the Republicans. Who the hell in his right mind would want to run a store like that? At least we got some sort of keeper down there now. So it feeds and nourishes his low-grade ambition; believe me, we could do worse."

"And also lines his pockets," Laura snorts.

"Well, we're not paying off, believe me. It's not worth it with Minkus. I know. That's why Howie's spending so much time with personal appearances in Sinnemok. Only the party. . . .

(Haven't we been over much of this material already? Let's get them through Alton quickly and onto the fishing. The groomed slopes of the Ferstock ski area rise on their left as Bryan follows the highway that will take them up into the wild, unexplored territory behind the mountain.)

It wouldn't be that wild or unexplored. He is heading for a favorite trout stream that runs down the other side of Ellis Mountain and is on the back side of Yost County, near the county line. The small town of Hunnicut lies nearby, with an enrollment of twenty-seven Democrats and thirty-nine Republicans. There is no direct route into Hunnicut within the county, the State Public Works Department never considering it sufficiently rewarding to complete the highway spur, and the pavement stops just four miles short of the town's limits. One must take a circuitous route through three other counties in order to drive into that remarkable, small square faced with the brick replicas of Philadelphia town houses that some unknown team of carpenters and masons duplicated from journeyman plan books nearly two hundred years ago.

(So they follow the smooth black surface of the state highway

*that curves around Ellis Mountain, the ski area becoming a point
for the road's circumferential route, and on up toward the small
town of Hunnicut where runs the clear, cold stream and pond
that Bryan considers his favorite.)*

"But who are the Liberals going to endorse next week?"
Bryan might ask her. "I suppose Matt has that one all sewn up.
He should have."

"I don't know," Laura shrugs and sits low in the seat, nearly
resting her cheek against the top of the open door. A glistening
streak of stream pursues them; darts suddenly to disappear in
the brake and scrub, then reappear to stretch wide in a leisurely
fashion before vanishing for good into a marsh of swamp maple
and pussy willow.

"Bored with politics already?" Bryan asks her.

"I only promised to help with the petitions," she replies.
"They'll be done in a couple of days. Is this where we're going?"
She points to the stream by the road.

"Just a couple miles ahead. There's a natural reservoir. But
what are you doing this for? Belief? Affection for Wriston?" She
is leaning over the front seat, waking the boy in the rear. "Everyone has a reason," Bryan says.

*(Can we cut to the pond? Perhaps there would be a scene first
between Bryan and the small boy, the bait box opened between
them, the dry flies and other lures fascinating to Laura's son.
He makes the mistake of reaching out to touch the bright feathers, the glitter.*

*"Hands off," Bryan would snap. His tone would be neither
gentle nor harsh, but sharp enough to bring a quick glance from
Laura. She sits on a large boulder to pull on the waders. "I'll
find one you can play with, but you keep out of this box. Okay?"
he would tell the boy, and she might have been ready to defend her son. After all she had taken him on dates before, probably; and often outings with other young men, and there had always been a conscientious effort to include the boy; to cut the
pattern of activity to his size.*

*"Here," Bryan says in a normal tone of voice. "Take this one.
This is the good stuff," and he puts a colored sinker into the
boy's hands. "Now your spot is over there," he directs him to a
shelf of rock by the pond.)*

McArn's Pool, sometimes called Devil's Mirror or simply The

Hole. Elevation about 1,200 feet. A doughnut conformation, this large, round body of crystal-pure water is rather shallow, no more than two feet deep, except for the hole in the center where the depth has never been measured. There are old tales of men being lost there.

Clumps of hardy, thick white birch grow around the edge, roots yet untouched by the blight that has decimated the species in the valley below. Laurel establishes a soft picket reinforced by the punky barricades of fallen giant trees. Bastions of huge boulders shine with the polishing received from the tumbling press of ice that pushed them way up here long ago. In short, it is the sort of place that makes an honest painter of a Frederic Church.

(As to Bryan's equipment. His pole would not be especially long but it would have a resiliency, a playful stiffness in his hands that would be uncommon. The line would be a twenty-pound test nylon caught up on a compact reel that could lay it out deftly and indefinitely, or so it seemed, and had never once backlashed.)

It is more likely that Bryan is the sort of fly fisherman who would use a bamboo rod with a single-action Hardy reel. The line—there's no such tensile—would be a double-tapered silk, H-D-H. One—two—three casts are made, dimpling the pool's shallow perimeter, the rod whipping back and forth to flick the line, tease the flat shallows with the feathery touch of a Roger's Tip; these motions perhaps to prepare the pond as much as they were to practice the fisherman. A final expert cast places the ragged pink lure exactly in the center, putting it down right over that primeval, bottomless hole. It falls like a baby's breath, not even disturbing the gnats and mayflies floating like pieces of lint on a polished mirror.

(While all this is going on, Laura would probably be standing to one side, boots fitted and holding the net that Bryan had shown her how to use. Little Jake squats on the flat rock by the water, studying the pebbles, the small pieces of quartz that inlay the pond's floor. Laura perhaps takes a closer look at the surroundings. The shelves of rock, the fallen timber and thick underbrush might harbor snakes. Several large bluejays swoop over the clearing, swing back and land on the lower branches of

a giant ash. Stillness seemed to drip from the leaves. Then the great rainbow chose to strike.)

It would not be a rainbow, not here, but more likely a brown trout – a ten-pound monster, that takes the lure some six feet into the air with him, still held loosely in his mouth before it sets-up in the sidewall of that great underslung jaw, looking back over powerful shoulders at the man on the other end of the line with an expression that seems to say, "Here we go again."

Also the term "strike" is not exactly right. This trout does not strike and if Laura had not been so busy looking for snakes or observing the birds and the trees, she would have noticed Bryan tensing, legs bent slightly, as large hands played the rod and line on supple wrists. You might say that Bryan could almost hear the fish coming. Something stirred in the black, cold depths of that bottomless well, a viscous sigh so subtle that it was only discerned by the delicate, feathered fly lying on the surface, transmitted through the line to the antenna of the pole. The fish would have begun to move, first swimming in figure-eight patterns, then settling into the counterclockwise grooves of an ever-steepening chandelle, going faster and faster as he nears the surface as if the water were easier to move through as it became more luminous.

(But all would be unchanged above. The forest breathes heavily. The gnats speck the water's surface, oblivious to the catastrophe gyrating beneath them. Laura still looks around for snakes, picks at snarls in the net. Little Jake noodles in the shallows. Bryan teases the line with his left hand, his right points the rod.)

The trout, a glistening, twisting missile the color of old straw, leaves the calm surface with a frugal precision that scatters only a few diamondlike droplets, arches high in the air in a silent, intense reenactment of that primeval transfer from water to air. Before reaching the apogee of his flight, the great mouth closes on gnats, water, Roger's Tip, and air, and the line begins to slide into the corner of his mouth, to pull and rationalize the inevitable failure as a bird. All ten pounds of him come crashing down with a fearful, awkward, walloping splash. Ka-PLUSH!

Zing, goes the reel under Bryan's thumb, as the rod takes the strain of the first plunge, a graceful arc shivering with an excitement all its own. Sudden slack as the fish makes a second leap, this one a thrashing eruption, wasteful of its energy to scatter water drops for the jeweler sun. Bryan takes up some line, plays it around the shallow perimeter, permits the fish to dive deep again where it hesitates, the great head perhaps rocking back and forth to dislodge the stab of barb and then, a decision or plan of action reached in the murky depths, options fast slipping away, one more grand rush will be made for the pearl screen that separates one world from another. Bryan senses the desperation in the abrupt slack of line, a rapid unstringing before another sinewed spasm. He braces himself, the muscles down the back of his thighs knot, cramp.

"Here it comes," he shouts rapidly taking up line. And Laura is unaccountably, unconsciously beside herself, jumping up and down, slapping the net against the tops of the waders, rushing up to Bryan who seems turned to metal save for the trembling pole, then pulling away, circling him—moving first to one side of him and then the other as if to get a better view of the contest.

"Wow! Wow!" is all she could say. "This is wild. Wow!"

And the fish has just plummeted again, but not so deep this time nor was his flight so high-arched, nor so economical of motion but a sloppy seesaw motion and then splash! All fell quiet. Bryan reels evenly, the great shape is pulled nearer, almost swimming toward them as if to submit to his own capture, and when close enough, Bryan would motion Laura to move in with the net.

A spate of thrashing on the pebbly shallows proves passivity to have been a ploy, catching both off-guard as Laura is about to bend over to scoop him up, thinking how similar to a shark. Perhaps they all look alike. There is a final, desperate struggle, Bryan's rod perhaps not able to take much more.

"Wow! Wow!" Laura shouts, very close to it, trying to capture it, yet also strangely afraid of it.

"Go ahead. Go on," Bryan says. He would be panting the sweat running all the way down his legs.

"Can you hold it, can you hold it?" she might ask, eyes bright, larger than ever.

"Yes, yes. Go on. Go ahead."

Neither of them would be aware of Little Jake, crying frightened by the sounds and the flashing, unnatural display as Laura reaches for it and screams triumphantly.

(Let's cut to Julius' Place where they might be sitting in a back booth waiting for the fish to be prepared. Or Bryan might only leave a number there and then they'd be off on some other errand; perhaps to the printer's to see if some new brochures are ready or he might call on some workers and committeemen in the county.)

". . . .issues." Bryan's voice. Julius has walked to the end of the bar to stand directly beneath a television set on a raised shelf. A horse race is in progress. "There's always been the same issues in this country – the main one being black and white. In fact, not just this country – the same issues are all over the world. You can't support a candidate just because he's supposed to *have the issues* as if they were a winning poker hand he carries around with him.

"Look at it this way. We've always had the same issues in this country, basically, but it's the way different personalities have reacted to these issues that's important. When people vote or react to the issues – or what they think are the issues – rather than for the personality, we get into trouble."

"Like when?" Laura.

"Well, like 1968, for example. Law and order, remember? That was the issue, people voted on that and forgot all about the personalities involved. Disaster. Now in 1960, for example, they went for the personality. Let me give you another example. Adlai Stevenson in 1952 was talking about the issues. He was the issues man. But people voted for the Ike-personality – and it may surprise you, but I think it was a good thing. We needed a rest then, a breather, and it also kept the Republicans sane. But 1956, the roles were reversed – Ike was the issue candidate and Stevenson by now the personality. Bad judgment was used in 1956. People reacted, voted, with a phony objectivity – when they should have responded to the personality."

Laura would look down at her nails, perhaps she had broken one in the struggle with the trout. Bryan looks ahead, finishes his beer and looks around for Little Jake, finds him squatting in the corner, petting an old basset hound owned by Julius. "And 1964?" Laura says finally.

"Oh, Christ," Bryan throws up his hands. "Who knows about 1964?"

". . . hold it? Can you hold it?" she asks, eyes bright, larger than ever.

"Yes, yes. Go on. Go ahead," he says, panting, the sweat running all the way down his legs. She circles him, moving first to one side of him and then the other as if to get a better view of the contest. . . .

"Wow! Wow!" she shouts, so very close to it. . . .

(We've already been over this. Let's put them at the end of the day. He might take her to the grassy precipice that overlooks Sullivan's Corners, and the whole valley.)

Bryan has parked the car off the road. They walk along the old railroad cut, with hands outstretched to shield their faces against the lash of maple saplings growing like buggy whips from the deserted roadbed. They trip on honeysuckle tangles. Older trees form a natural arch above this man-made aisle from which hang the gnarled vines of wild grape, the frayed halyards of lost standards. The boy might swing on these vines, his gleeful pipings stilling the anonymous chatter of the forest.

They sit on this overlook, one or two buildings of Sullivan's Corners discernible through the trees, a part of the highway visible and a milk truck upon it. He tells her how that truck, or one like it, was partly responsible for this abandoned railroad bed. There was no need for a milk train twice a day when the same sort of truck could pull up to each farm, plug in the hose, and draw off the milk. If a farmer didn't have to take his cans down to the milk depot twice daily, there were also fewer occasions for him to amble over to the general store afterward, to sit around and make a small purchase or maybe order some feed or fuel. So, the store closes up and then the only reason to go into the village will be to mail a letter at the P. O. which is operated these days out of the remodeled front porch of the postmaster's home. And that's probably not for long, the government hopes to move everything over to a rural route that's part of the Leix postal district.

"What's funny?" Bryan. Laura is laughing. She would stretch skyward and the green eyes, shuttered with amusement, seemed to slant even more with the gesture. "C'mon, what is it?" he asks as she continues to laugh, though it might please him to see her so relaxed. Perhaps the episode with the trout has made her more easy with him.

"You're funny," Laura. "You're wasting your multiple skills, your diverse store of knowledge." She would look down at the descending railroad grade. The remains of a trestle are still suspended in the gap of a ravine like a spider walking an invisible thread.

"You ought to join Vista or something like that," again Laura. "You could be your own Vista or Peace Corps. Wow, what a course you could give! Ecology is very big now and you could give a dissertation on the flora and fauna. Throw in a seminar or two on the transition of a rural community and while you're picturing the decline of store Cheddar you could pick up the allusion and develop a dissertation on practical politics. How to fake a proxy, for example.

"Or how to dump an absentee ballot or the efficient twist of an arm," a laugh, a check of breath in which to review some mental tabulation. "You're really something," she adds. "Professor Thomas J. Bryan's Basics 101. How to make it with grace. Also how to make it with capital Grace, too. Because that's what this has all been about, isn't it? A little exploitation in the name of education." Bryan's laughing now and he might reach out to her but she would have rolled away and stood up quickly, suddenly not so amused.

"Jakie!" her voice. "Jakie!" The boy answers from near the road behind them.

"The Compleat Angler," Bryan's voice and he's probably, smiling, accepting her reasoning.

"You work all the angles, that's for sure." Perhaps her mind came once again to the image of that great fish, and she could see his strong, thick fingers holding its glistening length as she, under his direction, gently worked the hook through the gasping mouth. The water's explosion of mirror like splinters are still embedded in her mind, the slivers working into her imagination, and she would remember saying softly, "Wow, oh, wow," as the quivering . . . "That's it! Of course, that's what happened!"

(What's it? What happened?)

"That's it," Laura would say, straightening.

"What's it?" Bryan would ask as she stood up and approached him. Were it not for the smile, a look of revelation, she would appear angry.

"I knew there was something funny about that fish you caught this morning," she would say and though not shaking her finger at him, her tone of voice would fit such a gesture.

"What was funny about it?" he would ask, unknowing.

"Ooh, I knew there was something about that big scene. Tell me," she was close enough to poke his shoulder. "You've caught that fish before, haven't you? How many times have you caught that fish before? C'mon, tell me. How many times?"

"Well, I don't know," Bryan answered, perplexed. "Maybe a couple of times."

"Couple of times!" Laura exploded. Now she did seem angry. "Why I bet you've trained that fish to chew on that hook. Even that's a goddamn act, one more put-on, one more lousy, fucking, machine-made technique to get . . . how many girls have you gone through this routine for? How many?"

"That's not true," Bryan answered, trying to laugh, also getting up because she kept edging closer to him, as if she were about to push him off the bluff. He saw she had become serious, perhaps without meaning to herself. Her eyes avoided his, shifted around and over his head. "You can't believe that," he added. "Wait a minute. You don't understand . . ."

"Oh, I understand," she snapped back. "Okay, answer me this one: why did you put him back, let him go? If you've caught that fish and put him back before, why did you do it this morning?" And while he was trying to put together an explanation that would make sense to her, she would add, "If it wasn't all an act, why don't you really catch him sometime, really catch that fish and eat him?"

. . . WHOPPA-WHOPPA-WHOP-CHINGA-CHINGA-CHING-CHING. ". . . Madame Chairman . . . Lissen. Wait a minute. Stop. Lissen. I haven't, I mean, I'm not, I mean, you'll have to . . . GIVE A HAND TO HOWIEEEEE . . . so we can go home to our . . . admittedly, Laura, our form of democracy establishes the perfect setting for mediocrity. Witness our present leadership. But it is also, as Mr. Churchill advised us, the best style of government we have available. There's something else, too, Matt Wriston crosses his legs and smiles. It is also a form of government which seems to maximize, at least so far, the most potentials for Good Luck . . . curious why you are seeing this Bryan. There has been talk, I'm afraid, Laura, and some of our people have expressed no little concern about . . . standing across from Ferguson's headquarters on Wentworth Avenue, just checking on who might be coming and going. It's early yet and it being Memorial Day, you know, there aren't that many people on the street. They had fixed over the old Thrift-penny Store like they planned to move in for good, repainted the front, new lights inside. Sure is great to have money. They've got a different band with them than at the rally at the Buy-Rite lot, but those five little girl cheerleaders are the same on the platform they've built on the sidewalk. There's a few kids around and a few people inside, Bryan and some of the hired help – and sure enough, there are the Whalen boys, big as life, strutting around importantly and acting as if they were useful. They don't see me, of course.

"Oh, it's great to have money like this kid Ferguson. Makes me sick to think of a good man like Matt Wriston losing out just because of the money. In a few hours that whirlybird will show up and drop him right down here in front of his headquarters. There's an ordinance against that sort of thing and they've prob-ably paid somebody off. I suggest to Matt we should raise a stink about that but he says to let it go. That's the sort of guy he is.

"Anyway, after his speech out at the cemetery, I tell him I saw the Whalen boys at Ferguson's headquarters and he just nods kind of sadly. Then I tell him about her – that niece of George Stamski – walking down the street and right into the storefront. That sort of surprises him. She's got on one of those pants suits except its very short, looks like a skirt, but it made you wonder what she had on underneath. She goes into the store and Tommy Bryan comes right up to her and they go over by themselves and talk.

"Couldn't tell what they said, because actually they were standing behind one of those big posters of Ferguson with his hand out that was plastered on the front window. Then after a while, she leaves – I think she lives just down the street over the Ace Cleaners – and he watches her go, smiling a little and pull-ing on that busted nose of his. .

"And then I have to go to check the arrangements for Matt's

speech at the cemetery . . . nicest Memorial Day ever. Honestly. We listened to that lovely talk Mr. Wriston made at the Legion Arcade, he's a lovely man, and then Aunt Mary and me
tended the graves. I had expected to see Laura there because
she said she was helping Mr. Wriston but, no, she wasn't there.
But we had finished Mama's and had moved over to the Stamski
plot to do Uncle George when Little Jake comes barreling out of
the blue and nearly knocks us down. These kids are something,
aren't they? I tell you.

"So I look around and see Laura at Frank's plot, kneeling beside it—not praying, mind you, not Laura—but kneeling there
just like she's thinking about something. Laura was always like
that, don't you know. And standing to one side, behind her, is
this man just standing and looking down at her with this funny
expression on his face. They're together, in some strange way,
you know they're together, but later when they come by where
Aunt Mary and me are, Laura doesn't introduce him. Wouldn't
you know?

"Just as cool as anything, she is. There's a slight grass stain
on one knee. She's wearing silvery stockings and a short white—
well, it looks like a sailor's pea jacket, except it's white and has
a big black scarf but it only comes down to—and this was Memorial Day too. Isn't she something? Honestly . . . Matt said
that after the designating petitions are filed next week, nominees
have three days to decline and then three days after that the
Liberals' committee on vacancies has got three days to name a
substitute, which he feels pretty much is going to be him. I don't
know why they go to all this trouble; this farmer the Liberals
nominated the other night is a nobody. I tell you why don't they
come out and give it to Wriston in the first place—or even Ferguson for that matter. That's right! Why are you so surprised?
Remember what they did to poor old Frank O'Connor in '66?
What was the figure? Well, I heard a half a million bucks. It's for
sale right now and you can bet that Tommy Bryan's down there
talking to Roger Young with a blank check in his pocket on Ferguson's bank. Well, old Matt's got a few up his sleeve too, so
don't be surprised if he gets the nod. Sure, it's worth it. In this
race, the Liberal line will amount to about fifteen-hundred votes
in the district, and this is going to be a close one against
Green—that could make the difference. Those Liberal bastards

know it too, which is why they're holding everybody up. You know what I'd like to do—over a hot stove, buddy—every one of those Liberal bastards—yea, and put the Whalen boys beside them—then, right up to here . . . " . . . CHINGA-CHING-CHING-CHING-WHOPPA-WHOPPA-POP. . .
(There seem to be a lot of loose ends that should be cleaned up. The fish episode, for example. Was the fish caught or not? There is a scene alluded to in her apartment that is not clear. Also, there's this report of her talking to Bryan in Ferguson's headquarters and then we have another scene of the two of them at the cemetery, presumably several hours later. What has happened in between?)

It would all be speculative. For example, we don't know what they said in Ferguson's headquarters and that would largely determine the ensuing action. She may have gone there only to inquire about some article she had left in his car during the fishing trip. Or perhaps, Tommy Bryan had raised objections to some of the petitions she had handed in for Wriston a few days ago, had had the secretary of state disqualify them for certain irregularities; signatures not signed the same way as printed on the enrollment lists, or dates missing or maybe some petition sheets have the names incorrectly totaled. Laura comes down to object, to abuse him for . . .

(No, that wouldn't be it. That doesn't seem to be in character with Bryan to be that petty. Also, that sort of tactic might lose more votes than it would gain. No, something else must have been discussed behind the poster picture of Howie Ferguson. It is Memorial Day. A week, perhaps ten days would have passed since the fishing trip. It would be late morning but already warm, and Laura had slipped on a terry-cloth, one-piece culotte that buttons down the back, to walk down the four or five blocks to the storefront headquarters of Howie Ferguson. She'd pause in the doorway, one sandaled foot toeing the heel of the other, looking at the workers inside, the grandmotherly types laying out pastries, heating water for the large drip coffeepot. A couple of men she recognized as committeemen were stacking brochures, bumper stickers, filling boxes with pins and plastic ball-point pens with the slogan, **Give a Hand to Howie.***)*

Bryan would not be in sight and she would feel awkward in the doorway, perhaps wondering now if she should have come.

Then he appears from behind the temporary partition halfway back. He would not see her immediately, perhaps going to the corner to talk with several men, then he would turn around and see her, as if someone had said, "Who's that girl?"

He would put down a paper cup of coffee, perhaps close up a notebook or stuff a few papers in his pocket and come to her. "Well, are you coming to join us or should we go in back and search you for a bomb?"

"What time does Apollo drop in?" she'd say.

"Not for a couple of hours. Why?"

Her eyes survey the interior, looking, it would seem, for some image or vision that would calm them, induce them to rest. "What is it?" he might ask. "What's the matter?"

(Yes, then they would have to move out of the doorway, away from the campaign workers, people and children off the street, coming and going. They walk to one of the large plate-glass windows, where Ferguson's large picture screens them from Wentworth Avenue.)

"As you can see, our volunteers are busy on the phones," he might say. Half a dozen women are using a bank of telephones installed along one wall.

"Volunteers? At how much an hour?" Laura might reply. "It's terrific the loyalty and enthusiasm that money can buy."

"Oh, it's going to cost a lot more than that," Bryan would say. Her expression would be solemn, her eyes making a careful inventory of his face; creased brow, broken nose, tired eyes, long cheeks, wide mouth, small chin.

"Listen," she might say, and her mouth would twist to one side, the eyes shift to the back of the room, then return to his face. The green irises seem to enlarge as he looks into them. "Listen, I was wondering if you might be interested in a little mutual exploitation?"

(No, no, no! She wouldn't say anything like that! Is there any need to include anything they say to each other at the Ferguson headquarters? Let them disappear behind that poster, as previously described, and that's it.)

She may have said only something like, "Listen, Little Jake is over at my sister's and my car is having its tires changed — I'm finally getting that done — and I was wondering, if you have time later on, would you drive me over to Marie's and then take us out to the cemetery. We could go late, so you wouldn't have to hear Matt Wriston speak."

(OK. Run that one.)

"I always enjoy listening to Matt Wriston," Bryan might reply. "You misjudge me and I don't underestimate him. But sure. OK. Howie is due in around three, the rally will be about an hour and then he's off to Cade County for a clambake and another rally down there. I can get away from here around four. Okay?

(But why is it approximately a half hour later he is seen leaving headquarters, strolling down Wentworth in the direction of her apartment? He could have gone only to Keesler's Pharmacy, one block down, perhaps to buy a package of mints. Or maybe to use the public phone booth.)

With all the banks of telephones just described at the headquarters?

(For a really important call, say a confidential call to Pug Connors, Bryan might prefer the privacy of an outside phone.)

Perhaps it might be better to imagine him climbing the steps of her apartment. The Ace Cleaners being closed on Memorial Day, there's a mood of desertion to the building except for the music blaring from the second floor.

Bryan distinguishes the sounds of more than one saxophone playing over a rhythm section. Instinctively, he would know not to knock, that the door would be open, and he would find her in the living room, bare feet planted apart, blowing on the saxophone, hunched over a player with a stack of records, the amplifier turned up. She owns a large tape recorder one with a triple-head, so that she can record and simultaneously play back the sounds of Coltrane or Byas or Hodges or Young, along with her sometimes clumsy, sometimes inspired mimicking. It is an enveloping, crazy effect; an infinite mirroring of slightly askance sound.

Her back would be to him, though she had glanced sideways, would know he had arrived. Nostrils flared as her classic mouth assumed an ovalness around the vibrating mouthpiece; her fingers deftly fingered the instrument. She would blow a spiral of notes, perhaps in welcome.

Bryan goes to the sofa, sits down, and his eyes close to savor the maximum amount of pleasure from this brief, unexpected recess. Not a jazz fan, but the sounds seep in. Then the sounds of her playing lose the track of harmony, awkwardly shunted off by the hard-driving brilliances on the record. He would open his eyes, look at her. Paradoxically, she looks as if she might fly off into space were her feet not pressed flat against the floor. The tension pulls the long muscles of leg and thigh, slimming the length of limb so that her legs momentarily lose the pleasing plump line that might forecast a future shapelessness. But on this particular afternoon in May, they are nicely proportioned for the rest of her, the backs of the knees succulent and . . .

The rhythm section would be laying down a beat for the solo piano while Coltrane and she took a break, one foot pat-pat-patting on the bare floor, black hair coiling, recoiling on itself like oil on water as her head bobs and shoulders swing back and forth in a tight arc—one hand would reach out to the top of a bookcase nearby, to an ashtray with a cigarette. She would hold the cigarette, light it, take a long drag, put it down, holding the smoke, letting it . . .

(If this is supposed to be marijuana, don't you think it's a rather gratuitous introduction? Would it be part of her character or rather only a self-indulgent listing of contemporary paraphernalia?)

It would seem to be very much a part of her character. A twenty-two-year-old girl who before she had reached voting age, at once the symbol of everything and nothing, had been made both a widow and a mother. Whose background urges her to join a society which she has learned to suspect, to doubt. The sixth ward could easily be thousands of miles away; on the other hand, she's not at ease with her contemporaries either. She's not really one of them. Even the music she plays, somewhat archaic and certainly not typical of her group. Something else she has learned, has taught herself. All these things, put together, would make it seem very normal for this girl to wrap herself in sounds, to get quietly stoned on Memorial Day. Not for any of the dime-store mysticism or the so-called mind expansion qualities claimed by some of her contemporaries that approximate the equation, 0×10. She just wants to get high.

But Bryan is very conscious of time slipping by. The rally at headquarters down the street, the candidate's schedule, the continued checking with different people, and gradually the happy-go-lucky, spontaneous mood slips away, is gradually fitted to the structure he had made earlier.

Boredom and impatience meet suddenly in mutual attrition. Bryan comes to her; slowly unfastens the rather large buttons down the back of the one-piece culotte. She continues to play, eyes closed, harmonizing with the cool sounds of Miles Davis and Getz.

The material slips off her shoulders. The back would be smooth, a few freckles peppering the pale skin between the shoulder blades. She would wear no bra. She stops playing, though still holds the instrument, head swaying to the sweet-sour blends of the jazz, nor would she be able to play, for the garment is loose around her arms, imprisoning her hands, as it were, and she would be naked from the waist up except for the thin black cord of the lanyard around her neck. This final adornment would be removed as her hands fumble in the folds of jersey, unsnap a fastening and the instrument is placed on its stand. Her breasts bell as she leans forward. Her eyes would still be half closed, whether to savor the music, the marijuana or perhaps she did not care to look him in the face, and in fact her back would still be turned to him. Somewhere in her mind there might flash a picture of the trout, how his large hands held it, gently held it, and these same large hands held her now, hands that seemed powerful enough to crush the bones beneath the flesh they caressed. The thought pebbles her skin, the nipples within the rather large aureoles stiffen.

"Lissen," she says drowsily, "I'm not ready. I mean I haven't . . . I don't . . . you'll have to. D'ya understand? We'll have to . . ." but Bryan assures her, his hands turning her around so she faces him, eyes still closed, face lifting and the Botticelli mouth pursed to receive his kiss.

(Would it be likely that she is not using some contraceptive device? Though no longer a practicing Roman Catholic, would she yet have a residue of feeling against the use of such devices? How about the pill? Or is it possible that Laura does not practice the casual promiscuity rumored to be prevalent among her contemporaries?)

We might suppose Bryan to be a man of some experience. Tempered by the bluer fires of his forty years, he can exercise sufficient control to give her maximum pleasure with a minimum of risk. We can assume that all of the usual tactile, labial, manual, and visual methods, are employed. Perhaps during *coitus reservatus*, if you wish, we can imagine several positions being

used, a rapid shift from one to another in the best olympic tradition; a couple so strenuous the female can maintain them for
only a few seconds.

(All of this takes place in Yost City?)

Yokels are not always found in provincial beds. Laura's bed
would be part of a suite bought at the time of her marriage, and
includes a bureau, vanity table with mirror, a bedside table. The
bed would be three-quarter size and above it hangs a ceiling fixture of brass around which spreads a fungi-shaped water stain
from the apartment above. A slight breeze puffs a green window
shade to increase the intensity of light. The mirror of the vanity
table flashes a coded message to the cornice above the bureau.

GIVE . . . AN . . . . EEEEEEEeeeeee.

"They're starting," she says.

"Yes."

"Time to go."

"Yes."

. . . A HAND . . . TO . . . HOWIE!!!!!!!!

"You've lost the old push, Bryan," she says. "Ouch, don't
bite."

"All beetles bite," he replies, and turns over on his back, lying
across her legs to regard the ceiling. "I've told you that," he
adds.

"Where's the old enthusiasm?" she says. She raises up against
the headboard, pulls her legs out from under him as if crawling
out from under a wreck. She plumps a pillow behind her back.
"Now that the ballot box is about to be stuffed, you've lost your
enthusiasm." His skin is pale and covered with a thick quantity
of hair that had surprised her.

A slant of sun slips between windowframe and undulating
shade to flick his right side. The shoulders are broad and thick
but the belly would be flattened, flattered by his position. The
genitals are almost hidden in the dark hair between the heavy
thighs. Though his eyes are open, there is a somnolence in his
pose; the lay of his limbs, an elongated proportion of forearm to
biceps as if the whole arm had been stretched or perhaps it was
all an illusion caused by the afternoon light filtered through the
dark green shade of the room's one window.

"Where's that torch you're always passing around?" she says.

"More like a can of worms," Bryan answers. He slides an arm
across his eyes as if the light in the bedroom were too strong for

him. "Where's Wriston today?"

"I told you," she answers. "First at the courthouse, then out at the cemetery."

"Maybe we could do something this evening. Should I meet you there, at the cemetery?"

"I'll have Jakie with me."

"That's okay. Maybe we could take a drive up to Taylor Lake. I caught a pike there last year that weighed nearly five pounds."

"What did you use?" she asks.

"Some sort of a spoon probably." He would roll on his side, an arm supporting his head by her hip. "You've learned a few things from me, haven't you?" And she returns his smile, amused by the tone in his voice.

. . . TO . . . HOWIEEEEEEeeeeee . . .

The cheering downstreet rouses him, but his movements are studied, slow. Laura closes her eyes when he leans forward, offers her lips but he kisses her eyelids.

"Why don't you take a quick shower before you go?" she says. "You'd feel better."

"I feel better," he replies. He pulls on his shorts. "Ah for the life of a student activist," he says. "One day you ring doorbells and the next day you ball the opposition."

"*I find this frenzy insufficient reason for conversation when we meet again,*" she murmurs.

"What's that?" he asks coming to the bed, adjusting his tie. "That sounds like some kind of Women's Lib stuff."

"Bryan," Laura stretches out on her side. "Do you really think Howie Ferguson will win?"

"You saw the polls. He's coming up fast. It's a question of time now. If we have enough time. I think we do. If we had the votes that Wriston will pull, we'd be ahead."

"And if Wriston had Ferguson's votes," but she does not finish, for his expression convinces her the converse would not be true. "Maybe," she changes her thought, "Wriston is drawing votes from Cranston."

"You've got to be kidding," he laughs. "Okay, four at the cemetery," he bends over her again but she turns away this time. "Just two more weeks, Laura," he says, kissing her by an ear. "Two weeks more and this will all be over. Then we'll just have one candidate to worry about."

His steps skip heavily down the stairs to the near-silent street below. She might stretch, listen intently. Through the open window in the front room come the soughing of footfalls along Wentworth. Even the few cars on the street would sound extraordinarily muffled and well lubricated. Memorial Day. In two weeks the primary would be over and there would be a winner, a nominee.

(Isn't there a scene in the cemetery? Also, aren't we supposed to hear more about the Liberal nomination?)

CHINGA . . . CHINGA . . . CHING . . . CHING . . . WOW . . . "It's wild . . . he starved to . . . same issues, Laura. It's the reaction of the different personalities to these same issues that has . . . Let's suppose Matt Wriston looking down on . . . Jakie comes running over . . . Aunt Mary and me are busy arranging the flowers and then Jakie comes running over and grabs me, like he had not seen me just about an hour before, don't you know. And I look around and I see Laura kneeling by Frank's grave and this man standing behind her. She's not praying or anything, not Laura, but just kneeling there, and wearing this white dress that's made like a sailor's pea jacket and only about down to here. Honestly. She's just kneeling there, one hand sort of reached out to brush the grass growing on Frank's grave, and this man standing behind her just watching her and when she finally gets up, I see grass stains on the knees of her hose. Then the two of them walk toward us. Little Jakie has . . ."

Not an awful lot can be done with this scrap. We might expect Bryan to muse upon the yonkers buried in these provincial plots. He might try to put his own life into the brief parenthesis of dates on Frank Kuslowski's stone. He might be moved by Laura's casual, offhand consecration of her husband's grave, maybe she brought a small bouquet of flowers; on the other hand, he probably observes only the straightness of her back, the flare of hips into the compact, somewhat underslung buttocks. He could observe her running one hand over the crisp grass of the grave, amused that only an hour before she had taken a similar position beside him in bed; kneeling over him, idly running a hand through the heavy hair that covered his body as they chatted.

(If there is no record of what they said on either occasion it might be better to move on to a summary of Laura's meeting with Matt Wriston, concerning the Liberal nomination.)

New York State election law requires that if a nominee for public office wishes to decline the designation of a particular party, he has four days in which to do so after the designating petitions have been filed. Let's assume the petitions – those lists of names that were filed on May 15th – that would be a reasonable date – declinations would have to be made by the 19th, so that means Laura and Wriston could have talked this over sometime between the fishing segment and Memorial Day.

The Liberal Party had nominated one of their own members as a candidate for Congress, a rather well-to-do dairy farmer whose name is unimportant. It was a Van Something-or-Other. Wriston's reaction was to assume the Liberals wished to bargain in the four days before the declination deadline. He and Ferguson had both appeared at a joint caucus held by the Liberal Party in the area. He felt that he had come off best in the exchange of views. Wriston's past record, his defense of various liberal causes. His long-standing attitude toward the war. All of these points led him to expect their endorsement of his candidacy. The Liberals had enthusiastically supported him when he ran for Assembly in 1962. You might say some of his best friends were Liberals.

But new leaders had taken over; aggressive, junior chamber of commerce types, that were strangers to Wriston. He had heard the treasury was pretty low – that perhaps the nomination was up for bid. After all, he should have been the only logical choice on grounds of issues and past positions. He feared Ferguson's bankroll; therefore, asked a lawyer friend to feel them out. This would be Hiram Stone, a former member of the executive committee of the Liberal Party. Wriston told Laura that Stone brought back the word that they would consider the proposal and so he made a quick assessment of his financial reserves. He was still paying off the note that had financed his Assembly campaign; however, there was his wife's Coca-Cola stock. He had planned to use some of it for a collateral loan to pay for his congressional campaign. He could borrow a little more to take care of the Liberals.

So Wriston had waited by the phone. A day went by. Then another. There was but one day left for this farmer to decline and for the Liberal Party committee on vacancies to submit the name of Matthew B. Wriston as nominated. Every hour of the last day, Wriston asks his secretary to call Albany and check if the declination form had come in. Ready for publication was a brief, warm acceptance statement he had put together. At five o'clock, he himself called the secretary of state's office. There was probably some mistake. He called Hiram Stone who called his contact; perhaps the courier with the forms had been delayed en route to Albany. But there had been no mistake, no accident. There was no declination. In November, the Liberal Party line would carry the name of this farmer, Van Something-or-Other.

*(The previous section with Bryan in Laura's apartment still does not sound right. Laura was seen talking to Bryan at Ferguson headquarters and maybe all she did was ask for a ride to the airport. Maybe Bryan **did** just stroll down to Keesler's Pharmacy to make a phone call. To have them run through a series of* **italicized** *acts on a warm afternoon does have an appeal but it might be more self-indulgent than objective.)*

Accept much of what is already down; the player, the tape, Laura playing the saxophone against the records. Even the stick of grass, let's leave that in. But not Bryan. He would not be in her apartment. Laura might be alone, a condition she's grown used to, even courts. No school books were in evidence before and these would be neatly stacked on the kitchen table. Perhaps this morning she had finished typing one of her last term papers at Cade State; Marxist Thought Related to Syndicalism. Everything was done, stacked on the table, ready to go the next morning. As before, she would be in the living room, playing the alto against the sounds of Don Byas, pausing to suck on the oolong, quietly getting stoned on a dreamy Memorial Day afternoon.

She might leave the equipment going, the tape recorder receiving the music from the record player and playing it back almost simultaneously, place the tarnished Conn on its rack and do some few chores around the house. She might even take a short nap on the sofa, waiting until four o'clock rolled around and Bryan would call for her. Little Jake would be at Marie's.

Maybe the idea of a bath would appeal to her. The night Wriston had told her about the Liberal Party nomination, she had put down fresh linoleum on the small floor of the closet-sized bathroom working as he leaned in the doorway, talking. Strawberry-colored swatches of oilcloth were tacked, fastened around the sink, the small stand beside it and a low stool. The same material had been used to skirt the old bathtub. The walls were an off-white.

As the water ran, she would reach back, undo the large buttons of the one-piece culotte so that the garment slipped off her shoulders, down over her arms to entangle her hands. She fumbled in the folds of the material and unclasped the belt at her waist so that the garment falls around her feet and she would be naked except for the thin black cord of the lanyard which still hung from her neck; she had forgotten to remove it when she unfastened the saxophone.

(OK – Go on – Run it.)

She might dump some bath oil in the steamy water, and sit upon the low stool by the tub. Ugly toes, she might think. All of those worn, wrong-sized shoes handed down to her and originally bought for Marie Patrovich who has beautiful feet but is an old maid at thirty-five and who now takes care of Little Jake for her. So maybe it all evens out, Laura might think. But her sister's legs were bad – thick, shapeless trunks, and she sometimes studies her own to see if their trim lines, the succulent nook behind the knee, were changing, though what she could do about it she did not know.

She might turn off the bath taps, feeling her skin pebble, anticipating the contact with the hot water, the rather stubby tips set in the dark aureoles of her breasts stiffening. Don Byas would be crooning, joking, swinging on the recorder and tape, as she stepped into the bath, sliding down into the slippery, aromatic water – eyes closed as a phrase of the alto turned over and over in her mind like a golden leaf in autumn sunlight – she could also hear some cheering from down the street, from Ferguson's headquarters. She lay low in the tub, the water up to her neck – the blue-black hair piled high on her head – her hands floating or sinking, idly paddling about the oily water as if disconnected from the rest of her and she would be listening to the music, smiling and aware she was smiling. GIVE . . . AN . . . EYE . . . I . . . I . . . I . . . iiiiii

Bryan would have gone to Keesler's Pharmacy not just to buy some mints but also to return a phone call. As he had watched Laura Kuslowski walk away, amused by her directness – she had come right out and asked him for a ride to the cemetery that afternoon—one of the workers told him he had a phone call.

"Hello."

"Oh, hiya," a distant voice, casual. "Lissen, I want you to call me back. I'll be at home. But wait about half an hour. And call from outside. So the number doesn't show up on the phone bill. Okay, pally?"

So in approximately thirty-five minutes, Worthy Kershaw sees Tommy Bryan stroll out of Ferguson's headquarters and down Wentworth Avenue, though no one really sees him in Keesler's Pharmacy. Sam Keesler is on duty, the store is open even though it's Memorial Day.

"Hello, Tommy Bryan," the druggist could say. "Who's winning? Who's the next President?"

"What are you doing open on Memorial Day?" Bryan would say, selecting a package of mints and receiving change.

"Ah, the dead can take care of themselves," Keesler might say. "Who's going to get Mrs. Simmons her paregoric if she needs it? Only this morning, I had an insulin prescription." And he shrugs and returns to the crossword he had been doing.

Bryan goes to the phone booth in the front corner of the store. Standing beside it, as if waiting for a call, is the cardboard cutout of a smiling girl wearing a bathing suit. She holds a camera. On the other side is a glass-doored cabinet with shelves stacked with jars and boxes.

"Pug?"

"Yeah. Lissen, Pally, we got some trouble."

"Oh?"

"Yeah. Captain Billy has just slipped into a coma. It looks like he's finished. Nobody knows what will happen down there. It's an unsettled situtation down in Cade. Some of his boys are already fighting among themselves."

(What happened to Laura in the bathtub?)

. . . is a glass-doored cabinet with shelves stacked with jars and boxes. As he dials the number, Bryan can look through the pharmacy's front window and across the street to Hancock's Furniture Store. The large plate-glass windows carried the image of the cheerleaders jumping up and down, reflected from downstreet like a billiard cushion shot. . . . GIVE . . . AN . . . EEEEEEeeeeeeee . . .

"Pug?"

"Yeah. Lissen, pally, we got some trouble."

"Oh?"

"Yeah. I had lunch with Joe Kruger yesterday and he told me that Minkus is boasting all around down in Sinnemok that he had been set up on this primary. Kruger said that Ernie even showed him a thousand-dollar bill he was carrying, saying there was more to come after the votes were counted."

"For Christ's sake, who would it be?"

"Well, figure it out, pally. It's not Ferguson, is it? You would know that? And Billy Brown wouldn't have to, not with Minkus. Right? So that leaves one left. Right?"

(Joe Kruger would be the Republican county chairman of Sinnemok County, and a good friend of Pug Connors. They see each other regularly to compare notes. Is Laura still in the tub?)

There's even a third possible conversation. As Bryan stands in that phone booth, watching the images of the cheerleaders downstreet flash on Hancock's window like fish leaping from a pool at evening, Pug Connors tells him that the turnout at the Green River rally, where Ferguson had just left, had been very small.

"Of course," Pug is saying, "that prick Worthy Kershaw is town chairman up there and he's right up Wriston's ass. He's had a hard-on for me since I didn't recommend his nephew for a rural carrier up at the Leix post office, but for Christ's sake, I can't please everybody and the kid was some sort of a pervert anyway. He had a history of exposing his privates. Can you imagine how that would be – 'Here's your mail, Mrs. Brown, and take a look at this banana.' Jesus!"

"It's okay, Pug," Bryan finds himself saying, as if to excuse the county chairman for the poor turnout. "Don't worry about it. We've had Green River in the lost column from the beginning."

"Yeah, but I hate to let you down," Connors might answer, nearly whining with chagrin.

"It's okay," Bryan insists. "You can't run everything. You're not God."

"Oh, yeah," Connors says softly, as if this were news.

"But now I understand something," Bryan might continue. "I've been seeing this girl who has been working for Wriston.

The Patrovich girl, you know?"

"Yeah," Connors says guardedly.

"Well, she told me she had a long talk with Wriston the other night after the Liberals put up Van Arsdale as their nominee, and Matt kept saying things like, he who laughs last laughs best. Didn't seem worried about it, you know. Just kept chuckling and saying, he who . . ."

"Yeah, but I want to tell you something, pally . . ."

(Whatever they said, whatever the information conveyed to Tommy Bryan by his county leader, their conversation would be interrupted right now by the sound of the helicopter coming in low over Wentworth, bringing Apollo down from the mountain. Laura would hear it also as she steeped in the hot bath, hands paddling lightly, coming to rest on her belly, limbs about to dissolve in the slippery aromatic water.)

. . . WHOPPA . . . WHOPPA . . . CHINGA . . . CHINGA . . . CHING . . . stitching all the pieces together in the front room . . . down on Wentworth . . . hold it, hold it . . . yes, go on . . . go on . . . what . . . the . . . what . . . votes . . . votes . . . wow . . . wow . . . WOW . . . GIVE . . . A . . . HAND . . . TO HOWIEEEEEEEeeeeeeeeeee . . . tell you something, pally; he who laughs last is a sorry son of a bitch . . .

Playback

Friday

Alma, this morning: "That second planting of corn is going to tassel out, just like I said it would. I told you it was too early to plant it and then frost got it. Then we put this crop in too late. Do you want eggs?"

No, just some toast and coffee.

"No eggs?"

No, just toast and coffee.

"Everything's off schedule, put off schedule because of this business that Pug Connors has got you mixed up with. And for what? How much money is he taking from this boy, Ferguson. He's spending too much. People don't like that. All these billboards and mailing pieces. Everytime I turn on the radio there's one of your commercials. People don't like all that show of money in the candidates they vote for."

You mean like FDR? Lehman? Jack Kennedy? Rockefeller? How about George Washington?

"Here's some of Florence Marples' quince jelly. A little sugary but it has a nice flavor. It doesn't bother me anymore. The people down at the real estate office say they could sell this house tomorrow. That's what I'm going to do. I'm going to sell this house and go to Florida. I can buy myself a nice little trailer and set it up on a lot down there and be just as happy as a clam.

It's my house. I can do what I want to with it. It's not right to force people to live in a house this big all their lives."

Nobody said otherwise, Alma.

"It's just too much for me to take care of anymore. All this gardening to worry about. My knees hurt all last night from the weeding I did yesterday. It's not right to live in a house that's partly closed up, rooms not being used. Too many people need a house like this. People with families. Children. Here."

But I didn't want any eggs.

"They're good for you. Cooked in butter. It's like that garden out there."

What?

"This campaign of yours for this rich boy. I know, I know . . . he made it all himself but it doesn't matter. That's all he has and you know it, money. It's all this slapdashing about with helicopters and fancy promotions."

He's wearing out a lot of shoe leather too.

"Slapdash. Just like that garden out there. Worst garden we've ever planted. I'm voting for Matt Wriston, and no matter what all those big-shot polls tell you, a lot of people are going to vote for Matt Wriston. You'll be surprised."

No I wouldn't. Might give old Matt a vote myself. Up in Alton the other day, I'm going over Primary Day expenses with Ferguson; so much for poll watchers, so much for cars and something for some committeemen.

"Just buying people right and left," he says, laughing in the back of his throat.

No, I explain, these are men who already support him—for some reason, but who would have to take the day off from where they work to get the votes in for him. One works as a clerk at the A&P. Another manages the Montgomery Ward catalog store. And so on. They have to be compensated for the time they lose on their jobs.

"Oh," he says and seems disappointed. "Hey, hon." Helen is coming down the spiral staircase. She's lost some weight, leaner —looks terrific. The other day I caught her watching Howie as he was talking; her eyes were scrooched up like she was afraid of what he was going to say. "Did you transfer the money from that account?"

"Yes," she says, pausing halfway down the steps and looks out the big window. I hear it also, the whoppopping noise of the helicopter just coming over the peak.

"Here," he talks over the sound of the landing aircraft. "This should take care of it." And he signs the check and hands it to me. Our newspaper ads this week will cost around fifteen hundred dollars. Pug has got Chub Miller to head a Professional and Businessmen for Howard Ferguson Committee, so we'll funnel some money through him.

We walked down to the parking lot where the helicopter is waiting to take them to Sinnemok County. Howie is making the commencement address at a school down there and he and Helen both look like members of the class. She has dropped the hemline on her skirts — almost to her knee.

He's about to climb in after her, but turns around and pulls the manuscript of the speech partway from his inside coat pocket. It's the best one I've done for him. He's grinning from ear to ear as he taps it and I see his lips shape the phrase, "Words of Wisdom."

The truth of the matter is that I'm tired, pooped, exhausted. I'm too old for these games. I've drunk too much coffee out of paper cups, made too many phone calls, smiled down too many ugly, mean faces. I have some sort of spiritual indigestion, a cramp in my soul. The other morning I sat here and stared at the typewriter for nearly an hour before I could put together a simple press release about Howie talking at this high school commencement.

"In remarks made to the Haynesberry Central School commencement class, the congressional candidate said . . ." and that's as far as I got for an hour, even though I knew what the remarks were because I had just written them!

In remarks made to the finance committee, the minority leader said . . . In remarks made to the Yost City Rotary Club, Sherriff Connors said . . . In remarks made to the Tri-County Bar Association, assembly candidate Matthew Wriston said . . . too much. I've been remarking the obvious too long, but in politics one must always remark the obvious.

I seem to be going into a shuddering stall, all my garments loose, flapping. "Hey, boy, I'm sure glad you're on my side,"

Howie says merrily. "Wow, the things I've been hearing about you. You're one tough hombre, a real gunner." He meant to be complimentary, as if I had shot down all those stuffed heads from his wall, but I had to turn away from him, giving my grim smile. And that was no good because there was Helen standing on the other side, smiling also until she caught my eyes and then her expression became powdery. She's been looking at me differently, curiously, ever since.

Then there is this girl, L. In retrospect, that scene at the cemetery on Memorial Day resembles a story in one of those magazines that Alma is always reading, stories written by authors with three names like Ruby Mae Kuntz—and resembling long-winded advertisements for bath towels. Maybe that's what it really sounds like when people talk to each other.

"It was his letters," L. told me. She patted the little grass mound approximately over where Kuslowski's chest might be. "I couldn't believe they were from the same boy, that they were for me. *Your loving Frank*, that's how he signed them. And I began to wonder who is this guy, Frank, and why is he writing to me?"

She told me about the letters. How he would describe fixing up a helicopter with searchlights so on dull evenings they could fly over the Saigon dump and knock off rats, or anything else that was scavenging, moving. Then there was a lot more nasty stuff, the usual crap that happens.

"Every time I received one—and he always wrote pages and pages—I could taste the salt bread from our wedding, as if it had been in my stomach all along. I'd come home from school—down at Cade State—and the first thing I'd see would be that small brass door of the mailbox, and I'd run right by it, upstairs, if I saw something inside. You see I wrote him, regularly. I just didn't want him to answer, not these stiff, formal little notes about his company's body score. Did you ever kill anyone, Bryan?"

Her turn caught me unexpectedly, for my immediate response was to ask myself, When—Where? "I don't know," I finally told her. "It was a different kind of war."

The mailbox in the hallway became so stuffed she would have

to open it. A lot of promotions, a few bills, and usually a square blue envelope. "Some of this junk mail would have wild things printed on the outside of the envelopes, like *You've Already WON*, or *Your Winning Number Is Inside.* The one I liked best was *Fly Anywhere . . . FOR LIFE.* I still remember that one. And then somewhere in the pile of all this shit would be a letter from him, this stranger that claimed some sort of special relationship with me."

It's interesting that L. is rather parsimonious with words like that. When they *are* used there's no special emphasis. Unlike the upper-class Miss S. and her self-conscious practice of the Olde English. We were walking somewhere one day, and Miss S. suddenly stops and starts scraping one sandal on the pavement. "Oh, shit!" she says, "I just stepped in some dog doo-doo."

"I nearly went off my rocker that spring," L. said. She was on her feet. A green silk ribbon fluttered in the black hair as she brushed at her knees, slightly stained by the grass. "I'd read those full-color ads about winning a vacation cottage, or flying anywhere in the world for free and then there would be these other letters about what he called their ball games and what the scores were. There would always be something like 'Keep those cards and letters coming in, folks. Ha-ha.' Do you understand?"

I told her yes but it was only to say something. We walked down the path, this kid of hers chasing around among the gravestones then disappearing, but she doesn't seem to be worried about him. As if he's safer in this cemetery than that day we went to the pond and fished for sunnies. She was constantly hallooing him there. We locate him with some relatives, working over old George Stamski's grave. The nose has been chipped off of a weeping angel standing over him.

Remember that grade-school teacher—must have been about fifth or sixth grade—who was a classics nut? Most teachers had pictures of Washington, Lincoln, Longfellow, or Cooper above the oak molding near the ceiling. But this one had photographs of statues, Perseus, Apollo, Zeus, and others like that. They all had had their pricks knocked off. Most of them were without noses also.

But this girl really gets me. Maybe because I'm so weary, worn out. But the other night — the night of Memorial Day — she says to me, "Listen, Bryan, maybe what you need is a friend." Now what kind of talk is that?

We seemed to have something going. We've been out a few times, had a couple of good outings and the way she talked at the cemetery — anyway, I call her about ten o'clock that night after the kid is asleep, and she says, "Maybe what you need is a friend." She sounds like I have wakened her, or it's more likely she's high on something.

She has the record player turned down very low. The boy is sleeping in a cot at the end of her bed. And she's got that saxophone hanging on her but she's not playing it, not blowing any sound out of it, that is, just her fingers playing on the keys as if she were making music. Ticky-tack,-tack, tack, and rattle, as she follows the soloist on the record, eyes closed perhaps to keep the sound completely inside her head.

During a piano solo she turns around and looks at me, almost smiles, tiptoes down the hallway to check on the kid and comes back by way of the kitchen, carrying this scrap of paper which I kept. "The desire for education," it says "should not be suffered to disturb in any way the existing class system, by awakening in youthful minds the impulse to acquire unnecessary knowledge which cannot be applied in practice."

She's been watching me read these immortal words, her mouth closed over the reed and fingers manipulating the brass keys of the instrument. And when I don't say anything, she pops the mouthpiece from sullen lips and says, "I found that in a book the other day."

"Oh, yeah?"

"You know who said that?" I give up. "He was a minister of education — dig that, a minister of education for the Czar!"

"Well, what can you expect?" I say, but she doesn't hear me because she's turned away to pantomine the big finish on the record; sax, piano, drums, and bass.

I have not mentioned that she was smoking one of those homemade cigarettes when I arrived and naturally offered me some. That's all I need in the condition I'm in. So she gets me a beer from the refrigerator and pours herself some more California Chablis and resumes her silent fingering.

What is the protocol these days? I mean in the old times of booze and the back seat, it used to be considered unsportsman-like, ungentlemanly to make out with a girl who was drunk. But what's the code today for a girl that's stoned on grass? Or does any of that matter anymore?

After a while she unfastens the sax and puts it on the stand, turns off the record player and turns on the tape recorder. She listens to the music, one ear cocked critically to pick up the low amplification. There's an odd dimension to this tape recording and I realize that it's the sound of her playing over a twice-recorded jazz combo. She's really pretty good. I'm about to say something like that, also ask why she's so interested in this kind of music, when she leaves the room. The apartment is small, so I can hear the unmistakable sounds of clothing being removed.

Kuslowski must have sent her this outfit from Hong Kong, maybe on his last R&R before he went back to shooting rats in the Saigon dump. Maybe the blade dropped off his helicopter because it had been nibbled through by some rodents at the base, a bit of counterinsurgency. The pajamas seem a size too large and the kimono overlaps her narrow waist half around again — everything of an emerald-green silk that sets off vibrations in her eyes. She sits on a hassock and puts her elbows on the coffee table, chin in her hands, and flicks those big eyes up at the wall just over my head.

She has this disarming way of never really looking at you when she talks, her eyes roaming all over the place, and then when you look away, and look back, she's staring right through your skull.

"Hey, listen to that," she says, her back stiffening, attention on the murmuring tape. "That's not such a bad passage." She picks up a hairbrush from the table and makes several strokes with it, puts it back. She looks up at the ceiling, follows the molding around, switches to the hanging lamp in the corner, and, then the green eyes deftly glance to the floor. "I'm not fixed for anything, you know."

"Fixed?"

"Sure. You know, the pill or anything like that. And anyway, I really don't feel like balling." And before I can say anything like, well, how about another beer, she continues in the same breath, "I'm through with Wriston."

"Oh?"

"Yes. Nothing dramatic. No great break. But it just took me longer to see what Harvey Washington and the others were talking about—it's no great thing to help build the pyramid. That's what participatory politics is all about. It's the oldest trick around. Like Moses, you know?" She seems even smaller in the folds of green satin. Her hair flows around the right shoulder spreads over her bosom.

"But it's more than that," she says. "The other day Matt was laying out my future for me, you know. About how he was going to get me in with some judge in Albany and all. Or how, if he did get to Congress I could become his legislative assistant and everything. And while he was talking I couldn't see the ground," she says, falling silent, studying the hairbrush in her hand. Whether from the effect of the marijuana or it's the illusion of the low light, but she seems hypnotized by the fibers of the hairbrush.

"What do you mean you couldn't see the ground?"

"I mean I got no sense of reality." She pauses to dah-dee-dah-DAH a passage on the tape, then resumes the rhythmic stroking of her hair. "Springhill Avenue. That's you. Wow, I remember as a kid coming up to Springhill, we must have been handing out circulars for my uncle, and I almost tiptoed. It was like peeking around the corner of the living room on Christmas morning."

"That's ridiculous."

"I know that now. But the point is that you've got a place there. Not just a house, you know what I mean?" she said with a preemptive exasperation, "but a place. Turf. Like Harvey Washington has a place with his friends and almost all the kids down at the University, they've got a place. But not me—this is what I was thinking when Wriston was talking the other day. He's fixing up rooms for me that I don't want. They'd be okay, but he's fixing them up, and I want to do it myself. Do you understand?"

"What if Kuslowski had come back?" I say and she looks at me and smiles wanly, the heavy upper lip in sensuous disproportion to the lower.

"I've thought of that. I never felt part of my neighborhood, of Slab City. I can't even speak Polish. Not that I was ashamed of my family, of what my father did. Quite the contrary. But the whole neighborhood; I never felt like it was mine. No, if Frank had lived, he would have to go with me somewhere or . . . else . . ." and the boy cries in his sleep, interrupting her, though she apparently was not going to say more.

"So what are your plans?" I ask when she comes back. "Are you going to seek the fellowship of some campus bomb squad or what?"

"That's not my hang-up," she says, sinking into the sofa, legs doubled under. "It's hard to implicate those thin copper rods my old man turned out with the promotion of technocracy. So I don't have any aggressive reactions to pull him down, however symbolically."

It's not easy to talk to girls these days. The old topics are out and you have to spend a lot of time at the library.

"You always go after the young ones, don't you," Pug Connors says the other day. We were driving up to Ed Van Buskirk's farm to talk him into organizing a Farmers for Ferguson Committee. "This little Kuslowski widow, now—she's a neat twist."

"You might find it hard to believe," I say, "but ours seems to be an intellectual relationship." Connors rolls his eyes and the car swerves slightly on Route 19.

"Okay," he says after several miles of stunned silence. "What do you two talk about?"

"It's hard to explain," I answer, "but the basic subject is about finding her a place to live." Our Great Leader nearly drives off the road with that one. "I knew you wouldn't understand," I tell him.

"Yeah, and you do?" he replies, and I look out the window. The roadsides and fields are overrun with groundhogs this year.

"I have a sister, Marie, who wanted to be a nun," L. said. She leaned forward to examine her nails. She was unaware the loosened kimono draped open. Anyway, the rules had already been established. It was no more than a negligent display; a natural insouciant tit.

"Those women in the Middle Ages. They really weren't being locked away or punished in those convents. More likely they were getting together, because they didn't like what was outside. You see," she picked up the brush once again and pulled it from the crown of her head all the way through her hair, "I'm not just talking about a place, like a street or a neighborhood. Harvey Washington has got his community on his skin. You see? You're a member of a machine, that's your turf. Even those jerks at the cemetery this afternoon, those Legionnaires with their wooden guns, they've got something going. But not me."

"Why don't you join a sorority down at the University," I said, and would you believe it, she seemed to take the suggestion seriously? She stopped brushing her hair, paused to give the suggestion a fair trial, and shamed me. I was also getting sleepy. The steady murmuring of the tape deck, the rhythm of the low-keyed jazz softly beat upon my weariness, softening up and straightening out all of the tangles. The calendar turned to June upon the midnight air.

"Initially, you asked me," she continued, "why I didn't join the groups that go for violence and I was trying to explain, to myself as much as to you." She had put the brush away and was plaiting her hair into one thick braid. "I agree with them, you know, about this being a consumer-collectivist society but I'm just not ready to blow it up. Hey, are you going to sleep? But I don't want to join it either."

"How come you're going into the law, then?" I say with my eyes closed. I am experiencing a clairvoyant weightlessness. I know it's not possible to get high from just being in a room where the stuff is smoked, and the windows are open besides. Still it was a strange sensation.

"I've been asking myself a lot of questions about that too," L. said. "Like whether it's something I really want to do or whether in some way my family pushed me into it. Or whether I'm only doing it as some sort of a class distinction."

I drifted off somewhere around here, though I vaguely remem-

ber telling her about the Judge's hope that I would join the firm;
Bryan and Bryan. The traffic outside tells me it's late morning
when I awake though I keep trying to tell myself it's not. I was
supposed to meet Ferguson at a dam dedication way up in the
county, and the minority leader was going to be there also. The
apartment was empty, silent. There was a note on the kitchen
door directing me to orange juice and instant coffee but I had no
time for that.

"Listen," I explain to Pug, "if we *had* got a picture of Howie
with the Old Man and we *had* got it in the papers, it would have
cost him votes not gained. You know how people around here
feel about New York City Democrats." The minority leader is
from Queens.

"You know what I think," Pug says, his eyes opening with the
wisdom of the world in them. "I think that Polish sausage is too
spicy for you. Your indigestion is not what it used to be and you
can't chew it up so well."

"Believe me, there's nothing like that going on. She's an interesting girl."

"Sure she is," Connors says. "Why don't you find a nice Irish
girl; settle down. Have a family."

"Oh, fuck off."

Captain Billy Brown is dead. Or if he's not, then he's in a bad
way, *non compos mentis*. That's the only thing that can explain
the crazy way some of those Cade County people are acting. If
he did die, who would know the difference? They could rig up a
dummy in that bed, plug in a tape with someone imitating his
voice, hook a rubber tube with a bellows on it to the cigar stub,
turn down the lights and admit visitors briefly.

The other night I was telling L. about my Big Tape Recorder
in the Sky theory. We had been listening to her tape deck play
back some Earl Hines over which she had put some of her own
music. I got her laughing with the picture of the little green men
landing on our blasted cinder still going around in space, finding

this small black box and playing back the tape. All they hear is "Aw, shit!"

"Maybe that's why all these people are so upset about the government putting us all down on tape—not that it invades a citizen's privacy under the Bill of Rights," I said, "but because it's somehow sacrilegious. You know, we've lived with a sense of invaded privacy for a long time; Santa Claus is coming to town, and he knows when you've been had. That sort of thing. But now it's man-made, and maybe that's why people are screaming; because of what goes on in the plain brown wrappers of our minds, we're suddenly faced with a double jeopardy, electronic and divine. Not only Santa, but Max Ears down the street is going to have a complete file on everybody."

"That's wild," Laura said. "You know, you could make a lot of money with that idea. The kids all read science fiction these days. Why don't you make a story out of that, I bet you could clean up."

But it was payment enough to make her laugh, payment enough.

The Arthursburg Baptist Abyssinian Church had their annual blowout yesterday. "What do you mean you can't go? I sent you tickets." Ferguson looks dumb, tongue pushed into his cheek like a cud.

"Well, shit, Tommy, I already got three picnics and a turkey supper I got to go to tomorrow. Why do I have to go to a boog barbecue?"

"Because everyone else will be there. It's a tradition in this area. Everyone goes. You've got to be there."

I felt sorry for him, for the sour look on his face. One of the hazards of this sort of campaign is the pounds of sticky mashed potatoes, cardboard turkey, and gelatinous dressing a candidate must consume with obvious satisfaction. "Say, this is first-class," was Matt Wriston's pet phrase while sampling the gooey slush. He did it very well.

"You come in, chat with the Reverend Hood, have a plate, talk amiably with your table mates, and then pay a call on the ladies in the kitchen."

"Are you going to be there?" he asks suspiciously. All this in

front of the headquarters we opened in Sinnemok, across from
Minkus' real estate office. It had been a small turnout, as I expected. One or two committeemen, a few guys from Wriston's
old campaign that I called to come over, and finally Minkus
himself breezed in, extending his hand for us to touch and
speaking down low in his throat.

"Of course it's a Wednesday night," the county leader said,
looking down the nearly deserted main street. His little eyes
kept switching from Helen Ferguson to a couple of the cheerleaders, as if he were deciding which one he would strip. "But
you should have seen Cranston's opening," Minkus smirked,
preparing us for some fantastic joke. "Two people, that's all.
And who were they?" He held onto Howie's arm to support the
mirth that wracked him. "Me and a drunk who stumbled over
from the Palace Bar."

"Yes sir, give a hand to Howie . . . give a hand to Howie,"
this old lady said, trotting up to us in tempo with "My Beautiful Balloon" playing on a record player. The rock band couldn't
make it.

"Howie," I make the introductions, "this is Florence Rocas
who's going to run your headquarters down here."

"Well, I sure appreciate you're helping me, Mrs. Rocas."

"Just call me Flo—if I can call you Howie. Yes, sir," she says
to no one in particular and still holding onto Ferguson's hand.
"He's my boy!"

"Do you want a picture?" Red Tompkins asks. He's been
skulking around us, camera in hand, a big-game hunter scouting a
chicken farm. So we set up a shot; Howie shaking hands with
Flo Rocas, Minkus leering up at Helen and one of the two
committeemen on hand on the other side.

"He's my boy!" old lady Rocas says. Blip goes the flash. Another historical moment recorded. What Howie doesn't know is
that Flo Rocas is Ernie Minkus' sister's mother-in-law and we're
paying her $2.50 per hour. We also rented the storefront through
Minkus' real estate outfit, and the commission was a little more
than the usual ten percent.

"I'll have to check around," Pug Connors tells me. "There's
going to be one sweet fight down there when Captain Billy pas-

ses on, that's for sure. But I think what you picked up in Arthursburg was just some jitters. Cranston is losing ground, and
they're worried." We were clanking along in the pickup truck. I
had offered to use my car but he wanted to use the truck, maybe
to make the visit to Van Buskirk an official one. "Our boy
scored pretty good, I hear."

With some it's a way of stealing one hand into the opening of
the suit jacket to smooth down the tie. Others have a peculiar
way of waving a hand, a shy waggle of fingers. Some tug at an
ear and yet others have a brisk style of confrontation; hand
snapped out, grip made, eyebrows jerk up and the mouth set in
the grimace of a comic mask, which might be the most honest
pose of all.

I watched Howie arrive at the Abyssinian. He came in nearly
kicking his toes, looking around like he was sizing up the oppos-
ing team on the court and then he shook hands with someone.
And there was the trademark. When he put his hand out, the
long arm was held stiffly straight and he compensated by pulling
his right shoulder back, as if to make room for the greeting in a
confined space. It was awkward-looking but there was also
something genuine about it. Man to man. And awkward is sometimes good, especially around here.

I'm sitting over in the far corner of the church basement.
Long tables covered with white paper have been set up, plates
and cutlery rattle. This sitting is about half white and half black.
Some of Harvey Washington's boys are working the tables, efficient, unsmiling, and smooth. I'm sitting with the assistant treasurer of Cade County, the fire marshal of Cade County, and the
commissioner of jurors of Cade County. Without their titles it's
hard to tell them apart. Like the pros they are, they have the
wall behind them, so they can safely see everything that goes on.

"Evening, gentlemen, we're glad to have you join us."

"Reverend Hood."

"Hello, Reverend."

"Do you have everything you want?"

"Oh, wonderful, Reverend," the fire marshal says. "As always, the best food anywhere. Just terrific." He wads up a piece
of roast pork and shoves it down his gullet.

About then Howie comes down the stairs, followed by Helen

and then almost immediately by Matt Wriston. They must have pulled into the parking lot together. Reverend Hood goes over to greet them. Howie gives him the stout-fellows-together grip. Matt gives his casual but not unfeeling bony clasp, looking out from beneath that Cro-Magnon brow, "Hello, hello, hello."

There's an unwritten rule that no real campaigning is done at church suppers, except one or two Catholic churches where the priests are politically oriented, but those candidates who don't show up at the Arthursburg Abyssinian for a plate of greens, roast pork, and sweet potatoes usually hear about it in November. Helen Ferguson is carrying on an animated conversation with a black matron, apparently knowing her from someplace else, and Howie looking down on them with that gagged look. I wish he sometimes did not always look so much of a rube.

"How's your boy doing, Bryan?" the commissioner of jurors asked.

"We're coming up, I guess," I answered. "Of course it's down here we've got to cut it."

"Oh, I don't think you got anything to worry about down here," the man said, looking sidewise at the assistant treasurer of Cade County. They exchanged small smiles, and I felt my breath get short, as if I were suddenly flung up several miles. It could be a put-on, they're like that. On the other hand, they're not the kind of freebie loose-tongues who talk just to hear the noise.

"Do you think so?" I manage to get out, manage to sound casual, but they're a wary bunch and their heads, in unison like cattle at a feed trough, bend over their plates. "How's Captain Billy?" I said, just to change the subject, if not the predicate. It was as if I had kicked them under the table. All three heads bob up, one with gravy running down his chin, another with mouth of half-chewed meat, and the third with a small dab of sweet potato between lip and nose, an exotic mole.

"He was fine the last time I saw him," the fire marshal said. "When did you last see him?" he asked the assistant treasurer.

"Why just a few days ago. He was fine," the assistant treasurer agreed.

"I heard he was just fine," the commissioner of jurors concurred.

"Howdy there, boys," Ferguson said, coming over with his plate of food. I see Helen across the room already sitting down, chatting with several ladies of the congregation. Making the introductions, I see Matt Wriston start toward us, but there's no room and he takes a place at a table with a lot of children.

"Let me give you a tip, Howie," one of the three leans toward him. "You better go back an' get a little more on your plate, or the Reverend Hood might cost you some votes." There is only a small pile of collards and a dab of sweet potato on Ferguson's plate. He's pacing himself for the three or four similar dinners he must attend in the next two hours. Howie seemed wounded by the remark and hung his head mournfully over his plate, picked at the greens with his fork. I was about to defend him when I noted the corner of his left eye tighten up.

"I know it," he said softly. "But I tell you, I'll shoot them, but I'll be damned if I'll eat them." There's a sudden stillness in our corner. Finally, the assistant treasurer gets his voice.

"Eat what?"

"Groundhogs," Howie said simply, forking up some sweet potato. It was the fire marshal one had to feel sorry for, because he had just gulped down a wad of meat. Was it a put-on, his button eyes implored? They knew Ferguson was a big hunt-and-fish man. They also thought him to be a guileless dummy. I watched the fire marshal. He was making a valiant effort. The swallowed mass rose in his throat, past the esophagus, and there the man's true colors broke out. For rather than permitting it to spew all over the table, you could see him, by a sheer act of willpower, force the food up into his sinuses, into his inner ear, behind his eyes and whatever other cavities available in his fat head.

"He'll be blowing roast pork out of his nose for the next month," I told Howie. We were in the parking lot behind the church. Helen had gone to get the car, while Ferguson made his tour of the kitchen, chatted with Reverend Hood.

"Actually," Howie says soberly, "groundhog is good eating, but you have to soak it in vinegar for a long time before it's cooked. I got a few in our freezer."

I just called L. and she said she didn't want me to come over. I could hear the music playing in the background.

"Somebody there?"

"No. Nobody's here," she answers.

"Well, why can't I come over. I just want to listen to some music, talk over the day."

"That's just it," she says with a slight lilt, not quite a giggle. I can almost smell the stuff over the wire. "Maybe you should not come here anymore. It makes me feel bad, you know? Like one of those uptight CT's."

"We can change that."

"We've been all through that," she says, her voice is away from the mouthpiece. "Oh, hey, I auditioned today," she says brightly, coming closer to the mouthpiece and I pressed it tighter to my ear.

"Auditioned for what?"

"For a band. In Albany."

"You mean a dance band . . . playing music?"

"Yeah, sure. Just a minute, will you . . ." she says and there's a clunk as the phone is put down. The music rolls along in the background. The boy has probably had a dream of some sort and she's gone to comfort him. Except that she's gone for a long, long time. I have time to make some corrections on Howie's position paper on rural medical scholarships.

HOWIE: Something has just occurred to me. You're putting out the idea that scholarships be awarded to kids from rural areas to medical school. Fine. But why must they even become GP's? If the need is so critical as we've painted it, why not have some of them become like the old-fashioned midwives, or maybe like the armed services medical corpsmen? There must be some survey somewhere that shows the great number of cases involve things like broken bones, minor contusions, etc. Anyway, ailments capably handled by someone with the training, say, of a corpsman. Doesn't the article on the Mexican plan say something about this aspect?

Of course, you might get slammed by the AMA for such a suggestion as this. It might be better, if you think it useful, to keep it in the drawer until you get in.

Then I can hear this shouting or loud talking over the music, but it's hard to say whether it's on the tape—some sort of a blues singer maybe—or what. Where the hell did she go? Did she fall asleep, forget that I'm hanging on? The state chairman used to have an assistant who when he was being bothered by some hack would say, "Just a minute, So-and-So, I'm all alone and I've got to answer this other line." Then he'd put the guy on hold, checking back every minute or so to see if he was still on. Finally, there would be dead air.

"Hi, you still there?"

"Yes, where the hell were you? Who's that shouting?"

"Oh, it's one of those commercials on TV," she says. "Listen, I got to go."

"What's this about auditioning for a band?"

"I'll tell you later. Bryan, I really got to go. I've got a final in history tomorrow at eight. See you." And there's a click.

I don't remember any television set in her apartment.

Well, let's go over some figures. In round numbers, we have 8,000 enrolled Democrats here in Yost. Minkus had around 3,000 in Sinnemok. The big prize is down in Cade; 75,000, according to the Blue Book.

Few of that number will show up in a primary; say about half to be generous, and most of that will be an organization vote. We've got the city of Yost sewn up and nearly everything out in the county except for Green River and Hunnicutt, but Wriston is welcome to them.

I can't write Sinnemok completely off. Minkus probably doesn't know which way he's going yet, even though Wriston may have slipped him a card. He's waiting to hear more from Cade. So are we all.

On paper it looks impossible to overcome the clout that Captain Billy can swing. Say we get everyone in Yost *and* Sinnemok, that's still only 11,000 about. If the boys in Cade only brought out their hard core, about twenty percent of the total, they'd still come up with about 14,000.

The last poll indicates a terrific upswing of people knowing who Howie Ferguson is in Cade County. He's gone from a ten percent factor when we started out to a fifty-two percent last week. This door-to-door storming has paid off at that. Also, we're spending nearly five hundred dollars a week with the two radio stations in Hinton City, not to mention the newspapers. But can we assume the same people who recognize Howie's name will also vote for him?

"I want to tell you something, boy," the Judge said once. "To assume anything in politics is tantamount to assuming the position."

The other day in Arthursburg. Just as I put Howie and Helen into their station wagon the Cranston party wheels into the church parking lot. There are two cars, one of them with the emblem of the district attorney's office on the bumper and the other a sedan that belongs to the Cade County sheriff's office. The two black politicians in the entourage wear shiny suits and scuff the heels of their cordovans as they yell to acquaintances standing outside the vestibule. There are several of those bland-faced goons that I've seen around Captain Billy's house, wearing the same sort of silky suits. Their eyes search the lot, the roof of the church, the big maples in the front lawn. There's a good deal of joshing, cackling, calling to one another and to others attending the church supper. Also two, three, six, and then three more car doors open and slam, open and slam, slam, slam; seemingly many more doors than the two cars could possess.

I suddenly feel very sorry for Howie and for myself as well. The Flash from Alton looks just that; the Flash from Alton. His pretty wife is undoubtedly something you might look at in a supermarket, maybe even twice. There are no women in the Cranston party, and there is something very hard, very businesslike and very serious about the whole group.

"Hello there, Tommy," Cranston comes over, a cordial hand out. "How's that splendid mother of yours? Mrs. Ferguson, so nice to see you. How's it going, Howie?" He bends over to speak through the car window. "No, don't get out, don't get out.

I've got to go inside and you probably are behind schedule like me. Say, you're doing fantastic things down here. Everywhere I go, people say you've just been there. Making a lot of friends. Yes, sir."

"It was his attitude," I tell Pug over the clash and roar of Little Ben. "He obviously has the whole thing in his pocket. Or is damned sure he has."

"Who was with him?" Pug asks.

"Oh, just the usual bunch."

"Can you remember specifically?" he asks. He hangs over the wheel of the truck, steering with his shoulders.

"Well there was that Negro committeeman from the Bottoms."

"Wade."

"Yes. And he had another black committeeman, I suppose he was. Then there were those usual altar-boy hoods that are always around."

"Which ones?"

"Oh, how the hell do I know. Ralph or Jack or Tony or whatever their names are. They're all the same."

"That's where you're wrong, pally," he says, staring out the windshield.

"What's going on?" I say. "When do I get let in on the secret?"

"Here we are," Pug says, turning into the long dirt road that goes to Ed Van Buskirk's farm. "I'll tell you later." But he never does. But I'm wondering, why shouldn't Cranston be confident?

Saturday

We're coming down to the wire. Primary Day is a week from Tuesday; ten days to go.

I kept calling L. last night until nearly one this morning. No answer. Then later this morning, "Where were you?"

"Working." Of course I had forgot.

"Can I see you this afternoon?"

"I have to be at the restaurant at five," she yawns. I can imagine her stretching out in bed, wearing . . . what?

"That's early, isn't it?"

"Yes," yawns again, "but some of the girls want to start a union or something. So we're having a meeting."

"Well, how about lunch? I know a place that has great spiced crab." It also has a few cabins in the woods.

"I've already promised Jakie I'd take him to a cartoon show and that starts at eleven o'clock."

"Well, what time is it over?"

"Oh, I don't know." Something rustles. She's probably changing position or pulling the sheet up to cover herself. "Maybe around one o'clock."

"Well, could I meet you then?"

"When?"

"After the cartoon show."

"You mean with Jakie too?"

"Well, okay. What time are you taking him to your sister's?"

"Not until I was on my way to work." There's a long silence. Is she looking up at the ceiling, studying the water stain around the light fixture? Has she drifted back off to sleep? Or is she thinking about the same thing I am? "Bryan," her voice is fuzzy but also changed, as if she suddenly realizes she's talking to me. "Two o'clock. Okay?" Click.

Bart Keesler is as discreet as the doctors who send him their business. He knows from the prescriptions he fills who has what and, after nearly thirty years in business, he can usually judge whether the disease is fatal and how long the customer has to live. Nevertheless, I am not going to stroll in and buy a pack of Trojans like some sixteen-year-old kid.

I guess they don't buy them anymore either, judging from the amount of clap that's going around. But I mean a sixteen-year-old in my day. Who does buy rubbers these days? Anyway, it's a hell of a thing: there isn't a damn drugstore that I can think of where I can go without someone knowing me. It's silly I know but — I just can't do it. One of the minor but no less complicating aspects of living in an area like this; a commitment of any kind immediately becomes public when made.

Last night, Alma had pot roast which she warmed up when I came in. After we left Van Buskirk's, Pug and I went on a tour of the county, checking out some of the town chairmen we were sure of. Then he turned Little Ben south and we ended up in the late afternoon in Sinnemok at Minkus' barbecue in Flatrock. Howie was already there ahead of us, going from table to table, shaking hands, smiling, how-de-dooing. Behind him one of the cheerleaders was handing out favors, ball-point pens to the men and small kitchen sponges to the women. The sponges have a red hand printed on it with HOWIE die-cut into the palm. You can imagine the number of jokes we've had on this one.

They have a pretty good turnout. Ernie Minkus was moving around with his sense of importance barely under control. There's no sign of Cranston or Wriston, though someone has put Wriston's brochures around on the long tables.

"Fellow Democrats," Minkus breathed into the p.a. system. "We have a distinguished guest with us. A good neighbor of ours and one of the outstanding Democrats of the state, John Connors, chairman of the Yost County Democratic Party. Nice to see you, Pug." A splatter of applause from the people inside the pavilion.

Helen Ferguson stood near the beer counter, holding Howie's raincoat over one arm and chewing the inside of her cheek as she watched the scene. It's an off-guard moment, one of several I've caught her in lately. She's thinner, with faint blue shadows under her eyes. Rather appealing.

"Can I buy you a beer?" I said and she makes a sick face.

"This is our third barbecue today," she answered. "We have two banquets and a spaghetti supper tonight yet."

"You look great anyway. Only a week to go." She nodded slowly, watching Howie move down the aisle of barbecue eaters. He's developed a good style of pressing the flesh, a sort of hand-over-hand motion reminiscent of Rockefeller's without the impression you get from the latter of a short man tippy-toeing through chin-high water.

Minkus strolled over to extend his hand and take Helen by the elbow. He moved his hand to her waist, a brief stay, perhaps a testing squeeze, then the hand dropped, the large signet ring on the little finger ever so slightly brushing her flank, rustling her dress. All the while he talked about how well Howie was doing. Her face becomes pink and she's gritting her teeth underneath that Marilyn Monroe smile. He was called away to give a confidential ear to one of his people.

"Has he spoken yet?" I asked her.

"Yes. Just before you came."

"How did it go?" She shrugged her shoulders as if to say, fine—why shouldn't it? "Well, hang on, Helen. It's almost over." She looked at me with those big blue eyes.

"It's not almost over and you know it, Tommy. It's just beginning—no matter what happens on Tuesday, it's just beginning."

"Don't look at me?" I said. "He could have said no."

She shook her head. "He didn't have a chance. You guys," and her voice almost broke, she waves a hand toward Minkus who had just joined Pug Connors, "you guys. It's almost like you carry a disease that doesn't affect you but which you pass on to other people. You don't even know him!" she said with a peculiar laugh. I have to get her out of there right away, and she let me steer her beyond the glare of the pavilion lights. The golden light of the lowering sun seemed to restore some of her own color.

"Listen. Listen. Get hold of yourself."

"You all have an idea of what he's like and . . ."

"Helen. Now just settle down." She paused, takes a deep breath.

"I can barely remember what our life was like," she said after a moment. "Two months—just two months. Oh, I'm sorry," she said patting me on the shoulder and turned to walk in, laughed. "You know, I'm not much better than the rest of you."

"How's that?"

"Oh," she looked down at the ground, then quickly away, "I'd probably be in a better frame of mind if I could get him to myself now and then." Howie was at the temporary bar by the pavilion's entrance, waiting for us.

"C'mon, woman," he exhorted her. That's his style—the All-Star player firing up the team. "We got to get to Prussian's Run for that ham supper."

"Howie, Howie," her calm voice temporarily blanketed his anxiety. "That's not until seven o'clock; we have time to go home, you can take a shower, have a rest."

"But I got a date to meet Red Tompkins at that urban development in Hinton City. Right?" he asked me.

"That's right," I answered, remembering and somehow feeling guilty. "But we can change that until tomorrow."

"Naw, hell, let's get it over with tonight," he almost snarled.

"Also," Helen tried again, "Doreen's been with us all day, and we should take her home before we do the rest of the schedule."

"That's all right, Mrs. Ferguson," said the sixteen-year-old who wears the letter *H* on her sweater. She's having a great time, and you can see she just loves being with the candidate. "Tomorrow's a Saturday and I can sleep late."

"So what are we waiting for?" Howie said, swinging off toward their station wagon. It's got a big sign strapped on top of it, FERGUSON FOR CONGRESS. And this catches me up because the office is not mentioned on most of his materials, perhaps an unconscious but not irrelevant omission. Sometimes a race becomes more important than the office. But for Congress? Good Christ, what have we come to?

"You look terrible," Alma says when I sit down at the table. "Do you have to go out tonight?"

"Well, I've been up since three this morning," I tell her. "Had Howie down at the parking lot of the paper company to meet the changing of the shifts. He really went over very well. Almost all of the men recognized him immediately."

"Wait and see what happens during the real election," she says. "He won't get within a hundred feet of that place."

And that's probably true. During Wriston's campaign in '62, the management of the paper company wouldn't let him even stand on the same side of the road as the parking lot—sent out the company guards to drive us off—while they let Mr. Green come right inside the building. Of course, Matt had come down pretty hard on the pollution the outfit causes, but it is no secret how the management registers. They'll let Howie stand around during the primary, but it will be different in November.

"Where have you been?" I ask her. "This isn't your bridge club day?" Alma serves me my dinner all dressed up. "No," she says, sitting down to her coffee. "I've been downtown, talking to the real estate people."

"You're really serious about moving to Florida, aren't you? How do you know they'll let you plant a garden in that trailer camp?"

"You think this is funny, don't you," she answers. "That I'm some sort of funny old woman. But just wait and see. And for your information," she says, getting up to bring over a lemon meringue pie, "most of those places have one big garden that everyone helps out with, if they want to."

Well, it's her house. She can do with it what she wants to. But what the hell am I going to do with all that junk on the sun porch. Maybe I can give it to some university.

I kept calling L. from the pay phone at the Home Spot. No answer. She was working, of course, and I had forgot it. Hanging on to the instrument, listening to that buzz-buzz, buzz-buzz, I also think of Helen Ferguson. Maybe the mirror over the bed was her idea. All she was trying to do this afternoon was to get her husband alone for a few minutes. Perhaps they dumped Miss H. at a malt shop for a half an hour and found a secluded spot by the side of a back road. I pictured the two of them rolling around in the back of the station wagon, threshing about on the posters and glossy brochures, giving more than a hand to Howie. I hung up, feeling dirty.

". . . 'lone by the telephone, Tommy?" Tiny slowly turned behind the bar, black eyes following me back to where I had left my beer.

"Where is everybody?" I asked. The place was practically empty and this a Friday night. Just a few oldsters back in the corner, watching a Western on TV. "Where's Harvey Washington and his crowd?"

"They haven't been in in awhile," Tiny said. "They got exams about now, don't they? Probably doing their books." While he was talking, I noticed the few graying hairs on his close-cropped skull. "Say, I see by tonight's paper that the union council has endorsed Matt Wriston," he gave me that sleepy smile.

"Who needs them," I said, thinking, we do. "You're getting gray. You ought to dye your hair."

"Should I stick with black?" he asked.

I'm going up these clattery steps above the Ace Cleaners this afternoon, remembering old man Krueger who used to live on the third floor. He was one of the last of the old-timers when Pug took things over, never got out of his chair by the front window overlooking the street. But I stop at the landing on the second floor.

The door of her apartment is unlocked, I somehow knew it would be, and I walk in wondering if she is somewhere inside — waiting for me. And this gives me a partial hard-on, which in turns makes me sorry that I didn't drive somewhere to a distant drugstore. (Sudden image of myself, hobbling into a drugstore just across the Pennsylvania border, "A pack o' Trojans — quick!") The place is silent, no tape or record player going. In the living room, a note pinned to the sofa, *"Be right back."* There's a hiss of steam from downstairs. Somebody's pants are getting pressed.

Having never really been in the bedroom, and so as not to be a complete stranger if the occasion should arise, I check it out. It's a small room with one window that looks out over the W. T. Grant's parking lot in back. The dimensions were not designed to accommodate the bridal bedroom suite and were it not for personal items and pictures, the place resembles the backroom of a furniture store, a corner where stuff is stored to gather dust until the inventory sale. There's a double bed, a large bureau, two bedside tables, a vanity with mirror and a chair — all in heavy, blond modern. A small cot is set up at the foot of the bed, which cuts down on the maneuvering space even more.

How about that so-called teen-age orgy ring that the young Hancock boy was running in the backrooms of the family furniture store a few years back? Actually, he just let a few kids use the place in return so he could watch, I guess, since he's a little on the queer side. Demonstrations on the demonstrators. Wasn't one of Matt Wriston's nieces mixed up with that? She took off for San Francisco some time ago, disappeared.

So I am standing in the doorway of her bedroom having lustful thoughts when the phone rings. Now in similar situations in movies and TV dramas, the stranger alone in an empty apartment generally lets the phone ring and ring, all the while the tension building up, the background music becoming more suspenseful—and then when he finally picks it up, says hello, there's an ominous click on the other end.

The bell also sets off one of those *déjà-vu* experiences: I have come up these steps before, entered her seemingly deserted apartment, her presence is pervasive. The phone has rung before. Maybe these moments of extra-consciousness, or whatever they are, are part of the tape-recorder. Maybe they represent the points in the endless playing where the tape head shifted from one track to another. Perhaps these moments of *déjà-vu* are the places we expired during a previous run-through of the continuous tape. Did I pick the phone up in another version on the tape, or did I let it ring unanswered?

"Oh, hi," L. says. "Have you been waiting long? Listen, I'm here at my sister's. She had to go out shopping. I don't know when she'll be back. But I can't leave Jake here alone."

"No."

"I'll be there as soon as I can. Make yourself comfortable."

"Too bad you don't have a TV. I could watch a ball game," I say.

"Yeah," she says. "I had to give it back. I only borrowed it for a few days. See you soon."

BONNIE BOBBIN

and her

S-O-O-PER SEXTET

There's this glossy brochure on the table by the telephone showing a buxom blonde blowing into a trumpet and behind her is a six-piece all-girl orchestra. The upswept beehive hairdos date the picture, and the girls in the band wear black leotards with stylized abbreviations of a tuxedo shirt, wing collars, and black bow ties, hip-length black hose.

This swinging jazz-rock group is one of the hottest attractions on our list. Six outstanding girl musicians who can really break it down and who are knockouts each in her own right, and fronted by the one and only Bonnie Bobbin, formerly of the Cincinnati Symphony Orchestra.

You've heard them on Beverly Records, now hear them in person at your next Club Dance or Prom! A whole new repertoire fitted for the NOW SCENE. An expensive-looking, first-class production that is well within most budgets. Now booking for college and fair dates.

". . . folks in Cincinnati are talking how hard it is to keep their eyes off the brass section of the Symphony Orchestra, because of a curvaceous *fille* named Bonnie Bobbin who's good enough to play second trumpet . . ."

— *Danton Walker*

". . . both coming and going, the BB Super Sextette has got it: a tuneful eyeful or an eyeful tuneful . . ."

— *Variety*

". . . a socko attraction for any fair, college weekend or club date. The girls lay on the music and sex, hot and heavy and everybody comes back for more . . ."

— *Billboard*

The white truck of the artificial breeder was parked beside Van Buskirk's barn when we pulled up yesterday. Inside, there was this young guy dressed like an intern except for big rubber boots, covered with mud and grime. He has an arm shoved up the ass of a cow standing in stanchions, chewing her cud. The rest of the herd was outside.

"What are you two guys up to?" Ed Van Buskirk calls from the other side of the buggered Holstein. His face is already sun-burned and he resembles an advertisement for tomato soup.

Ka-Plop-Plop-Flop, goes the shit the man in white is scooping

out of the cow's lower intestine. Pug and I stepped back a few steps, very much aware of our low-cut, thin-soled brogans. The breeder wears a long plastic glove that comes up to his armpit.

"We just dropped by to say hello," Pug says to Van Buskirk, trying to ignore the sloppy, soft concussions at our feet. A card above identifies the cow as Jo's Sunshine Girl and that her milking record is 13,850 pounds.

"Here comes trouble, I said to myself," Van Buskirk smiles and gives the cow an affectionate slap on her flanks. She continued to chew as the breeder makes a final exploration of her anus.

"Lissen, Ed," Pug says, resetting his fedora along his brow. "You saw where the Liberals have put up Van Arsdale as their candidate?" The farmer glanced at the breeder, as if he were ashamed to be talking politics in the cow barn, but he nods. The man in white goes about his business with a professional indifference to surroundings, or the talk.

"Well, we were wondering if you would like to head a committee," Connors says, stepping gingerly around the other side of the cow next to Van Buskirk.

"What sort of committee?" the farmer asks warily.

"Well, you're well known in the area," Pug says. "Maybe a Farmers for Ferguson Committee. You wouldn't have to do anything. Tommy here will line up a few other names and we'll just have an ad in the paper."

"Oh, I don't know, Pug . . ."

"Say," Connors interrupts him before the man could say no. "Why is he doing that?" The rectal orifice and the vulva of the cow were being carefully wiped, disinfectant applied, and then wiped once again.

"To reduce the chance of bacteria contaminating the sperm," the breeder explains.

"The bulls in the old days sure weren't so lucky to have it cleaned up for 'em like that, were they," Pug nudges Van Buskirk who seemed to blush.

"And that's why there were so many aborted calves in the old days," the young man in white remarks disdainfully. Jo's Sunshine Girl, her parts sparkling clean, continues to ruminate, staring straight ahead. The wall in front of her station was papered with the centerfold nudes from *Playboy*, a mosaic of tits and

teeth—and there are others stapled overhead gathering dust and
flyspecks. I wonder if such a prodigal mammillary display is
meant to urge the cow on to even greater milking records.

"Hadn't thought of that," Pug says, though the gray eyes pass
over the boy in a way that says different. "Ed," he turns to the
farmer, "we need this favor."

"But don't you think—our names are similar, Van Arsdale's
and mine—that people will get us mixed up?"

"Let them," Connors replies, spreading his eyes open.

"Oh, I don't know, Pug," Van Buskirk says, holding the
cow's tail up for the young man in white, who has been making
final preparations. A kit box containing a large thermometer,
other instruments, disinfectant, gauze was on the floor to one
side. There was also a stainless steel container full of liquid,
water perhaps, with a plastic tube in it—like an enormously long
soda straw which he withdrew, replaced: somewhat anxiously
looked at the thermometer. He pulls the rod out again, examines
the substance in one end and then fixes a hypodermic plunger
to the other.

"Also," Van Buskirk continues, "I'm out of favor with the
Farm Bureau these days. My name appearing with Howie might
cost him some votes." Jo's Sunshine Girl shivers impatiently,
looks around to see why her tail was still aloft.

"Let's face it," Pug says , watching the freshly gloved hand of
the man in white gently part the vulva lips. "How many Democrat farmers are there around here? But I'm looking ahead after
this boy wins the primary. However, the Farm Bureau feels, Ed,
you are highly respected by most of the farmers around here for
trying to get that union going back then."

As Pug talked, about a foot of the plastic tube has been carefully inserted, tenderly pushed inch by inch into the cow's va-
gina until all but about six inches remains outside. The breeder
makes several rapid but no less careful inspections of everything. Then he stands a little straighter, puts his hand on the sy-
ringe, pauses, and presses the plunger home with an even pressure.

Perhaps there should have been a clap of thunder, a flash of
lightning. There was almost a mournful look on Pug Connors'
face and it would not have surprised me at that moment if he had
removed his hat and placed it over his heart. Flies buzzed, a

chicken cackled outside, and a diesel tractor roared hoarsely in the fields. Only silence inside the barn acknowledges the holy moment when the sperm was injected. Jo's Sunshine Girl could not care less. Her lower jaw continues to roll the cud around in her mouth and her velvet-eyed contemplation of the Misses February through October never wavers.

"Pug, I would like to," Ed Van Buskirk says, primly dropping the cow's tail after the plastic tube had been withdrawn.

"Lissen," Connors says, not giving him a chance to finish. "How's that boy of yours like that special school?"

"Well enough, I guess," the farmer looks away. "It's a long bus ride for him, that's all."

"I know but those special courses make it worthwhile, and you can thank Tommy Bryan here for getting that new legislation applied to—Carl, isn't it?—Carl's condition. Let the state pay for the special classes, right?"

The young man in white has closed up his kit and walks outside to his truck. He returns, boots flapping, but uniform still immaculate.

"Listen, Ed," he says. "Keep an eye on her and call me if there's any trouble."

"Does it always take?" Pug asks him.

"Hardly ever fails," the breeder says proudly. "Mr. Van Buskirk is using the best too. The sperm from this bull, Mountain Top Buddy, has thrown hundreds of calves with nary a dry run."

"You just want to use my name? I don't have to do anything?" Van Buskirk says, affectionately patting the cow on the rump and walking away. Pug is by his side, step for step.

"That's all. You don't have to do a thing."

"Well, okay," the man says. Jo's Sunshine Girl apparently just realized what had happened to her and cuts loose with a mellow "Mooh-ah!"

I was going to tell Laura about all of this but by the time she arrived this afternoon, it is already two thirty and she says she has to leave at three. She's wearing a sleeveless turtleneck jersey and slacks, all white. . . . It does me no good to hang around like this.

But I had the whole thing worked up like one of those modern retellings of old myths. Jo's Sunshine Girl was actually the fair maiden Io and the young man in white was Mercury, or Hermes, bringing Jupiter's sperm and performing this covert coupling under the multiple eyes of Argus — the blind nipples of all those tits on the wall ceiling. Such narrative allusions do not always amuse her.

"What is this outfit?" I ask Laura, holding up the brochure for the all-girl orchestra. "Something left over from Phil Spitalny?" She wrinkles her forehead — Phil Who?

"That's the band I auditioned for the other day."

"You mean this outfit," I say, looking at the picture again. There's something obscene about the group pictured.

"Oh," she laughs. "That picture was taken a long time ago. Even Bonnie Bobbin doesn't play anymore, she just organizes and gets the groups together. There are three or four of them traveling around, all going under the same name, playing for colleges and like that. They're all in their twenties."

"You mean you're interested in doing this?"

"Sure. Why not?" She sits on a hassock, a defiant posturing.

"But what about law school?"

"It doesn't seem so important anymore," she shrugs and looks at the floor. "I can't find an answer when I ask myself, why. Maybe later on."

"But what would you do about Little Jake? How would you take him with you?"

"Oh, that's easy," she says, excited. "Some of the other girls have small children and they travel with them too. Each outfit has a big bus it travels in, and we all take care of each other's children. And then when we're working, there's a woman who's kind of road manager who minds the kids."

"It sounds like fun," I say. Bonnie Bobbin's eyebrows are plucked clean, penciled in, and there's an enameled quality about her face.

"It is," she answers seriously.

"Sounds kind of dykey though," I say, and she laughs. "What's so funny about that?"

"Oh, I don't know," she says. "That really bothers you,

doesn't it. That idea." She stands up, hand on her hip and pushes them out at me. "What would you think if I went gay? Would you say it was a terrible waste? That's the term isn't it, a waste?"

"No, that's not what . . ."

"Well, how do you know I'm not gay anyway?"

"Well . . ."

"Hey," she suddenly darts away, pivots and takes a pose by the tape machine. "How would you like me to put on my little birdie costume for you. You ought to see me in it. Outasight, baby!"

"Cut it out!"

"I remember writing Frank right after I got this job at the bar, and I told him all about this corny costume and about these old guys drooling over it and you know what he wrote back? He wanted me to get someone to take my picture, wearing it, and send him one. How about that?"

"You've got me all wrong," I say, believing it. It may not be time to go but it's certainly no longer reasonable to stay. I can use a few hours making the rounds, sampling my own opinion poll.

"One of us has the other wrong, that's for sure," Laura says. She goes down the hall to the bedroom, there's some rustling of material and then she reappears carrying a plastic garment bag. She throws it over the end of the sofa. "You just won't take no for an answer and you should," she continues in a hurried voice. Her eyes have begun that dance about the room again. "So all right, it's been fun. Educational. Emotionally developing. You taught me about birds and fish and wildflowers." Her eyes pause, almost look at me but then flick away. "But, so what."

"Okay. I'm sorry. Good luck with the band."

"Bryan." She stops me at the door. "It's my exams, my family, I worry about Jakie. I'm changing my whole direction. Okay?" The small mouth broadens, hesitates; then shapes a marvelous smile. "My last exam is Tuesday afternoon," she tells me, not moving from the living room. "I'll feel better then. Tuesday night? What's on your schedule for Tuesday night?" Pug and I are supposed to meet Ferguson at his headquarters here on Tuesday night to go over ideas for the last week. But that will be early in the evening because Howie has to talk to a Democratic club in Cade County later that evening. So I nod — I can make it.

But make her? It's beyond my ability to transform myself into a swan, let alone a white bull. How would Zeus make out with some of these kids today? Golden rain? They'd wash their hair with him, then rinse him down the drain.

And yesterday, I followed that nice serious boy in intern whites out to his truck. He was putting his equipment away explaining to me, very proudly, how they put the bull's sperm into a solution, so that one ejaculation can be used to service many cows, not just one. Also, the scientific-hygienic method of impregnation he'd just demonstrated practically guaranteed the desired results.

He showed me the container of liquid nitrogen which kept the stuff at a temperature several hundreds of degrees below zero. "This tube contains the sperm from a Black Angus bull that's going over to the Butterfield Farms. This one," he fingered another of the long plastic wands. The frozen darts of Eros? "This one is from one of the all-time great Holstein bulls. This is rare stuff, because he is dead."

The obvious question: Who jerks off Jupiter? But I rephrased it for to say it that way would have embarrassed if not insulted him.

"Oh, well," he answered very straightforward. "They used to use an imitation vulva, mounted on two-by-sixes, but that didn't work out very well. The best thing they use now is to get another small bull and let the donor bull hump him until he's about to ejaculate. Then they pull him off and catch it, put it in solution and freeze it. It's a wonderful process to watch."

You suppose that's what they said about Zeus and Ganymedes?

Monday

Quiet Sunday. Quiet Monday. We're spending nearly a thousand this week in newspapers and radio. Pug said over the weekend that there really does seem to be some sort of a division in Cade County. And it was working for us, he thinks.

I'm tired. One week from tomorrow morning before the polls open, I'm heading for the mountains. I can get back around ten, time enough. Everything's all lined up. We've got six deputies, including both of the black ones, driving for us! Of course, they're off duty, out of uniform — but everybody knows. The idiot cards are ready at the printers. Howie is on the last line, which I've always preferred to the top — Wriston drew that. And it's going to cost us, but we've got workers with cars lined up in Cade.

Tomorrow, we start the last week. Tomorrow night I'll be with L. It sounds like we'll make out, but maybe Connors is right; I'm getting too old for this sort of thing. It's going to be hard to give up.

Wednesday

It started with a phone call to police headquarters, about six o'clock last night. Just as I'm finishing supper in the kitchen and am about to leave to meet Howie and Pug downtown. It was a young woman's voice, according to Sergeant McAndrews.

"This is the voice of the Ding-Dong Apocalyptic Party. We demand to interview all three of the Democratic nominees for Congress. We have seized and now occupy the Lafayette Hotel. We are holding our convention there in one hour, seven o'clock. Do not attempt to use force. We have fused dynamite and Molotov cocktails prepared. All three candidates are to appear before us in one hour."

Similar messages were delivered in writing to the *Sentinel* and to the radio station. No one had a clear idea of what the messengers looked like. So Yost County comes of age.

Just now.
"Annie?"
"Oh, hello, Tommy?"
"Annie, is there any word from Pug, yet?"
"Gosh, I don't know. Have you tried his office? He should be at his office." There's that old worried note in her voice.

Next. "Reclamation and Supply, Mr. Connors' office."

"Mabel?"

"Who's this?"

"Tommy — Bryan."

Oh, hello, Tommy. How's . . ."

"Mabel. Where is he?"

"He's at home, Tommy. He called in sick. Some sort of bug."

"Mabel?"

"Yes?"

"Thanks, Mabel." It's a bug all right. A bug called booze. That son of a bitch!

By the time I got downtown, the cops had completely surrounded the old hotel. They were dressed up like something out of the War Between The Worlds; plastic face masks, metal shields, helmets. All sorts of firepower. They had cleared the entire area around the Lafayette, but there must have been a couple hundred people standing across the street on the sidewalk.

"They're up there on the mezzanine," a cop told me. He pointed the muzzle of his shotgun toward the large windows along the second floor front. The shades are all drawn, but there's light inside. Several large sample rooms are there just off the balcony above the lobby.

"Who are they?"

"Some of those bums from down at the University probably," he replied, flipping down his face mask and striding away. I am reminded of Ivanhoe. Whoever they are, they brought their music with them and in between blasts of rock, they shout. They also cheer and sing over the music.

"THIS CONVENTION STARTS AT SEVEN O'CLOCK. TELL THOSE CANDIDATES TO GET THEIR ASSES UP HERE. YOU FUCKING PIGS STAY BACK OR THIS WHOLE BLOCK GOES SKY HIGH.

"TWO-FOUR-SIX-EIGHT — WHO DO WE APPRECIATE;PIG-SHIT, PIG-SHIT, PIG-SHIT!"

There was a wrangle over near the New York Café between

Sheriff Walden and Chief Perrina regarding jurisdiction. The chief wins. "We've got to play this cool," he was saying. "We can't go busting in there like some goddamn Hollywood movie. What if they do have dynamite and explosives in there?"

"They don't have any of that. They'd blow themselves up?" Sheriff Walden answered. He's up for re-election next year.

"How can you be sure?" Perrina replied. "I'm responsible for the safety around here. If you want to be of help, get your men to re-route the traffic."

"Hello, Carl. Tommy. Sheriff Walden." It's Matt Wriston. "This is a deplorable situation, isn't it," he says. His head shakes almost as if he were seized with palsy. "Deplorable."

The whirling red and white lights of the various police and fire vehicles freeze the faces of the mob, the storefronts, the plastic helmets and masks of the cops with a strobe effect.

HEY YOU, MATT WRISTON. HEY YOU, HOWIE FERGU-SON. HEY YOU, MR. DISTRICT ATTORNEY CRANSTON. GET YOUR MOTHERFUCKING ASSES UP HERE . . . ON THE DOUBLE . . . THE DING-DONG APOCALYPTIC PARTY IS GOING TO CHOOSE ONE OF YOU . . .

"The Ding-Dong Party?" someone behind us asks incredu-lously. There are guffaws and giggles.

"There's nothing amusing in any of this," Matt Wriston says, whirling on the anonymous crowd. "This is a senseless attack on the very structure that guarantees every one of us the freedom we enjoy. And it is tragic," he continues, raising his voice and fist simultaneously. I have to admire Wriston, he's ready all the time. "Tragic," he repeats, his fist smacking his palm. "Those young people inside are our children. Children. Yet they have become our enemies. Look at this array of armament here. Ready to shoot down . . . not the Red Chinese . . . not the Russians . . . not some other foreign enemy — but ready to shoot down our own children. Think of that, ladies and gentlemen! Who is responsible for this? It's no time for laughter."

Someone had shoved a bullhorn in his hand for the last part of his oratory, when he was saying, "ready to shoot down our own children . . ." Some people in the back cheered, apparently thinking it was a good idea.

PIGS EAT SHIT . . . PIGS EAT SHIT . . . PIGS EAT SHIT
. . .

"Where is Howie?" Matt asks me. "Maybe together we can make an appeal to them inside and avoid what I fear will be a terrible calamity."

"I don't know," I tell him. "I was supposed to meet him awhile ago, but the headquarters is dark."

"Perhaps he's planning to land on the roof by helicopter," Matt says, with a cunning expression.

"What time is it, Chief?" somebody asks. Perrina looks at his watch. It's ten minutes of seven.

"You're not planning to go in, are you, Matt?" The policeman asks.

"This is one endorsement that perhaps I might relinquish," he replies. The commotion in the street almost overcomes the twanging blare inside the hotel; whining police cars arrive or depart, the shouts and general stir of the several hundred spectators, the buzzing caterwaul of walkie-talkies in the hands and hip pockets of passing policemen, the magnified, unintelligible squawking of bullhorns that change a line of policemen here, reposition a barrier over there.

"What's going to happen at seven o'clock, Chief?" someone asks. He has no answer.

"Hope they go in and kill those little bastards," another voice says.

"Mr. Wriston," a young man with a microphone shoves his way through. "We wondered if we can get some of that statement you just made to the crowd here. Our camera is over there."

"Why, of course," Matt says, and there's just the slightest squint in his eye as he looks away from me.

The question is: if that Old Bull who carried Europa on his back is dead, is there any of his juice still around? We need to thaw it out real fast.

ALMA: "But you must eat something."
      "I'm not hungry."

"And you had no sleep last night."
"I napped a little bit at the hospital."
"Will he be all right?"
"Yes—he's in good shape. Physically."

I can remember almost the same dialogue a few years back except I'm the one that says, "You've got to eat something."

"I'm not hungry," Alma said.

"And you had no sleep last night."

"I napped a little bit at the hospital," she replied. We said no more until we got to the funeral home. I turned into the wide driveway and stopped under the old portico that used to shelter the Kelley family so they could get in and out of their fancy carriages in all kinds of weather.

"Tommy, would you mind going in first? I'll be in in a minute. I just want to sit here awhile." She handed me several folded sheets of paper. "He wrote everything down himself. What he wants."

"Hi-ya, Tommy."

"Hello, Sheriff."

"Lissen—is your mother there—I got some bad news for you. . . . The Judge has had an accident. He apparently tripped or something on those stairs at the hotel going down to the lobby . . ."

"Where is he?"

". . . found him at the bottom, unconscious. He was leaving the game, said he didn't feel well and apparently . . ."

"Where is he?"

"What is it?" my mother wanted to know. She had been reading in the living room but now stood in the doorway of the sun porch. "What's the matter?" I looked at her, as I listened to Sheriff Connors' voice; she had been expecting this phone call for a long time.

". . . at the hospital. And Tommy? It don't look good."

. . . STARTS AT SEVEN O'CLOCK. TELL THOSE CANDI
DATES TO GET THEIR ASSES UP HERE . . .

It is a few minutes past seven by my watch. Chief Perrina puts the bullhorn against his lips, a vain attempt to get the attention of the screechers inside. He turns his head, listens with a quizzical look to the wild music, the shouts and jeers from the second floor of the abandoned hotel. He lowers the bullhorn.

"Hear what I hear?" he asks one of his subordinates. The man looks puzzled, cocks an ear. "We've heard this before, haven't we?" the chief suggests. The scatological litany of the young is repetitive. There are, after all, only a few obscene words in the language that bring up the blood of the average citizen. For this reason, I suppose, no one had noticed it. I get the idea about the same time as the cops around me. We begin to smile at each other, the muscles in the neck ease up, that strange looseness in the bowels fading away. A plainclothes sergeant next to me laughs, thumps me on the shoulder. "How about that?" he says. "It's like a record." But the smile dries up, his eyes become buttons on loose thread as one—two—three BANGS crack from the hotel.

"SNIPERS! SNIPERS!" There are screams from the crowd on the sidewalk. People fall to the ground. The cops move together, take cover, a piece of rehearsed choreography.

POP! the first canister of tear gas crashes through a window on the second floor.

Helen Ferguson is just coming around the corner of the house as I make the top of the steep driveway. This afternoon she's been puttering around in the rock garden behind the house, but she looks as if she's been pulling a plow in ninety-degree heat.

Without speaking, I follow her inside. She's been cleaning house too it seems. Pillows are neatly stacked, also all those books, manuals, reports that used to be scattered over the carpet are in prim piles. They are overdue at the library. The phone rings. She answers, waving me upstairs. Howie is fine, thank you, she says.

The candidate is flat on his back in the circular bed, arms behind his head, morosely staring at the ceiling. When did they remove the mirror? Which one of them took it down and why? Perhaps its incongruous rectangular shape over the round bed was finally too much for his sense of harmony or maybe it's installed somewhere else for a different perspective.

"Howdie, Chief," Ferguson says, leaning up on his elbows, and the ice pack falls off. His smile is lopsided, a good-natured dog that's been kicked once too often in the same side of the head, and the bruise that covers the right side of his face supports the illusion. The eye is swollen shut and is green, purple and black. There's a stitched gash from the eye down to the chin. He returns the ice pack to his face after permitting me an inspection.

"How do you feel?" I ask.

"I'm okay, except I don't think I'll be able to smell anything for a couple of weeks." His voice gets hoarse as he talks. He has to pause for breath. "Some show, huh?" The one good eye regards me with double intensity. Helen has come into the room and leans against the wall. "Haven't heard from Pug," Howie says. "Where's he got to?"

"Oh, he's out working the precincts. He told me to tell you just to rest and be thinking about your victory statement next Tuesday."

"Shit," he says, his tongue curls around a back molar. Then, "Really?"

"Yes," I nod, avoiding Helen's look.

"Waste of time," he says, falling back on the bed. "I really tore it, didn't I?"

"This won't make much difference," I say, somehow trying to believe it myself.

Apparently, Howie had been driving down to his headquarters for our meeting in a pickup truck with a CW receiver. It was set on the police band so he heard the alert. He got to the alley behind the hotel before the cops sealed it off, pulled into the old coal yard, and simply hopped, climbed, and vaulted the four or five fences to the back of the Lafayette.

What was in his mind? He says he thought that if he could get to them first, he'd be able to talk to them, cool the situation. Come up with their support, plus the gratitude of regular citizens. After all, there were not that many years between them. Not many years, maybe, but a lot of miles. I have a theory. He was bored. He had been kept in a shirt and tie for nearly two months. Had his language, his pet expressions edited for two months. Been told what to say, who to talk to, where to go. He

had been taken out of the woods, off of his mountain and mounted dumb and glass eyed as were the animals on his living-room
wall.

It took nearly forty minutes between the time he forced the
window in the rear and when he opened that door into the display room in front. Forty minutes of cautious heel-and-toeing
through the dark, each step selected, set down as if he were
crossing a grove covered with dry leaves. Every time he stood
by a doorjamb, breathing easily, quietly, he could hear the yelling on the second floor and the old building vibrated with the
rock music. The noises outside were another world: sirens, amplified orders, the mumbling of the milling crowd. The interior
was bathed in a pearly light, as if all were underwater.

The back window opened onto the pantry. He made his way
slowly through the dark kitchen, one hand out, to protect against
a scrap of lumber or empty container, a counter edge, to stay
them noiselessly as he edged by. Now to cross the large hall
where his victory party had been. He dropped into a crouch and
crept along the baseboard and came to the swinging doors that
opened into the lobby.

He pushed one slightly; it squealed. He said he held it half-
opened for several minutes, the cramp spreading in his shoulder
muscle. He listened. The bunch above had not heard, too busy
shouting out the front windows. It sounded like the amplifier
was about to blow a fuse. The carefully thought-out, precise
moves that became extreme caution delighted him.

In the lobby now. If he used the wide stairway at the rear, he
would be instantly spotted from the front should one of them
suddenly open the door, come out on the balcony that overlooks
the lobby. He was standing beneath the overhang. It is the only
way to get to the upper floors. The rooms in front adjoin it. The
light from the impromptu convention hall of the Ding-Dong
Apocalyptic Party spills under the doors, filters down the air
space, and reflects upon the small hexagonal white tiles of the
lobby. The floor glows like the bottom of a shoal. There is no
furniture, not even a front desk anymore, that could be climbed
upon. The plywood cubicles that had been rented to a watch
repairman and an accountant take up most of the floor space.

He considers climbing on top of them, but he's afraid their
plasterboard ceilings would not hold him. He decides to shinny

up one of the balcony's supporting posts, an ornate trunk of wild grape thick with clusters of cast-iron fruit; the vine and leaves twining into an esplanade that forms the encircling railing of the balcony. Hand over hand, he pulls himself up the slick column, fingers gripping the hard bunches of grapes. What if the balustrade at the top were rusted or had become loose from the rotting wood? He hooks one hand through razor-sharp tendrils and gradually, legs still wrapped around the column, transfers more and more of his weight. The metal weir creaks, seems to pull slightly away, but it supports him.

Now both hands hooked in the leaves and shoots of the paling, he must pull up his weight, put a foot over. He said it took him several tries, each attempt seemingly more impossible, more difficult, until with a desperate pendulumlike motion, he catches the heel of his right shoe over the top. He has to rest on the floor once over.

Din piles on din in the front rooms, just fifteen feet from where he lies on the floor. The obscenities are shouted, the music blasts. He can hear them moving around inside, he said. For the first time, he is a little nervous. How will they react when he comes through the door? Should he knock first? Were they black? White? Who were they? He hears cheering outside the building, right then. More sirens. The whine and crackle of amplified voices. Why were they cheering? A hanging mob, no doubt.

Well, fish or cut bait, he thinks. He gets up and walks naturally along the balcony. It has just occurred to him that if they were asking to see him, why the commando approach? It had been fun. Somehow more of a test than any of the experiences of the last two months.

. . . STARTS AT SEVEN O'CLOCK. TELL THOSE CANDIDATES TO GET THEIR ASSES UP HERE, a young man's voice screams from inside. It cracks unappealingly. Other voices join in. PIGS EAT SHIT . . . PIGS EAT SHIT . . . Howie waits until they pause to catch their breath. He knocks and opens the door at the same time.

In the open doorway. Several small explosions above him. Instinctively he ducks, hands over his head. He slowly stands up—blinking. Can't believe what he sees. At that moment the first gas canister smashes the window in front of him, striking the right side of his head, ripping open his cheek and knocking him down, stunned. Exploding tear gas fills the old display room as the tape recorder continues to run, the music, screams and challenges blaring through a speaker wedged in an open window . . . THE DING-DONG APOCALYPTIC PARTY IS GOING TO CHOOSE ONE OF YOU . . .

•

"You should have seen the news last night," Alma says this morning.

"I was there," I tell her.

"Sure shot off a lot of tear gas. Some of it even floated up here. I could smell it." The cops had pumped over two dozen gas canisters into the hotel before Perrina could get them back under control. "The man on the news said it really did sound like shots inside. Did it?"

"They were good-sized firecrackers and a couple of them may have exploded together. The device was rigged to the door so when it was opened, a string was pulled — like one of those party poppers."

"It's a wonder your man wasn't shot dead when he came to the window. The camera had just swung up to the front of the hotel when you saw the shade being pulled off and this person standing in the broken window. Couldn't tell who he was or what he was doing. He had this thing in his hand . . ."

"Yes, I know." Near me a civilian tried to wrestle a riot gun away from a cop, shouting — Gimme that, gimme that . . . I'll kill those little bastards when he saw Howie at the window. They finally had to put manacles on the man's legs and arms, drag him away. Howie, choking, gasping in the searchlights and the blood pouring down his face, kept trying to shout something over the pandemonium. He finally held up the silent speaker, and pointed to it. He had a silly grin on his gory face as if he had just bagged a trophy shot. The upturned faces of the multitude, the cops poised for more battle, they stared back at him. For a moment the only sounds on Wentworth were the mechanical whirring of the revolving emergency lights, a sighing sound.

"It's just too bad," Alma says this morning.

From the *Register Herald* editorial this afternoon:

The Democrats are always good for a show in their self-destructive primaries. However, it will be difficult for them to top the act they presented last night in the city of Yost. The results of the bizarre circumstances could have been tragic, as it is, they are merely ridiculous.

It is unfortunate that Howard Ferguson chose to react to a potentially serious crisis with the derring-do of a storybook hero, because up to now, his candidacy had appealed to us most.

Admittedly, his campaign techniques were both flamboyant and extravagant and his various ideas, though agreeable enough, were not startlingly new. On the other hand, we liked his youth, his enthusiasm for people and his obvious eagerness to serve. He also seemed apart from the Brown machine.

However, his melodramatic performance last night indicates a hint of immaturity that has us second-thoughting. Democratic voters next Tuesday seem to have a dilemma; whether to leave Dick Tracy in the funnies or nominate him for Congress.

Of course this is a standard trick of Republicans; to say, I *was* going to vote for you but now . . .

Also, the Hinton paper has been taking its own polls too and they know what we know. That Howie would do damn well against Assemblyman Green.

Howie has read the editorial too when I see him today. Or maybe someone called him. "Well, I guess this gives Cranston a clear shot at it," he says. He pushes his feet over the edge of the bed and struggles up.

"We still have a week," I tell him. "After all, a lot of people think what you did was sort of heroic."

"Yeah, sort of," he answers with a sneer that hurts the sewn-up cheek.

"You mustn't get up," Helen tells him. "The doctor said to be careful because of the concussion."

"Christ," he says, looking at his feet. "What a fucking waste."

I tried to get Connors from the hospital last night. He was at none of his hangouts. No one had seen him. I also thought of L. and called her but she didn't answer. Maybe out watching the fire. Or maybe just out.

While I was standing by the pay phone in the corridor, Helen comes out of the elevator. I had one of the deputies go for her up in Carthage where she had been talking to a Women's Club meeting.

"He's okay," I start to comfort her.

"Okay!" she snapped. I forgot how tall she is, her shoes making her more so. "What do you mean he's okay? Is there anything that's not okay with you?" She started to say something more, but turned away and went down the hall to the recovery room.

I tried another number where Pug might be.

UNLIKE MOST PEOPLE, the Judge's will and testament read in part, I DO NOT DESERVE ANY MEMORIAL TO MY EXISTENCE. NOR DO I WISH ANY MARKER, STONE OR TABLET ERECTED ON ANY SITE THAT WOULD REFER TO MY PRESENCE ON EARTH EITHER BY NAME OR INFERENCE. MY ASHES ARE TO BE DISPOSED OF IN THE MANNER SET FORTH BELOW. A SMALL GATHERING OF FRIENDS COULD BE PERMITTED, IF THEY SO DESIRE . . .

My mother busied herself most of the morning with the flower arrangements on the altar. Since there was no coffin, there were a lot of flowers—I had a wild thought. I had been sitting in the back pew, going over the seating chart with the two city detectives that were going to be head ushers that afternoon. It suddenly came over me we'd have to get rid of those flowers later on. The old phrase came into mind. I pictured myself, a much younger version of myself—or maybe some other kid entirely, dropping off baskets of gladiolas and roses and lilies to nursing homes, hospital wards, and sickrooms all across the county, across the state, or even across the whole country. "Compliments of Judge Bryan and all your friends at the Yost Democratic Club."

That afternoon those of us who were the official mourners, no pall to bear, were waiting in the sacristy for the procession to form. We talked about the weather, the large turnout, about the different personalities appearing at the entrance, and shown to their seats. Some had arrived with police escort, and it had been rumored that Kennedy was sending Sarge Shriver. But I didn't believe that.

Pug Connors looked pretty good, only a slight flush under and around his ears. His eyes were clear and he moved among us, adjusting coat lapels or brushing dandruff from a blue serge shoulder; the captain readying his troops. There was a knock at the door. Not Shriver but the secretary of state.

"Hello there, Pug," he said, moving in, taking my hand, "Tommy, the governor sent me down here, but I would have come anyway, you know that. Your dad and I had some great arguments, but he was always a credit to the people he served on the bench. I'll speak to your mother in a minute."

"Hey," Pug took him by the arm, "I want you to meet our next assemblyman from down here, Matthew Wriston."

"Why, I know Matt, sure." Vigorous hand-pumping, Wriston wearing that pained jack-o'-lantern smile. The organist moved from a moody doodling into the firm chords of the processional.

"Tommy, here, is going to run his campaign," Connors added quickly over the majestic melody.

"Splendid," the state official said, glancing toward me but still gripping the attorney by the hand. "Listen, Matt, between you and me: Green is supposed to be on my side but I just as soon . . . well, you know." He winked and turned a well-tailored back upon us, gripped another shoulder on his way out to rejoin the two state troopers in plainclothes, who had waited outside, anxiously.

With the secretary of state's sweat drying on my palm, I took my place in the double line of men who had been my father's associates and friends and who were now my associates and friends. It was, of course, a place in a ceremony for something already in ashes.

Finally got home about two this morning. Stayed at the hospital, outside his room — not wanting to intrude — until the young doctor on duty assured me he would be all right. Or maybe, I just didn't want to see Helen again, face to face. Anyway, back in the sun porch, kept trying to find Pug. Annie eventually answered the phone. Yes, Pug had come home but went out again. In the Cadillac about ten o'clock. No, she didn't know where he went. She never knew where he went. Would I please not call again until morning?

Kept calling Laura every ten minutes or so, in between times trying to figure out what to do next with Howie, Pug, Laura, Alma—me. It was a warm night. I open the French doors that face the side terrace. The old lilac came in bloom a few days ago and the June night is redolent with its heavy aroma, not one of my favorite smells and certainly not improved by the stench coming up from the city. In the open doorway, phone in hand, I see a tower of sparks spiral into blackness. An offering. One of the walls of the hotel probably.

Mattresses stored on the third floor had been set ablaze by an exploding gas canister and some forward-looking, progressive fireman had turned his back. As I dialed L.'s number again, the dilemma of the Hotel Lafayette was being solved before my eyes. The insurance company would be happy to pay off. The owners would be happy to collect. The urban renewal agency would be happy to get the land cleared. The mayor would be happy to condemn it. The aldermen in the third ward would be gratified with all the new voters eventually lodged in the new apartment units. Another wall must have collapsed, there was a tower of sparks and smoke. The Historical Society would not be happy.

L. never answered the phone but I kept listening to the steady buzz-buzz-buzz-buzz as I looked up at the sky. It also seemed on fire.

𝔉riday

Pug has disappeared like this a couple of times, just before an election, but he's not at any of the usual places. We might still pull this out, but I need him.

Ferguson has been getting a lot of sympathy in the last couple of days. But whether it will offset the other is hard to tell. Which is why I need Connors to start pushing the buttons.

Like today. I met that deputy Homer standing on the steps of the courthouse. I asked him if he was all set for Tuesday and his eyeballs sort of rolled up into his black forehead. "I might have duty," he finally said.

"You know what one of them said to me," Howie mumbled. I was driving him back last night from the meeting with a teamster local down in Cairo. His face still a godawful mess but it made some impression on the membership. "One of those guys said, Hear you been endorsed by the Ding-Dong Party. . . ."

They've traced the tape deck, amplifier and speaker components to a haul made on a music store in Hinton City a couple of months ago. No indication of who did it yet. Perrina says he doesn't have much hope of finding out unless someone betrays them, which is unlikely. No fingerprints, and the voices on the tape are unrecognizable. Of course, it doesn't matter who did it, does it? Them.

Strangely relieved that the electronic gear came from a burglary done awhile back. Why should I be? What does that prove one way or another? L.'s phone has been disconnected, according to the operator. She's probably tootling along with the other girls in the band, right now. Driving through the night in that bus, alternately minding each other's brats while passing around a roach. Well, you can't win them all.

"Look at this," Alma says when I get home tonight. She's holding the evening *Sentinel.* There's a piece down at the bottom of the front page. Not much of a story but the sort of headline that kills:

KERSHAW SAYS "DING-DONG"

CANDIDATE NOT FOR HIM

Worthy Kershaw, the influential Democratic town chairman of Green River, said late today that he was endorsing the candidacy of Matthew Wriston for his party's nomination for Congress.

Reached at his home, Mr. Kershaw said, "I've always been a Democrat and will always support the best Democrat candidate. That man is Matt Wriston." When asked about the candidacy of Howard Ferguson, the popular town chairman replied, "He's the Ding-Dong candidate, isn't he? I'm supporting only Democrats."

". . . painfully regret Worthy's statement," Matt Wriston tells me. There's music in the background, some sort of symphony. "It's the sort of thing I have attempted to eschew throughout this ordeal. How is Howard, by the way?"

"He's fine. But where did Kershaw get this . . . you know as well as I do, Matt, Worthy Kershaw can't put more than three words together at a time." There is no answer, only a scherzo of playful strings, some woodwinds. "Matt?"

"Yes, I'm here."

"Who gave Worthy this little speech?"

"I assure you, Tommy, I don't know. I would do anything I can to correct the impression that I encourage or endorse such slanders."

"How about a statement from you, discrediting Kershaw?"

"I'll be happy to. However, this is Friday. I won't be able to get anything in the paper now until Monday—if they use it then. The primary is the next day. As you know this vile poison will have been at work all weekend."

I know. I taught you that little trick myself, you prick!

Strangely, no word from Cade County. Jack Cranston must be delirious, quietly picking up all the pieces. Maybe I ought to send him a few clippings from the papers around here—just to keep my name in.

This evening: "Annie?"

"Oh, hello, Tommy. Have you tried the office?"

"Annie, it's ten thirty at night."

"Well, they sometimes work late you know. Payroll and all."

"They're not working late." Silence. No music in Pug's house. I refuse to say anything more. I'm determined to make her say something. Anything. It sounds like a hiccough on the other end, then her voice comes through, slurred.

"I don't know . . . I don't know. . . ." The line goes dead.

Monday

I spend the afternoon with Ferguson at his house. Nothing is held back. Frankly explain to him what will probably happen tomorrow. He sits on the ledge around the fire pit, tongue caught in his teeth, holding an ice pack to the bruised side of his face. He looks like he had been kicked in the balls too. Helen is standing at the window, looking out at the mountain.

"Well, shit, what about all those polls?" Howie said.

"They were taken a week, ten days ago," I answered. "I may be wrong—you never know. But I just want you to be prepared. With Pug not . . ."

"Where is that son of a bitch? He gets me in this and then he bugs out. Does he want some more money? What does he want? You know his people, don't you? You've been making the contacts." He gets up, moves to another quadrant where the large checkbook rests on the cushions. "How much will it cost? Christ, I might as well go broke. How much do we need, Tommy?"

"It's not that," I said. "It can't be done that way. They have more to look out for than a little cash."

"Okay, how about you?" he said. The surgeon did a very neat job on his cheek and if there is a scar it might appear to be a deep dimple.

"What about me?"

"Listen," he said, coming over, sitting down. "You don't want to be a fucking bureaucrat hack the rest of your life. We got a big operation going up here and we need someone to do our publicity, be our public relations counsel. You know? You can do it, you know the numbers to call." Then in the silence—I was unable to speak or look him in the face—he shouted, "For Christ sake, help me!" The phone rings, and rings. Helen moves on bare feet into the kitchen, answers it. We hear her say she appreciates the call, that it is good news and thank-you. I'm on my feet ready to get out of there.

"Who was that, hon?" he asked. She moves back to the window as if she were studying some particular part of Ellis Mountain.

"That was your headquarters in Yost," she said evenly. "The *Sentinel* has just come out. They have a front-page editorial endorsing you."

"Wow! Listen to that!" he jumped up. "This isn't all over by a long shot."

"I said I could be wrong," I told him.

"Hey, you old son of a bitch, been working behind the scenes on that newspaper and not saying anything about it, eh? Maybe that's where Connors has been; back there pulling the old strings." His one good eye is like a steel bearing. He clapped his hands. The team's behind but the timekeeper has made a mistake; there's another whole period to go! "How about that?" He clapped his hands together again.

"Get some rest," I told them both. Helen has now come around, she's agreeable to bidding me farewell, anyway. "It's going to be all right."

Normally this is my favorite time in an election—the twenty-four hours before the ballots start being counted. There's nothing to be done and you can only relax, think about the things you should have done or should not have done. Oddly, in this quiet interval, a euphoric myopia occurs.

It's peculiar. I've seen the most unsuitable candidates, hopelessly outnumbered, haplessly equipped, strut about on election eve—actually believing themselves the winners of what has been a beautifully engineered, perfectly organized campaign. Remember Darly Morrison when he ran for mayor of the city of Yost? The Republicans only have a two-to-one edge in the city in the first place. Then Darly has that unfortunate speech impediment when he gets excited, which the opposition gossiped about. Then there was that old rumor about the unpaid bills when he had been comptroller.

"Boys," I remember him saying election eve, "we haven't *mithed* a trick." And he congratulated all of us on the coming victory. Pug took out an envelope from the filing cabinet; i.e., from his inside coat pocket, wrote something on it and showed it to me.

"Want to bet? By twelve hundred votes," he had written, which turned out incorrect. Darly lost by 1,187.

And guess who I get a card from today? From Buffalo.

> Sorry about stand-up but had to join band here at the U. But for the best, right? Toronto tomorrow, K.C. next. Jakie fine. Good luck. I *mean* it.
>
> L.

And on the other side? A big picture of Niagara Falls! Bu-tee-ful!

Tuesday

Alma found him. She called me into her upstairs domain of tulle and organdy, said she had been going through some old appointment books of the Judge's and came across the name of this place where they sometimes went if they were in the capital on business. She had called the place and was told Mr. Connors was there.

"Are you going to Albany now?" she asked when I take the slip of paper from her.

"The place is open all night, isn't it?"

"You can't wear those," the attendant says, motioning me around the counter and through an office that smells of chlorine and soap powder. I follow him down a corridor lined with old green lockers, doors askew, some missing, and into a second room where there are banks of wire cages. Naked light bulbs burn hazily in the moist air that weighs heavily in the lungs. The attendant is garbed in a baggy pair of soiled white trousers and a tank-style undershirt. He hacks, drawing a tenacious strand of mucous from his head, steps delicately to a spitoon in the corner, and spits. "It's the change of weather. It always gets me," he apologizes.

Before he left his cubicle and the tabloid opened neatly on the counter, he had picked up a large, towel-like robe and a pair of wooden clogs. He hands these to me now, licking his lips.

"Change into these. If you got anything really valuable on you, you can leave it with me. He's in there," he adds, waving a hand toward the large pair of swinging doors at the end of the locker room. I strip, select a wire cage for my clothes, and put on what was given me.

The clogs echo hollowly in the tiled chamber and I am enveloped in billowing, hot vapors that make it impossible to see how large the room is, that blur everything. Lights pulse in the gloomy firmament of the ceiling and water splashes somewhere against a ceramic surface. It's like walking into the waiting room of a deserted suburban railroad station where the last custodian forgot to turn off the furnace and never repaired the leaking water fountain.

Or perhaps it might be something else, for as my eyes become accustomed to the scudding wisps of steam, I make out three rows of marble slabs, like the tops of picnic tables, tiered around the room in the form of a small arena. Aisles of steps, evenly spaced, go from floor level to the top row and it is on a slab up there I see this bundled, amorphous shape. So it comes down to an either-or situation; either he missed the train or he's too early for the chariot race.

He's prepared for a wait of some duration, for food and drink have been brought. Several trays are stacked on the floor beside him. The top one bears a sandwich in wax paper, a large, plastic-looking apple—also wrapped in plastic and two quart cartons of buttermilk. Maybe he thinks my footsteps are those of a fellow steamer, because he does not move or acknowledge my clatter up the six or eight steps to his humid perch. I take the marble seat in the row beneath him and speak his name conversationally. He sits up with a disarming suppleness, an alacrity that makes me wonder if I had been expected.

"Oh, hiya, pally," he says as the robe falls to his waist. The large rib cage is covered with very white skin. I am taken back, not prepared for the age of the body. He yawns, scratches the thinning hair plastered wetly on his dome and asks, "What's today?"

"Look," I'm trying to soften the blow for Howie yesterday. "There's been some talk lately that the district is going to be reapportioned anyway. So whoever wins tomorrow, and say

Green is beaten in November, it would only be for one term. The Legislature is Republican, and when they reapportion, you can damn well be sure they're going to make it impossible to get a Democrat elected to Congress from around here."

"But who were they?" Helen Ferguson wants to know. All the while we've been talking, she's been standing in the corner — thinking just one thing.

"At the hotel? Who knows. We'll probably never know."

"But why?" she asks, her pretty face nearly plain with exasperation.

"Why? Maybe just to put a finger in the air, a thumb to the nose," I tell her. "I don't think they intended these results," pointing to Howie. "They probably expected no results. Creative playtime."

Pug sits up to draw the terry-cloth garment over his shoulders and rather nicely slip his feet into the canvas straps of the wooden sandals. He bends down, picks up one of the cartons of buttermilk, rips open the top and takes several gulping swallows. Some spills over his whiskered chin and drips on the nearly hairless pale chest.

"You picked a hell of a time to go on a drunk," I say.

"Now, Tommy, where's the old generous self," he soothes me. Water splashes in the white obscurity, several pipes hiss and bang.

"Well, for Christ sake, what a time to desert Ferguson. Don't you have any feelings about him at all? What have you done to him? You've practically wrecked his life, you've certainly changed it. The other night he could have been killed and all the while . . . you . . . ."

"Let's not get carried away, pally," he says, standing and easing by me like a spectator suddenly bored with the program. There's a comic majesty about him, the togalike bathrobe and the buttermilk carton clutched in one hand. He carefully clops to the floor below. "He'll make a splendid sheriff," he says.

"What do you mean sheriff!" I finally find my voice in the oppressive wetness. In fact it's a yell that reverberates in the tiled cavern. He stands below, the robe held together with one hand, statesmanlike, sipping from the quart carton.

"He's had marvelous exposure this time around," he says. "I

bet there's hardly anyone in Yost County who doesn't know him, hasn't met him. You've done a terrific job with him. And all that swooping around by helicopter, that's great stuff! I bet we could get the board of supervisors to buy one for the sheriff's office. Wouldn't that be something? Do you really think he's congressional material — right now? Maybe later, but now?" Sometimes as he spoke, a grayish scrap of vapor passes over him, envelops his face so he resembles a headless statue. Then his eyes would seem to burn through, evaporate the mist.

"Hot damn," he says. "Just think of that. Come next year we take over the sheriff's office again."

"That's a bunch of bullshit," I say. "After playing Errol Flynn the other night, who's going to vote for him for anything."

"Now, now, Tommy," Pug says gently, his words rising up on the soft clouds of steam. "Not for Congress, I agree. But for sheriff, now that's different. Besides, a year will have gone by and what seems foolish this week will to most people, a year from now, seem courageous. I tell you, he's a natural."

"But he won't run for sheriff," I say. Pug has gradually disappeared again moving into a vapor bank on the far side.

"How do you know?" he replies, the voice echoing deceptively near, right by my ear. There's a chuckle. "Why don't you ask him?"

"No, no — not this time." There's no answer. "Pug?"

A smacking of lips, "Yes." He materializes in an unexpected place, to my left. "Let him recover from the hurt he's going to have today. By the way, I hear he got cut up. A scar like that could be a visual reminder about his stand for law and order, eh? He'll love it, I tell you. The kid's got the bug, you know that." And once again, he turns, disappears then reappears on a slab in the first row, across the floor from me.

"Do me a favor, will you?" I ask, awkwardly clopping down the steps to his level. "Can you tell me how this is supposed to come out? Who have you guys decided on to win this primary?" He tilts his head back to finish the buttermilk then throws the carton away, wipes the back of his hand across his mouth. His laugh rattles around the room, some pipes crash and clank.

"Why that's obvious," he says. "Jack Cranston is supposed to win, but whether he will or not is another question. You got me there."

"From the beginning, he's been the winner? Then why all this business with a primary?"

"Well that's Wriston's doing. You see, Tommy," he stretches out on the marble. "The story I get is that Captain Billy wanted to get Cranston into Congress just to move him out of the DA's office. Maybe Jack heard too much with his wiretaps or something. Who knows why? But the angle was, put him in Congress and two years later with the reapportionment, he'd be just another civilian. Maybe Cranston was making a play for the organization too. Who knows?"

"That doesn't wash. Why would Cranston give up a sure thing like DA for one term in Congress?"

"He may not have known about the reapportionment plans until it was too late, until the deals were made. Who knows?" He is on his feet again, pacing the perimeter of the floor. "Anyway, old Matt Wriston really . . ." and his voice fades away as he walks in an ever-widening radius. The clogs scrape against cement like the hooves of an animal shifting in a stall.

I locate him, in the shower room, just stepping beneath one of the silvery heads. He sets the knob and slowly turns under the torrential downpour of cold water, briskly rubbing the big, pale chest and the narrow buttocks. His legs, like his arms, are unusually slender. Wooling his face, squeezing water from his eyes, he steps out and says to me without looking, "You ought to try that. Makes a man out of you." Leaving the shower running, he pulls the terry-cloth robe back over his shoulders, and pushes through a swinging door into the hot swirling mist of the steam room once more.

"But what about Sinnemok County? Minkus has always gone with the Brown organization. Why would he get behind Wriston?"

"Well, you don't know this, but Ernie Minkus wanted a no-show at the Assembly last year—it paid fifteen G's but the old man wouldn't recommend him for it and that really burned him. He's been waiting to get back at Captain Billy ever since." He reaches up and pulls me down beside him on the bench.

"You know Matt Wriston pretty well," he continues, crossing rather pudgy ankles. "It's not one of his MO's to pay off, is it? No, it's not. So the money that Minkus said he got from Wriston more likely came from Cranston. It was made to look like it came from Matt. I'm sure Ernie Minkus thought it came from Matt."

He sighs and rises to his feet, leaving me on the bench. He moves to the left, dematerializes in the steam and I hear the tear of heavy paper. The second carton of buttermilk. The sandals clop-clop up near the ceiling, going clockwise around the line of the top row and finally coming to a halt at the three o'clock position. There's a resounding belch and it's as if this venting clears the atmosphere around him as well, for he reappears on a top platform. A small towel has been draped over his head like a worn magistrate's wig.

"So the old bunch is breaking up," he says. His words bounce against the obscured ceiling. "Captain Billy is indisposed. Cranston and/or Cy Miller, the same thing, see their chance. They'll let either Howie or Matt Wriston win the primary and they'll pick up the pieces of the organization in Cade. Howie was probably their choice." He starts to laugh, his belly shaking the terry cloth, as he stretches out on the marble shelf, grunting contentedly between chuckles.

"You asked who's supposed to win?" He murmurs through the towel pulled over his face. "Use your head, pally. Jack Cranston was supposed to win, how could it be otherwise. But the funny thing," and he pauses to get his breath, "what with the business at the hotel the other night, he just *might* win now." I wonder if he'll roll off the top row, come bouncing down the marble steps, a whooping, big ball of glee.

"Why couldn't Wriston take it now?" I ask.

"Well, of course, he could," he says, suddenly serious. "If the people in Cade County can get their people realigned quick enough. We'll push him, too." We listen to the dripping water, the clank of expanding or contracting pipes. "What time is it?" he asks after awhile.

"It's about two in the morning," I tell him.

"The lull before the battle," he says, one last chuckle and then he's silent. He seems to have drifted off.

"There's another possibility," I say.

"Hmmn?"

"That money Minkus was flashing around. Maybe it came from Howie Ferguson."

"Very possible, very possible," he says, eyes closed. "But it doesn't matter, none of it matters." He seems to doze in the dripping silence. Then, "Just think, Tommy. Little old Yost County. We're going to take over the sheriff's office next year and we might even get a Congressman this year. That's what matters."

He stops me at the door, his voice ballooning in the heavy air. "And do me a favor, pally. Call Wriston and Howie and tell them I'm with them. Best of luck, you know. Tell them that I have to stay neutral right now but after today, no matter who wins, they'll have me behind them, 110 percent. Tell Matt that especially. Okay? Oh, and Tommy — remind me to your mother?"

•

I've just turned off the desk lamp. The sun has been up for a couple of hours. Just for the hell of it, I call L.'s old number. "Iyamsorry . . . the number you have reached has been disconnected." I know that, dummy. She's on her way to Kansas City.

I feel several pounds lighter, abnormally alert and fresh. Awake. It's been a dream. Pug Connor's words have evaporated in the clear light of morning. The elaborate joke at the hotel last week has given us a good shot at sheriff next year and just might hand Wriston the nomination for Congress. But who can say if this is the way it was supposed to turn out.

As I'm filing some clippings and bills, Alma comes down the stairs. She's all dressed up and looks rather attractive.

"I've told you before," I say, "you're only allowed one vote, no matter how pretty you look."

"What's the sheriff up to?" she asks.

"He thinks Matt Wriston might win," I answer.

"I could have told you that," she replies. "I have to get downtown to the bank," she says now. "Can you fix your own breakfast?"

"Sure. What's up?"

"Up? Nothing's up. I have to get some papers out of the safe deposit box for the real estate people to see."

"You're really going through with this, selling the house?"

"Of course," my mother answers and turns then comes back. "And I'd appreciate it if you could neaten this sun porch up a little bit. They might be showing it to some people and I'd like it to look nice."

If not the sole surviving juror, I was the only one to follow the Judge's last instructions. My mother not being up to it delegated the authority to me. The peepers were out and the mournful cry of an owl lifted now and then, a hair-raising croon if you weren't prepared for the sound or could not recognize it. I had a flashlight, but there was no need for it, for the light of a slim moon let me make my way down the old roadbed. Also the glow from Sullivan's Corners contributed to the illumination, particularly marking the cliff's edge at the end of the tunnel of trees.

It was only the second week of April but mayflies brushed at my face when I got to the small savannah above the crossroads. All I could see were the several new mercury lights that had been installed in the village. The abandoned store and the one or two buildings still there were camouflaged by the heavy, new growth of leaves. Bugs bothered my face, tickled around my nose, prompting a consideration which made me test the wind. It was from behind me, and that was all right. Anyway when the container was upside down over the valley, nothing seemed to fall out of it nor, in the gloom, did I see anything. Maybe it had been empty all along. However, the metal canister made a satisfying clunk — clank — crash down the gulley. I was halfway back to the road before the forest recovered its voices.

"Now what?" Rosie said. She leaned against the car door, smoking, looking up at the few stars that were just appearing. I had a Ford convertible then and she liked to drive with the top down.

R. L.—About my age, which would make her about 34
when I had her. Worked on the local newspaper for a
time. "I've got freckles," she said shyly, the first
time in the buff. She sure did! A mantle of brown
that spilled over her shoulders and halfway down over
rather girlish breasts. Gave her a doelike-animal
quality; put together with rather timorous brown eyes.
Rather exciting. The trouble was she was too old when
I got to her. She approached a fuck with a rather
simple meat-and-potatoes attitude which eventually
turned me off. But a nice, bright girl all in all.
She left for the city and works on some magazine. I
think.

"Now," I said getting in the Ford, "I just have to pay a call in Green River and then we're off to Julius' for the best spiced crab you've ever tasted."

"What's in Green River?" she asked, moving over on the seat.

"Are you a reporter tonight or a girl out for spiced crab?"

"Do I have a choice?" she laughed, pulling back. Rosie was very sensitive. "Okay — off the record, Scout's honor."

"Well, off the record, Scout's honor, there's a town chairman I've got to feel out on the candidacy of someone who's going to run for the Assembly."

"Who's that?" Rosie asked, lighting another cigarette. She smoked too much.

"Matthew B. Wriston."

"No kidding?" she said. "He going to run for the Assembly?"

"Off the record," I reminded her. Then she started to laugh; a merry giggle with the prospective tinkles of the old maid she would no doubt become. "What's so funny?"

"Oh, you just go round and round all the time, don't you?" she said. "It's always politics with you, always. Round and round," she repeated to the night air as we came into Green River's town limits. "I bet you can't tell your beginning from your end."

I always brought a few big candles whenever I went to Julius' place because the lighting he had in the cabins, one bare bulb dangling from a two-ply wire stapled to the roof beam, was not terribly romantic. I was lighting a second candle from the one sputtering in the saucer when Rosie came back from the bathroom. She fished out a cigarette and bent over to light it from the new candle's flame. Apple-sized breasts swayed under a lacy brown stole of freckles. (In fact, now that I think about it, she was really a pretty good girl.)

"You know, you're right," she said, getting back into bed, climbing over my feet and dropping a hot ash on my thigh. The mattresses in those cabins were so dry they could go up before you could cross your legs. "Those were the best spiced crabs I've ever had." She giggled, puffed. "They're the only ones I've ever had. And something else. You may have converted me?"

"Oh?"

"I must admit he was very impressive on television tonight.

Righteous anger. He's right, a raise in steel prices would be inflationary."

"Not only that," I replied. I could span her shoulder blades with one hand. "They signed an agreement with the unions for benefits rather than wages and now turn around and raise their own prices. It's really the steel industry thumbing its nose at the Presidency—at the nation. But I have a feeling this speech tonight will change their minds. They've made the mistake of underestimating him, of what he can do as President. He's not in awe of them. He can't be pushed around." Rosie was sitting up as I stroked her smooth back. She even had a few freckles way down low. "Understand?"

"Yes," she said, nodding her head and very serious as if I had just set her whole life straight. She took a final puff on the cigarette and put it to smolder in the saucer full of melted paraffin. She turned and pulled the sheet up over us. "I didn't vote for him, you know," she whispered. Then "What if the sheriff should raid this place and find you in bed with a registered Republican?"

"I could say that I'm changing your mind?" I said.

"How?"

"Reasoned argument."

"Yes."

"Unequivocal examples."

"Hmm."

"Incontrovertible proofs."

"Yes."

"And this."

"Oh, Tommy," she whispered in my ear, her arms stretched out, hands grip the headboard; ". . . I can't wait until 1964."